Highly-acclaimed, *Thirst* has been described as 'The best Antarctic thriller since *Ice Station*'. To write *Thirst* Larkin travelled to Antarctica and learned about crevasse rescue and Antarctic survival. After the success of the first novel, *The Genesis Flaw*, Larkin gave up a climate change consultancy role to become a full-time author. L. A. Larkin lives in Sydney and London, and teaches mystery and thriller writing.

www.lalarkin.com
www.facebook.com/LALarkinAuthor
@lalarkinauthor

D0552574

8000342012

By L. A. Larkin
The Genesis Flaw
Thirst
Devour

Thirst

L. A. Larkin

CONSTABLE • LONDON

CONSTABLE

First published in Australia in 2012 by Pier 9, an imprint of
Murdoch Books Pty Limited

First published in Great Britain in 2016 by Constable

1 3 5 7 9 10 8 6 4 2

Copyright © L.A. Larkin, 2012

The moral right of the author has been asserted.

A CIP catalogue record for this book
is available from the British Library.

ISBN: 978-1-47212-589-7

Printed and bound by CPI Group (UK) Ltd, Croydon, CR0 4YY

Papers used by Constable are from well-managed forests and
other responsible sources.

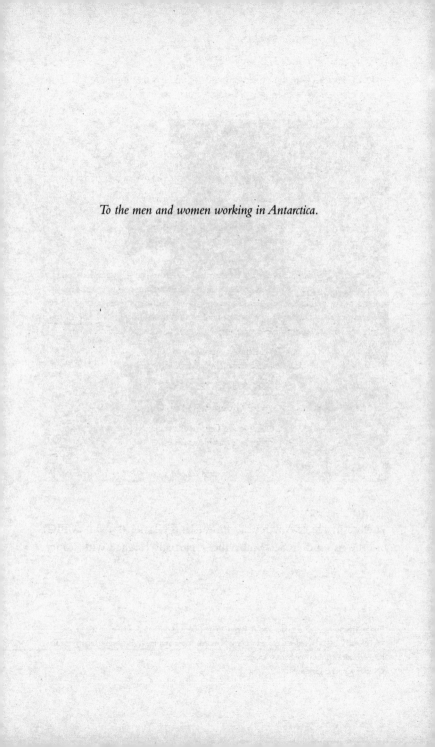

To the men and women working in Antarctica.

Satellite image of Antarctica's Pine Island Glacier (known as PIG) and the Amundsen Sea Embayment, partially clogged with sea ice.

Image: T. Scambos, J. Bohlander and B. Raup, 1996. *Images of Antarctic ice shelves*, accessed
16 February 2012. Boulder, Colorado, USA: National Snow and Ice Data Center. Digital media.
http://nsidc.org/data/iceshelves_images.
Overlay adapted: Larkin, M.

A few years from now …

T MINUS 5 DAYS, 2 HOURS, 53 MINUTES
5 March, 9:07 am (UTC-07)

Pine Island Glacier, Antarctica, 74° 55' S, 101° 11' W

At minus thirty degrees Celsius, the trickle of blood on Mac's beard froze rapidly.

'Wh— what do you want?' he stammered, spreadeagled on his back.

His masked attacker didn't respond. In the struggle, Mac's prescription goggles had been torn off, so the man pointing an assault rifle at him was a terrifying blur.

Minutes earlier, Mac had been helping Dave to remove fragile scientific equipment from the camp's red, domed pods, known as 'apples'. The Walgreen Crevasse project was complete and they were shutting down camp for the winter. The snowmobiles were loaded up, and Mac, chilled by the winds, had started swinging his arms and stamping his feet. His initial excitement at swapping shifts with Luke – the project's glaciologist – had waned as the intense cold clawed at his bones.

Now his heart was racing and sweat trickled down the back of his neck. His ribs had been broken by a savage blow from a rifle butt and every breath was torture. A few metres away, near the crevasse edge, Dave lay with his arms raised, two guns trained on him. The last of the four strangers was unarmed and watched from a distance. He was the leader – it was clear from the way the others deferred to him.

'Who are you?' Mac asked, dumbfounded. There were no other field sites for at least a thousand kilometres, and he knew the nearest station, Li Bai, was currently unmanned.

Still no response. Had they heard him above the katabatic winds that hissed down the mountain and across the glacier, blowing stinging spindrift into his face?

The leader moved closer. As he bent over Mac, some of his features came into focus. He rolled his balaclava up and away from his mouth, revealing thin lips and sparse black hairs on his boyish chin. 'Did you report our presence here?'

His voice was surprisingly deep. Authoritative. Some kind of accent … American?

Before Mac could answer, his interrogator gestured to the nearest subordinate, who kicked him in the kidneys. Mac convulsed, vomiting bile.

'Answer. Did you radio your station?' the man yelled like a drill sergeant.

Panting, and with his eyes now watering, Mac could barely make out the black blobs of his shattered two-way radio on the ground. They hadn't had time to call for help. Dressed in white, the strangers had been virtually invisible. When they appeared out of nowhere, Mac and Dave had simply gawped. In Antarctica, there was no reason to assume strangers were anything but friendly, part of the international research fraternity. And they never expected visitors to be armed.

'Yes,' said Mac, hoping his lie would be believed. He had made his scheduled call to Hope Station at 09:00, but that was ten minutes ago.

The man in charge glanced at the radio shards, then leaned closer to Mac's face. His small but perfect teeth were unnaturally whiter than the glacier. His eyes studied Mac's with clinical precision. 'I don't believe you.' He smiled, stretching his lips so thin they almost disappeared. 'And you're from Hope, the Australian station?'

Mac just managed to shake his head, although his body shrieked in pain. The last thing he was going to do was lead them to his mates.

4

'I see.'

The man walked to where Dave lay, pocketed his working radio and then kicked the sole of his captive's boot, as if inspecting a car's tyres. Dave kicked back but his assailant jumped aside and issued orders in a language Mac didn't understand. Two of the attackers kneeled on Dave's arms, one on each side.

Young and fit, he struggled hard. 'Get off me, you fuckers!'

'Did you radio Hope Station?' the leader called to Mac.

One of their attackers – wide-framed and short-legged, like a bulldog – pulled off Dave's hood to reveal a mop of light-blond hair. He moved with the speed of a man used to combat.

'Let me go!' Dave yelled, kicking and writhing.

Mac struggled to go to the aid of his friend, but his guard shoved a rifle muzzle in his face. The broad soldier straddled Dave's chest and slapped him twice. In the second or so it took Dave to recover, his assailant took hold of his head, a hand on either side, and twisted it sharply to the right. Despite the whining wind, the crack was unmistakable. Dave no longer moved.

Too late, Mac shouted, 'No! No, we didn't. For God's sake, we never radioed.'

As the tears ran down his face and onto the hair at his temples, they froze in tiny pear-shaped beads of white.

'That's better. Your hesitation cost your friend his life. Don't treat me like a fool.'

Unable to speak, Mac stared in horror as Dave, still in his safety harness, was dragged to the crevasse lip and thrown in. The ropes pinged tight, as the three metallic anchors, hammered deep into the ice, strained under his weight. For a fleeting moment, Mac imagined Dave hanging like a macabre marionette.

Mac was yanked to his feet, the pain in his ribs like an ice pick in his side. Two men held him fast. As they pulled him towards the crevasse, Mac's terror mounted. Its mouth gaped a few metres wide, and it plunged into a deep and jagged V-shaped chasm.

He managed to tear an arm free but a rifle butt hit him between the shoulder blades and he crumpled, yelping. Mac peered down into his turquoise tomb. Faced with imminent death, all the fight drained from him and he released the contents of his bladder.

'Please don't,' he begged. 'I won't say anything, for God's sake.'

'Do you promise?'

'Yes, I do, yes. Not a word. Please, I have a wife and daughter.'

His captor barked instructions. Mac's smashed radio was dropped into the crevasse, then the men used hammers to dislodge the ice screws still holding Dave's weight. Once loosened, they zipped across the surface and disappeared into the depths, taking the ropes and Dave's body with them.

'A tragic accident. This poor man,' the leader gestured towards the crevasse, 'tried to save you. But unfortunately his anchors didn't hold. Such heroism.'

'No, not down there!' cried Mac, attempting to pull back from the edge. 'No! Don't let me die down there!'

The leader placed a gloved hand on his shoulder. 'My friend, this is not personal. In fact, we probably want the same thing.' He paused. 'I don't want to hurt you.'

Mac was released. He could barely stand but a glimmer of hope gave him strength and he staggered round to face his aggressor.

'But you see,' said the leader, gesturing to his second-in-command, 'it has to be done.'

A kick to the stomach propelled Mac backwards, and the lip of the crevasse gave way beneath him. He was too stunned to scream. With a thud his body bounced off an ice ledge and into the blue void.

The other side of the Pine Island Glacier

Suspended from a ten-metre rope as casually as if he were sitting on a swing, Luke Searle stabbed his crampons into the crevasse's glassy wall. He removed his XL-sized inner and outer gloves and ran his fingers across a striking stain in the ice. It felt as smooth as polished granite. With the care of a diamond-cutter, Luke used the blade of his ice axe to chip away a tiny piece. He rolled it between his warm fingers. The ice melted slowly, releasing its gritty contents.

During all his years studying ice, he had never seen anything quite like this. Engrossed by his discovery, he ignored the barely audible voice coming from the two-way radio strapped across his chest. Not only was Luke abseiling in an unknown and potentially unstable crevasse, he was alone and had not bothered to alert anyone at Hope Station to his whereabouts.

Above Luke, the ice walls shone a milky, opalescent white. Below, the ice morphed from the palest sapphire-blue to dark titanium; here the sun penetrated for the briefest of glimpses, and then only at the height of summer. In front of him, a horizontal black line as thick as his arm ran through the ice like the licorice in an allsort. A circle of ice crystals clung to his balaclava's mouth slit and to the tips of his eyelashes, as the

7

moisture in his breath froze.

This was Luke's first day off in three months. His research into accelerated glacial flow was complete, his report submitted. But his love affair with ice didn't stop simply because his project was over. Antarctica would soon be plunged into six months of darkness; before that happened, Luke wanted to investigate his theory that a sub-glacial volcano had erupted two thousand years ago, dropping a layer of ash onto the ice that, over time, had been buried.

'Maddie ... ten ... you read? ...' his station leader called through the radio, every few words missing. Her persistence worried him; it might be something urgent. Luke scraped some frozen ash into a sample bag, sealed it and then ascended rapidly to the surface to improve his radio's reception.

'Luke, this is Maddie on channel ten. Do you read? Over.'

Luke crawled over the lip of the crevasse and away from the fragile edge. Still on all fours, he pulled the radio close to his mouth. 'Maddie, Luke here. Receive you loud and clear.'

'Luke, I know this is your day off but Mac's having problems with his snowmobile and might need you to go out there and fix it. Everything's packed into the trailer but the clutch is slipping. Over.'

The overwintering team was small so each member had to be multi-skilled and Luke's other role was station mechanic. He checked his watch: 09:19.

'No worries, Maddie. I'll give him a yell now.'

'Thanks, Luke. And by the way, it would be helpful if we knew where you were.' She sighed.

Inside the entrance to Hope Station hung a chess-like board covered by small hooks; on every hook hung a plastic tag bearing a station member's name. When someone left or returned to the station, they had to turn their tag. There was also a book in which they were to record their name, time of departure, destination and intended time of return. Luke had done neither.

'Maddie, I can look after myself.' As if to reinforce this point, Luke rose to his full height of six foot three.

'I know you can. But I need you to set an example.'

'Roger that.'

'Luke, I shouldn't be saying this on the radio, but has anyone told you what a pain in the arse you are?'

He smiled. 'Yes, you have – several times. Oh, and my ex. And my previous boss, too, now that you mention it.'

'Yeah, well, at least I'm not the only station leader you pay no attention to. But, we've got to work as a team here. Out.'

Luke stowed his abseiling gear with expert speed, slung his pack on his back and, having removed his crampons and secured them, slid his boots into his skis' bindings.

'Mac, this is Luke on channel ten, are you receiving? Over.' He waited. 'Luke to Mac, radio check, please.'

Nothing. He glanced up the mountain to the VHF repeater tower, which resembled a long ladder pointing at the sky. His signal should definitely reach the field camp because the repeater extended its range. Perhaps the silly bugger had left his radio in the field hut. He tried Dave instead, but still no response. Surely one of them should hear his voice?

He tried Mac again, and at last a response came. He could barely understand it, however, because it kept cutting out, the gaps filled with brief silence. It sounded like, 'Mac to Luke. Receiving you weak and intermittent. Over.'

'Mac, what's wrong with your snowmobile? Over.'

A pause. 'What … you mean?'

'You radioed in. Is the clutch slipping again?'

'Negative. The clutch is …' Then nothing.

'Mac, can you repeat?'

'The clutch is fine.'

Luke frowned, surprised. Maddie wouldn't have asked him to check if it hadn't been important. 'You sure?'

'Clutch … working now.' Still the voice kept dropping out.

'Roger that. Mate, you sound like your head's in a bucket of water. I can hardly hear you. ETA still midday?'

'Mac to Luke … midday.'

'Roger that. Radio me if you have any problems.'

'Will do. Out.'

This was odd, but Luke decided to give Mac another call once he was back at the station.

***

Half an hour later, Luke slid to a stop and removed his balaclava and goggles to reveal blue-grey eyes, prominent cheekbones and weathered olive skin which belied his thirty years. His unruly black hair was sorely in need of a cut.

His home for the last five months was a structure raised above the ice on sixteen hydraulic legs. Hope Station's silver metal skin gleamed in the anaemic sun. From where Luke stood, it looked like a cross between a giant silverfish and the Eagle lunar lander. All the living and working quarters were under one roof; the fuel tank, wind turbine, water-recycling plant, fire hut and satellite dish were separate from the main building.

The station was positioned to one side of the mighty Pine Island Glacier and faced the sea – at least, it did in the summer. It was now Antarctica's autumn, and the fractured sea ice was fast thickening into an impenetrable barrier. In a few weeks, Pine Island Bay would be covered in an unyielding icy crust. It swelled out from the continent so much that, in the depths of winter, Antarctica bloated to double its size.

Luke closed his eyes. All he could hear was the occasional pop and crack as mountain ice surrendered to gravity, moving imperceptibly downhill towards the glacier. The stillness filled him with an energy that made his skin tingle, as if every cell in his body was being recharged. In Antarctica, especially when he was away from the day-to-day clatter and chatter of cramped station life, he felt exhilarated. Here, his thoughts had a pristine clarity.

He inhaled the sparkling sub-zero air and opened his eyes. Leaning on his ski poles, he gazed in admiration at the glacier's endless white moonscape, which reached deep into the heart of the vast West Antarctic Ice Sheet. In the opposite direction, it met the Amundsen Sea, its giant ice tongue extending out over the water as if it were licking the salty brine.

The last supply ship had left a week ago, not to return until October. Maddie Wildman, the ball-breaking station leader, had waved a confident farewell to the ice-breaker's crew, the pompoms on her fleece hat swinging as her arms described wide arcs. But Luke had seen her apprehensive glance at Craig, the oldest of the over-winterers, before she beamed a huge smile again. Craig had his arms folded across his knitted-by-my-wife-it's-ghastly-but-I-love-her jumper. Tubs, the youngest, was all bravado – he had dropped his pants, and received a blast from the ship's horn in response. But once the ship was nothing more than a smudge in the distance, Tubs had gone unusually quiet.

Over the years, Luke had watched the ship depart with relief. For him, Antarctica was home. But since the birth of his son, Jason, this relief had been tinged with guilt – and, more recently, with apprehension. There was something his six-year-old was keeping from him. As Luke pulled on his headgear and skied downhill, he felt an urgent need to talk to him. But, given the time difference, that would have to wait a few hours.

He deftly wove around rocky outcrops until he was within hailing distance of the station. Craig waved at him from the top of a ladder, where he was working on the roof of the fire hut, which housed emergency fire equipment and survival supplies. He was the station carpenter and fire chief.

As Luke headed towards Craig, three black and white Adélie penguins cut across his path. Beaks first, they slid on their bellies down the gentle incline towards the beach, oblivious to Luke's presence.

'Hey, mate,' Luke called out to Craig. 'Need some help?'

'Nah, I'm just about done here. You, on the other hand, might need some yourself.' Craig jerked his head behind him.

Luke glanced at the station, searching for a clue. Everything looked normal, including the Australian flag which had been snap frozen mid-flap for the last few weeks.

'Maddie wants to see you.' Craig climbed down the ladder, nimble for a man in his early fifties, and slapped Luke's shoulder. 'Good luck,' he said, with a mischievous smile.

Luke nodded and hurried on. Before he'd even removed his

skis, he heard Maddie's husky voice calling his name. She always sounded as if she had been shouting above nightclub music all night, but nothing could be further from the truth. Expecting a reprimand, his grip on his ski poles tightened a fraction. He peered up at the metal walkway, which ran the length of the raised building.

Maddie leaned over the railing and looked down at him. Her copper-coloured hair spiralled out from under her beanie and over her shoulders. 'Congratulations, Luke,' she said. 'Your paper on dynamic thinning won the Seligman Crystal Award. We're very proud of you.' She smiled and carefully stepped down the slick steps.

Luke tore off his balaclava. 'It did?' he asked, incredulous.

'Yes, and so it should have. I haven't told the others yet – wanted to let you know first. We'll be having a big celebration tonight.'

'Woo hoo!' Luke punched the air. He couldn't wait to tell Jason.

Maddie was five foot eight, muscular and slim. She adopted a no-nonsense stance with arms folded as her green eyes scanned his face. 'Did you talk to Mac?'

'Yeah. He said the clutch was working again, but I think I'd better get over there and check it out for myself.'

'No need. If he said it's fine, I'm sure it is. Let's not waste fuel on an unnecessary trip.'

Luke hesitated, wondering if it was worth arguing. They already disagreed over so many issues.

'Okay, you're the boss,' he replied, raising his arms in surrender.

Still, something didn't feel right.

T MINUS 5 DAYS, 1 HOUR, 50 MINUTES
5 March, 10:10 am (UTC-07)

74° 52' S, 100° 30' W

To Robert Zhao Sheng, Antarctica was a hellhole, made only just bearable by his executive chef and the billions he would earn exploiting it.

He dabbed his mouth with a napkin and pushed away his half-eaten breakfast: porridge liberally sprinkled with brown sugar. His lip curled in disgust at the muddy black coffee. How he longed for *oeufs florentine* and a double-shot espresso. His chef did his best, but after weeks of frozen, dehydrated and boil-in-a-bag meals, Robert was suffering real hardship. Much like Robert Falcon Scott, whose diary he had been reading on his iPad.

As he leaned back in his chair, he grinned. How his competitors would squirm with jealousy when his story of courage and survival in Antarctica was on the front page of the *Wall Street Journal*. He glanced at his video camera, still on its tripod at one end of his ten-person, super-insulated Weatherhaven tent. He was recording history in the making. It would be wall-to-wall coverage on all networks.

'Ha!' he said, throwing his head back.

In the world of private equity, this was unique. No one else would be able to tell of survival against such odds, of personally leading a pioneering project that would bring the world an invaluable resource – not to mention make him more money than he could ever spend. But spending it wasn't the point. As they say, he who has the most when he dies, wins.

Robert frowned. The winds roaring down the Hudson Mountains buffeted his tent and intruded on his reverie. He glanced at his new platinum Jean Dunand watch, the only one in the world, which had cost a little shy of eight hundred thousand US dollars. He had four minutes until a call with his father, General Zhao Yun, a fellow investor in his brainchild. Robert turned up the volume of Vivaldi's 'L'Inverno' concerto, from *The Four Seasons*, to drown out the wind's annoying moan.

He stared down at the heater at his feet and thought of the times he'd looked down from his luxurious office at the jungle of Hong Kong's streets. As Senior Managing Director and Chief Investment Officer of the Hood Group, a global private equity firm, Robert's job was to find opportunity in chaos. Gold in the dross. He liked to target companies in trouble and force them to sell. Not only was it vastly profitable if done well – and Robert did it very well indeed – but it was fun watching them try to squirm out of his embrace. Of course, he did it with style and panache, even if behind the scenes his staff would schmooze, blackmail or intimidate – whatever it took to ensure that the Hood Group maintained its reputation as *the* private equity firm of the Orient.

Occasionally there were murmurings about the Hood Group going too far, with the politicians or the press – spokespeople for the great unwashed masses – calling them a 'vulture fund'. But Robert was no ordinary predator. He had built the largest corporate art collection in the region, sponsored the symphony orchestra, and his foundation contributed to a portfolio of worthy causes. Patrons like him were needed, even if the ungrateful recipients despised what he did. His philanthropy was a reminder to all of his wealth and power, and – most of all – of his impeccable taste.

Robert smiled to himself. 'I put the *private* back into private equity,' he said aloud, not caring if his men outside heard.

He loved to boast that a significant proportion of his company's capital came from individuals – the new and rapidly growing class of Chinese billionaires.

It was time. Robert silenced the music, wishing he could silence the winds too. He was reminded of a production of *King Lear* he saw when last in London, in which the old king raged against the winds. Robert brushed the thought from his mind. The king was a fool and should never have given away his kingdom. Robert glanced in a mirror and combed his hair, parted slightly right of centre, Clark Kent-style. He was less well kempt than usual, but thought he looked rugged, like a great Antarctic explorer should.

Robert dialled into the secure teleconference and nodded at his father's image, which filled the screen. It was after midnight in Beijing, though the General still wore the pine-green uniform of the People's Liberation Army. He dropped his chin a fraction in acknowledgement of his son. Their traditional heartfelt greeting. Robert's interactions with his father were like strategic moves in the Chinese board game of Go, each constantly trying to outwit the other.

'So you ordered your first kill. Congratulations, my son,' said the General. 'Did you enjoy it?'

'No, Father, I did not. Their deaths were unnecessary. Captain Wei made an error.' It was hard to look imposing in the skin-tight thermals that stretched over Robert's puny body but he leaned towards the screen, trying to fill it.

The General raised a greying eyebrow, looking at Robert over the frames of his bifocals, which rested high on the puffy skin of his cheekbones. 'I doubt it.'

Robert had never seen any warmth in his father's eyes, let alone any sign of approval. It didn't matter to the General that in the financial world Robert was famous – or rather infamous – or that his net worth could wipe out the debt of many third-world countries.

'My men are under strict instructions to keep away from Hope Station people,' Robert replied. 'Two of Wei's soldiers were at the Fitzgerald Fissure. We believe MacNamara and Cox spotted their snowmobiles. They should have taken more care to conceal them.'

'From what I hear, the Australians were racing their snowmobiles and strayed from their Walgreen Crevasse campsite.'

As usual, Robert kept his partly lame left hand hidden under his right. His grip tightened, his knuckles whitened. 'Father, I know that Gao Wei was once under your command, but now he reports to me. He can have only one commander.'

'He works for Hung Security, and I selected him for this job,' the General growled.

'And I *own* Hung Security. So I own Captain Wei.'

The mercenaries with Robert were from a private security and military contractor, one of the Hood Group's investee companies. A number of them, including Captain Wei, had been in the People's Liberation Army, and had never forgotten what the General had done for them.

'Do I have to remind you, son, that you are a civilian commanding some of the most highly skilled soldiers in the world, and you are doing so because of me? If I wish to talk to Wei, I will do so.'

'This is *my* project.' Robert began to grind his teeth.

'This is war, Robert. We cannot be discovered.'

'It's *business*, Father, and I like to use a little more subtlety.' His breakfast churned in his stomach.

'They had to die.' The General paused. 'So do the others.'

'No. We can jam their communications. They won't be able to tell anyone anything.'

'The hacker is trustworthy?'

'Totally. I've used him many times. He used to work for our government. Goes by the name of Eye.'

'Eye?'

'Yes. An affectation. He can look into anybody's system, no matter how secure. He's hacked into the Pentagon several times.'

'And how long will the jammer last?'

'Maximum eighteen hours.'

'Not long enough. You know what you have to do, and I expect you to do it.' The General ended the call.

Robert stood suddenly and his chair fell backwards. He grabbed a two-way radio and yelled into it: 'Captain Wei. In my tent, now!'

Wei soon appeared, dressed in a white parka and waterproof trousers. He didn't salute but stood to attention. His frame was wide and squat, his face, flat and hard. His small eyes appeared like black marbles. 'Sir?' Captain Wei said.

'The two idiots who allowed themselves to be seen by the Australians have caused us a great deal of trouble. Halve their food rations.'

'Sir, in these sub-zero temperatures, if their rations are halved they won't have the energy to do their job.'

'Two days, half rations, and I expect them to do their job. Perfectly. Now leave.'

Robert righted his chair and sat down, ready for his next call. He might be stuck in the middle of nowhere but he still had a portfolio to run. He didn't need the video-conferencing facility so he used his satellite phone to call the chairman of the largest missile manufacturing company in Asia, an idiot who'd had the audacity to reject Robert's offer to buy the floundering company. How could anyone fail to make money from missiles?

'Who is this?' The voice was sleepy.

Robert introduced himself in Mandarin, the preferred language of the chairman, but he could just as easily converse in Cantonese or English.

'How dare you call me in the middle of the night!'

'Listen to me. I'm going to buy your company,' Robert answered. 'I've got money and time. I am patient. But next time, I'll be buying it for half what's on the table today.' The contempt in his voice was unmistakable.

'I repeat,' said the chairman, 'the company is not for sale.'

'You're in trouble. And believe me, I can add to the pressure. Your share price is down thirty per cent in three months – who knows how long your banks will be patient? Time is ticking. You will sell.'

Grinning, Robert ended the call and made a mental note to organise a press leak about a board member's fondness for expensive call girls. He then cranked up his Vivaldi and returned his attention to Hope Station. The problem for its remaining residents was that their time was running out too.

Hope Station, 75° 10' S, 102° 3' W

In the lab, Luke found that his samples' chemical composition was remarkably similar to that of volcanic ash from Mount Erebus, Antarctica's most active volcano. But Erebus was well over a thousand kilometres away. Excited, he decided to return to the crevasse tomorrow with his field assistant, Dave.

On his way to a storage facility, Luke ducked into his room. When he turned, he found Maddie standing in his doorway. 'Can I come in?' she asked.

Luke involuntarily clenched his jaw. Maddie lived her life on station with the predictability of a metronome, whereas he was as unpredictable as spindrift, blowing every which way. They seldom saw eye to eye.

'Sure.' He gestured towards the chair.

As Maddie entered, her eyes darted to the wall above his bed. Luke saw a pained expression flicker across her face.

There were no photos of people in his room. His only one of his son was in a drawer. On his walls were four crayon drawings, each signed 'Jase' in large, wobbly letters. In one, there were two stick people, a little boy and his mum with long yellow hair. They stood next to a square house with a triangular red roof. At the edge of the page, another stick figure sat alone in a large yellow circle, next to an igloo-shaped house, with blue waves encircling the island. This, Jason had decided, was where Daddy lived, not realising there were no Inuit in Antarctica. The paintings reminded Luke that Jason had been unusually cagey when they'd last spoken.

'Luke? You okay?' asked Maddie.

'Fine,' he said, focusing back on her.

'I said, amazing photo.' She nodded at a photograph of an albatross. 'I remember that one. Followed the ship for three days.'

Luke raised his eyebrows. 'Coming from an ornithologist, I'll take that as a compliment.'

Maddie had several roles, including station leader and microbiologist, but in what little spare time she had she loved to study Antarctica's birdlife.

'Ornithology's just a hobby. Look, sorry if I've been a bit abrupt lately. Got a lot on my mind.'

'You mean the bird flu?' asked Luke, relaxing. The one thing they did have in common was a love of birds.

'Yes. I can't believe it's reached Antarctica.' She brushed away a speck of something on her arm, as if trying to brush away her anxiety.

'What did Charlie say? Have you heard any more from him?'

Maddie cupped her chin in her hands. 'Well, it's kind of bizarre,' she said. 'I've known him years. But since he arrived at Whalers Island, he's gone all weird.'

'Maybe he feels he can't tell you everything. That it would upset you.'

'I'm already upset, Luke. There are one hundred thousand pairs of Adélie penguins nesting there. Quarantining the whole island is a tough call. I mean, you can't stop them fishing. They need to eat, and so the flu spreads.'

'So what was weird about Charlie?'

'His last email was … stuffy, kind of formal. Then I heard nothing. He's not replying to any of my emails.'

'Okay, that's not like him.'

'I'd give anything to go over there and help out.' Whalers Island was in the Amundsen Sea, twenty nautical miles away.

'You want to check it out? I'll take you there.'

'Are you serious?' Her voice was high-pitched with excitement. Then she shook her head. 'No, I can't do it. I don't have time to waste on a jolly.'

'But this outbreak could decimate penguin populations.'

'I know, but we can't go on the island.'

'No, we'd stay in the boat and keep a safe distance. But at least you could see Charlie and talk through the radio.'

He watched her consider his offer. Whenever she was unsure how to respond, she twisted her hair into a bun and secured it with whatever was to hand. This time it was a pen. He always wondered how it stayed put.

'Too risky, Luke, and I should just get on with running the station.' She stood and headed for the door. 'Well done again for winning the prize. You annoy the hell out of me most of the time, but I'm very proud of you.'

Maddie left before he could respond, almost colliding with Tubs. The station chef charged into the room. His head of blond curls, his dimpled smile and his short, plump body gave him the appearance of a mischievous cherub.

'Hey, my man,' he said, high-fiving Luke. 'The award thing is awesome.'

'How did you …?' The grapevine was as fast as ever. 'Thanks.'

Tubs, who was always on hyperdrive, continued. 'So, party tonight. Cooking up a feast. Big juicy steaks, medium rare, just how you like them.' Tubs rubbed his pudgy hands together in excitement.

Luke couldn't help but laugh. 'I hope to God Maddie doesn't make a speech.'

'She has to! From what I hear, this is a big deal. So, you're a rich man now?'

Deep in thought, Luke didn't answer.

'Hello? Anybody there?' said Tubs. 'I said, any prize money?'

'Yeah, but I won't be spending it.'

'Are you kidding me?'

Luke stood, dwarfing his friend, and smiled. 'Fancy a boat trip?'

T MINUS 5 DAYS, 1 HOUR, 1 MINUTE
5 March, 10:59 am (UTC-07)

'What would you know about the risk I'm taking?' sneered the General. 'All you do is play with numbers.'

Only his father would dare to speak to him like that. Robert's boot swung back and forth in irritation, tapping the makeshift floor of his tent. He felt like punching the monitor that framed his father's bloated face. Instead, he took a deep breath.

'Wrong, Father. I make things happen – things other people consider impossible – and I make a fortune from it. My good investments make so much money that the inevitable losses are just the price of doing business. You talk about risk, Father? Well, risk is my life. You think this man in Sydney threatens our project? Then, yes, we must eliminate that risk. But another death? Why not just keep him quiet until the tenth of March? It won't matter after that.'

'Son, you focus on making this project a success. I'll send King to deal with it.'

Robert had heard of King: a Caucasian operative his father had used before. He moved on quickly.

'Father, I've always made it very clear this project is a high-risk venture. Our new technology could fail, our costs could blow out or the international community could stop our operations. Any number of things could go wrong. This has never been done before. But private equity is a high-wire act. Only someone as smart and experienced as me – only someone with my connections and resources – could have spotted this potential gold mine in Antarctica. We're on the verge of launching a whole new industry! Never before has this resource been so desperately needed, nor has anyone invested the millions necessary to make it happen. We will be national heroes.' Robert's gaunt face stretched into a triumphant smile.

'That's all very well,' the General replied, 'but it must make us rich. Rich enough to be safe. For you, this is merely a business venture. I, on the other hand, have put my life on the line. I have gone behind the Party's back. Only a few hand-picked men know. If word gets out I could be tried for treason.'

'Nerves of steel, Father.'

'Don't patronise me, you paper-pusher.' Robert had only ever heard panic in his father's belligerent voice once before, and that was when he had discovered his wife dead.

'I have staked my reputation, Father. And when you have one hundred and sixty billion US dollars under management – as I do – reputation is *everything*. It was that reputation that got us the four hundred million to make this project happen.'

'Don't lecture me, boy! In the scheme of things, four hundred million is small fry to you.'

'True, but we won't fail.'

Robert waited for his father's phlegmy, agitated breathing to slow down.

'So what are you doing about Hope Station?' the General growled.

For once the winds had died down, and Robert's tent – which resembled an oversized forty-four-gallon drum cut in half and laid on its side – felt too quiet, and his father's voice too loud. 'My hacker has been monitoring all their communications. The alarm hasn't been raised. The jammer is about to be activated, and I have a plan to deal with the six residents.'

'Well, get on with it,' grumbled the General. 'And watch out for

22

Luke Searle. I have read his file. He lacks discipline and challenges his superiors, but he's a born survivor. Seven seasons in Antarctica, experienced mountaineer, has trekked through the Karakoram … He survived a three-day storm by digging an ice cave.'

Thanks to his hacker, Robert had watched Searle's email traffic and paid particular attention to his regular Skype calls to his son. In any campaign, Robert always tried to identify his enemies' weaknesses. Searle's was his son. But Robert would keep that to himself for now. If his plan worked, there would be no need to exploit it.

'I agree, but Madeline Wildman is the leader. She is disciplined, tough—'

'Pah! A woman! Don't be ridiculous. Now, eliminate them or I will order Captain Wei to do it.'

As their phone conversation ended, Wei's voice barked over the two-way radio. 'Captain Oates to Commander Scott. Permission to wake the baby?'

It was Robert's idea to adopt the names of Robert Falcon Scott's team. It was unlikely their radio transmissions would be overheard, but this way their identities were safeguarded. Besides, he enjoyed the association with the heroic Scott. Wei's message meant that he was within a kilometre of Hope Station and ready to activate the jammer. The captain wouldn't be spotted: his white parka, hood and salopettes gave him more than adequate camouflage.

'Scott to Oates. Permission granted.'

In his mind's eye, Robert could see the small wooden crate filled with fancy-dress clothing, stored at Hope Station. Hidden inside was a radio and satellite jammer, placed there many months ago by King, who had also planted key-loggers into three laptops bound for Hope Station so that Robert could monitor the keystrokes of Searle, Wildman and the now dead communications officer, MacNamara. The jammer resembled an early 'brick' mobile phone, but instead of one long antenna, it had four. King had selected the fancy-dress crate because he knew its contents were unlikely to be opened until the winter solstice celebration on the twenty-first of June, by which time his employer's mission would be complete.

'The baby is awake, sir,' said Wei.

Robert turned to his communications officer, Huang Feng. 'So it'll jam for eighteen hours if it's inside, in the warm, but what if it's stored outside? How long then?'

Huang was almost hidden by the laptops, sat phones, handheld GPS and GPR units, surveillance binoculars and other equipment that was piled on his table. 'Batteries don't cope well in extreme cold. It could be as little as six, sir.'

'But it will block all frequency bands?'

'All those used at Hope, yes.' Huang looked at his monitors and scratched his shaved head. 'Sir, the jammer doesn't appear to be working.'

'Why not?' asked Robert, his voice perfectly calm.

'I don't know yet, sir. The battery could be dislodged or perhaps drained.' Huang looked nervously askance at his commander. 'I'm working on it, sir.'

Robert radioed Wei. 'Captain Oates, are you sure the baby's awake? Confirm.'

Wei responded with an affirmative.

'The baby appears dead,' Robert told him. 'Keep one of your men on watch. If a search party leaves Hope, alert me.'

'Will do, sir.'

Robert now addressed Huang. 'If it's the battery, how do we solve it?'

'Someone has to find the jammer and replace the battery, which means entering the station.'

'Time to call in a favour.'

T MINUS 5 DAYS, 29 MINUTES
5 March, 11:31 am (UTC-07)

Luke blinked, his thick black eyelashes sweeping away the sting of salt. Dodging chunks of sea ice, he managed to keep the twelve-person inflatable rubber boat, a Zodiac, at a reasonable speed as they approached the brooding bulk of Whalers Island.

Circular in shape, the island was a volcanic caldera, with asphalt-grey, icy crags punctuated by bleak beaches of black volcanic sand. A burst of red between the jumble of icebergs and smaller bergy bits caught Luke's eye. He squinted into the murky distance; it had to be the *Professor Basov*. She was always the last tourist ship of the season and usually dropped anchor for one night inside the island's hidden harbour. But with the bird flu outbreak, she had clearly kept a safe distance. Luke had hoped the *Basov* might be in the area: a chance to catch up with his mate, Vitaly Yushkov. He wiped his sunglasses with a gloved hand and placed them back on his wind-chafed face. Tubs sat on the bulbous side of the boat, grinning with delight, with one hand gripping the rope.

Luke revved the engine and leaned into the rush of air, one leg forward to stabilise himself. The sun broke through the clouds and lit up the submerged section of a truck-sized piece of floating ice, which glowed a dazzling turquoise. A three-metre leopard seal sunbathed on the icy raft. Its mouth, wide enough to engulf Luke's head, seemed fixed in a permanent Joker's grin.

'Look at the size of that,' called Tubs, pointing.

'They get even bigger,' Luke shouted back. 'The females can reach almost four metres.'

The seal, so sleek and fast in the water, lumbered towards the ice's edge and slid in.

As they moved around a three-storey-high iceberg shaped like a dented teapot, the predominantly white *Professor Basov* was revealed. Now Luke could clearly see the brightly painted funnel – with its horizontal stripes alternating red, blue and black – and the garish red lifeboats, raised high on the upper deck. The ice-breaker, five storeys high, with rust stains down its bow like a nosebleed, had dropped anchor. Luke spied tiny figures on the decks and knew the tourists were enjoying the breathtaking views.

As they approached the vessel, Luke spotted Vitaly Yushkov leaning on the railing at the stern. Over his powerful wrestler's body, the tall Russian wore a navy-blue boilersuit, from which a wide neck and a head of closely cropped fair hair protruded. Despite the cold, his head and hands weren't covered. He was smoking a cigarette, which he stubbed out on the deck under his salt-stained boots, and kicked the stub into the ocean.

When Luke was close enough, he hollered, 'Hey! Stop littering, you old bastard.'

Vitaly didn't deign to respond. He didn't even move his head but he must have glanced down in their direction, as he straightened and waved his muscular arms in the air. Luke waved back and used his two-way radio to request permission to board the ship. The gangway was lowered, and with the Zodiac safely secured, Luke and Tubs went aboard. They stepped into a shallow pool of disinfectant to ensure they didn't contribute to the spread of any infectious diseases.

Vitaly opened his arms wide and caught Luke in a bear hug. 'My friend. Good to see you.'

He pushed Luke away as quickly as he had embraced him. 'You bring me a gift?' he demanded, folding his arms across his broad chest.

'What? So you can litter the ocean some more?' laughed Luke. 'Now why would I do that?' Luke unzipped his windproof jacket and retrieved a packet of cigarettes from his inner pocket. 'But I guess if you want to kill yourself, who am I to stop you?' he joked, as he threw the packet at Vitaly.

'Ha!' said Vitaly, as if to say he knew all along that Luke had them concealed on his person. He popped the cigarettes in his boilersuit pocket. His sapphire-blue eyes then focused on Tubs.

'This is Tubs, the best station chef I've ever known. He can really cook,' said Luke. 'Tubs, this is my good friend, Vitaly Yushkov. I did a stint as a tour guide on this ship. If it hadn't been for Vitaly, I would have thrown myself overboard.' Luke glanced up at the tourists watching them, thankful he was not at their beck and call.

'If you are a friend of this big guy, then you are also my friend,' said Vitaly, embracing Tubs, who wriggled free as soon as he could without offending the Russian. He wasn't comfortable with man-on-man hugging.

The arrival of two strangers had captured the attention of several guests, who hovered nearby, whispering to each other in their diverse languages. But because the Russian crew didn't fraternise with the tourists, the onlookers kept a polite distance.

'Why you come here?' Vitaly asked.

Luke smiled. Vitaly had always been direct. 'I wanted to take a look at Whalers and talk to Charlie, our guy in charge of the quarantine. You know, see how he's going,' he said, moving to the starboard side of the ship. Vitaly and Tubs followed.

'We cannot visit the island,' Vitaly said. 'It is this bird flu. The tourists, they are not happy.'

Luke nodded and tried to raise Charlie on the radio. No response. He frowned. 'Must be out of range. I'll try again later.' He looked at Vitaly. 'How about a coffee?'

'Of course.'

'Still like paint stripper?'

'Worse. I take you to Captain first.'

Vitaly then clomped up the steel steps of each deck until he reached the bridge. It was midday – way too early for Captain Dmitry Bolshakov to

27

be at the helm, Luke thought. He had expected the captain to be sleeping off the alcohol that ran through his veins pretty much twenty-four/seven. Luke stepped forward to shake his hand.

'Luke.' From behind his white handlebar moustache and ruddy pockmarked skin, Bolshakov smiled. He wore a light camel-coloured uniform, complete with gold-braided insignia on his epaulettes. Luke could smell the alcohol on his breath.

The bridge was warm, the old radiators still pumping out a comfortable heat. Luke gazed around. Nothing had changed since his time on the *Basov*. The heavy grey equipment with large dials dated the ship to the 1980s; she'd been built in St Petersburg.

'Still deftly steering the ship away from danger?' Luke said. He remembered seeing the captain stand steady as his ship corkscrewed through terrifying seas, despite having consumed a bottle of vodka a few hours before.

Bolshakov shrugged. 'Of course. So, you visit us. Why?'

At that moment a short-haired, compact man with bulbous eyes entered. He moved with the agility of an athlete, each step a controlled bounce. 'I saw you come on board. I'm Alrek Tangen, from Norway. Have you come from Whalers?' His English was near perfect – educated, fast-paced, no-nonsense. Alrek put out his hand to shake Luke's and then thought better of it. The hand was swiftly retracted.

'No, Hope Station. Luke Searle and Warren Grigg.' Luke used Tubs' real name. 'So there's no danger we've brought the virus on board,' said Luke, anticipating Alrek's concern.

'Good,' Alrek said, shaking their hands in turn, with new-found enthusiasm. He then took a step back and fidgeted from foot to foot – he clearly had more energy than he could expend. 'Didn't want the ship quarantined, you know. Must keep the guests happy. So?' he asked, waiting for Luke to explain his uninvited presence.

'Visiting old friends,' Luke responded, flicking a smile at Vitaly and Bolshakov. 'And I was wondering if you'd seen any activity on Whalers? Our station leader is worried. Communication with the AARO quarantine team has been … limited.'

'Arrow?' asked Vitaly, misunderstanding the acronym.

'Short for Australian Antarctic Research Organisation,' Luke clarified.

Bolshakov handed Luke the binoculars. 'You look.'

The bridge afforded Luke a high vantage point. He scanned the nearest beach and could make out small black and white feathery bodies strewn over the grey sand. He swallowed hard. It looked like a massacre. Maddie would be devastated.

Alrek said, 'I've seen men in orange coats walking along the beach.'

Luke felt reassured that men wearing AARO colours had been seen. He was about to radio Charlie again on the island when he heard Maddie's voice. 'Luke, Tubs – this is Maddie. Do you read? Over?'

Luke pulled the radio close. 'Maddie, Luke here. Receive you loud and clear.'

'Where the hell are you?'

Tubs winced. She didn't sound happy. Luke could hear Vitaly chuckling behind him.

'On the *Professor Basov*,' he replied. 'Checking out Whalers Island.'

'Shit, Luke. I made it clear you weren't to go there.' Luke saw Alrek raise an eyebrow. *Sure*, he thought, *she hadn't wanted to go*, but he knew Maddie would see this as another example of his impetuousness. Maybe now was not the time to point out that he had turned his tag and written, clearly and neatly, his intention to visit Whalers Island in the book.

'Luke, we need you back here now,' she went on. 'Mac and Dave haven't come back, and they're not responding to radio contact.'

T MINUS 4 DAYS, 22 HOURS, 40 MINUTES
5 March, 1:20 pm (UTC-07)

Luke had ten minutes before the briefing. He tore off his salt-spattered parka and went to Skype, hoping Jason might be online earlier than they'd arranged. He was.

'Hey, little buddy,' Luke said, staring into his son's questioning eyes that were so similar to his own. Like his father, Jason preferred to observe people rather than engage with them. Jason's laptop was on a low plastic table, so Luke's view of his bedroom was limited to a glimpse of a sheet with penguins on it and a large green Lego tractor sitting on the floor.

'Look what I did.' Jason disappeared from view. A few seconds later he returned with what looked like a boat made of cardboard, painted orange with black portholes, which he placed between himself and the monitor so that Luke could barely see the boy's face. 'The Big Orange!' Jason shouted and giggled.

As it was Sunday and only 7:22 am in Melbourne, Jessica was probably still asleep. But Luke didn't want to dampen his son's excitement. 'The *Aurora Australis*. That's fantastic, Jase! Did you make it at school?'

Jason nodded, his face bobbing in and out of view. 'Tell me the story, Daddy.'

Luke checked the screen clock. He didn't have time, but his son's eager face won him over. Luke's fondest memory was of storytime, when Jason would snuggle under his arm and gaze up at him, open-mouthed.

'There's a very big ship that's painted bright orange, and it's called…'

'The Big Orange!'

'That's right. And it travels to a land of ice called …' He waited for Jason to chip in.

'Antarg … diga.'

'Antarctica, yes. And the ice-breaker goes up onto the sea ice and then it crashes down and cracks it—'

'Boom! Boom! Boom!' Jason shouted. Jessica wouldn't be asleep for much longer.

Luke raised his finger to his mouth, as if to say, *Hush*, and continued. 'And on the sea ice live lots of seals and—'

A woman's voice cut in. 'Keep the noise down, will you?' Then she leaned over Jason and pushed aside the cardboard ship so she could see Luke.

'If you have to talk this early, can you try not to get him so excited?' Despite her scowl and their unhappy history, Luke was still drawn to her translucent skin and full lips. Before he could say anything, she continued, 'We need to talk. But not now. Finish up, will you?'

'Jess?' called Luke.

Luke heard her voice and then a man's. Or was it the radio? Jason frowned.

'What's the matter, Jase?'

Jason looked down and wriggled about in his chair.

Luke knew he shouldn't ask his son the question, but he had to know. 'Does Mummy have a friend staying?'

Jason looked around the room, chewing his lip, and then nodded.

'Time to stop,' said Jessica from the doorway. 'Say goodbye.'

'Bye, Daddy.'

'Bye, Jase. Love you.'

Jessica severed the connection. Luke glanced at his hand on the mouse. It was shaking.

31

'Briefing,' Maddie called from the door. 'In the dining room, now.' She was gone.

Luke stood. His legs quivered as if he'd run a marathon. He had broken out in a sweat and his thermals clung to him.

Craig passed his doorway. 'Hurry up, mate.'

In a daze, Luke changed his top and then ran down the corridor.

In the dining room, the tension was palpable. Even Luke, who was calm when it came to rescues, felt his stomach tighten when he entered. Tubs was leaning against the wall, his folded arms resting on his ballooning stomach. Luke slid onto a bench. Sue Sadri, the plumber, plonked down next to him. He received a static shock as her arm brushed his. She stayed close regardless, gnawing at what remained of a fingernail. Short and squat, with a tattooed neck, she resembled a wrestler in pink. Craig was opposite them, with a mug of tea in his callused hands.

Maddie stood in front of the group, hands on her hips. The doctor, Frank Stone, was not far from her side. He was a man who took particular pride in his long, bushy beard, trimming it each morning as if he were training a bonsai. As a result, he'd earned the nickname Bluebeard, shortened to Blue.

'It's now four hours of zero radio contact,' Maddie began, 'and an hour and a half since Mac and Dave missed their midday return-to-station deadline. Given how reliable Mac is' – Maddie glanced at Luke, as if to emphasise the difference between the two men – 'we're now into SAR.' A search and rescue. 'At this stage, I'm not going to send more than three people out.' Her voice reverberated across the near-empty dining room. It was built to seat forty. The six who were present scarcely filled one corner. 'Luke is leader. Blue, I'd like you to go on this one, and Craig.'

Luke looked up, frowning in surprise. She looked at him again. 'Yes, Luke, I'd like you to lead. You know the Walgreen Crevasse better than anyone, and you're the most experienced abseiler. If they're in trouble down there, we'll need your skills to get them out.'

Very few people had ever set foot on the Pine Island Glacier – or PIG, as it was affectionately known. Luke had spent more time exploring its two hundred and fifty by forty kilometre expanse than any other person. Even their Chinese neighbours and friends at Li Bai Station spent most of their time focusing on the West Antarctic Ice Sheet, and only one of their scientists had ever joined Luke onsite. Luke knew all about the glacier's dangers, including the Walgreen – or Wal, a jagged crevasse that ran inland for ten kilometres – where Mac and Dave had been shutting up shop for the winter.

'I need you to stick to SAR protocols. No deviations. Got it?'

'Got it,' Luke replied. 'Has a locator beacon been activated?' All Hope Station vehicles had these; once a beacon was activated, any of the other station vehicles would be able to locate them.

'Nope.'

Curious, he thought.

Maddie began her briefing. Luke knew she had to issue instructions and run through safety procedures, but time was wasting. 'Maddie,' he cut in, 'we have plenty of light to get there today. Clear skies and the sun's low angle means we'll get nice long shadows. So no problem spotting slots. We should get going.' Shadows from icy peaks and troughs sometimes indicated a crevasse hidden under a shallow layer of snow, sometimes called a slot.

'There's a storm brewing to the south that could be heading our way. I want to wait an hour to check its direction.'

'I don't want to wait,' replied Luke. He noticed out of the corner of his eye Sue's jaw drop slightly. He shook his head, struggling to be diplomatic. 'I mean, I'm worried. If there's been an accident, the faster we get there the better.'

'I agree,' Maddie replied, 'but a SAR in a blizzard is too dangerous.'

'It'll take an hour to reach the camp. We've got to get going now. If we wait and the storm hits, we won't be going anywhere.' Under the table, Luke dug his fingers into his thighs, exasperated with Maddie and furious at himself. Why hadn't he made that second call to Mac?

'And if it does hit?' Maddie asked, pacing back and forth. 'I'd be putting the three of you in danger, and that won't help Dave and Mac one iota.'

Maddie closed her eyes, clearly trying to hide her annoyance. When they opened again they flashed a warning at Luke, a message she'd aimed at him several times over the past few months. Luke ignored the admonishment, momentarily fascinated by the woman glaring at him. He gazed at her stunning green eyes and the light freckles on her skin.

Luke focused back on his argument. 'If the storm hits and we're at the camp, we'll shelter in one of the apples. Plenty of food and medical supplies there. And we'll hopefully know more about the boys by then. If we're caught out on the ice, we'll shelter in our tent and wait it out. Either way, we'll be closer to finding them.'

'No, Luke, I can't allow that. We'll wait an hour and then decide. Now, let's run through SAR procedures.' Her tone allowed no further discussion.

Frustrated, Luke clenched his jaw and stared fixedly at the wall map, trying to regain his composure. Antarctica looked like a giant stingray, with its 'tail' curling up toward Argentina. His eyes traced the coastline to the base of the tail. A tiny dot marked Hope Station. To help locate their field site, Tubs had pinned a tiny plastic pig, the size of a fingernail, that dangled from a key ring. This had been on their second day, and Luke remembered wondering what their new chef was up to.

'Are you trying to tell us something?' he had asked, nodding at the pig, a wide smile on his face.

'Nah, it represents PIG 1 – you know, our camp.' Tubs had followed this comment with an *oink*. 'It's my lucky pig. Comes with me everywhere. Thought I'd share the luck.'

I hope it's working, Luke thought now. Mac was the worry: as their communications officer, he knew a lot about radios, computers and satellites, but not so much about surviving on an ice sheet. And if Mac was in trouble, why hadn't Dave – the more experienced field assistant – called for help? Luke fidgeted. Something was definitely wrong.

Deep in thought, he didn't hear Maddie's question. 'You got that, Luke?' she asked, waving her hand in front of him to attract his attention. Sue kicked him in the ankle.

'What?'

Sue pointed at Maddie, who raised her eyes in exasperation.

'Sorry, what was that?' said Luke.

'I said the key to survival is teamwork. And no heroics, okay?'

'Okay.'

Maddie continued with her briefing. *Damn protocols*, Luke thought. Precious minutes were ticking by. He stood up abruptly. 'Maddie, no disrespect, but I've done more search and rescue than anyone here, and I know how dangerous this glacier is to cross—'

It was Maddie's turn to cut in. 'Yes, Luke. We all know you think the PIG is the next Larsen B. So its instability is exactly why it's not safe to cross without good visibility.'

The other station members' faces moved from Luke to Maddie and back, as if following a tennis match.

Luke shook his head. 'What I'm trying to say is that I can get us there. If they've had an accident or they're hurt, they're going to need a doctor as soon as possible. Tomorrow could be too late.'

Blue spoke up. 'I know it's against protocol, but Luke is right. If they're injured and we wait out a storm, they may not survive the night.'

Maddie folded her arms, eyebrows raised in surprise. The doctor was cautious by nature.

'Craig, Sue? What do you think?' she asked.

'I'm with you, Maddie,' Craig drawled. 'No point having five in trouble instead of two. But if they're not safely inside the apple, the boys are unlikely to survive a blizzard.'

'Sue?'

'I'm with Luke. He could be there and back by nightfall, and we'd all sleep better knowing the guys are okay.'

Maddie looked up to the ceiling and chewed her lower lip. 'Okay, get kitted up and we'll reconvene in fifteen minutes. Craig, can you check the latest forecast? If it's okay, you guys can go.' She looked at Craig, who nodded his approval. 'Make sure you carry extra fuel and check over the tent before you pack it. And call in on the hour, every hour.'

Luke headed for the door.

'Wait,' Maddie called. 'I want you to double-check the

recovery kit and each one of you to go through your survival bags. And harnesses on. I want you all attached to your snowmobiles and the snowmobiles linked. Don't go losing any of my expensive gear,' she joked, trying to defuse the tension.

Blue rose to his feet.

Luke turned to him. 'I'll meet you and Craig in the garage. Sue, can you get the snowmobiles ready?'

'Sure,' she said.

'Blue, you got everything?' Maddie asked. 'You'll need a stretcher in case we have a serious injury.'

'Yup, got one. I'll be able to do most things, except operate,' he replied, his brow furrowed with anxiety.

'Doc, the guys will be fine,' Luke said. 'Don't worry.'

Luke took long, determined strides down the corridor to his room. Sue followed, at a trot.

'Luke,' she called.

He slowed but didn't stop.

'Give Maddie a break,' Sue said, working hard to keep up with him. 'She's just looking out for you guys. It's her job.'

Luke stopped. 'I know, I just want to get moving. I can't help thinking something is wrong, and it's my fault. I should never have let Mac go.'

She grabbed his arm. 'He asked, remember? But that's not the point.'

'Look. Maddie was frosty with me from the day we met. On the *Aurora Australis*. And that was before we discovered our very different approaches to station life.' He started walking again and Sue bustled down the corridor with him.

'I know, but she *is* the station leader and you just can't do whatever you want. She's responsible for us all.'

Luke placed his arm around Sue's shoulder and gave her a hug. 'Mate, I appreciate you looking out for me. But I need to focus now. What Maddie does or doesn't think of me doesn't matter.'

Within minutes, he was dressed in multiple layers and on his way to the drying room to collect his boots. He passed the mess. 'Tubs,' he called out.

Tubs' head shot up like a jack-in-the-box from behind a sofa where some small boxes were stored. Luke guessed he was rummaging through the party supplies crate.

'I appreciate the thought, but let's find Mac and Dave before we think about a party.'

Tubs stumbled to stand, hands in his pockets. 'Right you are.'

'What's up?' asked Luke.

'Nothing.' Tubs looked down and then shuffled sideways. He handed Luke the tiny pink plastic pig. 'Take this, mate.'

Luke smiled and put the pig in his parka pocket. 'Thanks, Tubs, but we won't need luck. It'll be fine.' Luke gave him a playful punch on the arm. 'I'll be back for dinner, so get those steaks marinating.'

'You reckon the guys are okay?' asked Tubs.

'They're okay. I'll find them,' Luke said, faking an optimism that he didn't feel.

Luke took the lift down one level to the garage. On the way, he zipped up his orange parka and put on his mask, goggles and gloves. Sue had already fired up the snowmobiles. Maddie reluctantly gave them the go-ahead. Luke double-checked the vehicles, then his survival bag and lastly the recovery kit, with its rescue equipment that included an ice hammer, shovel and rope.

'So you scientists have your uses, then. Not just good at winning awards,' Sue joked, leaning on the handlebars.

Luke smiled. 'Well, this one, anyway. Man of many talents.'

'Seriously, mate, well done.' Sue blushed like a ripe peach.

Luke winked, then turned to Blue and Craig. 'Okay, time to harness up.' Each man stepped into his climbing harness, which was then linked, via three metres of rope, to his snowmobile. Between Luke's vehicle and Blue's was a Kalkis sled carrying equipment, and between Blue's and Craig's was the stretcher. All the vehicles were linked together by rope.

'Time to get moving.' Luke nodded at Blue, who was already astride his snowmobile.

'Ready,' said Craig.

Luke switched on the ground-penetrating radar, or GPR. Raised above his head on a pole, it was designed to detect sub-surface features such as hidden crevasses. The data was fed to a small monitor on his handlebars. It was working fine. He then tested the two-way radio strapped across his chest. 'Luke to Blue. This is a test.'

'Read you loud and clear,' said Blue.

'Luke to Craig.'

'Craig here, go ahead,' he replied.

Luke then addressed them directly. 'Guys, we'll travel twenty metres apart and keep the ropes taut. The GPR should tell me where the crevasses are, but I'm gonna stop and look around a lot. I'll be searching for hidden slots. Okay?'

'Luke, I'll be yanking your chain all the way,' Blue joked, his chuckle muffled by his bird's nest of a beard.

T MINUS 4 DAYS, 21 HOURS, 35 MINUTES
5 March, 2:25 pm (UTC-07)

Blue followed Luke like a car behind a tow truck. Five minutes earlier, the sky had been a brilliant, clear cornflower-blue. But they could see the storm building, the clouds ominously dark. Antarctic blizzards were infamous for both their savagery and their sudden and unexpected arrival. Luke slowed and then halted. They had made good progress, but ahead of them the pristine uniformity of the ice shelf was morphing into a swirling mass of airborne ice. Above the monotone of the engines, Luke could hear the winds gathering speed.

Blue pulled his warm neck tube away from his mouth. 'We should go back,' he said. 'We can't rescue anyone in that.'

'It's only another kay to the camp, and we can't outrun it,' replied Luke, gazing at the distant storm.

Craig shook his head. 'Luke, you know the rules. Not in a blizzard. We either turn back or put up the pyramid and wait for it to pass.'

Luke stared in the direction of PIG 1.

'Doesn't look that bad to me.'

'Don't be so bloody stupid,' said Blue. 'Absolutely no way. I say we get inside our tent. Now.' His voice, a deep baritone, was urgent.

Luke looked at the ropes that tied their snowmobiles together.

As the lead vehicle, if he fell into a crevasse, the other two should be able to take his weight and pull him back out. Alone, he would plummet to his death. And he couldn't manage a rescue alone. He would need Blue and Craig if someone had to be hauled out of a crevasse. He had to persuade them to keep going.

'I can't do that, Blue,' said Luke. 'If they didn't make it to the pod, they won't survive the storm. I need you with me.'

'You're mad, Luke. You're putting our lives on the line,' Craig snapped.

'Then I'll go on alone.'

'You're a stubborn bastard, aren't you?' Blue said, thumping the handlebars.

'Put yourself in their shoes. What if they're wounded? Can't get to shelter? They'd be praying we'd come and find them. In that storm, they won't last long.'

At that moment, Maddie's voice called over the radio. 'Luke, this is Maddie. Do you read?'

Luke made no move to respond.

'Luke, do you hear me? The blizzard is right in your path. Get the tent up and wait it out. Over.'

'Ah, to hell with it,' Blue grumbled. 'If we're going on this suicide mission, let's get on with it. But we've gotta go real slow. I don't want to end up in an icy grave.'

'You're both out of your minds. But I can't leave you in the shit now, can I?' said Craig. Then he muttered, 'Good fucking job this is my last season. Won't get another posting.'

'Thanks, guys. I owe you one.'

'You owe me a hell of a lot more than that. I must be fucking mad,' mumbled Blue. 'And what are we going to tell the boss?'

Luke pulled the radio close to his mouth. 'Maddie, this is Luke. Weather looks fine here. We're continuing to PIG 1, only another kay to go. Out.' He dropped his radio back to his chest and revved the engine. He ignored Maddie's remonstrations, knowing he'd be in deep shit when he returned. But he couldn't let Mac and Dave down. 'Keep really tight,' he said.

'Gotcha,' replied Blue.

'I ain't losing you,' said Craig.

As the wind grew stronger, tiny particles of ice were whipped up into the air; it was like entering a cloud of shrapnel. Luke could no longer see the sky. At least it wasn't a complete whiteout – at least he could see the front of his snowmobile. They slowed to a crawl.

The adrenaline spread like fire through Luke's body. He could feel the wind buffeting him and marvelled at the unstoppable force of nature. He felt alive, just as he had when monstrous waves had lunged at the giant ice-breaker that had transported him to Hope Station. He craned his neck to check on his team. Blue might be nervous but he was doing fine, and Craig was clearly unfazed.

Luke accelerated gently, checking his GPR monitor. He'd be relying on it to get them there, since visibility was virtually nil. But it couldn't detect surface boulders, so to avoid them he'd have to rely on memory alone. They were coming up to a large glacial 'erratic' – a boulder stuck for thousands of years in the ice.

In the howling winds Luke pressed his radio close to his lips. 'Craig, Blue, this is Luke. Moving right. Erratic ahead.'

Neither man acknowledged the message. They probably couldn't hear him above the winds. Luke repeated his warning, and first Craig and then Blue said they'd received it. They steered to the right. The boulder, as high as a house, appeared almost out of nowhere.

'Luke, this is Blue. I can't see you.'

Luke braked. 'Roger that. Just follow the rope. I've stopped moving.'

'Luke, can you hear me? This is Blue. I can't see you.'

Shit. He hadn't heard Luke's response. Luke tried again. The rope didn't move and Blue didn't appear. The air was so thick with ice that it was like trying to see through cotton wool, but Luke could just make out the beam from Blue's single headlight. He drove round in a narrow arc and found Blue crouched forward over his machine, his gloved hands rigidly gripping the handlebars.

Luke pulled up parallel and stopped. 'You all right?'

'Not sure,' Blue replied. 'Feeling claustrophobic, like I can't breathe. All this ice in the air. Can't see a thing.'

Luke hesitated. He knew he wasn't good at looking after people. In fact, he hated it. Luke's solitary childhood had taught him to simply get on with things, because nobody else was going to do it for him. His French father, a head chef, had been too busy running his kitchen, and his Australian mother too busy chasing new lovers. Luke had learned to look after himself but never anyone else. Why in God's name had Maddie put him in charge?

'You'll be fine,' he told Blue. 'All you have to do is follow the rope. Real slow, I promise.'

Luke led the way and, to his relief, Blue followed. They were approaching another rocky outcrop. This time, Blue stayed so close that his snowmobile might have been a dog sniffing another's tail. The second boulder was much smaller, but still large enough to wreck a vehicle and seriously hurt the rider.

For Luke, though, this was familiar territory, even in a blizzard. After five months monitoring the gashes opening up across the glacier, and the alarming acceleration of its flow towards the sea, he knew its features intimately. The Walgreen Crevasse was widening by a metre each week. He'd targeted another one for his summer research: the Fitzgerald, which ran parallel to the Walgreen but, at twenty kilometres, was much longer. The two crevasses were like train tracks, with a strip of solid glacier between them.

Ahead, a narrow snow bridge over a crevasse separated the search party from PIG 1. Luke had crossed it many times and knew it was strong enough to support their snowmobiles. To the untrained eye, it looked solid, if slightly sunken. But a few metres below the snow bridge there was a deep void. Last year, a colleague had accidentally fallen into a crevasse like this because he'd strayed from an approved travel route. Luckily, he'd survived.

Luke halted. Blue stopped and waited, then Craig arrived too. The wind speed was picking up – it was now around sixty, maybe even seventy kilometres per hour – and Luke had to lean into it as he shouted into his radio. 'Luke to Craig and Blue. I'll go first. It's safe. I've used this bridge before. Over.'

'This is Blue. Can't we go around?' His words were almost lost to the roaring winds.

Luke held the radio as close to his mouth as possible. 'Say again?'

'Can't we go around?' Blue shouted into his radio.

'Luke here. Take too long. Storm's getting worse.' Luke paused for a moment, considering what might go wrong. 'It should be sound, but if the bridge collapses and I fall, you'll have to brake and turn your snowmobile over to take my weight. Blue, you're next in line – can you do that?'

'Affirmative,' said Blue, but Luke was worried he might panic again.

'Craig, are you happy with that?' Luke shouted, seeking reassurance from the more confident man.

'Craig here. No worries, I've done this before.'

Luke pulled away at a crawl. The snow bridge was twice the width of his vehicle, but with such poor visibility it felt to Luke as if he were crossing a knife's edge. Buried beneath the thick layers of his clothing, his heart galloped. He was across in a few seconds but it felt like a lifetime. With his brake on, he radioed Blue. 'Safely across. Your turn now.'

The response was slow. 'Blue to Luke. Will do.' Was it the wind that made his voice sound weak?

Luke couldn't see across to the other side of the snow bridge but he could see the rope didn't move. He waited. Still no movement. Then suddenly the rope zinged tight. His heart almost missed a beat. Had Blue fallen? Luke immediately turned his snowmobile on its side and dug his ice axe into the glacier surface. This would enable him to hold a snowmobile's weight if necessary. 'This is Luke,' he radioed. 'What's up, Blue?' He wouldn't allow his voice to betray his agitation.

No response.

'Blue, can you hear me? This is Luke. Are you in trouble?'

Still no response, but then the rope loosened. Luke released a breath he hadn't realised he'd been holding. Through the swirling snow and ice, the red snowmobile and its orange-clad driver materialised like an apparition. He was across the bridge. Blue sped up and stopped behind Luke.

'Blue, what happened?' asked Luke, still clinging to his buried ice axe.

'Nothing. Just taking my time.' He nodded at Luke's upended

snowmobile. 'Good to see you're looking out for me.'

Luke gave him the thumbs-up. He guessed that Blue had mistakenly reversed in a moment of fear, but he didn't want to embarrass the good doctor. Craig appeared shortly afterwards. Luke righted his snowmobile and retrieved his ice axe.

'Nearly there,' said Luke. 'Look out for the marker flags.'

The field site was little more than a generator and two red, domed pods, with porthole windows. The apples were just big enough to house two scientists amongst the equipment and provide shelter, food and emergency supplies. Radiating out from the apples were poles, dug into the ice at each of the four points of the compass, with red triangular flags that helped the scientists find their shelter in bad weather. Luke spotted the first flag and immediately felt a surge of relief.

They stopped outside the first apple. The whole site was covered in a layer of snow. Even though visibility was improving as the storm began to subside, tracking footprints was impossible. Luke opened the hut door and stepped inside, hoping to find Mac and Dave sheltering inside. But the men weren't there. Luke checked the second apple. Nobody.

'Where could they be?' asked Blue. They no longer needed to use their radios; the wind had died to a low whine.

Luke looked around. There was no other shelter. The three men walked around the site, searching for clues, but found nothing. Mac's and Dave's snowmobiles were still parked next to the generator, packed with research equipment. Luke checked inside the pods again and realised their radios weren't there. They must have them. Luke tried calling them but received no reply. In fact, he heard nothing at all. Not even a signal.

'Craig, try your radio, will you? Mine's gone dead.'

Craig tried calling Luke. 'Dead as a dodo.'

'Mine too,' said Blue. 'What the hell is going on?'

Luke's heartbeat sped up. He removed his mask. He felt suffocated by it. The cold slapped him in the face and helped him focus. The radios were the least of his worries. Luke stared out into the never-ending whiteness. Where would they go without their snowmobiles?

He grabbed the binoculars and scanned the ice sheet. If they were out there and hurt, they'd be buried under snow by now. He lowered the binoculars. No, it had to be an accident.

His eyes moved apprehensively in the direction of the Walgreen Crevasse.

Robert admired himself on video at the Chinese Polar Institute's indoor mountaineering centre. Hadn't he surprised his instructor, who had mistakenly assumed his damaged hand would hold him back! He stood and stretched, knocking the remaining Hope Station two-way radio to the floor. He picked it up.

'Mac to Hope. Receiving you weak and intermittent,' he said in his best Australian accent, reliving the moment of his subterfuge.

'Sir,' interrupted Huang, 'I can confirm the jammer is working. Their radio and satellite communications are down.'

Robert leaned over the officer's desk. 'Are you absolutely certain?'

'Yes, sir. Your contact must have fixed the jammer.'

'Everybody has a price. The secret is to know what it is.' Robert paused. 'And the internet? No emails? No tweets?'

'Already fixed. Hope Station cannot send a message to the outside world.'

'How does it work? I know the Eye bypassed AARO's firewall, unnoticed, some time ago. One of our many safeguards. Then what?'

'On your command, he has gained domain admin rights over AARO's headquarters in Kingston.'

Robert's thin brows frowned and the comms officer blinked nervously. 'Drop the jargon and get on with it,' Robert ordered.

'Yes, sir. Once our hacker's on the network he shuts down the routers at both Hope and at AARO's headquarters by deleting the routers' configuration and operating system.' Robert frowned again. Huang sped up, 'Both routers can be fixed – and we know at Kingston they have already done it – but they can't fix Hope Station's remotely. It can only be done by someone at Hope who knows what to do, and without their comms officer, they have no hope of fixing it.'

'Are you sure there's nobody who can?'

'There are two who might try,' replied Huang. 'Maddie Wildman, who seems quite IT-savvy, and Luke Searle, who's into computers. But if they don't know where the IOS file is stored on the server, they can't solve the problem.'

'IOS?'

'Internet Operation System. It makes the router work. They'd have to find the IOS file and then load it onto their switch hardware.'

'So if the hacker has complete control, he should delete the IOS file off the station server so there's no chance they'll find it.'

'He could do that, sir.'

'But surely Hope will have hardware backup? Disks?'

'General Zhao ordered King to remove them from the crate before it left Kingston. Hope Station has no backup.'

Robert nodded approvingly. 'Delete the software backup too.'

While Huang issued instructions to the hacker, Robert checked his emails. One alerted him to a live video feed from Whalers Island. He clicked the link and saw a grey sandy beach, strewn far and wide with the bodies of penguins. Against the ashen backdrop, the strikingly crisp black and white of the dead Adélie penguins' feathers dazzled him. He nodded as if he were appreciating one of the priceless masterpieces hanging in his Hong Kong office.

'Whalers Island,' he said aloud. 'The secret haven of hunters in days gone by.'

He clicked an icon and a three-dimensional map of the island appeared. He moved this new image to the top-right of the screen so he could still follow the live feed.

The hidden interior bay was large enough to contain Pearl Harbor. It could only be entered through a narrow breach in the sea cliffs, which was hard to find; hence it had been christened Deception Point. Robert traced the entrance to the inner sea with a long slim finger. Once a ship was inside the hidden harbour, it would be shrouded in a rank cloud of sulphur-laced steam that seeped out through the rocks. His finger moved to the bay where the Australian Antarctic Research Organisation's quarantine team had set up camp. He stabbed his finger at the words 'Whalers Bay'.

'A secret haven indeed.'

Robert closed the map and returned to the video. He watched as the cameraman moved inland, following the valley the penguins had used to return to their nests. At regular intervals he saw large red signs in English, Spanish and Mandarin: 'Quarantine. Do not enter.' He laughed. Robert had always marvelled at how easily the masses obeyed orders, especially signs forbidding something.

The cameraman spoke, complaining of the stench of ammonia from the pink penguin faeces that littered the thousands of nest sites. Nothing moved in this graveyard, except the feathers of the dead birds fluttering in the wind. The cameraman swore as he noticed movement, and Robert leaned forward in excitement. It was a penguin, barely alive, but unlike any other Adélie penguin. Instead of having a dazzling white chest, this bird was all black except for a small white patch around its beak. It was trying to walk but kept falling forward. Its mouth foamed.

'A genetic anomaly: an Adélie without the white feathers,' Robert said aloud. 'Come on, my ugly duckling, you can do it.' He clenched his right fist and cheered the penguin on. Terrified by the human closing in on it, the penguin, now on its belly, struggled to stand but was unable to. Blood filled its eyes, and its beak opened and closed, as if gasping for air. Some minutes passed until, finally, the bird died.

'Weakling,' Robert muttered. But, of course, it was hard to recover from strychnine poisoning.

T MINUS 4 DAYS, 20 HOURS, 56 MINUTES
5 March, 3:04 pm (UTC-07)

The storm had subsided but the silence filled Luke with dread. Without speaking, he started to disgorge the contents of the recovery kit. Before he got close to the crevasse's edge he had to anchor himself, and if either of their missing colleagues was in the chasm, he'd need to set up a pulley system to raise him. Luke was so desperate to get set up that it didn't occur to him to tell the others what he was doing.

'I'll give you a hand,' said Craig, who knew what Luke was up to.

Luke looked up, remembering his companions.

'You think they're down there?' asked Blue, nodding towards the Wal.

'I hope not, but I'm going to take a look. If they're not, we'll do a line search, using that pod as the fixed point. Here, help me get the anchors in,' he said, handing Craig the ice screws and ice axe.

Luke calculated where the three screws – each the length of a standard hammer – should go. Craig cleared away the loose surface ice and screwed them into the solid stuff. Luke threaded ropes through the eyes of the screws and knotted them, using a three-pronged fork pattern.

With the anchor system in place, Luke hooked his harness to it and switched on his head torch. He walked towards the lip of the crevasse, scanning the area for any sign of anchors that Mac and Dave may have used. Every AARO expeditioner received crevasse rescue training before leaving for Antarctica, Luke knew, so Mac and Dave would have followed these same procedures. Dave, in particular, as he was a keen mountaineer. He and Luke had often spent their time off abseiling into crevasses, which everybody else thought was utter madness.

So, if either Mac or Dave had set about a rescue, why were there no anchors?

Luke peered down into the darkness. The first few metres of icy walls shone blue, but the colour darkened until he couldn't differentiate between the walls and the space between. The overcast sky made it difficult to see into the depths. He used his head torch to search the ledges, but it was like shining a light at multiple fractured mirrors. It was nigh on impossible to fathom the actual shape of the space without entering it. But Luke knew this part of the crevasse well. Despite his sense of foreboding, his mind flickered fleetingly to an image from a movie he'd watched with Jason, when Superman's crystal fortress was destroyed. He pushed the mental image aside, annoyed at the distraction.

As he shone his torch at a ledge to his right, he spied something orange. His head told him that it had to be one of his friends, but he didn't want to believe it. He kneeled closer to the crevasse's lip and moved the torch's beam slowly over the orange shape. There was no doubt it was one of their men, and he wasn't moving.

'Dave! Mac! Are you down there? It's Luke – I'm coming to get you.' He waited for a cry, a moan, a banging, anything. 'Oh, God,' whispered Luke.

'What can you see?' called Blue, kneeling behind one of the anchors.

At first Luke couldn't answer. He shook his head. 'Someone on a ledge, six metres down, not moving.'

'I'll get kitted up and go down,' Blue shouted, quickly standing. 'He might be badly injured.'

Luke left the lip and raced towards them. 'No, I need you helping Craig with the pulley. It'll be tough work lifting him out.'

'I'm the doctor. It makes sense. I'll get geared up.'

'No!' Luke shouted. 'I mean, I'm stronger,' he said, seeing Blue's startled face. 'I can help from within the crevasse. He'll need you once we get him up. Okay?' Luke tapped Blue on the arm but didn't wait for him to agree. 'Craig, let's get a Z-system set up.' This was named after the Z shape formed by the rope between the pulleys. As a result, it would feel like they were only hauling one third of the victim's actual weight.

Craig nodded.

'Mate, I can tell you're angry but this is not your fault,' said Blue. 'So calm down a bit.'

Luke tested their handiwork and ignored Blue. 'Craig, you're heavier,' he said. 'Tie the rope end to your harness. It'll help you bear the weight. Blue, get yourself hooked to the anchors. I need you at the lip, relaying signs.'

'Luke—' It was too late. His leader was already heading for the Wal.

Blue hastily attached his harness by rope to the anchor and joined Luke.

'The lip looks pretty solid, so we shouldn't get much rope burn,' said Luke as he swung his legs over the edge and lay on his stomach.

'Ready, Craig?' Luke called.

'Ready!'

Blue watched Luke expertly manoeuvre himself down to the same ledge as the man in orange. He bent over the body and, in the semi-darkness, shone his torch at the lopsided head. It was Dave, his blond hair stained by a pool of frozen blood. His head had landed on a sharp, protruding piece of ice, and the point had split his skull open.

Luke wanted to retch but he wouldn't allow himself. He removed both layers of gloves on his right hand and touched the man's neck. It was a useless action. There would be no pulse.

'Luke?' Blue called out. 'Are you all right down there?'

'It's Dave.' His choked words were absorbed by the ice walls. Luke remembered his survival training. If you fall into a narrow crevasse like this one, it's hard to be heard from the outside. He went to use his radio and then remembered it didn't work. He tried shouting but his voice was a hoarse whisper, his throat dry, as if he had laryngitis. 'Found Dave.'

'Alive?' asked Blue.

'No.'

Silence, except for the creak of his rope.

'Can you get him out of there?' called Blue.

'Yes,' said Luke. *But I can't save him*, he thought.

'Need the stretcher?' asked Blue.

'No,' Luke said. Stretchers were for the living. 'Lower another line.'

Another rope came down. Luke tied it under Dave's legs and then around his chest. Checking that all the knots were secure, he indicated for them to start lifting the body. As the rope tightened, the body twitched as if still alive. Dave's torso lifted a few centimetres but his head hung back.

'Stop!' yelled Luke. 'He's stuck. Lower him back down.'

The blood had glued what was left of Dave's head to the frozen ledge. Using the pointy end of his ice axe Luke carefully chipped away at the blood, red splinters bursting out into oblivion, the noise reverberating through the chamber. All the time Dave's blank eyes stared at him. Luke kept chipping away but Dave's split head remained stuck to the ledge.

'Shit. I can't move him,' Luke called.

Luke could just make out a muffled conversation between Blue and Craig at the surface.

'Luke, Craig says you know what to do, so just do it, mate,' shouted Blue. 'Dave would forgive you.'

Luke looked up to see Blue's bird's nest of a face looking down at him. 'No way. I'm not pissing on the poor bastard. Jesus fucking Christ!'

'You can't leave him there. Just do it, Luke.'

'No way.' Luke used two Prusik loops to climb up and out of the crevasse. He was panting. 'I'll boil some water and use that.'

'Stay there, I'll get water,' said Blue. He scuttled to the pod, where Luke knew he'd have some snow melted on the little cooker within a few minutes. The doctor returned with a sealed thermos of hot water, handing it to a pale and silent Luke, who lay back on his stomach and dropped down into the crevasse again.

Luke carefully poured the water around Dave's head and then tenderly moved the skull away from the ice. A pink stream trickled over the ledge and down the walls.

'Okay. You can pull him up now. Nice and slow.'

The dangling rope above gradually tightened until it pulled taut with Dave's weight. Slowly, Dave began to rise, as if he were standing of his own volition. But his head hung to the right at an odd angle and his blue eyes bulged. Luke held out his hands to stop the body swinging too much. If it did, it might knock Luke off the ledge. Luke watched as the dead man rose above him and disappeared over the lip of the crevasse.

'I have him,' said Blue. Luke heard a muted, 'My God!'

'Throw down the rope. I'm searching for Mac,' Luke shouted.

'Mate, we're losing light. Too dangerous. In the morning,' said Blue.

'Throw down the rope,' Luke repeated slowly, trying to maintain his calm. He stared up but couldn't see what was happening at the surface. He hoped Blue was removing Dave from the bonds.

'Will do,' said Blue. Luke could hear the reluctance in his voice.

It took a few minutes for the rope to reach Luke. He used the torch to look deeper into the crevasse. Below him, the ice became like black onyx, glinting in the torchlight as if winking mockingly at him. He was shivering now, his sweat cold on his skin.

'Blue, I'm going deeper. You may not be able to hear me.'

'Not a good idea!' screamed Blue, as Luke lowered himself further into the V-shaped crevasse.

The walls closed in so much that Luke could touch both sides. Then he saw Mac. He appeared to be looking up, his mouth slightly open.

'Mac, mate, I'm coming for you. Hang on!'

Luke sped up his descent. Now the walls were only as wide as his shoulders, and a sharp protrusion tore his parka. At last, he hung directly above his friend. Mac was wedged between the pitch-black ice walls, with only his upper torso visible. He was trapped like a cork in a bottle. Luke stretched out his hand to grab Mac's parka.

'Mac? Mac? Come on, talk to me.'

Mac's eyes stared upwards, empty of life, bloodshot. At the side of his mouth, a ruby-hard capsule of frozen blood glinted in the torchlight. His skin was a greyish blue. Removing his gloves, Luke took his friend's limp wrist and checked for a pulse, knowing it was useless. The skin was cold.

Luke dropped the arm in shock. The realisation hit him that somehow Mac's broken body had survived the fall. He had suffocated to death, unable to move his chest to take a breath. A terrifying and lonely way to die. Luke covered his eyes for a moment, and for the first time since his son's birth they became watery.

He rubbed them roughly. A rage was building up inside him. He wanted to yell out but he couldn't. This was all his fault.

The slate sky lay like a heavy burden on the silvery station. Carefully, Luke and Craig each towed a body. Blue followed at a respectful distance, like a funeral attendant following a coffin. Not a word was spoken. They were on autopilot, each man dealing with his own grief. The wind had subsided, and not even the surface ice blew around. It was as if Antarctica itself was grieving with them, making their journey home as easy as possible.

With the communications blackout, Maddie, Tubs and Sue had kept watch for their colleagues' return, unaware of the situation. Maddie was the first to race down one of the two retractable exterior staircases, closely trailed by the others. They ran to the stretchers, their steps determined and hopeful. But when Maddie saw that both men's faces were covered, her hand shot up to her mouth and she bent forward and cried a muffled, 'No!' Seeing her so full of anguish, it was all Luke could do not to bawl like a baby.

Blue and Craig carried Mac inside on the stretcher. Exhausted and shivering, Luke took Dave in his arms. He laid his friend's body gently on the operating table so that Blue could officially pronounce death, with Maddie acting as coroner. She was refusing even to look at Luke. He went straight to his room and shut the door.

After a hot shower, he paced the room, asking himself the same two questions over and over: if he had been at the field site, would Mac and Dave still be alive? If he'd made that second call to Mac, would it have made a difference?

There was a knock on the door. Luke ignored it, unable to face anyone.

'Luke, it's Sue,' a voice called. 'Can I come in?'

'I …'

Sue continued to speak through the door. 'Luke, I'm so sorry. But I need your help. It can't wait.'

Luke opened the door. He was as pale as the insipid wall paint. 'What's up?' he asked, filling the frame and denying her entry.

'All comms are down and we can't fix it. And with Mac gone …' Her voice faded away.

Luke's mind only half-engaged with her words. He couldn't stop thinking about Mac's forlorn stare. 'I thought it was just the radios,' he said eventually.

'No, nothing's working. No phone, email, internet, nothing. It's like the ANARESAT link is down.' Each Australian station had a satellite terminal, which together formed the ANARESAT system, providing telephone and internet access.

'Have you done the obvious – rebooted everything?' asked Luke. Sue nodded.

'Checked the antenna? Any storm damage?'

'Did that, but Craig's taking another look.'

'It's not possible,' said Luke, 'unless the satellite has gone down or something, and then all our stations will be offline.'

'Can you take a look? You used to build radios, right?'

'Yes, but that won't help if it's an ANARESAT or IT problem.' Luke realised he needed a distraction. 'I'll take a look.'

'Um, have you checked your phone messages?'

Luke glanced at the phone by his bed. He was lucky to have one in his room complete with voicemail.

Sue tugged at her baby-pink fleece awkwardly. 'Yours was the last communication.' She spoke in a rush. 'I logged it but didn't listen to it.'

Luke dived for the phone and listened to his message.

A few seconds of silence. 'Daddy?' It was Jason's voice, whispering. 'I want to tell you a *big* secret.' Another pause. Breathing. 'Mummy is getting married. His name is Gary. I'm going to have a baby brother.' He sounded excited. 'Don't tell Mummy. Daddy?' Luke heard his son's breath and then nothing as Jason ended the call.

Already fatigued, Luke shut his eyes and shook his head.

'Luke? You okay?'

He could just imagine Jessica's sneering voice saying, 'Jase gets a proper dad now.' Jason meant everything to him. Now he was about to lose his son to this bloody Gary. And who the hell was he? Luke needed to talk to his son, but he knew he couldn't. He slammed his palms onto his desk, the noise like a whip cracking. His laptop jumped and his headphones fell to the floor.

Sue stepped closer. 'What's happened?'

Luke shook his head. 'It's personal.' He never spoke about his dysfunctional relationship with Jessica, or his long-distance relationship with his son.

Sue chewed her lip. 'When you feel up to it, can you check in with Maddie? She's already tried rebooting, so you two need to talk.'

Luke was sure he was the last person Maddie wanted to see. 'Is she in comms?'

'Garage.' Sue beat a hasty retreat.

Luke's head was spinning. He had lost two friends today, and now he was going to lose his son too. In a daze, he pulled on his fleece and headed for the industrial lift that linked the living quarters to the garage.

He arrived at the garage level, and from the weldmesh lift cage he could hear voices. Luke peered into the vast expanse of the garage. All the tools were hanging in their place, and the rotary snowplough and snowmobiles were parked neatly. His eyes opened wider when he glanced at the bench he used to repair equipment: two white body bags were lying there side by side.

At first he was appalled at Blue's insensitivity. Then he shook his head. Of course the bodies couldn't stay in the surgery; it was too warm and decomposition would set in, whereas the garage wasn't heated.

'You know, I'm almost glad that comms are down,' Luke heard Maddie say, her voice a croaky whisper. 'I just don't know what to say to their families.' She moved to the feet of the dead men and Luke saw her profile: it was as if her freckles had been washed away. She looked totally drained.

Blue shook his head slowly, his back to Luke. 'It's hard, I know, Maddie. It's the worst thing about being a doctor. All you can do is tell them the truth: it was a tragic accident, and while we're not sure who was trying to save who, they died heroically.'

She hugged herself and nodded. 'You know, all these years I've wanted to be station leader, I never thought I'd have to report a death, let alone two. My God, Blue, that's a quarter of my team. How did I manage to lose two people?' Luke heard her voice crack, then her head dropped further forward and her hair fell over her face.

Blue stepped forward and took her into a fatherly hug. 'It's not your fault. It's nobody's fault,' he said soothingly.

Maddie pulled away, wiping away her tears with the flats of her hands. 'Mac should never have been there. God, how am I going to explain this to his poor wife? And they've just had a baby.'

'Mac chose to be there, Maddie.'

'Luke should never have agreed,' she said, her voice rich in sudden fury. 'Mac wasn't experienced enough.'

Luke pulled open the lift doors and stepped forward. 'You're right.'

She strode over to him, her chin jutted forward. 'Jesus, Luke! It was *your* fucking research. You should've been doing it. Dave was your assistant.' A bitter tear escaped her left eye and trickled down her cheek. She wiped it away fiercely. 'And when we get the fucking comms working, I'm the one who has to tell their loved ones they're dead. I have to hear their agony. While you just hide away in your room as you always do and let it all pass by. God, you make me sick!' she seethed, her sodden face red and blotchy.

'Come on, Maddie,' interrupted Blue. 'You don't mean this. It's your grief talking.' He tried to grab her arm and she pulled it away.

'They were beautiful guys, Luke ...' Her voice trailed off and she ran from the garage.

Silence. Luke stayed rooted to the spot, staring at the body bags. 'You know she doesn't mean it, mate,' said Blue.

'The problem is, Blue, she's right.'

'Don't do this to yourself, Luke.' Blue put a pudgy hand on the taller man's shoulder.

'We've got to get them home, Blue. I'll call the *Professor Basov*. She's leaving tonight ...' Luke roughly ran his hands through his dark hair and then tugged at it in frustration. 'Shit! I can't make the call, can I?'

'We need to get comms working as a matter of urgency.'

'If we miss the *Basov*, we're stuffed. There won't be another ship till October.'

'The *Aurora Australis*? Or is she already in Hobart?'

'Hobart,' said Luke. 'She could make it back here, if only we could contact AARO. But who knows how thick the ice will be by then? The bay gets clogged easily.' Pine Island Bay was U-shaped and so was prone to thick sea ice. Luke paused, thinking. 'If I leave now, I might catch the *Basov* before it weighs anchor.'

Blue stepped closer. 'Don't be a fool. It's getting dark out there.'

Luke glanced at the closed garage doors.

'Stop this, Luke. You'll kill yourself. It's probably minus forty out there and you won't be able to see a bloody thing.'

'Oh, Christ,' Luke said. 'It could be seven months before their families see them.'

'Maybe. If it's going to be months, you also need to face the fact that we are going to have to preserve their bodies. That means building an ice shroud or placing them ... well, it means the freezer, I'm afraid.'

Luke's head shot up and he opened his mouth to object, then shut it again. When he spoke, he tried to control his emotions. 'No way. I'll build an ice shroud. We can't put them in the freezer. It's ... it's like they're pieces of meat.'

'Let's see if we can raise the *Basov*, shall we?'

Blue patted Luke's shoulder again, squeezed it reassuringly, and left. Luke went to the heads of the body bags and tenderly unzipped the longer one. Thankfully, Blue had closed Mac's eyes. When Luke had seen the look of helpless desperation in them, it had cut him to the quick. Now he looked at peace. Luke stood there for a long time, staring at his friend's face. An image of Mac's wife, Marie, popped into his head. God, he wouldn't swap places with Maddie for anything.

'I'm sorry, mate,' he said softly. 'If I'd known …' Luke focused on the small cross around Mac's neck. 'We'll do you a ceremony in the morning. Blue can say a few words from the Bible and we'll play that bit of music you like – you know, that song "Yellow". You always said you'd want that played at …' He stopped again, remembering the times he'd shared with Mac at his artist's retreat – a tiny hut they'd built together. Luke would take photos while Mac painted, each enjoying the other's taciturn company.

From his pocket, Luke took the lucky pig Tubs had given him and placed it next to Mac's head. 'There you go, mate. You're not alone now.' Luke then carefully zipped up the body bag; the little pig rolled close to Mac's ear.

Luke turned and headed for the comms room. He had to find a way to reach the *Professor Basov*.

Sydney, Australia

Almost seven thousand kilometres away, in a time zone on the other side of the international dateline and eighteen hours ahead of Hope Station, a bespoke tailor was ending his working day.

Sixty-year-old Jack Woo was tired but he gave his last client his undivided attention. He nodded every so often to demonstrate that he was listening as the chief executive officer of one of Australia's largest listed companies talked animatedly about his frustration with his board. Lenny Reid did not use names but Woo knew exactly to whom he was referring. Woo made it his job to know such things; it was one of the secrets to his successful twenty years as a bespoke tailor. Woo read the *Australian Financial Review* and the *Australian* every day just so he could engage his corporate clients in conversation.

The other reason for his loyal client base was the sanctity of his small rooms on Castlereagh Street: his clients knew that whatever they revealed to Woo would go no further. That was why he had so many big names in the corporate world: CEOs, CFOs, COOs. Politicians and diplomats too. But he was more than just a very fine tailor. His clients left his shop feeling relieved, having vented their frustrations to the quiet Woo, who always nodded and smiled sympathetically. Occasionally, he would make an observation that would stop his clients in their tracks, surprised at the clarity of his insight. But tonight Lenny Reid's verbal vomit was becoming tiresome.

In Woo's hand was a triangular piece of chalk, which he used to mark the alterations to a jacket. He worked quickly and systematically, leaving tiny white marks on the charcoal pinstriped super 150 fabric.

The jacket, if you could call it that, hung together with giant child-like threads, and the uninitiated might find it hard to imagine why this man was happy to pay fifteen thousand dollars for it. But under Woo's craftsmanship, these pieces of cloth would become a suit so perfectly fitting Reid's body shape that it would be remarked upon in the highest of Sydney's social circles.

'Sir, how does it feel across the shoulders?' asked Woo, as he glanced into the mirror to watch Reid's expression. Woo, a small man, was dressed impeccably in a navy-blue suit, a pink shirt and a striped tie. His head was shaved so closely that no regrowth ever showed, and his bifocals sat halfway down his nose, giving him the air of a sage.

Reid shrugged up and down a few times to test the suit's manoeuvrability, and then crossed his arms in front of his chest. 'A little tight. I must be putting on weight,' replied Lenny laughing, expecting Woo to contradict him.

'Sir, I don't think so. You simply carry a bigger burden on your shoulders,' Woo said on cue, without taking his eyes off the suit.

'That's right, Woo. I feel like I have the fucking board on my shoulders,' bemoaned Reid.

Woo noticed a stray pin under the chaise longue and picked it up. He stuck it in the felt hedgehog pincushion attached to his wrist. He was meticulous about such things and would have a word with his seamstresses tomorrow. They should never leave pins on the floor. Reid's booming voice was giving him a headache so he decided to change the subject.

'And how is your lovely daughter? She is getting married soon, I believe?' Reid usually softened at the mention of his daughter.

'Yeah, the wedding's a year away but the whole house is full of bridal magazines and this poncy bloody events organiser. My home is not my own.'

'Ah, but she will make a beautiful bride, sir.'

Reid stopped frowning and turned his head to the side to look at Woo. 'She will,' he said softly, smiling at the vision in his head of his daughter. He remained silent for the rest of the fitting.

Woo removed the suit and took it to the seamstresses' workroom, leaving Reid to get dressed. Woo, who had fled China as a young man, momentarily thought of his only child, Wendy, who lived in Melbourne. He would love to see her happily married too.

'And your daughter – how is she?' Reid called over the partition.

'Well, sir, thank you. Very focused on her career. I'm sure you understand.'

'No time to visit her old man, huh?'

'Unfortunately not, sir.'

While Woo waited for Reid to dress, he made his way to a tiny kitchenette that was hidden from the view of his customers. He removed the ice tray from the freezer and, as quietly as possible, dropped one ice cube into a crystal tumbler. He checked to see that Reid was still in the changing room, then took a bottle of Macallan single malt whisky from a cupboard over the sink and poured himself a drink. This was his little treat before the train ride home to Parramatta. But he wouldn't taste it until his client was gone.

Reid made his way to the shop door and Woo followed. 'Ready in a week?' asked the CEO, knowing full well that they had agreed on three weeks.

'Certainly, sir.'

Woo opened the door and Reid strode off into the busy street.

★ ★ ★

As Woo farewelled his client and locked the front door, another man silently entered through the rear, from an alley often used by the seamstresses for a quick 'smoko'. This door was only locked when Woo left for the night. The intruder, known only as King, moved inside, spotted the glass and grinned. Men of routine were so easy to kill.

King unwrapped a tablet from its foil and dropped it into the whisky. It fizzed briefly. The intruder then heard the tap of Woo's leather soles on the polished wooden floor and left, shutting the door quietly with his gloved hand.

The alley was strewn with large commercial bins. But someone had been careless with a bag of food scraps, which had exploded over the concrete. King almost stepped on a plastic Coke bottle as he ducked behind a bin. Sweat soaked his shirt armpits.

After a minute or two he peered through a tiny window into the rear of the shop. King saw the tailor sitting in a leather armchair that, he guessed, was for Woo's spoiled clients. Opposite the armchair, on a neat desk, a computer screen was filled with a map. At first King thought it was of the United States, but the tail was pointing the wrong way. Upwards, rather than down to Mexico. Then he realised it was Antarctica. This seemed strange, but his briefings only gave him what he needed to know and nothing more.

Woo swirled his whisky to coat the inside of the glass, then held it up to admire the toffee-coloured spirit. He brought the glass to his nose. King held his breath. The target took a sip and raised his eyebrows in surprise. Woo shook his head in disappointment but sipped again, soon finishing his drink. He got up from the chair and then suddenly doubled over, dropping the glass, which shattered on the floor.

Confident of the massive dose he had delivered, King watched the tailor's final throes. Woo grasped his chest in pain, as his mouth gaped hungrily for breath. He fell back into the chair as a second, more violent seizure engulfed his whole body. It was then that Woo noticed King. He mouthed, 'Help me!' King didn't even blink. The dying man clawed at the phone but couldn't quite reach it. Woo's terrified eyes stared at the man watching him die. A final spasm of agony, and he took his last breath.

King looked at the computer screen and then down at Woo, now lying motionless, surrounded by glistening shards of glass. From his jacket he pulled out a pay-as-you-go mobile he had bought for cash that day, and texted 'Job 209 complete. Antarctica on screen?' just in case this had significance. Many times he had seen what seemed to be trivial or irrelevant, only for it to prove to be vital intelligence. Always observe. It was a necessity in his profession. The killer left the alley and vanished into the throng of weary commuters.

Woo's lifeless wrist still carried the pincushion into which he had so carefully placed the stray pin a few minutes earlier. When his seamstresses arrived at seven the following morning, they would have more than stray pins to worry about.

T MINUS 4 DAYS, 9 HOURS, 17 MINUTES
6 March, 2:43 am (UTC-07)

Like the laptop in front of him, Luke was finally in sleep mode, slumped over the desk. His head of dishevelled hair rested on his crossed arms. He had tried everything he could think of to get the phone, radio and internet to work, but with no success. He knew there had to be a means of rebooting the whole system and reloading the IOS images program, but he couldn't find it anywhere on the server. And he couldn't find the backup disks either. Eventually, exhaustion had claimed him.

But his sleep had been sporadic. He'd woken twice from the same nightmare: Mac was calling his name, over and over, from inside the crevasse. Mac's arms were raised towards Luke, begging for help, as Luke stretched over the lip of the fissure, desperately trying to reach him. But Luke was too far away. He was calling to Mac, but something prevented him from abseiling down the steep walls. He thrashed about but couldn't get any closer.

Luke woke with a start to find he had knocked over his coffee mug, which fortunately had been empty. He squinted at the bright lights overhead, rubbed his eyes and checked the time: 2:43 am. The station was silent except for the low thrum of the generators and the rhythmic snoring of its occupants. Craig's was the loudest.

Even with his bedroom door shut, his guttural gruntings resounded through the living quarters like a sow at feeding time.

Normally, this would have made Luke smile, but not tonight. He yawned and resumed his search for IOS images on Mac's laptop, until gradually his eyelids closed and he fell asleep again. Something hit the outside of the sleeping quarters but the sixty-centimetre-thick aluminium walls, filled with polystyrene insulation, absorbed the sound. No one inside heard it.

Minutes later, Luke coughed in his sleep. He coughed again, this time more violently, and awoke. Where was he? His eyes stung and he was surrounded by a haze. He breathed in and it made him choke. He shot his hand out and hit the laptop, which lit up like a Christmas tree. Yes, the communications room. But why no power, except for the equipment still running on batteries?

A scream that sounded like an animal being torn apart pierced his eardrums. He stood so fast that his chair toppled backwards. He clocked the smoke seeping under the door. Fire. The station was on fire. Their worst nightmare. Luke had no idea who that scream came from, but it was excruciating. A man's voice. He realised it had to be Tubs, Craig or Blue.

Luke opened the door and was met by dense, acrid smoke. The emergency floor lighting provided a dull glow. At the end of the corridor, the door to Craig's room was a hole surrounded by a circle of flames. Luke ran to the bathroom, seized a towel and turned on the shower tap. The nozzle only dribbled. Why wasn't there water? The towel was damp, but not enough. He threw it into a shower cubicle to mop up whatever moisture was left.

With the wet towel over his head and arms, Luke approached the archway of fire that was the entrance to Craig's room. Above the doorway the roof was alight with golden waves that appeared to flow into the smoke-filled room. Backdraft, Luke realised. When Craig had opened his door to escape, the flames had been sucked into the vacuum. Luke ducked low and charged in.

Craig was rolling on the floor, his hair and clothes alight. Despite the thick smoke, Luke saw that Craig's face was red-raw with burns, waxy and ghoulish. Luke threw the towel over him to starve the flames of oxygen. Craig stopped moving and Luke coughed as the smoke burned his lungs.

He pulled the towel away. Craig's face had melted, and not a hair on his head, beard or eyebrows remained. His hands were like gnarled claws, twisted in agony, the skin bubbling. The poor man moaned and then was still. Luke touched the raw flesh of his neck to check for a pulse but there wasn't one. Luke stepped back, then, horrified, he noticed his hands were covered with bits of Craig's skin.

'Luke!' A voice called, hoarse and unrecognisable.

Luke felt lightheaded and confused. A flaming piece of timber from the ceiling collapsed, landing an arm's length from him. Adrenaline and panic fought for supremacy of his body. The heat felt as though it was singeing his skin through his clothing. The towel was now useless, so he picked up Craig's desk chair and held it over his head as he ran though the doorway.

In the corridor, Luke dropped the smouldering chair. Tubs had a fire extinguisher and was spraying dry powder onto the flaming walls. He only had on his candy-striped thermals – he'd been sleeping in them – and, incongruously, his expedition boots. It had been drilled into them that in an emergency they had to put on their boots. They couldn't walk outside without them.

'The others?' Luke shouted.

'Exit 1,' Tubs spluttered. 'Craig?'

'Dead.'

Luke's eyes were streaming caustic tears and he could barely see. Tubs stopped his useless attempts to quell the fire and the two stumbled down the corridor towards the exit. As they passed the kitchen, another part of the ceiling collapsed behind them. The cold night air was sucked in, further fuelling the flames. They turned a corner to see Blue in shorts and an open parka hurl himself at the door. It didn't budge. Sue, dressed in pink brushed-cotton pyjamas and hiking boots, was kicking at it.

'It won't budge,' yelled Blue above the roar of the flames.

'Maddie?' coughed Luke.

'Went to check Exit 2,' shouted Blue.

'Shit!' said Luke, glancing back down the burning corridor.

'The door, Luke!' screamed Sue, her round face creased with fear. Luke shook his head. How could it be jammed? Tubs had shovelled away the snow yesterday. Luke threw the full force of his weight into the door. Fit and strong, his broad shoulders had no impact. And again. The door creaked but didn't budge. Tubs tried to ram it open with the fire extinguisher but it held tight.

'Exit 2?' gasped Blue.

Luke nodded and they ran, crouching low to avoid the suffocating smoke and flames. Why wasn't the ventilation working? They stepped around burning debris. The heat was unbearable but Luke knew the smoke would kill them first. They reached the first internal fire door and shut it behind them. This would give them ninety minutes, as long as the fire was only at one end of the station.

Sue fell to her knees. She couldn't breathe. The smoke was everywhere. Luke pulled her to her feet and held her up. He had never realised how short she was till then, having always thought of her as one of the lads. He now realised how her personality had made her seem larger than life.

'Get to Exit 2 and look out for Maddie,' Luke said, wheezing. He dragged Sue past the mess and the kitchen, towards the laboratories. 'Maddie,' he tried to shout, but his voice was strangled and weak.

The further they stumbled towards Exit 2, the thicker the smoke became. *Not good*, thought Luke. Like an apparition, Maddie staggered though the smoky darkness towards them.

She fell to her knees, gasping for breath. 'Exit 2 won't open.'

They were trapped.

T MINUS 4 DAYS, 9 HOURS, 4 MINUTES
6 March, 2:56 am (UTC-07)

'Both exits are blocked,' Maddie said, coughing. 'Fire's coming from both directions.' She was wearing the same clothes as last night. She must have fallen asleep fully dressed. 'I was about to ... try the lift.'

'Power's out,' Sue croaked.

'Break a window?' suggested Luke.

'Triple-glazed. Take ... too long,' Maddie coughed.

Luke's mind worked with hangover-like slowness, and his lungs felt as if they were being torn to shreds. He peered into the inferno of flames coming at them in a pincer movement.

'Lift shaft!' he said. 'Follow me.'

They moved deeper into the stinging smoke like drunks, tripping and falling. Luke shut another fire door but the conflagration seemed to be all around them. At the lift, Maddie leaned against the wall, unable to stand.

'The ladder,' Luke said as he tried to open the maintenance door to the lift shaft. It was locked and the key was in Maddie's office, on the other side of the corridor fire door. 'It's locked – I'll get a knife. The kitchen.'

Blue grabbed his arm. 'I'll go. You'll need to carry Sue – I can't,' he said, nodding at Sue, who lay semi-conscious on the floor.

Blue lurched back down the corridor in the direction of the kitchen.

'Lie low,' Maddie directed them. 'Avoid the smoke.'

Before anyone could respond, an explosion shook the whole station, throwing them to the floor. It tore at their eardrums. Debris hurtled through the air. Luke felt something hit him in the back and bounce off. *Ting, thwack, crack,* as metal, wood and glass fell around them. The heat felt like a blowtorch. Maddie shrieked. Luke looked up and could see she was hugging her left calf.

Disoriented, Luke's balance was shot to pieces. Tiny shards of glass were embedded in his hands. What had exploded? What in God's name was going on? The fireball had come from the direction of the kitchen, but Luke didn't want to believe Blue was dead. Tubs had been thrown against the wall and lay winded.

Maddie sat up, her hands trembling as she stared in shock at the triangular piece of metal protruding from the side of her leg. Sue stared blankly at Luke, her mouth opening and closing like a ventriloquist's doll. She was impaled on a length of steel pipe.

'God, no,' said Luke, crawling towards her on all fours.

Sue tried to say something, then her mouth stopped moving. He couldn't find any pulse, and for an instant he felt completely overwhelmed. His head dropped forward onto his chest. Tubs was now sitting up, stunned. He touched his face and stared at his bloody hands like a child fascinated by a strange new toy.

'Luke,' pleaded Maddie. He stared at her, his face blank, uncomprehending. 'Luke!' she said, louder this time. 'Help me!' He moved at last and kneeled at her side.

'Get it out!' she screamed, holding her leg and rocking backwards and forwards in excruciating pain.

'Not now,' he gasped. 'You have to stand. Come on! There could be another explosion.'

'You fucking bastard!' she screamed. 'Get it out!'

The encroaching smoke was getting thicker, as though moving in on its cornered prey. Luke smelled diesel and petrol and his alarm increased. On his knees, barely able to see through tears thick with soot and grime, he searched for another piece of metal, feeling his way through the detritus. His hand landed on one and he stood weakly, almost collapsing into the lift maintenance door. He forced the piece of metal into the gap between the door and the wall, and using brute force, broke the lock. The door swung open.

Unsteadily, Luke peered down the lift shaft. The air inside was pretty clear and the ladder was still there. Their first bit of luck. 'Tubs, snap out of it. Help me lift Maddie.'

Coming out of his stupor, Tubs helped Luke. They placed their hands underneath her armpits and pulled her up. She leaned against the wall.

'Can you climb down the ladder?' Luke asked her.

'I'll have to,' Maddie managed to say. 'We can't leave Sue.'

'She's dead, Maddie.' He coughed. 'So is Blue.'

She looked back at the source of the explosion and nodded.

'I'll go first,' Luke said, 'so if you slip, I'll catch you. Tubs, you go last – and shut the door behind you, for God's sake. Keep the smoke out.'

Tubs choked out a 'Got it'.

Luke started his descent, relishing the clearer air in the lift shaft. Maddie took her first step down the ladder, using her stronger leg first. One way or another, her wounded leg had to bear her weight, but it was clearly agony as the metal dug into the muscle. She groaned with each step.

'You're doing well. Just a little bit further,' Luke called up to her. The thought flashed through his mind that Craig had built the ladder but wasn't with them. He pushed it away: they weren't safe yet, and they'd have to break through the maintenance door at the bottom of the lift shaft. Luke looked down at the bare steel roof of the lift, which was stationary at the garage level. The gap between the cage and the shaft walls was just wide enough for a person. Luke reached the bottom rung.

'Hang on while I get this door open,' he called up.

Maddie's trouser leg was soaked with blood. She clung to the ladder, gulping air as she rested on her good leg.

Luke leaned his back against the lift cage and kicked at the shaft door. It opened easily as it was designed to open outwards. What greeted Luke took his breath away. He'd hoped the garage was free of fire, but the wooden storage containers in the corner were burning, as was the snow tractor. The flames were dangerously near the snowmobiles.

'Hurry!' he yelled. 'Get down here!' Fearing more explosions, the panic in his voice brought the limping Maddie and then Tubs quickly to his side.

Luke knew the sound of gunfire, but it was so totally unexpected that he was slow to react. No station had weapons and military action was banned. As a bullet fizzed past his right ear he grabbed Maddie and they plunged to the ground.

Tubs hit the floor with a thud. 'Jesus! I'm shot. I'm bloody well shot,' he screamed, clutching his chest.

The gunfire started again. It was coming from somewhere near the main garage doors.

'The snowmobiles,' whispered Maddie.

The keys were still in them. The quad bikes were further away, and even if they had been able to cope with soft snow – which they couldn't – their tyres were on fire. It had to be the snowmobiles. Through the thick, foul smoke, Luke tried to locate the shelf under the workbench where he stashed his tools. He couldn't help but glance at the two white body bags, raised above the flames as if on a funeral pyre.

'Can you drive?' he asked Maddie.

She nodded, clutching her leg.

'We've gotta get into the work overalls, otherwise we'll die of cold,' he said, nodding at the bright-yellow, all-in-one waterproof freezer suits hanging on their hooks. They were used by all mainten-ance staff for outdoors work and were fleece lined for warmth. Tubs, in particular, who was only in his thermals, had no hope of surviving without them.

For a moment Luke was wryly thankful for the smoke that was their only protection from the gunman. 'Wait here,' he said, and crawled on his belly across the floor to the freezer suits. Above the crackle of the flames, Luke heard radio chatter – it wasn't in English. He reached the legs of the first overall, and, still prone, he tugged at the material. But the all-in-one suit stayed on the hook. He yanked harder and the loop of material at the collar tore free. He did the same with two more, then bundled them under his arms and crawled back to Tubs and Maddie.

Bullets zinged over Luke, the shooter unable to see his target. Tubs was lying on his side, his grey thermal top soaked with dark blood that seeped through his fingers.

Luke paused, horrified, then pulled himself together. 'This'll hurt, mate, I'm sorry,' he said, pushing Tubs' legs into the overalls and then rolling him from side to side as he pulled it up. Tubs gagged with the pain.

Maddie tore at the waterproof material with her teeth, yanking apart the stitching on the left leg so she could get both the shrapnel and her leg inside. She struggled into her suit, using her hands to force her wounded leg inside.

'Follow me,' Luke said to Maddie. He looked at Tubs. 'Mate, when I bring the snowmobile near you, you gotta get on, okay? Can you get up?' Tubs nodded, the bloody stain now hidden by his yellow suit.

Luke crawled along the floor, followed by Maddie. He grabbed a hammer and threw it at one of the metal storage containers at the other end of the garage. The gunman opened fire at the container and Luke scuttled towards the snowmobiles hoping to reach the furthest one with the full tank, but the gunfire turned in their direction. He jumped on Mac's snowmobile and Maddie took Dave's.

Luke sped off and, leaning over, pulled Tubs onto the seat behind him. Tubs yelped in agony. Briefly checking that Maddie was okay, Luke charged for the open garage doors and the source of the gunfire. It was suicidal, he knew, but he had no choice. He heard shouting outside, angry and sharp.

Luke burst out of the garage, followed by Maddie, and began driving in a zigzag, which Maddie mimicked. Without goggles, the raw polar air tore at his eyes. They needed headlights, but Luke knew that would make them an easy target. As they careened into the darkness, the shooting began again, this time from several directions. Luke glanced back and saw the silhouette of a man shooting at them. Behind him, the station was burning in startling oranges and reds.

'Stop,' panted Tubs, slouching forward.

'We can't stop,' called Luke over his shoulder. He could just make out Maddie, accelerating ahead of him. He called out but she didn't hear, so he gunned the engine to catch up to her. He waved at her to get her attention and she slowed.

'Go to the fire hut – emergency supplies,' she shouted.

Luke made a cutting motion at his throat and they killed their engines. 'Too close,' he said. 'They'll find us.'

'Then where?' she asked in desperation.

'The Zodiac,' he replied. They had no other options. With their station destroyed and the emergency hut out of bounds, their only hope was to escape in the Zodiac. How they would stay alive after that, Luke had no idea.

'No,' Maddie said. 'We need shelter – Mac's hut.'

Of course. Built a few months ago, it wasn't on the plans or any map. It was on a pebbly beach they'd christened 'the Nest' because of all the Adélie penguin nesting sites in the area. It wasn't far from where they'd left the Zodiac.

'Perfect,' Luke said, nodding.

'Got to lie down,' said Tubs, whose grip around Luke's waist was weakening.

'Not long, mate. Keep your head down out of the wind.' Luke pulled Tubs' arms tighter around him, and Tubs groaned but hung on. Maddie had moved off.

Before he followed, Luke took one last look at Hope Station. Their home had been turned into a hell on earth.

Robert stares at the woman's face and wants to be sick. It is covered in black burn marks. Yet they weren't caused by flames. Each mark is circular in shape, and there is a constellation of them on her left cheekbone and around her nose. The marks continue down her neck but they are lighter in colour – pinker, more raw. The more intensive burns, caused by repeated applications of electric batons, are darker.

The woman, in her thirties, is shackled tightly to an iron bed, naked. She was probably beautiful once. Atrophy has set in as she has been in the same position for seven days. She cannot move even a centimetre. But her eyes follow the boy, Robert, and his father.

Robert looks behind him and he recognises the uniform of the People's Armed Police, Beijing.

'And this one?' asks General Zhao. Robert remembers he is on some kind of ghoulish tour but has no idea how he got there.

'Falun Gong, General Zhao.'

'Name?'

'Woo Ling.'

'Has she renounced?'

'She will. The Death Bed is effective.'

The General turns to Robert, pointing at the captive. 'These people killed your mother!' he shouts.

The yelling woke Robert from his fitful sleep. He stared up at the fabric of his tent. His lamp still burned through the darkness. Why had he dreamed of the woman again? Was it the fire? Her burns? Was that the connection?

He unzipped his sleeping bag to discover his thermals were soaked with sweat. He tore them off and pulled on fresh ones, followed by salopettes and his parka. How he missed his crisp monogrammed shirts and his luxurious suits.

He looked at his watch; it was almost six thirty. He radioed his chef and demanded coffee and pancakes. Perhaps food would make him feel less wretched. Minutes later, as Robert ploughed through his hearty meal, Wei arrived to deliver his report.

'The fire still burns,' he said. 'By mid-morning it should have burned itself out, and then we will start checking through the debris to confirm the body count.'

Robert looked up and wiped the sticky syrup from his lips with a napkin. It had been an inferno of incredible reds and yellows against the black and starry sky. Quite beautiful. It reminded him of an Uluru sunrise he'd enjoyed on his one and only Australian visit. *Rather apposite*, he thought.

But the failure to eliminate all of the Hope Station inhabitants troubled him. He had been assured by the General that the blaze hadn't been spotted from space – there were no spy satellites over Antarctica at the time; most satellites orbit the northern hemisphere.

'But we know that two, perhaps three, escaped,' Robert said.

Wei, whose white coat, trousers and face were smudged with ash, dropped his chin a fraction. 'Yes, sir. But we believe that at least one has been shot.'

Robert dropped his knife and fork onto the plate in disapproval. 'Brilliant! A bullet is traceable, you idiot. You must find the survivors, and if you have to shoot them, remove the bullets and incinerate them. I don't want it known they were shot. I need your men to remove every shell and every bullet from the station and the surrounding area, and the door bolts too. This fire was an accident, a tragic ...' Robert abruptly stopped speaking. 'Or was it?'

He leaned back, his hands behind his head, his director's chair at an angle. 'Or was it the act of a madman?' His mind quickly calculated the pros and cons of his new idea. 'Leave the bolts.'

'Sir?' Wei frowned.

'Just do as I say, Captain.'

Wei was about to leave when Robert called him back. He wiped his hand over the soldier's face and smeared the dirty residue over his own cheek and down his parka. Wei blinked in confusion but remained mute. With Wei dismissed, Robert checked his face in the mirror and scraped the sleep from his eyes with his finger. He was impressed by the grubby, battle-scarred man staring back at him. He pulled a comb through his coarse hair and then patted it into place, but not too much.

He switched on the video camera.

'March sixth, zero seven hundred hours. Robert Zhao Sheng. This is my video diary, embargoed until March eleventh.' He spoke in Mandarin. Later, the footage would have subtitles in English and other languages.

'My beloved country, I am proud to be in Antarctica, working for our greater good.'

Robert couldn't help thinking, *Above all, mine.*

'My men and I work tirelessly to keep on schedule. We battle raging winds and temperatures as low as minus forty. We risk our lives to save our people.

'Despite my good fortune to be the son of General Zhao ...' he said, marginally nodding in the necessary, if galling, deference. He had made his own fucking fortune, clawing his way to the top and tearing the guts out of anyone who got in his way. 'My mother's family are poor farmers,' he continued, 'I know only too well how our people suffer. My work here will change the lives of millions of Chinese. This will be my legacy.'

The last phrase was heartfelt. Robert knew he would go down in history as China's saviour. Through his diary – his version of the truth – he intended to out-hero Scott, Amundsen, Shackleton, Byrd, all of them.

'I have no doubt that once our project is revealed, there will be a global outcry,' he continued. 'Signatories to the Antarctic Treaty will condemn us and demand we cease our activities. But the loudest voices will be the ones most envious of our initiative and ingenuity. Mark my words, those whining countries, so quick to condemn, will follow our lead, eager not to miss out on the bounty.

'I hope that until stage one is complete, and this footage is made public' – *and ruthlessly marketed*, he thought – 'our presence in Antarctica will remain secret. So it may surprise some that, at great risk to myself and my mission, I ordered the rescue of a nearby station which has tragically burned to the ground: Hope Station.

'We have kept away from the Australians, quietly going about our business, until last night, when I heard an explosion. Leaving my tent, I saw an ominous orange glow on the horizon. By the time we got there, the main quarters were a raging inferno. My guess is that their gas cylinders exploded. I tried to smash a window and eventually broke my way through, but the fire was too fierce and I couldn't enter. It was a terrible sight.'

He dropped his head and then lifted sorrowful eyes to the camera.

'A tragic day. It seems that all have perished. Needless to say, we will preserve the bodies for burial but as there is nobody left alive, I have made the difficult decision not to contact the relevant authorities until the eleventh of March, when stage one of my mission will be complete. Much as it grieves me – and my heart goes out to their families – my priority has to remain this project. My people's needs come first.'

Robert switched off the camera, satisfied that he had shown the right mixture of compassion and dedication to his cause. Best of all, he had turned murder into a noble rescue attempt. But as the memories from last night's fire filled his head, his smug expression disappeared. He raised both hands and gave his scalp a vigorous, almost violent massage. He could still smell the stench of burning flesh.

'Reputations. And now lives,' he said aloud, leaning forward and cradling his head.

For a long moment he remained still. Was he now as bad as his father? Then, like water through sand, his remorse seeped away. He lit a cigarette, inhaled deeply and focused on practical matters. It was time to ensure the right person was blamed for the disaster.

Robert had studied Wildman's writing, and her style was easy to mimic. With degrees from Harvard and Wharton, Robert's command of English was often better than that of native speakers. He composed an email:

To: Matt Lovedale, chief of station operations
From: Madeline Wildman
Subject: Luke Searle

Hi Matt

I'm increasingly concerned about Luke Searle's erratic behaviour and want to ask your advice on managing the situation.

As you know, in his recent performance appraisal I highlighted his lack of adherence to station rules and his poor social interaction skills. He is a law unto himself, even if brilliant. On numerous occasions I have spoken to him about the importance of being a team player and why station procedures must be followed. Until recently, he's taken my comments good-naturedly, even if he's tended to ignore them.

But now he's showing signs of aggression and mood swings. He shuts himself in his room for long periods of time and avoids the company of others. We had planned a party tonight to celebrate his award but Luke reacted badly and said he wouldn't attend. I have spoken to Blue and he is of the opinion that Luke is showing signs of mental illness.

Please advise on a course of action.

Best wishes,

Maddie

This was how she always signed off. A shame – Madeline was a beautiful name.

Robert leaned back to reread his work and then composed a

similar email from the doctor. As Sun Tzu had written in *The Art of War*, all warfare is based on deception. Satisfied that this would plant a seed of doubt about Searle's sanity, Robert sent the emails to the Eye, whose task was to ensure they reached Lovedale. Robert stressed to his hacker that it must appear as though both Maddie and the doctor sent their emails last night – before the fire. Lovedale, a busy man, must have overlooked them.

Luke Searle was going to be the perfect scapegoat.

Luke heard a moaning sound as he woke. He turned over and a sharp pain shot through his shoulder. He, Maddie and Tubs were lying on a wooden floor only two metres square, which had forced Luke to spend the night curled up with his knees against the wall. Tubs and Maddie were under the sleeping bag Mac had used to wrap himself in when painting. Luke had slept in his freezer suit.

The hut was a simple structure, with wooden walls, floor and roof, and one window that opened outwards. Inside was an easel and stool, paints, watercolour paper, brushes, a heater and a spare sleeping bag. Suddenly Luke began coughing convulsively and had to sit up. His lungs wanted to be rid of the toxic filth from the fire.

'You … all right?' asked Tubs. His voice was weak and wheezy, his face pale.

Nightmare images from the fire filled Luke's head: Craig's raw and hairless face, Sue's limp body, the explosion, the men shooting at them. The coughing fit subsided but his mouth was bone dry and filled with the bitter aftertaste of smoke. No doubt they all reeked of it. He looked sideways at Tubs who was lying on sheets of Mac's watercolour paper, used as insulation against the cold that seeped up through the floor.

'Don't worry about me,' Luke replied. 'Let me take a look at you.'

He moved to a kneeling position but his legs were numb and he couldn't keep his balance. He stood stiffly and stamped his feet on the floor to get the blood moving.

Tubs gritted his teeth in agony and Luke realised he was jolting the thin floor. He kneeled again, having regained some feeling in the form of pins and needles. 'Sorry, that was dumb. Let me look at you. Can you sit up?'

Tubs tried moving, then groaned. 'Fuck me, that hurts.'

By the time Tubs was in a sitting position he was wheezing badly, barely able to get enough breath. He coughed, clenching his eyes shut. His mouth was bloody.

Maddie was now awake, blinking, trying to get her bearings. Her freezer suit was several sizes too big, and this, on top of her wound, made it difficult for her to move.

Luke gingerly pulled back Tubs' sleeping bag and unzipped his freezer suit. A hole, like a large cigarette burn, marked the entry point of the bullet through Tubs' clothing. The inside of the suit was soaked in blood.

Before they slept Maddie had done her best to cover Tubs' wound, using gauze and bandages from a snowmobile's basic first-aid kit. She and Tubs had shared the painkillers. But the kit didn't contain the sutures, antibiotics and morphine they needed and they were out of bandages.

'Let me see,' said Maddie. She winced as she shuffled nearer. She carefully lifted off the dressing. Tubs' wound was weeping a little. The bullet had created a perfect circle between his lower ribs.

Tubs craned his head down to look at his injury. 'Holy shit!'

Luke hadn't thought it possible, but Tubs went paler still.

'Can't breathe …' he mumbled, and then, exhausted, he began to cough again. This time he spat out blood. The hole in his skin hissed and frothed.

Luke and Maddie looked at each other in concern.

'He needs stronger painkillers. Morphine or pethidine, and antibiotics,' Maddie said.

Luke shook his head. They had nothing stronger than Panadol.

He searched the hut for anything useful. He picked up some sketch paper and masking tape and kneeled next to Tubs.

'We can use Mac's painting paper, tear it into squares and create a fresh pad for his wound. It's the only semi-sterile absorbent thing I can think of. The rags in here are too dirty. We can use masking tape to hold it in place. What do you think?'

'That'll do for now. But we'll need more than that.'

'This is all we've got,' he replied, gesturing around the hut. 'No station, no communications, no doctor. But we do have a camping stove with enough fuel for three hours, so we can melt ice and rehydrate, and we've got shelter. I can get us food. Penguin, seal. It could be worse.'

'Love your optimism,' Maddie said. Her face was grubby from the smoke, making her green eyes seem strangely bright as she looked at him. 'But we can't last long like this, and Tubs needs proper medical attention.'

'Hey, guys, down here,' Tubs gasped. 'I'm not dead yet.' He attempted a smile, but his lips were clenched tightly as he fought the pain.

Luke had never watched someone die before. He could see Tubs weakening fast, as if his body was gradually shutting down and his force of will was the only thing keeping him alive. He dreaded to think about the organ damage the bullet must have caused.

'I'll go back to the station,' he said. 'Salvage what I can. Find medical supplies.'

'No!' Maddie and Tubs said in unison.

'Too dangerous,' Maddie continued. 'They'll be there, expecting us to do just that. It's suicide. They want us dead.'

'We could stay here for a while if they don't track us down,' said Luke, 'but Tubs needs treatment. I might even find some way to call for help.' The floorboards shook as he stood. 'I'm going.'

'Luke, why do you have to be so bloody impetuous?' Maddie flung her arms up. 'I'm telling you, it's madness. They'll kill you, and then where will we be?' Her voice grew more urgent. 'I can hardly walk, Tubs can't move – how would we survive without you? Think, Luke!'

85

'What choice do I have?'

'I'm station leader. Well, leader of what's left of us. And you're my responsibility. I'll go back for supplies. I can manage the snowmobile fine. You just have to get this shrapnel out of my leg,' she said, looking down at the metal protruding from the torn snowsuit.

'I'm not removing it till I know I can stem the blood loss. If it's severed an artery you could bleed to death.'

Maddie frowned. 'And I thought I was the cautious one. Look, Luke, it's my leg and I want you to take it out. Now!' Her anger was building.

'I'm not going to be responsible for your death.'

'You will be, if you go back to Hope,' she snapped.

Luke swallowed. 'I need to think,' he said, stepping outside. He shut the door quickly to keep what little warmth there was inside.

The anaemic morning light did nothing to brighten his mood. Without a hat, Luke's head felt as if it were being squeezed in a clamp. The cold air scratched at his sore throat and he coughed hard, bent double. As he straightened, he peered towards their gutted station. A dark slash of smoke in the sky looked like God's finger pointing to the destruction. He scanned the mountainside, the glacier and then out to sea. No sign of the killers.

As he turned the ignition of the first snowmobile to check its fuel gauge, he considered their options. They had to put their energies into a plan that would give them the best chance of survival and rescue. Pine Island Bay was getting clogged with ice but an ice-breaker could probably still get through. But they had no way of calling for help, not nearly enough clothing to keep warm, and only enough fuel for a few hours. Capturing and killing animals to eat would be no mean feat, with nothing but Mac's rusty penknife as a weapon. They could be facing months in permanent darkness, with temperatures as low as minus forty degrees Celsius at night, the wind chill making it feel far colder. He knew their odds of survival were dire. But he needed Maddie and Tubs to believe they could live long enough to be rescued.

As he searched for a solution, he pulled out a bit of glass from his hair.

The immediate worry was Tubs' health. Luke suspected the bullet had punctured a lung, and if that was right, he didn't rate Tubs' chances unless they could get him to a hospital soon. And Maddie's prospects weren't good either – she might bleed to death and risked infection if the metal was left in her leg. Luke had to find a way to contact the outside world. Perhaps the cause of the comms blackout had been rectified? Perhaps it had been a problem with ANARESAT? He had to return to Hope.

Luke coughed again, his eyes watering. His heightened breathing had triggered the attack. 'Focus, man, focus,' he said to himself. 'You can do this.'

The fuel gauge of the first snowmobile indicated that it was almost empty, but it might have enough. Just. He turned off the engine quickly. As Luke approached the second snowmobile, he noticed that his right foot was colder than the left. He lifted his boot; the sole was torn – not good. To his relief, he found the second vehicle had more fuel.

The door opened and Maddie limped out. She leaned on a snowmobile seat. 'Someone should go back, I agree. But it has to be me. What use am I wounded? I can't hunt for food. Tubs stands a better chance with you. So I go. Do you understand?'

Her expression revealed nothing of the fear she must be feeling.

'I understand your logic,' Luke said. 'But you're assuming they're waiting for us. Maybe they aren't. There's no shelter for them there – they'd have gone back to their camp to survive the rest of the night.' Maddie tried to interrupt but he continued. 'I'm not wounded. I can carry more weight than you. I'll be in and out fast.'

Maddie hugged herself. She stared off into the distance for a moment and then looked him in the eye. 'Luke, I'm instructing you not to go. I'm going to rehydrate first, then I'm off.'

'Why do you have to be so bloody stubborn? You're injured!'

She turned her back on him and began to stagger back to the hut. She paused and then faced him, her voice hushed. 'I think the bullet's in Tubs' lungs,' she said, leaning on her good leg. 'Did you see the wound frothing? And the wheezing? I'm worried he's bleeding into his chest.'

'I was thinking the same.'

'I need a plastic bag.'

'Why?'

'It's called a flutter valve, I think. Anyway, we have to allow the blood to come out of the hole but stop him sucking in air through it. I need to tape down three sides of the plastic. He breathes in, the plastic creates a vacuum. He breathes out, it allows blood to escape.'

'I think Mac kept his paper in a plastic bag. I'll look. Maddie?'

'Yes?' She was shivering badly.

'Don't let him know how bad it is,' said Luke. 'We've got to keep him positive.'

She nodded.

Back inside, Maddie managed to tape a section of plastic over Tubs' wound. They watched it lift and then seal, just as she had described.

'Good job,' said Luke.

He and Tubs made eye contact and Luke saw his panic.

'It'll be all right, mate. You'll see. We'll be rescued soon. Now, I'll get some ice and make tea. Mac kept a stash here.' Luke grabbed the billy can. 'But, my friend, I need your boot. Mine's ripped,' he said, lifting his right foot. The sole of his boot hung like a floppy tongue.

'Take the boots from a dying man, why don't you?' Tubs joked. His lips were now almost blue.

'Dying, my arse. You're just lazy, as usual,' Luke replied with a big grin, then gently removed Tubs' right boot. 'Small feet, mate? Could be a tight squeeze.'

Luke crammed his larger foot into Tubs' boot.

Tubs stared at him, like a child frightened to be left alone in the dark. Had Tubs guessed what he was about to do?

'Geez, stinky socks,' Luke said to Tubs, trying to lighten the mood.

Tubs half-smiled. 'Yeah … damp dog meets smelly cheese.'

Luke stood, the billy in his hand. 'I'll give the vehicles a check too,' he said. 'I may be some time.'

He shut the door behind him. He hoped they hadn't noticed that he had unintentionally used the famous last words of the late

Captain Lawrence Oates, one of Robert Falcon Scott's men. On the doomed return leg of their expedition to the South Pole in 1912, he had left their battered tent, saying, 'I am just going outside and may be some time.' He had not returned.

Luke scooped up some snow and left the billy on the doorstep. He then straddled the snowmobile with the fuller tank. Before Maddie could open the door, he sped off in the direction of Hope Station.

T MINUS 4 DAYS, 1 HOUR, 33 MINUTES
6 March, 10:27 am (UTC-07)

Luke rounded the promontory, the snowmobile's engine a quiet purr. In a few minutes he would be able to see the station – and anyone guarding it would be able to see him. A marksman on the raised station platform could easily take him out. Would he ever see his son again?

His heart rate was up and his hands trembled. He focused on slowing his breathing to steady his nerves. To push away the mounting fear, he made a mental list of the supplies they'd need: bandages, antibiotics, antiseptic, painkillers, sutures, boots (preferably large), fleeces, gloves, hats, sleeping bags, food, ideally a tin opener, knives to kill and cut food, shellite for the camping stove … and, by some miracle, maybe some of their comms gear, if it had not been completely destroyed.

The closer Luke got to the station, the more hopeful he became. Yes, they could survive. If Shackleton and Mawson had survived for years with vastly inferior clothing and limited food, then so could they. And the fire may not have devoured every room. Perhaps something in the comms room would still work?

Then he smelled the aroma of burned wood and fuel, and his empty stomach heaved. Despite the wind, the turbine didn't move.

Had it been switched off last night? Gradually, the satellite dish came into view, followed by the two-storey-high fuel tank. Luke slowed, anxious to be as quiet as possible. A few more metres and he saw what was left of Hope.

The station looked like a black beetle with its guts hanging out. It was still raised on its hydraulic legs but the outer walls of the living quarters were half their normal height and the roof was destroyed. The garage doors had remained open. The workbenches still stood high and proud, like altars. He could just make out the plastic body bags, which had melted like white paint over the dead.

It took a minute or two for Luke to recover. He focused on a familiar motif on the diesel tank. Months before, Mac and Luke had painted a three-metre-high kangaroo doing a thumbs-up on the tank's side, cheekily announcing their nationality to any ship that found itself in Pine Island Bay. He remembered the fun they'd had painting it. Now, the kangaroo's oversized thumb and cheesy grin was glaringly out of place amongst the carnage.

Luke looked up at the living quarters, searching for movement. He guessed he was still out of gunfire range but he couldn't be sure. The sky was the kind of exquisite blue that he'd only ever seen in Antarctica. It didn't seem right that the sky above their burnt-out home should feign such purity, given the horror that had happened beneath it. The brightness of ice all around made him squint. Without snow goggles or sunglasses, Luke knew that snow-blindness would set in. He added eye protection to his salvage list.

He tentatively accelerated toward the wreckage, constantly scanning for places in which the killers might hide. No gunfire. No shouting. He finally stopped just inside the garage entrance and cut the engine, hiding the snowmobile from view.

Luke dismounted and looked towards the metal steps leading up to Exit 1. They were free of ice, due to the heat of the blaze. Despite his painfully tight borrowed boot, he raced up the steps, keen to get inside. He stopped in front of the door, dumbfounded. It had remained shut last night because bolts had been attached to its top and bottom. Crudely drilled at speed, the screws had been forced into the door and frame at odd angles.

It took Luke a few seconds to grasp fully that someone had sealed the doors to prevent their escape. It had been cold, calculated murder.

'Bastards,' he breathed. He staggered along the deck in search of another way in. The large window of Craig's room was shattered but Luke hesitated, the memory of Craig's charred and twisted body all too vivid. Remembering that his brilliant-yellow freezer suit was designed for maximum visibility, he stepped through the open window. The room was still smoking. Before he had a chance to look around, the stench of burnt human flesh caused him to gag. He saw Craig's blackened skeleton, its flesh stripped away, and retched violently.

Bent forward, Luke tried not to think of the agony Craig must have suffered. He tried not to think of Craig emailing his wife and grown-up kids every day, exchanging photos with them. A gruff man with a soft heart. Luke wiped his mouth with the back of his glove. But he hadn't felt the fabric against his lips and cheeks; the skin on his face was numb. He needed to protect his extremities – especially his sockless feet – fast, otherwise frost-nip and its more serious successor, frostbite, would set in. Luke knew that frostbite didn't just incapacitate – it could kill.

He straightened and placed a hand over his nose and mouth and systematically checked through what was left of Craig's room. There was nothing worth salvaging from the rubble.

'I'm sorry, Craig,' Luke said. He had to move on.

T MINUS 4 DAYS, 1 HOUR, 16 MINUTES
6 March, 10:44 am (UTC-07)

Tubs' room was gutted. On the smoke-stained walls, Luke noticed a photograph, curled and singed at the edges but miraculously mostly intact. It was of Tubs with his mum, dad and girlfriend, taken on the beach at Wallaby Point. He remembered Tubs talking about his hometown and his childhood sweetheart, Carley. Tubs was over-wintering in Antarctica because the pay was good and they were saving for their wedding. Luke peeled the photo off the wall and put it in his pocket.

The wardrobe door came away in his hands. Inside, the synthetic fabric fleeces, parka and outer leggings had perished. His hope of finding clothing was declining rapidly. However, Tubs' daypack, dumped at the bottom of his wardrobe, was still mainly intact. Some of the straps were brittle but it would do for now. Luke threw it over his shoulder.

Maddie's room was a burnt-out shell, as was Sue's. Luke's room was next.

His wardrobe was nothing more than a black hole. But under his bed frame and carbonised mattress he found a spare pair of boots, with a double pair of used socks inside. He whooped with excitement, forgetting the need for quiet. Sometimes being untidy paid off.

Luke sat on the stinking carpet and pulled off Tubs' boot, as well as his other one. He pulled on both pairs of socks, rubbing his numb feet, then laced up his fresh boots. He tied Tubs' boot to the daypack, then turned to his collapsed desk and kneeled down. The drawer was jammed shut but he managed to yank it open. The notebooks inside were browned and crisp, his sunglasses' frames were warped and the lenses cracked. Reaching to the very back, he pulled out a curled-up photo of Jason as a baby. He was in his father's arms, and Luke was looking down at him adoringly. Luke had taken this photo with him wherever he went: it was a record of the first time in his life he had felt such overwhelming and unconditional love for another person. He put it in the same pocket as Tubs' family photo.

Blue's room was next. Luke found a parka and waterproof trousers in a crumpled heap at the bottom of the wardrobe – the ones the doctor had worn on the SAR mission. They would fit Tubs or Maddie. Luke checked the pockets and found Blue's inner and outer gloves. Bingo. But his large hand threatened to burst the seams so he peeled it off and stuffed both pairs in the daypack.

Then Luke remembered he had clothing in the laundry. How could he be so forgetful? The washing machine and dryer were still intact, although their paint had blistered and blackened. He opened the dryer door and found, protected from the flames, his thermals, socks, inner gloves, balaclava, inner trousers and a large fleece. He hastily threw all of it into the daypack, except the gloves, which he pulled on immediately. He spotted his canvas laundry bag, too, and grabbed it. This find should give all three of them enough clothing.

Luke moved to the comms room. The swivel chair he'd fallen asleep on was melted like a wilted black tulip. The desk had collapsed. The high-frequency radio was upended on the floor, and its front panel had fallen away. It looked as if someone had put a boot into it, but maybe there was a way it could be repaired … Luke decided to come back for it at the end of his scavenge.

Luke looked around for the two VHF radios, one, marine band, the other, aeronautical. Someone had taken an axe to them, as well as to the Iridium satellite terminal. The Inmarsat BGAN satellite terminal was trashed too. He looked for the handheld radios. They were crushed.

Luke tried not to let his rising panic overwhelm him. As a scientist, he believed there was always a solution; you just had to find it. Their survival depended on shelter, food and, ultimately, rescue – but how could he call for help? He scanned the room and found a compass in the debris. He held it up and pointed it due north – it still worked. He pocketed it.

Next, the surgery. The wall cabinets had burst open and spewed out their contents. Plastic syringes had melted like ice cream on a summer's day. Luke worked his way through Blue's surgery drawers and found needle holders and sutures. He combed the shelves for antibiotics, but only two vials were unbroken.

Then he remembered the safe that held the addictive drugs. Surely it would have protected its contents from the blaze? But the key – where did Blue keep the key? He spun around to Blue's desk and opened the top drawer, and there it was. The key clicked in the safe lock and the thick door opened. Luke grabbed handfuls of vials filled with morphine and pethidine. But he still had no syringes or intravenous drips.

Back at the wall cabinet, he found most things burned, shattered or melted. Then, out of the corner of his eye, Luke spotted a blackened backpack. The fabric had originally been red and the badge still had the brand 'Thomas' on it: an emergency medical pack. He ripped it open and found syringes in one of the pouches. In another pouch were painkillers, and in another bandages, antiseptic and sterile wipes. Placing his other finds inside the pack, he closed it and tied it using a sling, much as he would place a belt around a suitcase.

Wondering how long it would be before the killers returned, Luke dashed towards the kitchen. He came upon Sue and stood stock-still. He felt terrible – he had forgotten about her. Somehow the flames had not reached her, and she lay on the floor as if asleep. Her face and fluffy pyjamas were covered in a fine layer of ash. Her parted lips were black. He bent down and used his hand to close her eyes. Irrationally, he thought about trying to find a blanket to cover her. *Pull yourself together, man.*

When he saw Blue, Luke turned away immediately. There was little left of the doctor. It was as if an autopsy had been performed and he'd been left with his entrails hanging out. Luke managed to control his gag reflex this time. He thought that he should bury his friends, to give them back some dignity. But that would be like putting up a sign saying, 'I'm still alive. Come and get me.' It was, of course, impossible to bury them anyway. The ground was frozen solid.

Luke had worked, laughed, eaten and played with these people. He knew all about their families, their friends, their worries, hopes and dreams. And their loved ones had no idea they were dead. A sharp gust of wind chilled him to the core, awakening him from his grief. Tubs and Maddie needed him.

The kitchen had clearly been the epicentre of the explosion: there was a small crater where the gas tanks had once been. He clambered over the rubble and found a saucepan – into the canvas bag. All the plastic containers had melted, and the foods dripped down the shelves in congealing browns, reds, creams and greens. Cardboard packaged foods were nothing but black flakes, but some of the cans were fine.

He plucked tins of soups, stews, baked beans off the shelves and put them into the bag. In the large cabinet freezer he pulled out bread, several bags of vegetables and meat.

The cutlery had been blown across the room but some still remained in the sink drainer, including several knives. Luke nearly fell as he rushed to the general stores cupboard. Despite being highly flammable, a couple of bottles of shellite looked to be undamaged. He placed the daypack on his back and then pulled his arms through the straps of the second bag so it rested across his chest, balancing the weight. He carried the medical kit with one of his free hands.

Crash!

Luke turned around clumsily, his movement hampered. What was that? Was someone there? He ducked, and the tins inside the bag clanked together and dug into his spine. He couldn't see anyone. He kept his head low as he stepped over the remains of the kitchen wall and out onto the deck. He peered below. Were they hiding down there?

He approached the steps, his heart pounding and his mouth as dry as chalk. He poked his head around the corner: the steps were empty. He couldn't see anyone. He raced for the snowmobile but when there was no gunfire, his confidence grew. He strapped the bags to the snowmobile and decided to go back for the radio transmitter.

A figure appeared from behind the massive fuel tank. The person was wearing white, and Luke might not have noticed him if he hadn't been standing against the bright colours of the thumbs-up kangaroo. He had a gun but didn't move. Perhaps he hadn't seen Luke?

He had to leave the radio. He turned the ignition and revved the engine. Out of the corner of his eye he noticed an ice axe near the door. He accelerated, leaned down to pick it up and then raced out of the garage. Immediately machine-gun fire began, the noise like a frenetic jackhammer. Bullets tore at the ice around him.

Terrified, Luke ducked and accelerated hard, burning up what little fuel remained. The gauge was flashing on empty in angry red.

Tubs screwed up his young face as he coughed. The morphine hadn't yet kicked in and the pain was excruciating. Upon Luke's return, Maddie used the antiseptic wipes and placed a fresh three-sided sterile dressing over the entry wound. There was nothing more they could do. Tubs rested his limp hand over the photograph of Carley and his parents.

'Your turn, Maddie,' said Luke, looking at the shrapnel in her leg.

'Didn't you say you were followed?'

'Yes, but I detoured through an area littered with slots. It'll take him a while to get backup, and unless he knows the area well, which I doubt, I reckon we have at least an hour's head start, maybe more. The emergency medical kit has everything I need to do it.'

Maddie studied the piece of metal sticking out of her calf. What she could see was as wide as a credit card. She reached for a paintbrush and pulled her hair back, twisted it round and secured it in a bun with the paintbrush protruding from the top. Her thinking mode. 'Let's work out where we're going first.'

Luke crouched down. 'Have you heard of Bettingtons?'

'The abandoned British station? That's exactly where I was

going to suggest. I'm not sure how comfortable it'll be, though. I heard it was a bit of a wreck.'

'Don't think so – it was evacuated in a hurry in the nineteen-fifties. Apparently they left everything they couldn't carry.'

'It's at the southern end of Cranton Bay, isn't it?' Maddie asked. 'That's a long way.'

'That's what Craig told me. Probably seventy kilometres, as the crow flies.'

'Seven … ty!' Tubs rasped.

Luke looked at him. 'You'll be resting in the boat. You won't have to do a thing. We'll look after you, mate.' He focused again on Maddie. 'The Zodiac has spare fuel; the only problem might be hardening sea ice.'

Maddie scratched her head, deep in thought.

Luke continued. 'Craig showed me photos of Bettingtons taken a couple of years ago. Said it was like going back in time – mattresses still on beds, food still in cupboards. Like some English village cricket hut, complete with checked curtains. It was fine a few years ago, so there's no reason to believe it won't be now.'

'Yes, I remember,' she said, nodding. 'The Brits planned to use it as a base for dog-sledding survey parties in the embayment. But they couldn't do it because the sea ice is so unpredictable – sometimes solid as a rock, sometimes like porridge.'

'I think we must've read the same article,' Luke replied. 'How ironic that when their ship came to pick them up, the sea ice was rock-hard so they had to sled out to the ship. That's why so much is left behind: they could only take what fitted on the sleds.' It occurred to Luke that this was probably the most relaxed conversation he'd had with Maddie in the five months he'd known her.

She glanced at her leg and then at the hut door. 'Let's leave the operation until we're at Bettingtons. I think we should focus on getting away from here. If I'm in the boat, I won't need to use my leg anyway.'

'We'll have to cross Pine Island Bay. Then we'll follow the headland round into Cranton Bay,' said Luke. 'There's a risk we'll be spotted, but Bettingtons is our only chance of survival.'

'Tubs? Are you okay with this?' asked Maddie.

'We stay … here.' Every word was agony.

Luke replied, 'Mate, they're professionals, probably military. They'll find us here. I'm sorry, but we have to leave.'

Tubs nodded a fraction.

'We'll need plenty of energy. Tubs especially,' Maddie said. 'Have we got time to eat before we leave?'

'We'll have to be quick. I'll get the boat ready. Can you heat something up?'

When Luke returned, he found Maddie trying to get Tubs to eat some tinned stew she had warmed over the tiny camping stove. She handed it to Luke, who gulped it down.

Maddie shared the rest with Tubs, who could do little more than lick the gravy. 'Needs seasoning,' he said, trying to smile. 'Water.'

Maddie helped him drink some melted snow in a plastic beaker that used to be Mac's tea mug.

'Can't go with you,' wheezed Tubs.

'Of course you can,' said Luke. 'Try to eat some more.'

'Nah.' Tubs turned his head slowly to look at the photograph of Carley with his family. 'Can't see,' he breathed. Luke lifted the photo so it was in front of Tubs' face but still in Tubs' grip. 'Was gonna marry her.'

'You still are,' said Maddie. 'She's gorgeous. When's the wedding?'

'Jan … uary.' Tubs' words were slurred; the morphine was beginning to take effect.

'You focus on her, Tubs, on getting better for your wedding, okay?' said Maddie, but Luke could tell that she, too, realised Tubs wouldn't live till January.

Tubs' eyes flickered and then opened again.

'It's my … fault,' he said, as a tear spilled from a half-open eye.

Maddie cut in. 'Let's not go there again. It's not your fault. Just relax, okay?'

'They paid … money for wedding … God, what … have I done?'

Luke glanced at Maddie, confused. 'What's he mean?' He turned to Tubs. 'Who paid you? And for what?'

'A stranger,' he wheezed. 'I jammed … communications.

100

Didn't know … new batteries.'

'Maddie?'

'Luke, he said all this while you were gone. Over and over again. He says the comms blackout was his doing.'

'Mate,' said Luke, softly squeezing Tubs' shoulder, 'you're delirious. We'll get you in the boat and you can rest.'

Tubs grabbed Luke's arm with what little strength he had left. 'I didn't know … I'm so … sorry.'

Tubs coughed hard, droplets of blood splattering the sleeping bag. He lay back on his makeshift pillow. 'Must be them … at fire.' He opened his blue eyes wide at his last breath.

'Tubs? Mate?' called Luke.

Maddie reached out and touched Tubs' neck, feeling for a pulse. She gently closed his eyes and took his hand. Neither she nor Luke spoke for a while, as Tubs' loved ones continued to smile up at him from the photograph lying in his lifeless hand.

'Why does everyone I care for have to die?' Maddie whispered.

'It's not your fault,' Luke said. 'There's nothing you could have done to prevent this.'

'He was only twenty-four,' said Maddie. 'He had everything to look forward to. Wedding. New business. They were going to open a café on the beach. Did you know that?'

Luke stared blankly at the steamed-up hut window. 'It would have been a winner. Long hours and hard work, but he'd have made it.' Luke took the photo from Tubs' palm and unzipped his friend's freezer suit. He placed it facedown over Tubs' heart and pulled the zipper shut. 'There, mate,' he said. 'You've got them with you. You wait there, and when our ship turns up, we'll get you home.'

Maddie released Tubs' hand and pulled the sleeping bag up and over his face.

Luke could feel his eyes getting watery but he knew there was no time for grief. He stood. 'We've got to get going.'

'We can't just leave him like this.'

'We have to. He's safe here, but we're not.'

Luke hurriedly packed their bags. He couldn't allow his desolation to show. He wanted to watch over Tubs' body just as much as Maddie, but their enemy might arrive at any moment.

She stared at him, appalled, her grimy face streaked with tears. 'You're a cold-hearted son of a bitch.'

Her words were like a punch to the stomach.

'Goodbye, Tubs. We love you.' Maddie stroked his hand one last time, then struggled to stand. Luke went to help her but she glared at him and he backed off. As she tried to use her left leg she fell against the door, only just regaining her balance.

'I'm sorry, Maddie, but we need to take that sleeping bag,' Luke said. She was about to object but he persisted. 'He'd want us to have it.'

Reluctantly, she drew back the sleeping bag from Tubs' face and began rolling it as tightly as possible. Luke dismantled the camping stove and shoved it into the daypack, along with the pan. Maddie grabbed the first-aid kit and stuffed the spare clothes into the second bag.

'Ready?' he said.

Maddie glanced at Tubs' peaceful face. He looked as if he were just sleeping. 'We'll come back for you, I promise,' she said, her voice cracking.

Once in the Zodiac, Luke handed her their only pair of snow-goggles. He'd found them stuffed inside a jacket pocket.

'You have them,' she said.

Luke put them on and was grateful to cut out some of the eye-stinging glare. 'I drive, you navigate?' he asked, offering her the compass.

'Sounds good,' replied Maddie, pocketing it. She smiled grimly. 'Seems like we're working as a team at last.'

'Looks like it,' agreed Luke, smiling back. 'How the hell did that happen?' he joked.

But as he placed his arm around her so she could lean on his shoulders, his smile evaporated. Neither of them knew the exact location of Bettington Station. It would be pure guesswork.

Robert Zhao Sheng skidded the white snowmobile to a halt outside Hope Station. He turned off the ignition and flexed the fingers of his left hand; the outer three hardly moved, and they ached. He had taken great pains to ensure his men had not noticed his weakness as they crossed the glacier to arrive at Hope. The journey had given him the chance to listen to the allegro movement from Beethoven's Ninth Symphony. Such sublime music further lifted his spirits.

He was already on a high. The chairman of the arms manufacturer he'd wanted to buy had caved. It was only a small deal — five hundred million or so — but the company was worth at least twice that, given the opportunities his ownership of Hung Security would create. Synergy. What a wonderful word. And it was yet another victory for Robert. Life was about keeping score and staying ahead, and even from this cesspit of a place, he was still king.

Robert switched off his iPod, dismounted and removed his helmet and balaclava. He waited for Captain Wei and the soldier who had failed to kill the survivor to jog over. He had deliberately parked some distance away to avoid seeing the burned corpses. 'How many bodies do we have?' he asked.

'Including MacNamara and Cox, five, sir,' said Wei.

'So three are still alive, and one is clearly close enough to salvage supplies,' concluded Robert, lighting a cigarette, his movements deliberately slow.

'Yes, sir,' responded Wei, his head down.

Robert sucked on the cigarette and exhaled several times in rapid succession, creating rings of smoke. The rest he blew through his nose, in Wei's face. 'Identify the person who returned.'

'We believe it was Searle. A tall man. Grigg is rounder and shorter. And the only other person to escape was a woman.'

Robert nodded, speed-smoking his cigarette. The stench of burned flesh and petrol was wafting towards him on the wind. He had hoped the cigarette would remove some of the smell from his nose, but it didn't. 'Yes. I expected it to be Searle. But where are the others?'

He looked down as he contemplated this question. When he looked up again, both soldiers were observing him. They immediately dropped their eyes to the ground. 'What did he take?' Robert asked sharply.

'It's hard to tell, sir …'

'Food, medicines, what?' He was growing impatient.

'We're checking now, sir. Do you wish to check for yourself?'

Robert had spent his life watching his back, and he recognised Wei's challenge. He stepped to within centimetres of Wei's face. 'You think me a soft city boy, don't you?' Perhaps Wei, who was used to the unrelenting brutality of commanders such as Robert's father, had heard him vomiting after the first killings.

Wei didn't flinch. 'No, sir.'

'Follow me,' said Robert. His Dolce & Gabbana sunglasses masked his trepidation, but he had a point to prove. He led them up the steps to the outdoor platform, and he recalled his men sabotaging the generators and bolting the doors.

'Show me,' he commanded, and Wei took him to Craig's charred remains. Bile rose in Robert's throat but he swallowed it back down. He called over the soldier who had let Searle escape. 'Kneel,' Robert ordered.

The soldier hesitated for a fraction of a second, then obeyed.

'Why didn't you kill Searle, as you were ordered?'

'I tried to, sir, but he was too fast. He was leaving as I arrived.'

'Did you chase after him?' Robert was circling Craig's body.

'Yes, sir, but he crossed a snow bridge and then destroyed it. I couldn't get across. By the time I found a way around, he'd gone.'

'You followed his tracks?'

'As far as I could. He took a route that was riddled with crevasses. It was too dangerous to enter without the proper gear, so I radioed in and called for backup. Sir.'

'Liar!' yelled Robert. 'You're a sickening coward.'

Robert pushed the soldier's head down so that his nose touched Craig's blackened, stinking corpse. The soldier screamed and resisted. 'I should shoot you like a dog,' he said. 'You disgust me.'

Robert released his grip and stood up. He enjoyed the flicker of shock he saw on Wei's face. The soldier wouldn't fail him again. Robert's father had used the same technique on him as a child when he wet his bed. His mother would comfort him but his father was disgusted and pushed his face into it. Eventually, the fear of his father's torment outweighed his fear of the dark, and he stopped wetting his bed.

'Show me the others,' Robert ordered. Perhaps he was getting used to the smell of death as he no longer felt like gagging.

Wei showed him Sue, lying near the lift. Robert couldn't resist saying, 'Ah, nicely kebabbed', but his humour fell flat. They arrived at the kitchen. On finding Blue's dismembered body Robert's façade almost crumbled. He had to turn away.

'Searle took food, cooking equipment,' said Wei. He pointed to the fresh footprints in the ash, which led to the freezer; the lid was hanging open. A series of circles on the pantry shelves revealed that tins of food had been removed.

'What else is missing?' Robert barked.

'Medical supplies, possibly clothing, and he went into the communications room, sir.'

Robert's head shot round. 'And?'

'All the equipment was destroyed, sir. There's nothing left.'

Robert nodded. 'Which way did he go?'

'Towards the bay.'

'Why would he go there?'

'We'll know very soon, sir.'

Robert kicked Blue's body in frustration. The corpse jolted sideways; the guts, now mostly frozen, moved with him, like a macabre sculpture. Captain Wei instinctively took a step forward.

'Do you have a problem, captain?' Robert demanded.

'I … I wish to respect those fallen on the battlefield, sir.'

Robert guffawed, his head thrown back. 'What old-fashioned nonsense.'

Wei stared at him defiantly, his eyes angry. 'General Zhao insists we respect the dead, even if they are our enemy. It is a matter of honour.'

'We'll have time for honour once we're victorious. Until then, nothing else matters. And might I remind you that I own Hung Security. And that means while you're here, I own you too. Remember that.'

Wei looked down. 'Yes, sir.'

'Well, get on with it, man!'

Wei took off like a startled rabbit, rather than the well-seasoned soldier he was.

On the way back to his snowmobile, Robert passed the fuel tank and saw a sign still stuck to its side: 'Danger – No Smoking'. The irony was not lost on him as he glanced at the still smouldering station timbers.

The lawyer's office was tucked down an alleyway in Sydney's Chinatown. It was a little after eight in the morning – the day after Jack Woo's death – when Wendy Woo stepped into the office's reception area, which consisted of nothing more than two plastic chairs and some tatty real-estate magazines, piled neatly on a small and slightly chipped coffee table. There was no receptionist. The airless space smelled of yesterday's meal; no doubt it had wafted in from the nearby restaurants.

On the other side of the frosted glass wall of the only office of Chan Associates sat Anthony Chan, Wendy's father's solicitor of almost twenty years. In one sinuous movement, Wendy glided from the doorway to the chair in front of Chan before he even registered her presence.

'Wendy!' Chan's jaw dropped, revealing crooked lower teeth. 'But how did you …'

'I rode all night.' She sat before him in skin-tight black leather jacket and trousers, clutching a biker's helmet under one arm.

'What? From Melbourne? Why didn't you catch the red-eye?'

Wendy unzipped her jacket and threw it over the back of her chair. 'Had to do something. Couldn't sleep.'

Chan dashed around his desk to give Wendy a hug. She was surprised by this formal man's emotion, and she relaxed into his comforting arms. 'Oh, this is terrible,' he said. 'I am so sorry.'

Eventually, she pulled away. 'Thank you for calling me. I'm sorry I was ... rude. It was such a shock, you know.'

Jack's body had been found less than an hour after his death by a seamstress who had left her grocery shopping behind at the shop. She had first called an ambulance and then Chan.

He observed Wendy's wan face. She knew what he was thinking: Wendy, the source of her father's woes.

'Please take a seat. Green tea? I didn't expect you this early.'

'You're a creature of habit. I knew you'd be doing your paperwork early. Yes, tea would be lovely.'

Chan boiled the kettle and prepared the pot. 'I marvel at how someone as petite as you can handle those heavy motorbikes.'

Wendy ignored the comment. 'I don't understand,' she said. 'Heart attack? He didn't have heart problems. He never even went to the doctor. I just can't believe he's gone.'

Chan poured the green tea into thimble-shaped cups. Wendy sipped at it like a hummingbird. Except in Chan's eyes, this little bird was dressed like a man. The only thing feminine about her was her neat black bob and pink lipstick.

'He wasn't a young man, Wendy,' he said. 'And he worked very hard. Long hours, you know that.' He paused. Wendy had covered her face with her hand and was shaking her head in disbelief. 'And he loved you very much, you know.'

Wendy's hand jerked away from her face and her almond-shaped eyes narrowed. 'Our relationship is none of your business.'

Chan's eyes widened, a little shocked at her curt tone. He focused back on the matter in hand. 'The police needed someone to identify him. I went last night. I didn't want you to have to go through all that.'

Her frown softened. She looked over his shoulder at the groaning air-conditioner on the wall, which belched out a damp-smelling chill. 'Thank you,' she said, avoiding eye contact, embarrassed by her outburst.

'There will be a post-mortem today, only because he doesn't have any history of heart disease. A routine thing. It's nothing to worry about.'

She looked up, startled. 'I want to see him before they do that.' She blinked away a tear.

'I can arrange that. But are you sure, Wendy? They say the image of the dead haunts you forever.'

Wendy nodded and pulled a tissue from her pocket. 'Can I see him right away?'

'Well, I'll have to ask the Department of Forensic Medicine mortuary. You normally need an appointment, but I have a contact there so I'll see what I can do.'

'Please. I can't wait.' She wiped her eyes.

'Oh Wendy, I am so sorry for your loss. Your father was a fine man and a good friend to me. If you need anywhere to stay while you're here, you are very welcome to stay with me and my family.'

Her eyes roamed the room, locking onto anything but Chan's kindly face. She was trying hard not to bawl but his pitying look threatened to tip her over the edge. She glued her focus to a pile of paper files gathering dust on a side table. 'He's all I have,' she said. 'Had. There's no one else.'

Chan knew their family history. 'Then stay with us. You are always welcome.'

She looked up at Chan and clenched her teeth to control her emotion. 'No, I'll stay at Dad's. There's a funeral to organise, things to sort out. But thank you.'

'You have keys, of course?' he asked. She nodded. 'And to the business?'

'I'm not sure.'

'Strictly speaking, I'm not supposed to give you keys until the paperwork has been approved by the court. But as you are a director of the company, you are entitled to them anyway.' Chan opened his desk drawer and presented her with a bundle of keys tied together with a red ribbon.

'I'd forgotten I was a director. Dad did that years ago.' She fingered the ribbon. 'He was hoping I'd join him.' *And I*

109

disappointed him once again, she thought. 'What about the will? Shall we do it now, so it's over and done with?'

Chan blanched but quickly recovered. 'If you wish. You are the sole beneficiary.'

Wendy realised he probably thought her a heartless bitch. But this moment was agony; hearing the will would be agony; seeing her poor dad's body would be beyond agony, as would the funeral. So why prolong the pain with a will-reading at another time? Chan was looking at her sitting stiffly, behaving in a business-like manner, but he was unaware of the emotional war being waged inside her. She wanted to cry and scream and wail but she didn't want Chan to see her break down. So she took a big breath and held it, hoping that she could stifle the sob that was building inside her.

Chan opened a fat and frayed manila file on his desk. 'This is your father's last will, dated the second of July, 2008. In it he bequeaths his house and business and his worldly possessions to you, Wendy Woo. As I mentioned, there is no other beneficiary. However, since this will was made, your father re-mortgaged his house. Given the size of the loan, the bank virtually owns it. I am afraid, Wendy, there's barely any money set aside for the funeral.'

Wendy blinked in surprise and exhaled loudly, the sob that had been bursting to escape sounding much like a hiccup.

'What? You're saying he mortgaged our home? Why?' She was incredulous.

'I am. You didn't know?'

'How would I? We haven't spoken in five years.'

'Hmm,' muttered Chan, unsure what to say next.

'But why? Did he need money?' she asked, leaning forward. The house was probably worth one point two million and their original mortgage had been paid off years ago. She looked intently at Chan, who leaned back, uncomfortable under her stare.

'He recently invested in shares,' Chan said. 'He came to me for advice about buying shares in his name or the company's. I explained the legalities of both options and he bought the shares through the company, so you, as the sole surviving director, can do with them as you think fit.' Wendy opened her mouth to speak but Chan raised his hand. 'Wendy, in my professional capacity I could not guide your father on whether he should buy shares or not, but I warned him that the share market was a risky venture and that he should seek advice from a financial adviser.'

Wendy's cupid's bow lips parted, then shut. She was speechless and Wendy was seldom speechless. As an equity analyst for an investment bank, she could hold her own. But today she could barely hold up her head. 'But shares? Dad never took risks. This is absurd. It doesn't make any sense.'

'All I can tell you is that he was convinced the shares were about to rise in value in a big way. He said he didn't need professional advice and insisted there was no risk.'

'So what did he buy into?' she asked, shaking her head.

'Only one company. Dragon Resources Corporation.'

Wendy's eyes opened wide in shock. She rubbed her temples, revealing black nail polish. Her work portfolio was property, not resources, but she had overheard her colleagues talking about this company. It had two divisions: Dragon Oil and Dragon Mining.

'Why didn't he ask me?' she asked. 'I could have looked into the company for him.'

But they both knew why, and she flicked Chan a warning look. She didn't want to hear his answer, which she knew would only make her feel worse. 'It's madness to invest everything in just one company. How much did he spend?'

'I believe it was nine hundred and thirty-five thousand dollars.'

'Jesus fucking Christ!'

'Wendy!'

'What was Dad thinking?'

Chan frowned. 'Wendy, your father may not have been a professional analyst like you, but he was a sensible man and I'm sure—'

'I'm sorry, Anthony. Look, I don't need the money, you know that. But I thought I knew Dad. This is so unlike him. He was always so careful, so … predictable, reliable. Owning his home meant everything to him. Why on earth would he have put it all on the line to buy shares in one resources company?'

Wendy stood and paced the office. The air-conditioning unit churned feebly, and from outside a truck's brakes intruded. Perhaps the answer would be in her father's papers.

'Thank you, Anthony,' she said at last. 'You've been wonderful.' She shook his hand, careful to avoid another hug, unable to allow herself to be enveloped by the old man's kindness.

'Let me give you the details … the morgue.' Chan wrote down the address for her and she left.

In the alleyway, Wendy tucked the big bunch of keys into her jacket pocket, put on her helmet and straddled her black Ducati Monster. She loved its throaty roar. She revved the engine and accelerated sharply. Beneath the tinted visor, her face was wet with tears.

Luke stood tall, his hand on the outboard's throttle, powering the boat forward. He peered past the bow so he could pick his way between the irregular gaps in the pancake ice which floated like giant frozen lily pads on the water. His left shoulder was aching badly and he found it increasingly painful to stretch out his fingers when he switched hands on the motor. By taking a wide arc away from the glacier front, they seemed to have avoided detection by the killers. As always, Luke was in awe of the Pine Island Glacier, a mighty white wall as wide as eighteen Sydney Harbour Bridges. Now, heading out of the bay, he focused on trying to follow the shoreline, but the fast ice – which attached itself to land or grounded bergs – made it difficult to tell where the land ended and the ocean began.

They made good progress for the first two hours, but the further north they went, the slower the going. In the distance, Luke could see the two-hundred-kilometre-long Hudson Mountains poking through the ice. The range looked like a giant sleeping beast, its back arched to the sky and its white pointed tail stuck out into the sea as a promontory. Further inland, it bent round until it abutted the Pine Island Glacier. Cranton Bay and Bettington Station were on the other side of the headland, but where exactly, Luke didn't know.

The noise of the engine made it difficult to talk and after a while Maddie dozed off, oblivious to the frequent *clonks* as ice hit the boat's sides. Luke didn't need the compass yet, and besides, they had to use it judiciously because of their proximity to the South Magnetic Pole.

Just the two of us left.

He thought back to the day they had met aboard the *Aurora Australis*. Maddie's first briefing of the team had been in the bar, which was a good start. Her speech made everyone laugh. She chatted amiably to each of them, her words and presence visibly defusing the first-timers' nerves. But when she had reached Luke, the anger in her startling green eyes was obvious, despite her fixed smile.

'I hear you're a bit of a rebel,' she'd said. 'I've read the reports from Casey and Mawson.'

'Not really,' he'd replied, confused. 'I just get on with my job.'

That night, the ninth member of their over-wintering team had needed an emergency operation for a ruptured appendix. Blue was the only qualified doctor on board so Maddie had stood in as his anaesthetist. The next morning the grateful patient was airlifted back to Tasmania. *That took some guts*, thought Luke.

Bang! He'd hit a thick slab of ice. Maddie's eyes opened and then quickly closed again, unsure of her surroundings and shocked by the brightness.

'Sorry, the ice is getting thicker.' The whine of the engine became a low hum as he slowed the craft down.

'Where are we?' Maddie asked, struggling to sit up. 'God, I didn't mean to sleep. Must be the painkillers. What's this?' she said, feeling inside her freezer suit pocket. She held up someone's zinc cream. 'Could come in handy,' she said, dabbing a white streak down her nose, and offering the tube to Luke.

He shook his head. 'It's getting tougher to find gaps, but we have to keep going. We're way too far away.'

'Luke, why don't you take a rest and I'll drive?'

'That'd be great, but it means moving you this end.' Maddie was in the middle of the boat.

'I can do it,' she said, 'I was brought up around boats.'

'Were you?'

'Dad built boats. You and I never really talked.'

'No, we didn't.'

Luke released the throttle and let the engine stop. He tried uncurling his hand but it took several goes to flex his stiff fingers.

Maddie checked the compass as Luke sat on the edge of the boat, next to the engine, their bags at his feet. Apart from the soft wash of water against the rubber, there was silence. Luke took a tomato sauce bottle filled with water from inside his parka; he kept it there to stop it freezing. Luke drank sparingly and handed it to Maddie.

'Unbelievable really,' said Luke, looking around at the ice. 'There's water everywhere but only a sauce bottle's worth to drink.'

'Like the poem. You know, "The Rime of the Ancient Mariner"? How did it go?' Maddie frowned, trying to remember.

'"Water, water everywhere, nor any drop to drink." I know how that sailor felt.'

Maddie's smile was partially hidden by the thick collar of her parka, but Luke could see the upturned corners of her mouth peeking above the fabric. 'I didn't think you'd like poetry,' she said, handing him back the bottle.

'At school I was into anything to do with the sea and wildlife – oh, and ice, of course. I guess the sailor got what was coming to him after killing the albatross.'

'Yeah, I remember thinking that too. But literature wasn't my thing. It was biology. Apparently, as a kid I kept asking how, not why. How does the eye work? How does the phone work? I must've been a real pain.'

'Explains why you're so good at what you do. I've seen you solve problems nobody else could.'

'Thanks, Luke. I think that's the nicest thing you've ever said.'

'My pleasure.' Luke affected a bow, which made her laugh. 'So what are you doing *here* then, Maddie?'

Her smile dropped like a blind across a window. 'Oh, you know. It pays well. Adventure. No ties. The usual.'

Luke placed the bottle back in his pocket and leaned against the side of the boat. 'Oh-kay,' he said slowly.

Maddie's reply was a little sharp. 'What do you mean by that?'

'Nothing. Just from what I've seen, over-winterers tend to be either loners or running away from something.'

'And which one are you?' she shot back.

'Neither. Antarctica is my home.'

'Come off it, Luke,' she scoffed. 'Australia's your home. This is just a job.'

'No, not for me. This is where I belong. Don't get me wrong, I'm proud to be an Aussie, but I'm a bit of a stranger there. As a kid I ping-ponged from Australia to France and back, while my parents worked out how to deal with their mistake.'

Luke stopped, unwilling to disclose any more. He cleared his throat. 'This was the first place I really felt happy. At home.' He gestured around the bay, taking in the mountains behind him. 'It's just … gorgeous. And best of all, there are next to no people.'

'So you are a loner, then?'

'I just don't get other people most of the time. Best to keep my distance. Where's the harm in that?' He pointed to a patch of pink ice high up the Hudson Mountains. 'Look up there. Snow algae. Look at the colours: the pink algae, the white ice, the blue sky – it's breathtaking. It's untouched. Antarctica is like the Garden of Eden before man cocked it up. I want to keep it that way.' His face clouded over. 'Eventually, though, we're going to fuck this up too.'

He rummaged in a bag for some energy bars and handed one to Maddie. 'I mean, there's never been a murder here. Until now. Now the innocence of the place is gone.'

'You mean a bit like Cain killing Abel?'

'Exactly. I'm guessing all this killing is about money. Not sure how. There've been rumblings recently about Antarctica's untapped resources, so I'd have said mining, but if you wanted to mine here you wouldn't set up camp on a moving glacier.'

'I think I know where they're from,' Maddie said, chewing her muesli bar. 'Mainland China. One of the soldiers spoke Mandarin.'

'Are you sure?'

'I lived in Hong Kong for a while.'

Luke whistled. 'That's bad. China acceded to the treaty back in

1983.' Luke stretched his arms above his head and then shook his hands to encourage the circulation. 'I just can't believe the Chinese would do this.'

'Let's hope AARO works out there's something wrong and sends help soon.'

'They will. We just have to stay alive till then,' he said.

Luke prepared to help Maddie shift position so that she could steer, but she abruptly changed the topic. 'So what about your boy?'

'What about him?'

Maddie hesitated, her eyes darting about the boat, as if searching for the right words. 'Well, you've got a lovely little boy, so why do you spend so much time here?'

'What are you saying?' His voice had deepened – a clear warning for her to be careful.

'Well, he must miss his daddy, that's all, and it must be hard for you too, being so far away,' she mumbled.

'It is,' he said, frowning.

Maddie seemed about to drop the subject but then changed her mind. 'When you're back home, do you see him much?'

Her words were like sandpaper on his ever-raw guilt, and their earlier understanding evaporated. Luke leaned over the outboard motor and yanked the starter cable so hard that he nearly lost his balance.

'You've got me all wrong.'

The engine spluttered into life and Luke began to steer through gaps in the sea ice. He stared fixedly ahead. Behind his tinted goggles, his eyes betrayed his fury. Maddie didn't apologise and he didn't say another word.

Wendy wove the bike effortlessly in and out of Parramatta Road's heavy traffic and ran a red light. A car honked its horn as they nearly collided. She accelerated away, knowing she was driving recklessly but she had to get away from the morgue as fast as possible.

When she had first seen her father's body she'd felt angry with him, which had surprised and disgusted her. She'd wanted to yell at him for leaving her alone. Now she would never be able to make amends, and he'd never know how much she loved him. Wendy hated herself for that.

The mortuary official had given her some time alone with him and she had told him everything she'd ever meant to say, her warm tears falling on his cold cheeks and the frigid metal trolley. Then her regret had morphed into fury again, and the only way she knew how to vent her anger was to get on her motorbike and ride like crazy.

She broke the speed limit all the way and burned rubber as the bike screeched to a halt in Castlereagh Street. She caught her breath as she noticed the sign above her father's tailoring shop: 'Jack Woo, Bespoke Tailor', in baroque gold lettering on a black background. Through the glass shopfront, Wendy spotted a handwritten note on the inside of the glass door. 'Closed. Mr Woo passed away. Sorry for inconvenience.' She was struck by its absurdity.

As Wendy took the bunch of keys from her pocket, she realised she had forgotten to ask Chan for the alarm code. She dialled his number on her iPhone.

'It hasn't changed, my dear,' he replied.

'It's still "Lori"?'

It was reassuring that some things were still as they had always been. Although Wendy never admitted it, to this day her whole world was anchored to her reliable dad. Without him, she knew a shy Chinese refugee kid could never have dared to work for one of the world's largest banks.

'Yes, I remember you with that rainbow lorikeet,' said Chan. 'You'd only just moved here from Darwin. My, you were a skinny little kid then. You started feeding that bird and named it Lori.'

'Yes, he would sit on my shoulder. God, I was devastated when he disappeared. Dad said it was time to leave the nest but I always thought the neighbour's cat got it.'

Bidding Chan farewell, she tested a few of the keys. When she opened the door she heard the security alarm begin to buzz. She keyed in the code – 5674 – and to her relief the noise stopped. On her father's mobile phone keyboard these numbers spelled 'LORI'.

The shop's interior was unnervingly quiet. No humming sewing machines, no chatter from the seamstresses, no clients lording it about, no Dad smiling graciously. Despite the sunny day, the shop was dark; the tall buildings opposite prevented the sunshine from reaching the street. But Wendy did not touch the light switch.

This tiny shop used to be her second home. She recognised the fabric sample books that lay on the glass table. She ran her fingers across the ties on display, which hung from racks in every colour imaginable, then entered the room where the seamstresses worked, smiling at the familiar mannequins dressed in partially completed suits. As an only child she'd often played with the mannequins, giving them names. But the sewing machines were covered in plastic hoods, like shrouds.

Wendy went to open the door to the area where her dad had measured and pinned and fawned over his clients. She began to tremble: this was where he had died. The door creaked and she paused with it ajar. What would she see? She pushed it open further to find everything in its place, including the leather chair. *Don't be an idiot*, she told herself. *He had a heart attack. What do you expect to see?*

She stepped into the room, relieved that the broken glass had been swept away. Then she realised there was a large stain on the chair seat. She brought her hand up to her mouth and bit her finger as she guessed that the pain of the heart attack had caused her immaculate father to wet himself.

A sob escaped her and she slumped to the floor. 'I'm so sorry,' she whispered. 'I'm so sorry.'

The clock on Jack's desk ticked loudly as the minutes passed. Eventually, Wendy stood and washed her blotchy face at the kitchenette sink and dried it with a tea towel that had a whiff of whisky and aftershave.

She sat at her dad's desk and turned on his ancient computer. He had refused to update it; why spend the money, he'd said, when it works just fine? While she waited for it to warm up, she checked through his filing cabinet.

'Why, Dad? Who told you to do this crazy thing?' she said aloud.

Wendy found records of client accounts and orders for new fabrics but nothing relating to Dragon Resources. As the ancient computer laboured through its anti-virus programs, the screen wallpaper appeared. It was an image of Wendy and her father taken during Chinese New Year celebrations five years earlier – before their big row.

Ever since he and Wendy fled China, Jack had worked to free his wife and bring her to Australia. Every avenue had been explored: letters for clemency, appeals to the Australian government for help, Amnesty International. That's how they'd met Anthony Chan, who put them in touch with a human-rights lawyer in China. But after fifteen years of fruitless effort, Wendy had begged her father to stop. This had infuriated Jack.

'Selfish girl! All you care about is money. How can you abandon your mother?'

'She's dead!' Wendy had screamed. 'I can't do this anymore. It's killing me and it's killing you. I want to forget, don't you understand?'

'I will never give up!'

'Then you're on your own.'

They hadn't spoken since.

Wendy wiped away a tear. How she regretted those words. She took several deep breaths and started to work systematically through Jack's computer files. The shop was doing well but the mortgage on the home was for nine hundred and fifty thousand dollars, as Chan had told her. With further searching, she found details of the share purchase. Nine days before his death, Jack had bought seventeen thousand shares in Dragon Resources at fifty-five dollars per share for nine hundred and thirty-five thousand, after brokerage. Wendy checked the stock's performance: at yesterday's close, it was down three dollars since Jack's purchase.

Using her iPhone to access her company's systems, Wendy checked what the analyst covering Dragon Resources had to say. It wasn't pretty reading. Unlike most other oil companies, which were diversifying – some into nuclear, others into renewables or geothermal – Dragon Oil had been slow to change. While Dragon Mining was doing well enough, its costs seemed to be spiralling out of control, and the company was listed as a 'sell', and most analysts avoided 'sell' recommendations.

It appeared that, a few years ago, a private-equity firm had taken a majority stake in Dragon Resources, so Wendy was surprised to see that the company hadn't yet been kicked into shape. She'd never dealt with the Hood Group – they had no property clients and property was her area of expertise, and she only covered Australian companies anyway – but she had heard of their formidable success rate.

'This must be a real dud.'

She suddenly had an idea and checked the most recent websites her father had visited, but there was nothing much of interest. The very last page he had accessed was a map of Antarctica. *That's weird*, she thought. *Was Dad thinking of going on a trip?* She moved on.

She let her eyes wander around the room. Her father had loved tailoring. Wendy knew he would never have taken such a huge risk unless he was absolutely sure of himself. But how could anyone be sure that their shares would increase in value? Unless …

'What did you know?' she whispered.

Luke had managed to keep going through the sea ice for another half an hour but they were now hemmed in. He used an oar to smash a path to a rocky outcrop where he beached the Zodiac. He unloaded the bags and then helped Maddie out of the boat.

She checked the compass and then finally broke the stony silence. 'Luke, I'm sorry, I didn't mean—'

'Let's not go there.' He cut her off.

'So, which way?' she asked.

'We'll skirt the Hudsons as much as possible. But we'll have to cross that low ridge,' he said, pointing ahead of them. 'Bettingtons should be on the other side.'

'How far is it?'

'I don't know. I'm guessing six kilometres, so, depending on how well you can walk, it could be a two- or three-hour trek.' He scratched the dark stubble on his chin. 'Can you put any weight on your foot?'

Maddie pushed herself up and tried walking. She stumbled forward and Luke caught her. 'Holy shit!' she said. She grimaced and sat down again. 'I don't know how I'm going to do this.'

He kneeled in front of her. 'You'll have to hop. I'll hold you up on the other side. We'll take it slowly.'

'You're kidding, right? Hopping for three hours? Are you out of your mind?'

'I'm sorry but you have to. I'll take most of your weight. Once we're at Bettingtons we'll have food and shelter and we'll be safe. But we've got to get there first.'

She peered at the mountain as if weighing up her chances. 'Okay, I guess I'm hopping.'

'We can't take everything with us. We'll have to leave one bag in the boat. I can come back for it later.'

Maddie shook her head in frustration. 'I hate being so helpless. I like to pull my own weight.'

'I know.' He smiled. 'And I know you don't trust me. But give me a chance, okay?'

Her silence confirmed he was right.

When they had finished sorting and repacking, Luke put the spare bag in the Zodiac and checked the boat was firmly grounded between the rocky outcrops. He hoisted the other pack onto his back, fastened the waist belt and helped Maddie stand.

She hopped a few paces, leaning into his shoulder, then stopped. 'What about using an oar as a walking stick?' she suggested. 'Might be easier.'

'Good idea.'

He grabbed one of the oars, removed the rubber paddle and soon Maddie got into a rhythm. They passed a penguin colony and Maddie paused for a moment to watch some of them slide down the slope on their bellies. She was clearly in a lot of pain. Even the slightest jolt to her injured leg made her wince.

Luke removed his goggles and pulled them over her hat. 'Your turn,' he said.

She thanked him and pulled them over her sore-looking eyes.

They trudged on and soon a ridge of sharp rocks and small peaks appeared in the distance, piercing the ice sheet like islands in a vast white sea.

'Nunataks,' Luke said.

'Volcanic, aren't they?'

'In this case, yes. What we're seeing are isolated mountain peaks poking through the ice.'

Maddie turned her head to look at him. She was smiling. 'Great! So now we have a volcano to deal with!'

'Nah, these haven't erupted for over two thousand years.' Luke remembered his excitement at discovering volcanic ash in the glacier. That was only yesterday but it seemed a lifetime ago.

'Knowing our luck, it's about time for another blow,' she said, laughing to herself. 'How much further, do you reckon?' she asked.

'Maybe an hour. Do you need a rest?'

Maddie bent forward, puffing. 'You sure? Only an hour?'

'Yup. You can do that, can't you?'

'That's not too bad. Let's keep going.'

'You're doing really well.' Luke was lying about the distance. But he had learned the hard way that delusion could be one of the keys to survival. He had to make sure Maddie didn't get discouraged. And he had to keep telling himself that they actually could make it to Bettingtons. He refused to contemplate a night on the ice.

Forty minutes later, the ridge was closer but they still had a way to go yet. They stopped for a break. Maddie lay on her side, panting with exhaustion. 'Only an hour, you said. Geez!'

Luke set up the little stove to make tea. He had grabbed Mac's stash of teabags: only seven left. It looked like they'd have to take a leaf out of Sir Douglas Mawson's book and reuse them several times each. He helped Maddie sit up and gave her the cup of hot liquid.

'I've been thinking about … the killers,' she said, still short of breath.

'Yes?'

'Could they be from Li Bai?'

'No, these guys were military, not scientists. Unless someone at Li Bai discovered something important and Chinese soldiers were sent in to protect it.'

'Like what?' Maddie asked.

'That's where my theory falls apart. What could anyone want with a fracturing glacier?'

'What about oil or gas? Like in the Arctic.'

'Well, if it is that, it's going to be damn hard to reach. The glacier's constantly moving and cracking. Their drills would snap like twigs. And if they wanted to drill under the ice tongue and into the seabed, they'd have to use a submersible.' He sipped his tea and enjoyed the burning sensation as it slipped down his throat. 'It's got to be some really critical resource, something worth going to war over.'

'You think this could escalate to war?'

'I do. The Chinese Minister for Resources has visited Antarctica several times, and China desperately needs more coal. So maybe it's coal?'

'And what happens if their actions destabilise the West Antarctic Ice Sheet?'

'Then all hell breaks loose. Sea levels rise and the world goes into disaster recovery.'

Maddie shook her head. 'We have to raise the alarm. I mean, we're the only two people in the world who have any idea what's going on here.'

Luke turned away and started to pack up. 'I agree, but we may not be able to call for help. We may have to stop them ourselves.'

She tugged at his freezer suit so he faced her. 'That would be suicidal. All I meant was we should try to find a way to communicate with the outside world. That's all.' She peered up at him but he was lost in his own thoughts. 'Luke, our first duty is our own survival.' He didn't reply. 'Luke?'

'We'd better get moving. Are you ready for more hopping?'

Maddie nodded. 'Call me Hopalong,' she joked, trying to lighten the mood.

He pulled her up and she placed an arm over his shoulders for support. The oar was in her other hand as a walking stick. This forced Luke to stoop and bear most of her weight. The terrain was getting steeper, and the pink snow algae, closer. Surely they would cross the mountain ridge soon and see Cranton Bay on the other side?

'Looks like someone's sprayed ... raspberry cordial,' Maddie puffed.

'Amazing, isn't it?' Luke said, gazing at the pink mountainside.

126

They hobbled onwards. 'What if the man you spoke to on the radio … wasn't Mac?' Maddie asked. 'What if Mac was already dead?'

'Why would someone pretend to be Mac?'

'To stop us searching earlier … To give them time to shut down our comms and set fire to Hope.'

Luke stalled at the thought. 'What makes you think someone was impersonating him?'

Maddie glanced sideways at him. 'The more I think about it … the more I think somebody else … wrote Charlie's emails.' She gasped for breath. 'Just as someone pretended … Mac was still alive, so we didn't … have time to alert AARO.'

Luke nodded. 'I could hardly hear what Mac was saying … I guess somebody could have impersonated him.'

'Oh, God, Luke,' Maddie said with a shudder. 'Our quarantine team could be dead.'

Luke's grip on her arm tightened. More needless deaths. He swallowed as he tried to think. 'So that would mean there's a link between the Pine Island Glacier and Whalers Island. Whatever these killers are after, they need both locations.'

They continued their trek in silence. By now, Luke was carrying almost all of Maddie's weight. His thermals were soaked with sweat. In this climate, it would take a week or more for them to dry out. The sun was getting low on the horizon and he feared that they would have to spend a night out on the ice.

As they reached the ridge, Maddie's head sagged forward and she dropped the oar. 'I … can't,' she murmured as she collapsed.

'Sir, permission to speak.'

Robert glanced across his desk at his glaciologist, Li Guangjie, who stood with his shoulders hunched, his hands cradling an open laptop close to his chest, as his eyes darted to and from his leader's face. What a snivelling wretch! He reminded Robert of Dickens' Uriah Heep. 'What is it?' he snapped.

'I wanted to alert you to … to a potential, well, I suppose, it could be a problem.'

Robert sat up straight. 'A problem?'

'May I?' Li held out the laptop.

'Show me.'

Li scuttled round to Robert's side of the desk. On the screen were two black and white images, side by side – stills from video footage. 'What am I looking at?' asked Robert.

'As you know, sir, we have cameras at various strategic spots to monitor the Pine Island Glacier's movement. I took the liberty of monitoring the Thwaites Glacier as well.'

'Why?'

'Because they are sister glaciers, running parallel, both feeding off the West Antarctic Ice Sheet. The health of one affects the other.

Most importantly, they keep the West Antarctic Ice Sheet – which covers over a third of this continent – from sliding towards the coast.'

'Don't give me a geography lesson. Get to the point.'

'Yes, sir. This footage was shot a week ago at the Thwaites Glacier,' Li said, pointing to the first image. 'The other was shot this morning. Look here,' he said, pointing to the second image. He ran his finger under a black gash on white terrain. 'This crack has only just opened up. Last night. I estimate it's a kilometre long and a hundred metres wide. It appears very deep. If it continues to work its way across, well, the Thwaites Ice Shelf could snap off.'

'So what?'

'If, well …'

Li ran his tongue over chapped lips. It revolted Robert. 'Get on with it!'

The glaciologist glanced at the tent entrance then back to the screen. He screwed up his face – it looked as if he were constipated. Robert's features hardened. 'What are you hiding, Li Guangjie?'

The man wouldn't look at his leader. 'Nothing, sir. I just worry that if the Thwaites Ice Shelf collapses and we start blasting away at the face of the Pine Island Glacier, we might destabilise the whole region.'

Robert tilted his head. 'That's it? Nothing else? Look at me, will you!'

Again Li glanced at the tent entrance, then looked Robert in the eye, blinking rapidly with nerves. 'Well, if the Thwaites continues to crack, it could form an eight-hundred-square-kilometre iceberg, which would endanger our vessels.'

'Sit down, over there.' Robert gestured to the chair usually occupied by his communications officer. The glaciologist obeyed.

Robert stood. 'Okay, I agree, it's a risk, but the Thwaites Ice Shelf could take months, years to break away – am I right?'

'It's hard to be certain …'

'Exactly, so I'm not altering our plans when you can't be sure.'

'Um, our blast site is very near the Fitzgerald Fissure, sir. Sea water might flood in and cause further cracking …'

'Stop! Set up a camera to monitor this bloody fissure and

stop your wretched moaning,' Robert said, irritated. 'Now, let me remind you why we are here. We are saving the most populous nation on the planet from dying of thirst.'

Robert paused, letting his words sink in. He needed his glaciologist to be one hundred per cent committed, and the last thing he wanted was Li blabbing to his already jittery father.

'China's water shortage cripples us, cripples our industries, cripples our wealth and status on the world stage. Over two thousand five hundred square kilometres of our land turns to desert every year! We can no longer feed our people. Even the great city of Beijing, where I was born, is encroached on by sand, and the tree-planting – to stop this invasion – has failed. Our cities cannot provide enough drinking water. Beijing alone needs four thousand gigalitres of water each year. Our rivers are polluted: the toxic Huai and Liao threaten the safety of one-sixth of our people, and the Mekong and Yellow rivers are almost dry.'

'I know, sir.'

'Shut up and listen! The Party has tried many alternatives to generate water. Costly and inefficient ways. Each coastal desalination plant not only costs us three hundred million US to build and twenty million a year to run, but they are hugely energy-intensive. A proposal for a national pipeline grid, to pump water to areas in severe drought, was rejected – the cost was prohibitive and it simply robbed Peter to pay Paul. During the 2008 Olympics we tried seeding rainclouds. We claimed it was a success but it wasn't.

'I personally have explored the idea of buying land overseas – land above aquifers or at water sources – but no government in its right mind would sell. So I looked for a new fresh water source, and I have found it here!' Robert raised his arms high and spun around. 'We are surrounded by it. Water everywhere, locked in the ice.'

'Yes, sir, I understand this project's importance. That's why I'm warning you of a possible impediment.'

Robert placed a reassuring hand on the man's shoulder. 'I appreciate that, but this project continues as planned.'

The subordinate nodded.

'You are Captain Wei's cousin. You were picked for this project not only because of your impeccable credentials as a glaciologist, as well as your knowledge of explosives, but also because we believed you could be trusted. Can you still be trusted?'

Robert watched Li's face. He looked like he was about to cry. Pathetic!

'Totally, sir.'

'Good. Do not share this information with anyone – do you understand?'

'Yes, sir.'

'Dismissed.'

Robert checked his watch: just enough time to update his video.

'March sixth, eighteen twenty hours. Robert Zhao Sheng. This is my video diary, embargoed until March eleventh.

'Our preparation is complete. We are ready for testing tomorrow. Drilling has taken longer than we had anticipated, so we have had to work longer hours to keep to our timetable. Several of my men have reported frost-nip and soon may suffer frostbite, and we are low on food. A mistake by our logistics team.'

He glanced at a pile of bamboo baskets on his desk, which fortunately were out of camera shot. An hour earlier they had been full of dim sum.

'I am troubled that my men are showing signs of strain. They complain they cannot feel their hands as they drill but they are properly clothed. This places a huge burden on me as I have to double-check their work, abseiling into the crevasse, often having to order the men to correct mistakes. I think the isolation, the hardship and the critical nature of this project is not sitting well with Captain Wei. He seems distracted.'

Robert couldn't shift the feeling that Wei had another agenda. His devotion to the General was also a concern.

'This is a pity, because I was impressed by Wei's efficiency.'

Robert recalled how his team of ten had flown into Li Bai Station two months before his arrival on site. The team had to be small: the fewer people involved, the less the likelihood of discovery. His father had been concerned about Beijing, full as it was of politicians and bureaucrats terrified of their own shadows. They would surely try to stop them, so the project was strictly need-to-know. Not even the Hood Group was in the loop.

'Led by Captain Wei, our mission team and equipment were tractored, in a convoy, to this site. It took many, many convoys. Even our diesel fuel bladders, as big as double-bed mattresses, were tractored here. Quite a feat of endurance.' Usually, fuel bags were dropped from a low-flying plane, but Robert hadn't wanted to risk the occupants of Hope Station hearing the drone of the plane's engines.

'That was three months ago. Now I fear Wei might make a mistake that could cost us the project, so I have to watch him closely.

'I am also anxious about our glaciologist, Li Guangjie. He spent two seasons at Zhongshan Station on the East Antarctic coast, so I expected him to be hardened to the rigours of our existence here, yet he has become sullen and uncooperative. I am concerned he may be losing faith in the project. I remind him daily that we are here to save the people. Millions of lives.' He leaned closer to the lens for emphasis.

If anything were to go wrong, Robert wanted Li and Wei in the firing line, rather than himself. That was one of his golden rules: always protect your reputation.

'Sadly, I also have to report that on the night of the fire, one of my men saw a tall man leaving the station on a snowmobile. I am very sorry to say that I believe the tall man was Luke Searle, Hope's glaciologist. I, also, now believe he drilled the exit doors shut and set fire to the station. This man has a history of rebelliousness and unreliability. He disobeys his commanders and has abandoned his son in Australia, leaving the mother destitute.'

Robert liked that – who wouldn't revile such behaviour? And setting Luke up to take the fall was an easy way to explain the bolts and bullets. 'He has done seven summer seasons and over-wintered four times, so is it any wonder he has finally gone mad?'

Robert looked around him. 'Antarctica is desolate and ugly, the stations claustrophobic. He obviously couldn't face the coming months of permanent night. I have read of a similar story: an Argentinian doctor at Almirante Brown Antarctic Base was asked to stay on for a second winter. This request tipped him over the edge. He burned his station to the ground, forcing a rescue ship to take him home.

'Of course, I am a mere businessman, not a detective. But my man is certain of what he saw and the bolts on the doors make it plain something is amiss.'

Switching the camera off, Robert made a mental note to make Hope Station's scheduled call to AARO headquarters at nineteen hundred hours, so they would remain blissfully unaware of the disaster. Since the fire, he had impersonated Mac without raising suspicion. In future media interviews he would suggest that, again, it must have been the deranged Searle. Robert couldn't stop his mouth from twitching into a smile.

It was time to ensure nobody would live to contradict him.

Robert had guessed how his adversary's mind worked and had pinpointed the nearest shelter: Bettingtons.

Maddie lay prostrate on the mountainside, her eyes closed and her breathing shallow. She was beyond exhaustion. Luke kneeled and lifted her head and shoulders so they rested in his lap.

'Maddie, can you hear me? Maddie?'

Her lids half-opened.

'I need you to stay with me a little longer. Maddie? Stay with me, okay?'

No response.

'Maddie, wake up!'

Luke peered down the slope, searching for a sign of Bettingtons. The old hut's weathered timbers would be much the same colour as the slate-grey rocks at the water's edge, making it hard to see. But he had to find it: Maddie wouldn't last a night without shelter.

The low sun streaked the dark waters of Cranton Bay a vibrant blood orange. Something on the shoreline gleamed. Luke squinted. It had to be metallic. He remembered his conversation with Craig. Perhaps it was one of the diesel canisters he'd said were scattered about the hut? Luke guessed it was half a kilometre away, mainly downhill. Not far, he told himself.

'Hey! I can see Bettingtons,' said Luke, pointing towards the rocks. 'It's downhill from here. This is the easy bit.'

Her eyelids fluttered.

'I'm going to carry you. Can you put your arms around my neck?'

No response.

'Maddie? Put your arms around my neck. We're nearly there.'

He heaved her up into his arms and her head flopped against his chest, but she placed an arm over his shoulder. The bag of supplies dug painfully into his back. After ten minutes of hard walking, Luke was panting heavily. Dehydrated, his head pounded. His tongue felt swollen. With every gruelling step, his boots sank into the loose surface snow, his muscles on fire. He stumbled and almost dropped her. There had to be another way.

The slope down to the bay was getting steep. Luke gently placed Maddie on the ground and sat behind her, gasping for air. She was barely conscious. Luke put his legs on either side of her hips and pulled her towards him so her head rested on his chest. Locking one arm around Maddie's chest, with the other he pulled the bag as close as possible to his side.

Luke remembered sliding down hills like this as a kid in the Snowy Mountains. He hoped it would work as well now.

'Maddie, wake up.' He shook her. It was brutal but he needed her alert.

'What?' she said, dreamily.

'Try to lift your legs, Maddie, we're going tobogganing,' he called, as he kicked his heels into the snow to drive them forward. Their waterproof clothes offered a slippery surface he hoped would reduce friction. Nothing happened. Luke dug his heels into the snow again. His leg muscles locked as he forced both of them forward. Gradually, they began to slide. Soon gravity took over and they gained momentum. There was a risk they might tumble into a crevasse, but at this stage there was no other way.

'Like being kids again!' Luke shouted into her ear.

Jolted awake by the bumpy ride, Maddie relaxed back onto his chest.

'Woo hoo!' Luke shouted to the sky, laughing. They were going to make it. Using his boot, Luke steered them away from a boulder in their path. The heavy backpack was causing them to veer to the right, away from the location of the glinting metal. He tried lifting it off the ice but it was too cumbersome. They began to slow.

'Can you take the weight of the bag?'

'Yes,' she called back.

With every last bit of his strength, Luke swung the backpack up and onto Maddie, who exhaled loudly under the heavy load. He clung to her and the bag until their descent stopped. Luke pulled the bag aside and wriggled free from beneath Maddie. Shakily, he stood. He peered in the direction of the glinting object, and there was Bettingtons: a long faded-wood hut with a gabled roof.

'Look!' he cried, pointing at it.

'Thank … God,' exhaled Maddie, unable to move.

They were less than a hundred metres from shelter. He'd leave the bag there; the first job was to get Maddie inside.

'The terrain's pretty flat. I'm going to carry you over my shoulder.'

Luke raised Maddie up in a fireman's lift. She whimpered as her wounded leg hit his thigh. Their combined weight drove his boots deep into the loose ice. Every step was like wading through sand and his whole body shuddered with the exertion.

Just when Luke thought he couldn't go any further, he almost tripped over a pile of bricks partly hidden in the snow. He could hardly believe it. Bettington Station was raised above the bedrock on piles of reddish-brown bricks. Two rusty pipes ran up the side of one wall. Most of the windows were roughly boarded up. Discarded canisters, wire, planks and what looked like solidified paraffin oil lay strewn around. Three wooden steps led up to the door, which had no handle, just a hole for a key, long since lost. It had withstood seventy years of battering by the elements.

'Incredible,' Luke breathed.

He sat Maddie on the steps and pushed the door, which didn't budge. It was either locked, which he doubted, or the wood had warped, jamming the door. He thumped hard and it opened inward, the wood scraping on the floor.

Luke took Maddie up in his arms again. His legs shook so much that he stumbled and had to lean against the doorframe. Beyond a narrow, damp corridor was a room full of rusted hand-tools. Luke felt lightheaded, his strength almost gone. To his left was the dormitory, consisting of four bunk beds, with mattresses still on them. Although they were damp and stained, they looked heavenly.

The nearest bed had a pillow, and Luke placed the comatose Maddie on it. Draped over a chair was a grey army-style blanket. It felt damp but not wet, so Luke covered Maddie with it. The room was spinning. He had to lie down.

A heavy, ankle-length woollen coat hung from a hook on the opposite bunk. Barely able to stand, Luke took the coat, collapsed onto a bed and pulled the rough material over him. Forgetting Maddie's wound and the backpack still on the icy slopes, he lapsed into unconsciousness.

Despite the air-conditioning, Wendy's hotel room was hot and stuffy. She kicked off the sheet clinging to her body. The clock-radio's digital face told her in hard-to-ignore red that it was 1:01 am. She swivelled it round so she couldn't see the time anymore and closed her eyes. Having only had a few hours' sleep, she was wrecked. She could hear cars on the road outside her window, and then the *vroom* of an accelerating motorbike – an Aprilia superbike. A beautiful sound. Then her thoughts returned to her father.

Earlier that evening, she'd been to his house in Parramatta, intending to stay the night. But her old home was too full of memories. She'd wandered about the place feeling like an intruder, gingerly touching the framed photos, the leather of his favourite reclining chair, the neatly pressed sheets on his perfectly made bed.

She had run her fingers along the shoulders of his suits, all bespoke, all beautifully crafted. Every coathanger's hook faced the same direction in the fitted cupboards, and every suit hung equidistant from the next. There were plenty of photos of Wendy proudly displayed around the house, but there was only one taken of her before they fled China. It was by his bedside table, in a tarnished metal frame that looked as old as the photo. Her dad had managed to hide it among their meagre belongings as they'd clambered into the decrepit boat that carried them to Australia.

Wendy had brought the photo with her to the hotel. It was propped up in the middle of a circular glass table. She got out of bed and looked at the back of the frame. On it was scrawled 'Woo Ling, Woo Huo'. Huo was Wendy's given name until she arrived in Australia, when both she and her father had adopted Western names.

Turning the frame back around, Wendy stared at herself and her mother at a family gathering. She was twelve years old. An uncle, a wealthy factory owner, had given them a copy of the precious photograph. Her mother's long black hair swayed as she danced, holding the giggling Wendy by her hands.

That was shortly before Woo Ling had been arrested as a Falun Gong practitioner. Wendy hadn't learned until much later of the horrific torture she had endured because she refused to recant. Afterwards, Ling had been moved to Heizuizi Women's Forced Labour Camp in Jilin Province.

Wendy sat on her bed and hugged the picture. 'Oh, Mum. Dad's dead. I need you more than ever,' she said aloud. 'Please forgive me.'

A sob caught in her throat. 'I had to move on. It was killing us.'

She remembered opening the fridge in her dad's kitchen the night before. She had found his dinner already prepared and covered in cling-wrap. It was his favourite, Szechuan chicken. He loved the pepper and chilli. The memory had brought her to tears knowing that he would never eat the dish he'd so carefully prepared.

Wendy shuffled to the bathroom and blew her nose. The same question tormented her: why would her cautious dad, who'd always longed to own his home outright, mortgage it to the hilt to buy shares in a resources company? Especially a company based in a country he had grown to despise. It made no sense whatsoever.

She drank some iced water from the bar fridge and stood by the window. The curtains were open and she stared out over ugly houses and concrete office blocks. Most of the office blocks had their lights on, as if their employees were never allowed to go home. *What a waste of energy*, Wendy thought.

She flopped into the only chair in the room and began to gnaw at her already bitten fingernails. Something was wrong – it was driving her crazy. She catapulted herself from the chair and pulled on her jeans, boots and leather jacket. Picking up her helmet, she grabbed her father's keys and left the hotel.

Twenty minutes later, Wendy extracted a drop-file from the beige filing cabinet and sat on one of the seamstresses' chairs. Only the tiny office at the back of the shop was lit up by a harsh light bulb with no lampshade. Each file was carefully labelled with a client's name, address and phone number. Her father also recorded any personal information he'd picked up during conversations with the client, such as birthday, children's names, holiday destination and so on.

Wendy smiled. Her dad's clients had always been amazed at his memory for such personal details; they were flattered by his interest. Inside each file was a list of every order the client had made, and a hand-drawn sketch of the suit design. She ran her fingers over the sketch and sighed. When she was small, her dad would draw pictures for her. He had been an incredible artist but never had the time to enjoy his talent. Unbeknown to him, Wendy had kept a number of his sketches, which she had framed on the walls of her Melbourne apartment.

As she flicked through one file after another, she was struck by the highbrow nature of the clientele – a judge, barristers, a couple of government ministers, investment bankers galore, CEOs, CFOs. Wendy yawned. She was down to her father's last client file. She'd also checked every drawer and been through all his computer documents for a second time. The file belonged to Xu Biao, China's Consul General in Sydney. Xu had bought four suits over recent months, and another was ready and waiting to be picked up. The suit was single-breasted, dark-grey herringbone super 180 wool. Gorgeous, but not exactly practical.

According to her dad's notes, Xu had been in Sydney a year, and he had a wife and one child. There seemed nothing unusual about his file except her dad had written a series of numbers next to the man's name. She leaned back, intrigued. What could the numbers mean? With a Masters of Science in applied mathematics, she should be able to work it out.

She studied the three rows of numbers:

372466

74 52 100 30

74374373

First she considered the obvious options. Were the numbers a birth date, credit card or telephone number? With these ruled out, she suspected they formed some kind of code. She raised her linear eyebrows, fascinated that her dear old dad could be so devious. She instantly felt a twinge of guilt; she was being disrespectful. 'Sorry, Dad,' she said to the cream office walls.

She tried replacing the numbers with letters, using an A for a 1 and so on. That didn't work. She then looked at her iPhone keypad and tried replacing the numbers with the letters that sat below each number on the keypad. As soon as she'd worked out the first two letters were D and R, she knew instantly what the first row spelt.

She caught her breath. 'Dragon.'

So had Xu advised her father to buy the shares? She shook her head. Consuls and diplomats were basically spies. They manipulated the truth according to the dictates of the powers back home. Xu Biao would never have betrayed his country to help out a tailor, however much he may have liked him.

Exhilarated by her success, she attempted to discover the meaning of the second row of numbers, but it didn't work. She stared at them, tilting her head from one side to the other. The second line's sequencing looked familiar. Where had she seen it before? Why were there gaps between the numbers in the second row but not in the first or last?

Stumped, she turned her attention to the third row. She tried using her phone keypad system again. It took half an hour, but eventually she worked out that the word was probably 'shepherd'.

So, she had the name of the company, some indecipherable numbers and a third word that made no sense. She double-checked that the third row couldn't possibly spell something else. She shook her head. It had to be 'shepherd'.

As her dad always used to say, 'Leave it in the toaster and the answer will pop up.'

It was still dark outside. Exhausted, Wendy curled up on the chaise longue in the changing room and fell sound asleep.

T MINUS 3 DAYS, 3 HOURS, 15 MINUTES
7 March, 8:45 am (UTC-07)

Bettington Station, 74° 27' S, 101° 24' W

At first light, Luke opened his eyes to see green and white checked curtains framing a four-paned window. He imagined he was a child again, at his father's country cottage. But through the blurry panes of glass, which were dripping with condensation, the world outside was white, not the lush green of rural France. Then he remembered. He was lying underneath a heavy coat with scratchy wool and thick lining. In the 1950s, warmth in clothing meant weight. He sat up and banged his head on the wooden slats of the upper bunk. Rubbing his scalp, he contemplated his new surroundings.

The walls had once been painted cream, but they were now striated with rust stains where the damp had crept in through the roof. The ceiling was awash with black mildew. Wooden storage cupboards were built into the walls. Their doors hung wide open, revealing books, a stained pillow, a ribbed khaki jumper with patches on the elbows and shoulders, and a pair of old-fashioned long johns, once white but now stained a pinkish orange from the drips of rusty water. A small iron – also rusted – and a single leather lace-up boot sat on the floor next to a brown leather binocular case.

Luke smiled. Only the British would bother to iron their clothes in Antarctica. But he understood why they'd done it — it was all about morale, maintaining standards despite the hardship.

A paraffin lamp, speckled with powdery rust, sat on another shelf next to a pile of books and the box of a jigsaw puzzle. Luke could imagine the men living here, trying to create a little bit of England and entertain themselves with a jigsaw of a classic village scene complete with thatched cottages and lavender bushes. They had even painted the window frames and the bookshelves an apple green to match the curtains. Luke admired that. They had created a cosy home in spite of the extreme conditions.

He had no idea how long he'd been asleep. He checked his watch: 8:45 am. Then he remembered Maddie. He had to do something about her wound. As he stood, he groaned, and for a moment or two was unable to straighten his cramped leg muscles. He hobbled over to the opposite bunk.

'Maddie? It's Luke,' he said quietly, not wanting to frighten her, but his tone grew more urgent when she failed to respond. 'Maddie?'

Luke took her wrist and felt her pulse; it was strong. He lifted the blanket to check on her leg. There was no bleeding. Relieved, he began to laugh inanely. She woke with a start, squeezed her eyes shut a few times and then stared at the rough grey blanket lying over her. 'We made it?' she asked, her voice croaky, her lips paper-dry.

'We did. This is Bettingtons.'

She moved very slightly and flinched. 'God, it hurts.'

'Can you move your foot?' he asked.

The toe of her boot lifted a fraction.

'And can you feel your toes?'

'I'm not sure,' she replied. 'I think so.'

'I'm going to collect the pack, then we'll get that shrapnel out.'

She nodded as she scanned the room. 'My God, it's like a time capsule.'

Luke stood. 'Yeah, but it'll keep us alive. We're going to be fine here. Just fine.'

★ ★ ★

When Luke returned with the bag, Maddie had fallen back to sleep. He headed down the corridor hoping to find the rest of the hut in as good condition as the dormitory. With a crack, a rotten floorboard snapped and Luke's leg disappeared up to the knee. His knee locked and his ankle twisted slightly, but his boot prevented any injury. Once he'd extracted himself, he resolved to walk around their new home with more care.

Two shallow cupboards ran the length of the corridor wall. Inside were food tins, and many, although tarnished, appeared to be sealed. Luke picked up a large can of Scotch porridge oats and smiled. It was over sixty years old but there was a chance it was still edible. He spotted a tin of Cross & Blackwell herrings, and then one of Heinz baked beans, as well as jars of Marmite, honey and HP Sauce. Some of the tins were corroded or bulging, but others looked fine. Things were looking up.

The next room on the left was the kitchen. He paused in the doorway. Apart from the ubiquitous rust and mildew, the room looked as if the occupants had stepped out and would soon return. At one end of the room was a black cast-iron stove. Above the stove hung a washing line, and dangling from it was a pair of long johns, presumably left there to dry. Shelves on either side offered more books and games, as well as soggy matches, pots, pans and a tin of brown boot polish. The lid had been left off, and a stained boot brush lay beside it, as if the owner had left partway through cleaning his boots.

In the middle of the room was a large wooden table strewn with old magazines. He peered at the first one, *World Sports*, dated August 1952. Underneath it was a copy of *Reveille*, dated October 1952. Luke indulged himself with the idea of spending leisurely days reading them.

He kneeled and forced open the creaking stove door, wondering if there was any chance he could get it going again. He could keep using his little camping stove, but that would do nothing to warm the hut and fuel was scarce. Of course, smoke from the stove could draw their enemy to them, but he hoped they'd be too far away to see it.

'Bugger it,' he said, under his breath and went outside to find something to burn. He was hopeful that the killers wouldn't guess their location and that the mountains would hide the smoke.

The hut looked out to a bay covered in large pieces of fast sea ice, attached to the shore. Crabeater seals dotted the ice at regular intervals, as if they had staked a claim to their own tiny territories. From half a kilometre away, they looked like giant slugs. They lay perfectly still, probably asleep. Among them Luke noticed the darker grey of a much bigger leopard seal, long with powerful shoulders. Its floating island was stained with a trail of red, no doubt its last meal, probably a penguin.

Luke circled the hut so he could inspect the mountain slopes they had descended yesterday. Satisfied they were still alone, he focused on finding timber and soon discovered several discarded storage crates. The wood was brittle and broke easily. He then kneeled down to inspect the white goo that spewed over the rocks from some rusted tins. He sniffed it. Good, paraffin oil. Luke lifted a half-full ruptured tin and carried it inside.

He placed the wood and some of the paraffin in the stove. The wood was damp and would be hard to ignite; guiltily, he ripped some pages from a book and stuffed them in the stove. At first the paper burned weakly and died out. He tried again. This time the paraffin oil caught. He shut the stove door and hoped it would continue to burn.

Luke waited a few minutes, his arms crossed, and then opened the stove to find a homely fire burning. The warmth on his face emphasised how damp and chilled the rest of his body was. He went outside and filled two saucepans with snow, then placed them on the hob to heat. Next he stripped off his outer layers and peeled away his damp thermals. He quickly put his fleece layer and freezer suit back on, and then hung his thermals on the line above the stove, in place of the 1950s long johns, which he respectfully folded.

After clearing the table top, Luke returned to the bedroom, dragged a mattress to the kitchen and placed it on the table, which he then pushed closer to the fire. Back in the bedroom, he lifted Maddie, blanket and all, and carried her to the kitchen, where he laid her on the mattress. She stared, bewildered, around the room.

'Time to operate,' he said. His voice was upbeat but inside he was terrified. One false move and he might kill her. 'I'm no expert,' he continued, 'but at least it's not wedged in your thigh, which means it's nowhere near your femoral artery. If we do nothing, it's bound to get infected.' He knew he was jabbering. 'Maddie, are you okay with this?'

She pulled off her gloves and ran her fingers over her face. As she did so, she smudged some of the ash from her cheek across her mouth. 'You know what I'm looking forward to? Warm water on my face. I might feel human again.'

She was avoiding the decision. Luke took her hand and squeezed it. Her eyes wide with surprise, she looked down at his hand on hers, then squeezed it in return.

'I can give you morphine,' Luke said. 'It'll dull the pain.'

'You did the advanced first-aid course, didn't you?' She looked up at him, seeking reassurance.

Luke nodded.

'Me too, but this is real, Luke. It's my leg. All we practised on was a dead pig. And the injections were into oranges, not people.' She chewed her lip. 'I need to think about this.'

'Have something to drink.' He reused the teabag he'd kept and handed her Mac's old beaker.

'I could do with something stronger,' Maddie joked weakly. She sipped the warm liquid, considering her options. 'Oh, all right. Do it before I change my mind.'

'Right. I'm going to clean my hands,' Luke said.

Taking the smaller pan of hot water outside, Luke added some snow to cool its contents and then cleaned his filthy hands as best he could. On the way back, he detoured to the tools room, searching for some pliers. He was going to need something tough to grip the piece of shrapnel. He found a pair and pocketed them.

Back in the kitchen, Luke used antiseptic wipes on his hands and began to lay out everything he might need: gloves, sutures, needle holders, more antiseptic wipes, morphine, syringes, a vial of amoxicillin trihydrate, dressing, bandages. He was missing forceps and scissors but he would manage without them.

'You're not allergic to penicillin, are you?'

'No.'

She reached out and held his arm. 'I want to clear the air,' she said. 'You know, in case … I'm sorry about what I said. About your son. I just wanted you to know that.'

He smiled. 'Thank you.' She still clung to his freezer suit. The warmth of her hand on his arm permeated the suit, and he took it in his own. 'You're going to be fine, Maddie. I promise.'

He saw her fear and pulled from his pocket his most precious and private possession: the photo of him holding his newborn son. Luke felt awkward but handed it to her.

'Is that your boy?'

Luke nodded.

'He's gorgeous. Got your eyes – that same enquiring look in them.' She glanced up. 'You seem so happy.'

'Jase is the best thing that ever happened to me. And he's the reason I bang on about Antarctica's melting ice. I'm terrified about the kind of world he's going to grow up in.'

She handed back the photo. 'Thank you for showing me.'

'You got any kids?' asked Luke. He realised he knew next to nothing about her.

Maddie chewed her lower lip. 'Once.' She looked away and released her grip on his arm. Luke let her hand go, realising he had gone too far. When Maddie spoke, it was so quiet that he almost missed it. 'Becky. Becky was her name. She died.'

'I'm so sorry. I didn't know. I wouldn't have asked …'

'That's okay. It's a bit like you with Jason – I never talk about her.' Maddie wouldn't look at him. 'So I guess you were right. I am running away.'

Luke took her hand again. 'No need to say any more. I have a knack for saying the wrong thing.'

'No, Luke. I need to say this.'

He waited.

She swallowed. 'I couldn't bear the pity. And the constant reminders – her clothes, her toys, the photos. It made the pain worse. I had to get away.' Maddie fell silent.

Luke rubbed his chin, unsure what to say. 'When did she die?' he asked.

'Six years ago. Cot death. She was seven weeks old. I was only away from her for a few minutes but when I went to her room I knew. She was too still …' Her voice trailed away.

'I can't begin to imagine how terrible that would be,' said Luke. He felt woefully inadequate.

'Adam changed after that. My husband. Maybe it was the grief, I don't know. But he avoided me, never seemed to want to come home. And then one day he didn't. He said he couldn't cope. Needed to forget. The strange thing was that I understood.' Her eyes were watery and again she bit her lower lip. 'We were living in Hong Kong at the time because of his job. I moved back to Australia and then got a job here.' She smiled wearily. 'Antarctica is about as far away as I could get.'

Luke instinctively pulled her into his chest and wrapped his arms around her. 'I'm so sorry.' He held her in silence for a while. 'You know it's not your fault, don't you?'

'I wasn't there to save her, Luke.' She sobbed quietly, her face buried into his clothing.

'Is that what you meant about people you care for dying?'

She nodded.

'Maddie. You couldn't have saved Becky, just as you couldn't have saved Tubs.' She wiped her eyes. 'Now I understand why you asked about Jason, but it's complicated,' he said.

She pulled away. 'Life is.'

Maddie's revelation had stunned Luke, but now, unburdened of her secret, she appeared calmer. 'I'm ready,' she said.

Luke carried a pot of hot water to the table.

'Have you got thicker dressings, in case I start haemorrhaging?'

'You won't, but I'll look for a towel. Just a minute.' He returned with a threadbare tea towel. He pulled on the surgical gloves, his large hands barely squeezing inside.

Maddie stared at the implements laid out on the table. 'Oh God, I can't go through with this.' She covered her face as if trying to block out reality.

'Yes, you can. I'll give you morphine.'

Her hands fell to her side. 'Okay, but not too much. I want to know what you're doing.'

'First I'll cut your freezer suit back and clean around the wound.'

She winced at his touch. With that done, Luke picked up the vial of morphine, showing it to her. 'I need your shoulder, Maddie.'

She unzipped her freezer suit, and Luke helped her pull it down to waist level. He then removed her fleece. She pulled her thermal top down from the neck so the tip of her shoulder was showing. Luke wiped the fleshy bit of her shoulder with a swab. He then sucked the morphine into a syringe and expressed a small amount, checking for air bubbles.

'I'm impressed,' she commented, and smiled weakly. 'You doing something by the book – I never thought I'd see the day.'

'Yeah, well, some things are worth paying attention to. Ready?'

She hesitated for a second. 'I … well.'

'Trust me,' Luke said, holding the syringe up. He would wait for as long as it took her to say yes.

'You?' she laughed nervously.

'Yes, me. I know what I'm doing.'

'Go ahead.'

He pushed the needle through her skin, into what he hoped was her muscle, and then released the fluid. Maddie pulled her thermal top back over her shoulder.

'How long before it starts working?' she asked.

'Not sure,' he replied.

'Trust me, he says!'

They had to wait until the drug kicked in before doing anything more.

'So, why have you never gone for station leader?' Maddie asked. She wanted to talk. Keep her mind off the operation. 'This is your seventh posting, right?'

'Not everyone wants to be boss,' he replied. 'I'm happy doing what I do best – research. I don't want to have to deal with everybody's problems. I can't even sort out my own.'

Maddie appeared to contemplate his response. 'You really don't like people much, do you?'

'Sure, I like people, but in small doses. But you're good at all that relationship-management stuff. I've seen you.'

'Not really. I find it hard to let go. Some might say I can be a bit bossy.' She turned her head slightly, as if she had asked a question, but she was grinning like the Cheshire cat.

Luke laughed. 'Yes, I think bossy is about the right word for it, but I guess I gave you cause, huh?'

Her eyelids began to close.

'How are you feeling?' he asked.

151

'Sleepy. Good.'

He gently touched the skin near the wound with the scissors.

'I can feel that, but it's okay,' she said. Without the morphine she would have flinched. It was time.

'Maddie. You can tell me to stop at any time.'

'I'll tell you.'

He took the pliers from his pocket and clamped them over the protruding part of the metal.

'Holy shit! Pliers?' she asked, her words slurred.

Before she could protest further, Luke jerked the metal from her leg and dropped it on the floor. Maddie screamed. The last time he'd heard a woman scream like that was at Jason's birth. Maybe he hadn't given her enough morphine.

The wound began to bleed more than he had expected. *Muscle shouldn't bleed that much*, he thought. He threw the surgical dressing over it and then pressed the towel down on top, pushing firmly.

Maddie craned her neck up, horrified at the blood seeping through the towel.

'Maddie, stay still,' he barked. She stopped struggling.

Luke kept up the pressure. 'How's the pain?'

'It's more like a dull ache now.'

He was relieved to see that the stain in the towel had stopped spreading. He kept up the pressure until he was satisfied it was safe to take a look.

'Has it stopped?' she asked.

'Mostly. It's not an artery, anyway.' He glanced at her and smiled.

Luke picked up the needle holders with his right hand, and then used them to pick up the suture, careful to hold the U-shaped, bevelled needle in the middle of the U. He recalled how tough the skin had been when he sewed up the pig's leg. Then he noticed a tiny string of yellow fabric inside the wound.

'There's some of your freezer suit in there,' he said. 'I can't leave it – it'll cause an infection.'

He didn't have any tweezers or forceps, and realised he'd have to use the needle holders. He released the suture from the needle holders' grip. 'This may hurt a little,' he warned.

Luckily, Luke managed to clutch the end of the tiny piece of fabric and remove it quickly.

'That felt weird,' said Maddie, very drowsy now.

'I'm starting the stitches,' he said.

He picked up the suture again, pointed the needle tip straight down and pushed it into the skin on one side of the wound. He expected her to yell out but she said nothing. The morphine was finally working well. Luke remembered to curve his wrist so the U-shaped needle appeared on the other side of that piece of skin. He repeated the action, pushing the needle through the opposite piece of skin, then drew the thread through to close that section of the wound, then tied several knots, finally cutting the ends. That was the first stitch done. For a few seconds he admired his handiwork, and continued. He made five more stitches, careful to ensure they weren't too tight. Finally, he bandaged the leg and stepped back.

'All done,' he said.

Maddie was asleep. Her head had fallen slightly to one side and her hair tumbled over the edge of the table. The copper strands reminded him of the forests outside Lyons in the autumn, when the leaves turned to gold.

Luke gave her a shot of antibiotics and let her rest. He'd keep watch for the killers.

T MINUS 3 DAYS, 1 HOUR, 15 MINUTES
8 March, 4:45 am (AEDT)

After a much needed catnap, Wendy's metaphorical toast popped up. She had been trying to work out where she had seen the figures 74 52 100 30 before. The sequencing seemed familiar. Now she knew. They were coordinates. But were they north, south, east or west? Bleary-eyed, she found some instant coffee and made herself a strong cup. It was bitter but helped her focus. Then she tapped 74° 52' N, 100° 30' E into Google Maps.

That threw up Lake Taymyr in the Russian Arctic. Hmm. Wendy knew Chinese money sometimes funded Russian mining projects, but she doubted the Russian government would allow Dragon Resources to set up its own businesses there.

Wendy tried west. This took her to the sea off Bathurst Island in the Canadian Arctic. It was possible, but wouldn't the Inuit people notice an oil rig? She went to Dragon Resources' website and checked the locations of their oil and gas rigs around the world. Not one of their drilling sites, pipelines or terminals was located at either of these coordinates.

Then she remembered Antarctica in her father's browser history: an isolated and inaccessible continent, making it much easier to keep a project under wraps there. She tried 74° 52' S, 100° 30' E, but that was about as close to the middle of nowhere it was possible to get, while 74° 52' S, 100° 30' W was on the opposite coast, near the Pine Island Glacier.

Maybe the third word was the key. She tried googling 'Antarctica and shepherd' but all the hits were about whaling and the ship *Sea Shepherd*. Was she chasing phantoms? She'd never heard of any company mining or drilling in the Antarctic. How the hell would you drill through all that ice? Anyway, wasn't China part of the Antarctic Treaty? She was stumped.

Wendy double-checked the coordinates. She had been correct. They were either pointing to a location near what was known as Antarctica's 'Dome C' – one of the most hostile, inaccessible places on the planet – or at the Pine Island Glacier, which, being on the coast, was a little more accessible but still remote, even by Antarctic standards.

She googled the Antarctic stations. There was none anywhere near Dome C. In contrast, when she tried 100° 30' W, there was an Australian station virtually on top of the coordinates her father had written down. A Chinese station called Li Bai was a few hundred kilometres away. It was the only thing that looked like a connection.

The Australian station – called Hope – was researching the accelerating flow and rapid disintegration of the glacier, which, according to one glaciologist – a Luke Searle – was near collapse. She discovered that the Pine Island Glacier drained roughly ten per cent of the West Antarctic Ice Sheet. That didn't sound much, until she learned it was equivalent to half the land area of Germany.

'Okay, that's a lot of water,' she said quietly to herself.

Wendy gawped when she learned that the West Antarctic Ice Sheet alone was more than two-thirds the size of Australia. Gradually, her fascination turned to apprehension. Her exhausted mind was putting two and two together, and she didn't like the answer.

'Oh, my God, Dad! What did you …?' She stopped mid-sentence and stared wildly around the tiny office. She hadn't experienced this kind of panic since they had fled China. She was reminded of her mother's hushed tones when she'd discussed Falun Gong with fellow practitioners. But one of the practitioners was an informer and carried a bugging device. Wendy fell silent, wondering if her dad's office could be bugged too.

She threw open his hard-backed appointments diary and searched for Xu's name. The diary showed that May, the chief seamstress, had already called all the clients due to pick up suits that week, including Xu, to tell them the bad news. But the note in the diary was interesting: 'Gone to China. Invoice sent.'

Wendy stood and checked the rack of unclaimed suits to make sure she wasn't going mad. Yes, Xu's suit was still there. It was five-thirty in the morning but Wendy couldn't wait. May had worked for her father for many years and Wendy had her home number. She dialled it. It rang and rang.

'Come on, answer the phone.'

A hesitant voice said, 'Hello?'

'May, it's Wendy. I'm so sorry to call you this early but I have to ask you something urgent.'

'Oh, Wendy. I am so sorry. Mr Woo was a wonderful man.'

'Yes, thank you, he was. But tell me about one of his customers, Xu Biao, the Consul General. Has he gone back to China?'

'Oh, yes.' A pause. 'I called the consulate yesterday afternoon. They said he'd left Sydney and no longer needed the suit and to send them the invoice. I offered to courier it to China and they said no. No forwarding address. What a waste of a beautiful suit!'

Wendy's hands shook. 'Do you know when Xu left Sydney and why?'

'Only that he left the day poor Mr Woo was found.'

Wendy thanked May and ended the call. Her mouth was dry and her palms clammy. She suddenly felt very scared and raced to check both the front and back doors were locked.

The timing of Xu's hasty departure was unnerving. Had he told her father that Dragon Resources was in Antarctica? Is that why he'd been rushed back to China so fast and with no forwarding address?

Luke's view of the Hudson Mountains through the antique binoculars was a little streaky. Every time he checked for their pursuers and failed to see them, he relaxed a little more. Apart from the odd clang from the warm stove and the occasional creak of the roof, all was quiet.

Luke gazed around the wooden hut. He imagined Sir Douglas Mawson's men in their hut, woken each morning by the night watchman bellowing, 'Rise and shine! Porridge on the table getting cold!' Mawson had written in his journal of the jovial banter of his fellow expeditioners. Luke and Maddie might not be quite as comfortable with each other – yet. But at Bettingtons they could survive the winter and, most important of all, they had companionship. Luke now saw Maddie in a whole new light. He understood why, having lost a child and then her husband, she was distrustful of people in general, and of him in particular.

He looked at her peaceful face. Her mouth was slightly open, her regular breathing only just audible. Brave and feisty as she was, he saw a childlike vulnerability and felt surprisingly protective of her. She stirred and opened her eyes.

'Hungry?' Luke asked.

'I could eat a horse,' Maddie yawned.

'That's more like it.' Luke searched the bag. 'How about a treat?' he said, triumphantly holding up two frozen steaks.

'Now you're talking.'

'I might as well do some veggies too. Keep us regular.'

Despite feeling groggy, Maddie gazed at Luke in bewilderment. 'You're a funny one,' she said. 'Here we are, in the middle of nowhere, with killers after us, and you're thinking about keeping regular.'

'Someone's got to keep us healthy.'

Maddie wriggled up to a sitting position and stared at her bandaged leg. 'Well, at least I still have a leg,' she grinned. 'Thank you.'

'I checked it while you were sleeping. The bleeding's stopped but you're going to need to keep it still for a few days.'

The steaks sizzled in the pan on top of the stove, and the smell lifted their spirits. For a brief moment they could pretend their lives were normal.

'I had the weirdest dream. Probably the drugs. It was as if all the ice in Antarctica had gone. It was just a barren rocky landscape, and I was the only one in it. Horrible.'

'Just give it time,' Luke said. 'If we carry on pumping out carbon, Antarctica's ice will melt away, just like the Arctic.'

She looked up at him, startled by his comment.

'Okay, I exaggerate,' he said. 'It's already too late to stop the planet's warming. It's all about how much and how quickly. Slowing it is going to mean fundamental changes in the way we live, which the world isn't ready for.'

'So you think we're too late?'

Luke turned the steaks.

'No, not quite. We seem to have an uncanny knack of digging ourselves out of big holes. But atmospheric CO_2 is already over four hundred parts per million, and it's a big ask to get it back down below three hundred and fifty. Ice cover in the Arctic summer is almost gone, and Antarctica is already melting faster than we thought possible.' He paused and glanced at her. 'You've heard this all before, I know.'

'Not really. We used to avoid each other, remember? I

only ever got the tail end of your conversations.'

'Okay. We're in a feedback loop. Less ice reflects the sun, which accelerates warming. So we get longer, harsher droughts, increased desertification and food shortages. Water scarcity is already a problem at home, and it's huge in places like China, Africa and the United States. Jordan, Palestine and Israel are at war over the Jordan River. Large swathes of Europe, from Portugal to Ukraine, are at risk of becoming semi-desert. But people only react when there's a crisis and it's just around the corner.'

'Fear can be crippling,' said Maddie. 'People don't want to face it.'

'I understand that, but I worry about this place.' He nodded at the window. 'On top of everything else, with the race to drill the Arctic, now people are talking about exploration here. Once somebody finds a way to mine this place, everyone will want to get their snout in the trough.'

Maddie watched him, eyebrows raised. This was the longest speech she'd ever heard him make.

'Sorry, I get carried away sometimes.' Luke turned away, slightly embarrassed. He strained the vegetables, careful to keep the precious warm water. With his sleeve he wiped away the dust from two tin plates and started serving.

'You know, you should run for office,' Maddie said.

'Nah, politicians are gasbags.'

'Not all of them. Some see how important this is.'

'Some. Most don't want to risk their careers on such an unpopular subject,' he replied. 'And powerful people – those who don't want climate change taken seriously – pump millions into creating doubt and confusion. Just like the cigarette companies did. If you create enough doubt, people won't change their behaviour.'

'But speaking out is important.'

'Yeah, but I'm crap with words. I'm a backroom guy.'

'You're selling yourself short,' Maddie said.

'Nah. I'm happy to talk about glacier mass balance calculations or flow velocities, but I'm not so good at persuading people. I provide the evidence, like my paper.' He looked at her quizzically. 'You thought I was exaggerating, didn't you? That comparing the

PIG to Larsen B was over the top?'

He saw Maddie blush. 'Yeah, well,' she replied, 'for someone who'd barely speak to me, you had plenty to say to everyone else about it. I guess I felt left out. Petty, I know.'

He handed her a plate.

'This smells amazing,' Maddie said.

'You should try my *coq au vin* and *saucisson de Lyons*. I learned to cook from my French dad.'

'But your surname sounds English.'

'My dad's name is Philippe Seul, spelled S–E–U–L. It means—'

'Alone. Yes, I know. How fitting,' she said, rolling her eyes.

Luke ignored the teasing and tucked into the hot food. 'He's a chef in Lyons, the French capital of gastronomy – or so he used to keep telling me.'

'How did your parents meet, then?' Maddie asked.

'You really want to know?'

'I do.'

'Mum was backpacking through Europe. She ended up waitressing at his restaurant, and one thing led to another. Mum wanted me born in Australia so she went back to Melbourne and, to her surprise Dad followed. But it was a disaster. Anyway, when I was seven Dad left for France and took me with him.' Luke cut a piece of the steak and held it up, admiring its brown exterior and light-pink interior. 'Dad had caught Mum in the kitchen fucking his Melbourne business partner. Some pans went flying that night, I can tell you!'

'I'm sorry, Luke. That sounds terrible.'

'It happens.' He shrugged, concentrating on his meal, not wanting her to see his hurt.

'So why is your name not spelled the French way?' Maddie asked.

'That happened when I was enrolled at boarding school back in Australia. Dad sent me back when I was eleven and the school registered me as Searle. Mum didn't give a shit and I didn't want to sound French, so that's how it stayed. I made it official at eighteen.'

'So what happened in France?'

'Oh, Dad was really busy with the restaurant, my French was crap, I was lonely and I hated it. He put me on a plane and told

Mum that he'd pay for the school but that he didn't want to have anything more to do with me. I don't blame him. I was a little shit.'

'Geez, Luke, I do. You can't just dump your son because it's inconvenient.'

Maddie baulked when she realised the implication of her words.

The meat stuck in Luke's throat. He swallowed. 'You think I want to be away from Jason?'

'I don't know what to think because you won't tell me anything about him.'

Luke stared at the fogged-up window while Maddie finished her meal. She sighed. 'Don't worry about it, Luke. Another time. Just eat.'

Finally, he spoke. 'I'm ashamed.'

He looked down at his cooling meal, then put the plate on the floor.

'Of what?' she asked.

'I've failed him.' Maddie waited. 'I'd only known Jessica a few months when she fell pregnant. She lied … Argh, it doesn't matter.'

'Please, go on.'

'I found out later that she'd lied about taking the pill. I overheard her boasting to a friend about "snaring" me. Anyway, I cancelled my Antarctic trip and stayed in Melbourne so I could be there for the birth. I didn't move in, though; our relationship was really just the sex. We had nothing in common. I promised to support her and be a father to Jase, but I couldn't marry her.'

He paused. 'Despite everything, Jase was the best thing that had ever happened to me. But when Jessica finally grasped that I loved Jase and not her, she started finding ways to stop me seeing him. It was her way of punishing me. Two years later, I realised there was no point in being in Melbourne if I couldn't see my boy, so I moved to Tasmania to work at AARO's headquarters.' He looked at her. 'I'm a crap father.'

'Did you fight for access? Get a lawyer?'

'It was meant to be every other weekend, but Jessica would cancel at the last minute or say he was sick or some other excuse. I should have gone back to court but I'm not good at confrontation. Jessica knows that.' He paused again, 'I was weak. I gave up. I decided that if I couldn't be with Jase, I might as well do something worthwhile and earn some decent money for his education. That's why I've over-wintered four times. And the prize money will go to Jase too.'

He sighed. 'But I feel bad every day I'm away from him. Daily calls on Skype just don't cut it.'

'I didn't know you spoke every day,' Maddie said. 'Sounds like you're making the best of a difficult situation.' Lost in her own thoughts, she pulled her hair into a bun and then let it fall over her shoulders. 'Are you sure you can't make a go of it with Jessica?'

Luke stood and opened the stove door to add some more wood. He needed to do something.

'No chance,' he said. 'Think me a bastard, if you like, but I couldn't do to Jason what my parents did to me, arguing all the time. Hating each other. I didn't want to be the mirror image of *mon père*.' He spat out the last two words as if they were orange pips. 'Ironically, that's exactly what I've become.'

Luke turned to look at Maddie, his face wan. 'Anyway, she's marrying someone else.'

'How do you feel about that?'

'I'm pleased for her but I want to know who this bloke is. That he'll be good to my boy.'

'Yes, I'd want to know that. Have you spoken to Jason about it?'

'No, the comms blackout prevented me. I really can't get my head around Jase having a new dad.'

'You know, Luke, only you are his father,' Maddie said softly. 'But when we get out of here, maybe you should let Jason know you will always be his daddy. Find a way to spend more time with him.'

Neither spoke for several minutes.

'I'm sorry, Luke,' Maddie said, finally. 'I misjudged you. I thought you were neglecting him. You never talked about him or showed photos – you know, the normal stuff. I guess I was … well, jealous. You have what I can't have.'

'You can have another kid one day,' he said. 'How old are you? Early thirties?'

'Yeah, same as you. But no, I can't have any more children. There were complications at Becky's birth.'

They lapsed into silence again.

'So all that anger on the ship when we were coming to Antarctica and since, was about me as a father?'

She nodded. 'Mainly that. Oh, and the fact that you're a pain in the arse.'

They laughed together.

After lunch, Luke checked for any signs of activity outside. Satisfied, he did some more exploring. Inside a wall cabinet, he discovered coagulated medicines and, tucked behind the bottles, a solitary bar of soap. He raced the soap back to the kitchen.

'Would you believe it!' he said. He held out the soap, still intact after all those years. A faded mauve colour. He offered it to Maddie, who sniffed it tentatively at first and then beamed.

'It still smells of lavender. My God, we can wash! How incredibly civilised,' she said.

In a few minutes, he had two pans of snow warming on the stove. When the water was hot, he carried one pan to the table and placed it next to Maddie, then he took down one of the curtain rails and handed the curtain to her. She was still cradling the soap as if it were a baby bird.

Luke saw, perhaps for the first time, how stained with grime her face was. He had no doubt his was the same. Her tears had left streaks on her skin. 'I'll leave you to it, then.'

He decided to create a mental inventory of everything they could use at Bettingtons. His focus was on finding a power supply, as well as anything to cobble together to build a communication device. The tools room looked promising; he was amazed at how well stocked it was.

'Hey, Luke,' Maddie called. 'Your turn.'

Her face shone, her freckles like the decorative pattern on an ancient vase now revealed through polishing. She smelled of lavender, and he couldn't help closing his eyes and remembering his mother's garden.

'I never thought washing could feel so good,' Maddie said.

Luke took the second pan of hot water from the stove and set it down on the sideboard.

'Here – catch!' Maddie tossed the slippery soap at him and Luke fumbled. Maddie laughed.

With his back to her, he stripped down to his waist. As he washed his hands and arms, his chilled skin tingled. The sensation was so good that he sighed. He was aware of her watching him. Station life was never a private affair, but somehow her gaze now felt different.

'You've got a bad bruise on your back and shoulder,' she said.

'I'll live.'

'Nice back, by the way.'

Luke splashed his face, leaning over the pan. He wiped it dry with the curtain and glanced round at her. 'Pervert,' he joked.

She had her arms folded across her chest and wore a mischievous grin. 'I can't move, remember? So you're safe.' She threw her head back and laughed.

He smiled, enjoying her teasing, and pulled on his now dry thermal top.

'We're going to make it, aren't we?' she said. It was more of an affirmation than a question.

He perched on the table next to her. For the first time since the fire he felt genuinely optimistic. 'Yes, I think we are. There's so much stuff here. We can survive the winter if we have to.'

Maddie placed a hand on his, and he stared at it. 'Thanks, Luke. Thanks for everything.' She let go and immediately Luke wanted her hand back on his.

'My pleasure.'

She touched her nose and cheeks with the back of her hand.

165

'It feels like my skin is burning.' She looked flushed.

'It is getting warm in here. But it could be mild frost-nip.' He placed the back of his hand on her cheek. He nodded. 'It'll be fine. Nothing to worry about.'

He felt his body lean towards her, as if he wasn't controlling it. To his surprise she bent towards him, her eyes peering straight into his. They hovered for a moment, then he felt her pull back, closing in on herself like a flower shutting its petals at night.

'That wouldn't be a good idea.' She looked down.

Luke went to place his hand on her face again and she shied away.

'No, Luke.' She looked around the room, keen to avoid his concerned gaze. 'I need to rest.'

She wanted him gone. It was his turn to look away, as he didn't want her to see his disappointment. 'I'll go see if I can find a radio.'

At the very end of the corridor, Luke discovered a cupboard-sized room with a tiny desk and a chunky 1950s two-way radio, complete with headphones and a horn-shaped bakelite mouthpiece. The transmitter and receiver were encased in a black rectangular box with a grey face covered in dials. He cautiously pulled off the back cover and checked the six glass valves. They weren't smashed, but the chances that they were all working were very slim. He gave the rest of the radio's interior a cursory once-over; it looked in surprisingly decent condition. But a radio was no good without power.

He went searching for the station's generator. He expected it to be separated from the main living quarters, due to the noise and stench of diesel it would create, but he found it in the tools room next to the dormitory. He ran his hands over the generator's rusty exterior and then opened it up. His optimism waned. The pistons looked seized up and rusty, and he had no doubt the diesel inside would be a useless wax-like sludge.

He went back to the kitchen to collect the camping stove. Maddie's eyes were closed. He touched her shoulder to wake her but she didn't stir.

'Mads, wake up. I've found an old radio and a generator. I need you to keep an eye out while I try to get them working. Mads?'

'Sure,' Maddie replied drowsily, then she frowned as his words sunk in. 'Really? Are they repairable?'

'It's a long shot. If I can get them working, I might be able to send an SOS.'

'You know Morse code?' She rubbed her eyes.

'My boarding school caretaker was a ham radio fanatic. Lovely old guy. He taught me Morse code too.'

'And how to rebuild radios?'

'Yes. Murray was his name. I was such a misfit and he took pity on me. I was twelve. I'd sit on an upside down bucket and watch and listen in silence. Sometimes I'd help rebuild a radio, the old man indicating which part went where with a point of his finger. I remember the bucket clearly. It was blue.'

She crossed her arms and grinned. 'You certainly are a man of many hidden talents.' Luke watched as her expression became more serious. 'Do people still use Morse code?'

'Oh, yes. You'd be surprised. Especially radio operators on ships. They don't have to listen into the distress frequency anymore, but most do – out of sheer boredom, if nothing else.'

'Luke?'

'Yes?'

'Stick with calling me Mads. I like it.'

'Okay, I will.' Luke hesitated. 'There's something I've been meaning to ask you. Do you think Tubs betrayed us?'

'I've been wondering that too. I guess he knew he was dying.' The words seemed to catch in her throat. 'So, yeah, I do. Much as it saddens me.'

'I don't want to believe it. He was a good friend.' Luke perched on the edge of the table and tapped his finger on his lower lip. 'This must have been planned for ages. It takes serious money and power to get soldiers down here. It's the sort of thing only governments can do.' He left the thought hanging and gave a loud sigh. 'This is going to end badly. For all of us.'

'Can you send a warning along with the SOS?' Maddie asked.

'If I have enough power, but I'll have to focus on our location.'

'It might not be mining. What if they're here to test weapons? We don't know. But they have to be stopped. Promise me you'll try to raise the alarm.'

'Of course, if I can.'

Back in the tools room he shook the generator and heard a slurp as the diesel sludge moved. It was almost empty but there might be enough to run for a couple of minutes. He turned the camping stove on and held the flame underneath the sump to loosen the gloopy diesel. He hoped he wasn't wasting their precious shellite on a dud generator. He toyed with the idea of using some of the paraffin dumped outside. It would probably destroy the bearings, but it might power up the generator for long enough to send an SOS.

Luke turned off the camping stove and stepped outside to fetch an old can of paraffin. Back inside the hut, he used his hands to scoop it out of the can, funnelling it into the generator's tank. He wiped the residue on the rusted pistons, hoping it might help to loosen them.

This was going to be his one chance to send an SOS, so he had to have everything ready. He collected the radio from the cupboard room then scanned the desk and shelves for a Morse key. No luck, he'd have to tap two wires together instead.

Luke carried the radio to the tools room and placed it carefully on the workbench next to the generator. He connected the two. Now he had to get the generator's flywheel moving. It looked a bit like an old-fashioned sewing machine wheel, except it had a concave outer rim that took a thin rope snugly. The wheel wasn't budging. Luke found a small block of wood, positioned it on the top of the wheel and gave it a gentle tap with a hammer. He tried another tap. The wheel moved a fraction, then a bit further.

Luke breathed a sigh of relief. He took the rope and wrapped it around the wheel, then yanked it down sharply. But the generator didn't roar into life as he had hoped it would. He tried again, and again. He wouldn't give up – he *had* to send a call for help.

At last there was a splutter, then the generator sprang to life, complaining loudly. Luke whooped with excitement and swiftly checked the radio. Five of the six valves glowed orange: one was clearly broken. Desperate not to waste fuel, Luke switched off the generator.

Where would they have kept their spare valves? He charged back to the radio room and pawed through the desk. Nothing. Then he saw an old tea caddy on the shelf above. He opened it and found nails and string and pencils – and yes, right at the bottom, a valve, still in its cardboard box. Luke took the tin, as well as some rolled-up maps he saw on the shelf. He had to know his exact location.

He still needed an antenna. He ran outside and looked around, but he couldn't see any evidence of one; it must have collapsed years ago. He'd have to improvise.

He began inspecting the debris scattered around the hut, and at last found a roll of fencing wire. The roof was wooden and wouldn't short out the antenna. He uncoiled the wire and wound one end around some heavy pipe, which he then threw over the roof. The pipe landed on the other side of the gable's peak. He looped the other end of the fencing wire around a heavy rock on the ground, hoping the wind wouldn't blow the wire off the roof.

Back inside the hut, Luke leaned over the radio, extracted the faulty valve and, with great care, replaced it with the spare. He willed it to work.

The map of the Walgreen Coast and Cranton Bay gave him their coordinates. The generator wouldn't last long once it was restarted, so Luke planned his SOS message with care. He racked his brains but couldn't remember if W was 'dah–dah–dit' or 'di–dah–dah'. This was critical since, according to the map, they were at 101° 24' west. *Think!* He tried to imagine himself back in Murray's ham radio shack, tuning and listening. After what seemed an age, it finally came to him: 'di–dah–dah'.

Luke turned the radio dial to 500 kilohertz, the old international maritime distress frequency. It used to be monitored twenty-four hours a day, but nowadays, Luke would be counting on the few who tuned in. Its beauty was that it could be picked up as far as twelve hundred nautical miles away.

He started the generator again and the bearings made a terrible noise. *Not good*, he thought. *Gotta be quick*.

Luke pulled from the back of the radio the two exposed wires that should have been attached to the Morse key, if he'd had one. He began tapping the wires together. He was slow and tentative at first, keen to make sure he allowed enough of a gap between each element of code.

'SOS. 74° 27' S, 101° 24' W. Need rescue.'

He repeated the message several times, then expanded it to include the words 'one wounded'. The old generator was quaking. Fuel was critically low.

He began to doubt himself; what if nobody was listening on 500 kilohertz? What about 2182 kilohertz – the voice distress frequency? He could still transmit an SOS through it. It would be a fluke if anyone noticed his dits and dahs through all the voice traffic, but he had to try. He re-tuned the radio frequency dial and tapped out his message quickly.

'SOS. 74° 27' S, 101° 24' W. One wounded. Luke Searle.'

His hand was shaking so much that he wasn't sure if he was getting the dits and dahs right. Luke added 'murder' to the sequence, and managed to tap it out three more times before the generator shuddered and then stopped.

Then he heard Maddie, her voice frantic. 'Luke, they're coming. Luke!'

Wendy was stressed, and when she was stressed she ate chocolate. She bought two large bars from an all-night corner store – one milk chocolate, the other fruit and nut – and returned to the shop. She plonked herself in the desk chair and started to eat as she tried to calm herself.

She was halfway through the first bar when the realisation hit her with the force of a head-on collision: if her father knew about something the Chinese were up to in Antarctica, he was a security risk. And as an Australian citizen, Jack couldn't be spirited back to China as Xu had been. They would have had to find another way to keep him quiet.

She leaped up and began pacing the room, trying to order her thoughts. Was she imagining it all or was it possible that her dad had been murdered? She dialled Anthony Chan, but when she heard his voice she hung up. If she was right, she shouldn't involve anyone else. She might be endangering Chan.

If I was Xu, why would I pass on information about Dragon Resources? she asked herself.

'Money?' she said aloud. If Xu had confidential information about the company, it would be dangerous for him to buy its shares.

But if her father bought them in his name and they shared the profit, Xu could benefit from his knowledge without leaving a trail of evidence. But someone discovered what Xu and her dad were up to, and decided to stop them.

Wendy tried to calm herself. Once again she looked over to the rack of suits ready for collection; each suit was in its own black plastic cover, and a piece of paper with the client's name was taped to each coat hanger. She carefully unzipped the cover of Xu's suit and peeled it back. She couldn't help but admire the impeccable stitching around the buttonholes, the pockets and along the collar. She ran her fingertips over the tiny ridges of the collar's stitching, and to her surprise she felt a lump. At first she guessed it was a knot in the thread – but her father would never let such a fault pass his meticulous inspection.

She rubbed the lump, which was as big as an orange pip. 'No way,' she said aloud.

She rummaged through a seamstress's sewing box and found a cotton-cutter, to pick apart the tiny stitches. She pulled apart the collar, revealing a small pouch. Inside it was a device a bit like a computer chip. Wendy placed it in the palm of her hand and stared at it, mystified.

She took some deep breaths, then placed the device carefully on the desk and tapped 'bugging device Sydney' into Google. Websites supplying spy equipment to the domestic and professional markets popped up. Wendy searched for pictures of voice transmitters. She couldn't believe how many there were, and how easily available. And there it was: 'If you think your partner is having an affair, or you want to eavesdrop on your competitors, this is the listening device for you.' Once you had programmed your mobile phone number into the unit, you could listen to the bug's surrounding sounds through your mobile phone. It allowed you to eavesdrop on a conversation but did not record it.

Wendy sat back in her chair, open-mouthed. The diplomat hadn't fed the information to her dad at all – he had been spying on Xu Biao!

Hearing a bang in the alley, she jumped up from her chair.

'Who's there?' she called. She peered out of the shop's back window but saw nobody. *It must be all that sugar*, she thought.

She sat down and turned back to the website. She was partly in awe of her dad, partly furious and partly terrified. He must've used a similar bug in a previous suit and overheard conversations about Dragon Resources in Antarctica. It was obvious he'd heard enough to think that he couldn't lose if he bought shares in the company. Someone must have found the device. A heart attack? What could be more innocuous?

Wendy had to get out of there. She popped the listening device in an envelope, sealed it, and then taped the edges, placing it in the inside pocket of her leather jacket.

T MINUS 2 DAYS, 22 HOURS, 20 MINUTES
7 March, 1:40 pm (UTC-07)

Luke charged down the corridor, dodging the hole in the floor-boards, and peered through the streaky kitchen window.

'There! Snowmobiles,' said Maddie, pointing.

There was no mistaking the rectangular red shapes moving down the snowy slopes. They were using Hope Station vehicles. The snowmobiles merged and separated and then merged again, crisscrossing as if in a dance. But this was no joyful moment.

'I must've fallen asleep,' she said, her face flushed with panic. 'We have to get out of here.'

Luke was momentarily paralysed. He was an ordinary guy, living a quiet life. Until now. Suddenly, everyone around him was dead or wounded and he was being hunted by killers. He was forced to make life-or-death decisions. He made himself look out of the window again but still his mind didn't function. They were getting closer. He had to pull himself together. He had to act. No – he had to think first.

'Luke, we have to go!' screamed Maddie as she struggled off the mattress and swung her bandaged leg down to the floor.

'Wait!' He raised his hands to stop her going any further. 'They're probably twenty minutes away, so let's think this through.'

He breathed deeply. 'Okay,' he said, trying to focus. 'If we leave Bettingtons, we lose our only shelter. Without shelter we won't last. Can we defend the hut?'

'With what?'

He raced to the tools room, but a rusty saw and an axe were no match for men with guns. He spun around, scanning the equipment on the floor, then the shelves. A rifle on the wall. He picked it up. A Lee-Enfield bolt-action – the pride of the British army.

'I've found a gun,' he hollered.

'I'm getting my gear on,' Maddie shouted back. 'We're getting out of here.'

He had no idea if the rifle would fire, but without cartridges it was even less use than the axe. Where would cartridges be? Of course – with the station leader.

Luke charged into the station leader's room and turned it upside down. 'He must have taken them with him. Shit!' he yelled. He ran back to the kitchen.

'The smoke – they'll see the smoke,' said Maddie.

'Too late, they've already seen it.' Luke raced to the shelf and snatched their gloves and hats, which had been drying near the stove. 'We can't defend this place and we can't run. You can't run. So we have to hide.'

'No. I can run. I *have* to run.' She began hopping towards the door.

'Listen, Mads, please.' Luke held her arms. 'They have snowmobiles. And we're cornered. Beyond Bettingtons is the sea. The only place for us to go is onto the sea ice, and that's like playing Russian roulette. You don't have enough strength to balance. We must hide.'

'This bloody wound!' She took a deep breath. 'You're right, I can't make it on sea ice. But you don't have to stay here. You know the ice. You can hide out at sea. You should go.'

'I'm not leaving you.'

Maddie yanked her arms away from his hands. 'I'm still station leader, and for once in your life, Luke Searle, you'll do as I say!' She jabbed her finger into his chest. 'You are leaving. One of us must survive. Someone has to tell the world what's gone on here.' Luke opened his mouth to object but she cut in. 'I order you to run.'

Luke peered over her shoulder and through the window. The snowmobiles were close. 'I'm not going anywhere until we've found somewhere safe for you,' he said. 'And when they're gone, I'll come back for you. I know where you can hide. Now, wrap yourself tightly in your blanket.' The rock-coloured blanket would hide Maddie's dazzling yellow freezer suit.

'No way,' she said.

'Just do it,' his tone sharp.

She pulled the blanket around her. He stripped off his freezer suit, yanked on his now dry thermal leggings, pulled the spare parka and trousers from the bag, put them on, and threw the heavy old trench coat over the top. The parka and trousers were too small – they'd belonged to Blue – but they would have to do. Luke shoved a beanie on his head and stuffed his gloves in his pocket. He glanced through the window again. He could now make out three snowmobiles, which meant anything from three to six men.

Maddie leaned against the table, her blanket pulled around like a chrysalis, her hat low on her head. She looked like a sick child on a camping trip.

Luke reached his arms around her body, blanket and all, so he could lift her.

'What are you doing? Where am I hiding?' She struggled, trying to push him away.

'Stop fighting me, for God's sake.' Luke heaved her up, then staggered down the narrow corridor. 'Hold your leg in.'

After a sharp kick from Luke, the front door flew open and he stepped down onto the ice. He knew the killers couldn't see them because the front of the hut faced out to sea. The rear of the hut faced the mountains.

'Get under the hut with all the junk. There's no way they'll see you,' said Luke, kneeling down and placing her gently on the powdery ice.

'What if they burn it down?'

'They won't. One fire is an accident, two is too much of

177

a coincidence. Anyway, they'll be so focused on me that they won't be interested in the hut.'

'God, Luke – what are you planning?'

He didn't answer. Instead, he crawled into the narrow, ice-free gap under the hut. He used his elbows to propel himself forward. Apart from the columns of bricks that raised the hut's floor above the ground, the area was littered with debris: rusty pipes, wooden poles, old wooden crates, a rusted axe, a shovel, some wire. He cleared a place under the centre of the hut, arranging plenty of flat wood for her to lie on. He rotated himself around to face Maddie.

'Let's have you,' he said. 'Can you get under here?'

Maddie used her elbows to crawl forward. The boot of her injured leg snagged on a rock and she winced with pain. She managed to get most of her body underneath the hut when her blanket caught on a rock.

'Come on,' encouraged Luke. She was taking too long. He reached out and pulled her towards him in several jerky movements. Maddie stifled cries at the pain in her leg. When at last she was positioned beneath the centre of the hut, Luke wrapped her tightly in the blanket, both for warmth and to hide her bright freezer suit.

'God, Luke, I'm terrified,' Maddie whispered.

'Me too, but you'll be safe here. Just stay very quiet. Don't let them spook you.'

She nodded. 'Promise you'll come back. No heroics, okay?'

Luke remembered Maddie using those very words shortly before he left to search for Mac and Dave. It seemed so very long ago. He couldn't make the promise she wanted, but he could make a different one.

'I won't let you down,' he said. 'Now, keep very still. I'm going to hide you.'

As he started piling crates around her, she reached out and clung to his arm, and then touched his face. It was a single stroke down his cheek. He looked back at her and smiled.

'Go now,' she whispered.

Luke hesitated for a fraction of a second. He arranged a few more rusty canisters and wooden crates around her, until he was satisfied that she appeared to be nothing more than a pile of rubbish.

'I can't see anything of you,' he said. 'Just wait for me.'

'What choice do I have?' she joked, but he could hear the fear in her shaky voice.

Luke crawled away from her until he was free of the hut. He kneeled for a few moments to recover his breath.

'Luke?' Maddie called softly.

'Yes?'

A pause. 'Thanks.'

'Mads?'

'Yes?'

'I …' It was now or never. He wanted to say how he felt. *Spit the bloody words out, man*, he thought. 'You'll be fine. I'll be back for you.'

He stood up, cursing himself, and peered around the corner of the hut. Six men, maybe ten minutes away.

Luke sped back inside the hut. Despite what he had told Maddie, he didn't have a plan; he was making it up as he went along. Somehow, he had to lure the killers away.

In the kitchen he spun around in a circle, searching for inspiration. *Think, damn it!* He smacked his forehead. *Come on!* His brain felt scrambled. He raced to the tools room and found the map, then checked the contours of the local coastline. It gave him an idea. It was an implausible idea. Only a fool would buy it, but it was his only idea.

First Luke shoved the medical kit into his backpack, clipped it up and slung it on his shoulders. It also contained the remaining food from Hope; there wasn't enough time to pack all their supplies. He grabbed his freezer suit and the ice axe, and ran to the dormitory. He stuffed two pillows into his freezer suit, zipping it up, then seized the solitary leather boot and sprinted down the corridor and into the tools room. He found a hammer, some long, thick nails and a large coil of rope, which he threw over his head and wore diagonally across his body. He leapt through the front door, landing in the powdery ice outside.

'I'll come back for you, Maddie,' he called.

He bent over, pulled the boot onto his right hand and his thick glove onto his left, then he pushed the boot into the powdery top layer of ice, followed by his glove in the shape of a fist. He wanted to create the impression of two sets of footprints: his and Maddie's, one of them limping. It was a ludicrous concept, but it just might work. His mind kept telling him to flee, but he painstakingly walked a step and then pressed the boot and his fist into the loose ice. He continued doing this down the slope, crouching low, until he reached a cliff above the seashore.

Six metres directly below him lay a narrow rocky beach. It had no other access except via the sea, which was littered with thick slabs of shifting pack ice. He searched the bay for the leopard seal he'd spotted earlier. If it wasn't nearby, his plan would not work. He couldn't find it. His heart beat so loudly that he almost didn't hear the distant shouting. The hunters were close, but the hut still hid Luke from their view.

Luke spied the seal further out in the bay. It was in the water – perfect. He pulled the boot and glove off his hands, then opened the backpack and took out the meat. He tore at the plastic packaging with his teeth. The frozen steaks had begun to thaw in the heat of the kitchen, and the cold blood dripped into his mouth. He spat it on his freezer suit and then smeared the meat over the suit's outer surface and pushed some of it inside. He tightened the hood's drawstring to keep the meat in place.

He tossed the freezer suit 'body' onto the beach below. He intended to use the sea ice slabs as stepping stones, and carry it far enough out to sea that his pursuers wouldn't realise it wasn't a real person. Finally, he threw the remaining meat into the water. The leopard seal would pick up the scent almost immediately.

Luke wound the rope around a waist-high boulder and knotted it. It was old and frayed but he hoped it wouldn't slip or snap. He tied the spare boot to his pack and then lay on his stomach at the cliff's edge, his head facing inland. He cautiously slid over the cliff feet-first. The rope creaked but held. His arms were taking almost all his weight, plus that of the pack, and they burned like hell. He moved one hand and then the other down the rope until it gave way so fast that Luke didn't have time to dig his ice axe into the cliff. He fell backwards and landed badly.

Unconscious on the ground at the base of the cliff, and with blood seeping from a wound in his head, Luke was oblivious to the leopard seal swimming towards him. As he had predicted, it had found the scent of the raw meat, which now lay only metres from his defenceless body.

If the smoking chimney and the recently cooked meal hadn't been enough to tell Robert that his quarry had only just left Bettingtons, the Westerners' pungent body smell gave them away. He grimaced. Of course, Westerners themselves wouldn't notice.

Before studying economics at Harvard, Robert had only spent time with Han Chinese. His father had warned him that non-Han Chinese smelled like rotting corpses. Even with a daily shower. The General had exaggerated, his disgust fuelled by his hatred for all things American. To this day, Robert never understood why he'd been allowed to study in the United States. He suspected it had much to do with his father's shame: if Robert wouldn't join the army, then he wanted his wimpy son as far away as possible.

Robert recalled his white American roommate, Chet, who would come back from his morning rowing practice stinking of sweat. But even when the guy was showered and in clean clothes, Robert could still detect a foul meaty smell. And these Australians hadn't washed for days. Despite the cosiness of the warm stove, Robert had to open the window for some fresh air.

His men scurried like bull ants around the hut. Alone in the kitchen, he discovered the bloodstained towel. One of them was wounded. Good, that would make capture easier. He ran his fingers along the spines of books until he came across one that caught his eye: *An Approach to Landscape Painting*, published in 1950. He frowned with concentration as he turned the slightly curled pages, pleased they had escaped mildew. It illustrated how to sketch a landscape against a grid, how to handle perspective, and the principles of composition. He smiled at the English country scene, complete with neat hedgerows, creamy stone walls and a Saxon church. He had visited the Cotswolds once, and had been struck by a feeling that while the rest of the world had modernised, rural England had refused to budge. He pocketed the book as a keepsake.

Robert heard a crash come from the dormitory, and charged in to find one of his men trashing the place. The mattresses were on the floor, as were the books, clothing and games. A rusty oil lamp had shattered. Robert grabbed the soldier's collar and yanked him backwards.

'Show some respect! These early explorers were heroes.'

Robert held the man by the collar with his right hand and slapped him across the cheek with his left. Captain Wei, also in the room, stared at Robert, clearly dismayed that Robert felt it was acceptable to dishonour the dead but not the rubbish they left behind. In Robert's mind, there was a big difference between Hope Station and Bettingtons. He admired the early Antarctic explorers' single-minded determination and bravery, battling the elements to achieve their goal. The inhabitants of Hope Station, however, were his enemy. Any threat to his project had to be eliminated.

'Find the Australians,' he ordered. 'But do not destroy this place.' He released the man's collar and then gestured around the room. 'This is a museum. Would you trash a museum?'

'No, sir.' The man looked down.

'Wei, have you checked every room?'

'Yes, sir.'

'Then go outside and search.'

The soldier almost ran away, his boots tapping down the wooden steps. Wei followed.

Robert wandered to the tools room and noticed some maps near a decrepit radio. They were rolled up and bound by a mulberry coloured ribbon – except one. Robert unrolled it. Dated 1951, the Walgreen coastline had been incorrectly drawn. He smirked at the naivety of the error and then considered how unique the map was. It would look good framed and mounted behind his office desk. He placed it in his backpack and turned to see Captain Wei in the doorway, his fur-lined hood and goggles obscuring most of his face. Did Robert see a sneer, or was it his imagination?

'Sir, we found footprints that lead to a cliff edge and a half-eaten corpse in Hope Station colours. A seal is still eating him.'

'A seal?'

'Yes, sir. A leopard seal. There is very little left of him.'

'Seals don't attack people.'

'Normally not, sir.' Wei hesitated, unsure if he should dare to contradict Robert. 'I believe leopard seals are an exception, sir. A female scientist was taken a while back. A British woman.'

Robert bristled and pulled his shoulders back. 'Show me.'

★ ★ ★

Luke was nowhere near the leopard seal.

As Robert's men had searched the hut, Luke had been roused from unconsciousness by the sound of the predator dragging its huge body up the beach. His backpack had softened his fall but his head throbbed. Battling dizziness, he had set his pack on the beach as near as possible to the cliff to prevent it getting washed away. He had then picked up the stuffed, bloodstained freezer suit and leaped onto sea ice.

His first step had been terrifying. If the surface had collapsed, he would have lasted just a couple of minutes in the freezing water before his muscles seized up and he drowned. The ice slab lurched but it bore his weight. The further out he went, the more likely the killers would believe his stuffed freezer suit was a mauled body, and the less likely they'd inspect it. He had left the 'body' fifteen metres out from the shore, on a flat piece of pack ice, then he had hidden himself in a U-shaped iceberg that resembled a skateboard half-pipe.

This was where Luke lay now. If the killers were determined enough to follow, he hoped his camel-coloured coat might make him look like a crabeater seal. It was a faint hope but he clung to it. He pulled his legs in tight and tucked his boots under the fabric. He was on his side with his head resting on his right arm, which was now numb. He tried to move it a little to readjust the pressure, but his sleeve was stuck to the ice.

Luke was worried about Maddie and listened intently for any sign of her discovery. He was also aware that his berg might suddenly flip over, not only tossing him into the sea but in the process foiling his ruse and signalling his presence. Luke couldn't keep his head still as his teeth chattered. In the dip where he lay there was a pool of seawater, left behind from the last time the berg rolled. Luke was at its edge, trying to keep his woollen coat from getting sodden. He heard a shout and then another voice replying. Had they found Maddie? Silence again. He waited.

A voice barked an order. It sounded much closer now. Luke braced himself. His pulse pounded away the seconds and minutes. Eventually, the voices started to move away. He exhaled loudly, wondering if his luck would hold out.

★ ★ ★

Robert wasn't convinced. 'I can only see one body.'

Wei responded, 'Sir, the woman's probably been eaten. We have searched everywhere. There's nowhere else she can hide.'

'Hmm,' said Robert, looking around him. He had to be certain. 'Wei, widen your search along the coastline, and you and you,' he said, pointing at two soldiers, 'come with me.'

As he strode back to the hut Robert checked his watch. He had to leave in thirty minutes so he could oversee the explosives test. His radio sparked into life.

'Bowers to Commander Scott, are you receiving?'

'Bowers' was Tang Juwu, his explosives expert. Li, the glaciologist, worked with him, but his knowledge of explosives was inferior to Tang's.

Robert lapsed into Cantonese which was Tang's first language. 'Loud and clear,' Robert replied. 'What is it, Bowers?'

'I've been asked to confirm that the test will proceed at seventeen hundred hours as planned, sir.'

'General Zhao?'

'Yes, sir.'

Robert sighed loudly. 'Yes, seventeen hundred hours. Ensure all equipment and men are well away from the blast site.'

'Will do, sir.'

He remembered Li Guangjie's concerns. 'Do you have a camera set up to monitor the impact on the Fitzgerald Fissure?'

'Yes, sir.'

'Good. Out.'

Robert folded his arms across his narrow chest and contemplated the wooden structure before him. Were there any secret nooks a woman could hide in? He kneeled down and examined the space under the hut.

'You!' he shouted at his soldiers. 'Move all that crap out here,' he ordered, pointing to the rubbish under the floorboards.

They did as they were bid. Robert stayed on his knees, fascinated by the volume of building materials the British had brought with them.

'Sir! We've found her,' called a soldier. 'I think she's dead.'

'Pull her out, man!'

The two soldiers materialised with a body wrapped in a grey shroud, and lay it on the ice. Robert could just about see a pale freckled face, eyes closed. Was she dead or faking? The soldiers aimed their QBZ-97 assault rifles at her.

'Open the blanket and check for a pulse.'

One soldier pulled away the blanket as the other placed his hand on her neck. Robert was dazzled by Maddie's golden rivulets of hair. Her photos hadn't done her justice. As he noticed her bandaged leg, he heard a cry of pain from the soldier feeling for a pulse. Maddie's right fist had smashed into the soldier's face and he stumbled backwards in shock, his mouth bleeding. Her good leg kicked out at the other soldier straddling her, her boot connecting with his testicles. But the first soldier had recovered himself and was about to shoot her.

'Stop!' shouted Robert. 'Hold your fire.'

The woman was now trying to crawl away. He was impressed by her courage.

'Madeline Wildman,' Robert called out in English. 'Where do you think you are going?'

She stopped and turned to face him. 'Murdering scum! Get it over with,' she yelled.

He walked up to her, his arms open wide. 'You're safe now. Luke Searle can't hurt you anymore.'

Wendy waited for Anthony Chan inside the walled sanctuary of the Chinese Gardens at Darling Harbour. Before that, she had ridden around Sydney for an hour and a half, too jittery to stay in one place. There had been a short morning shower and her hair was wet but she didn't move from the bench. She watched a woman in her sixties practising tai chi with extraordinary fluidity and grace, but the woman's flowing movements only added to Wendy's sense of unreality. Surely this couldn't be happening to her?

Chan appeared almost to glide through the gardens like a phantom, as the moisture on the paved path began to steam in the heat. Despite the humidity, Chan was wearing a dark suit and tie, and as he sat next to her he wiped his forehead with a crumpled cotton handkerchief.

'I came as quickly as I could,' he said, his breath heavy and fast. 'You said it was urgent?' He glanced at her leather jacket folded on the bench but managed to suppress his normal look of disapproval. He also chose to ignore her untidy and wet hair.

Wendy scanned the faces of the people nearby. Nobody seemed to be listening to their conversation. Regardless, she moved closer to Chan. 'Anthony, my father trusted you implicitly.

I need to know you haven't betrayed that trust.'

'What? How can you ask such a thing? After all I've done to try to free your mother!'

For a moment she gave him a penetrating stare and then leaned close to his ear. She whispered, 'I think Dad was murdered.'

Chan's fine eyelashes fluttered. 'What can you mean?'

Wendy started to gnaw at an almost non-existent fingernail, then gave up. 'Dad was bugging a Chinese diplomat called Xu Biao. I found a listening device sewn into the collar of a suit Dad had made for him. I think that's how he learned about a new Dragon Resources project in Antarctica that was going to turn the company around, and that's why he bought all those shares.'

Chan's eyelashes continued to flutter. He took her hand and squeezed it.

'You don't believe me?' she said, yanking her hand free. 'I have the bug in my pocket …'

'Oh, my dear.' He shook his head. 'I'm afraid I do believe you.'

It was Wendy's turn to be stunned.

'Jack asked me never to tell you, but now I feel I must,' Chan continued. He turned away from her and looked at the ground. 'I don't know how he got the information, I swear. All I know is that he was desperate to raise a large sum of money and—'

'What for?' she interrupted, her voice raised.

'Hush. Keep your voice down.' Chan eyeballed a passing couple. 'Someone senior at Heizuizi agreed to release your mother and get her to Japan, where Jack was going to meet her and bring her here.'

Wendy gasped. She tried to speak but she had no voice.

'He'd exhausted all the legitimate channels. He was desperate. That's why he risked everything to raise the money.'

'She's alive?' Wendy asked, barely able to breathe.

Chan clasped her hand again. 'So your father was told. But after twenty years in that hellhole, I have my doubts. I'm sorry, Wendy. To survive that place … I mean, very few do. I think it was a scam, and I warned Jack. The amount of money they wanted was outrageous.'

'How much?' Wendy demanded.

'Two million dollars.'

'What?' Wendy's eyes narrowed in fury and she slapped the wooden park bench. 'Fuck! He should have told me. Fuck, fuck, fuck!'

Chan, who abhorred swearing, said nothing and waited for Wendy to calm down. With her head back, she looked up at the blue sky, her lips stretched into a wry, humourless smile. 'Fuck, I'm an idiot,' she murmured. 'I should have known he'd never give up. If I hadn't been so selfish, I might have been able to stop him. And now he's dead.'

'Nobody could have stopped him. Not even you.' Wendy made no response and Chan decided to focus on what was to be done. 'Wendy, if you really think Jack was murdered, you must report this to the police. But, doing so may not help your mother, if there is the remotest possibility she is still alive. If the Australian police reach out to their Chinese counterparts, who in turn talk to the prison … well, I fear your mother will simply disappear.'

Wendy's head spun round. 'Someone killed my dad! I can't just forget about it.'

Chan squeezed her hand. 'No, you can't, I agree. But where is your evidence?'

'I have the bug,' she said, tapping her pocket. She blinked a couple of times and sighed loudly. 'But you're right. It doesn't prove anything.'

'If you're serious about this, talk to the forensic pathologist who did the post-mortem. I have his name back at the office. He confirmed it was a heart attack but he may have missed something. And I don't know how you might do this, but I would strongly urge you to find out if Woo Ling is alive. Then consider if you want to start making waves.'

'I will,' said Wendy.

'Be careful, my dear. Be very careful.'

Luke heard a snowmobile fire up, then a second and third. He listened as the engine noise dwindled into the distance. At last, he sat up. His body heat had melted the ice beneath him and the woollen coat was saturated, which made it very heavy. If the soldiers were gone, he wouldn't need its camouflage anymore.

He attempted to stand but his legs were numb and the surface slippery, and he fell back. The berg creaked and wobbled from side to side like a seesaw. Luke held his breath, hoping it wouldn't tip over.

When it stopped swaying he managed to stand. He could see the snowmobiles on their way up the Hudson Mountains. He counted three red shapes. The hut was intact, and no soldiers appeared to have been left behind. He scanned the coastline. Nothing but seals. Thank God.

Luke took his first careful step onto a slab of wobbling pack-ice. Then another and another, heading back to shore. He spied the yellow freezer suit where he'd left it, the ice beneath it now stained a gory red. The hood had been torn off and the shoulder ripped.

Thankfully, the leopard seal was gone. Had it been enough to convince the soldiers they were dead? Luke turfed out the soaked pillows from inside the suit and carried it back to the rocky beach, where he collected his bag. He couldn't climb back up the cliff so he had to follow the fast ice along the coastline until the rock face dropped low enough for him to climb.

The effort drained him. His balance was getting worse and he was shivering. He slipped into the shallow water but recovered himself. After scrambling back over ice and boulders, he collapsed onto his knees not far from the hut's entrance. Doubled over and breathless, his eyes clenched shut, he gasped.

'Are you all right?' he called out. 'Maddie? It's Luke.'

No answer.

He opened his eyes and his heart almost stopped. The crates and canisters he had used to conceal Maddie were strewn around him. He wrenched his arms out of the backpack straps and clambered under the hut. It was as if a mini tornado had cleared a path through the debris, taking Maddie with it. Luke felt crushed with fear.

He wriggled back out and, still on all fours, shouted her name over and over. But it was hopeless. All that remained was the blanket she had been wrapped in. He stretched his hand out and touched the fabric, somehow expecting it to be warm – which, of course, it wasn't. Luke sat back on his haunches, his despair paralysing. Dotted around him were cigarette butts discarded by the soldiers. Their stink brought him out of his stupor.

Illogically, he wondered if Maddie might be inside the hut. He leaped through the open door and ran into every room, calling her name. Nothing. With a sickening feeling, he wondered if her body might be outside somewhere, discarded after they had killed her. Reluctantly, he left the hut.

He peered up at the mountains and watched as the snowmobiles became little more than moving red dots.

The first snowmobile was towing something, and he now realised it was a Kalkis sled and that Maddie was on it. But why take her? They'd killed all the others, and they must've believed him dead too. A dark, ugly thought crossed his mind. She was an attractive woman.

Luke's despair morphed into fury. There and then, he decided he must find Maddie. Yet it felt very little like a choice, more an instinctive reaction. If he had calculated his odds of success, he would never have considered it. But he wasn't thinking like a scientist. He refused to acknowledge that he would probably get killed. He had made a promise to Maddie – 'I won't let you down'. Then he'd run away and left her. He had to make it right. He would keep his promise.

'I'm coming after you,' he said aloud.

Luke was thinking more clearly now, and his breathing was calmer. It was then he noticed Maddie's tube of zinc cream lying next to the blanket. Had she lost it in the struggle? Or was she trying to leave him a message?

Luke crawled under the hut on his stomach and craned his neck, looking around. There was nothing but junk. He moved to the spot where Maddie had been lying. Rolling over to position himself as she had been, he instantly saw lettering on the underside of the hut's floorboards. It was so close to his face that, at first, it was unintelligible.

He touched the letter F: it was sticky and waxy. Zinc sunblock. It read 'FITZY GEN ZHAO'.

The first word was easy. Their camp must be near the Fitzgerald Fissure. That was a start, but the Fitzy was twenty kilometres long. And what of 'GEN' and 'ZHAO'? Maddie was obviously trying to tell him something she had overheard, but it made no sense. A military general in Antarctica?

Back inside the hut, Luke stripped off his soaked coat and hung his sodden boots and the freezer suit above the stove, which he loaded up with more wood. Both items would remain damp as they wouldn't hang there long, but damp was better than soaked. He couldn't survive the cold without his freezer suit. He assembled what he would need to take with him: food, what was left of their medical supplies, the camping stove, knife, ice axe, rope, binoculars and shovel. There was no tent but he took the blanket. He would be spending a night on the mountain and to survive it he would have to dig a snow cave to protect himself from the wind and cold. He knew all too well that his chances of living through such a night were slim, but 'slim' would have to do.

He eventually found a small box containing seven cartridges

for the Lee-Enfield rifle in a kitchen drawer, and cursed himself for not finding them earlier. But would the old rifle even fire, or would it blow up in his face? His last action was to leave a message, in case someone had picked up his SOS and come looking for him. Which he doubted. He was alone.

Thirty minutes later, Luke was on his way. He was now the hunter.

Luke kept up a good pace: not so fast that he would sweat too much, but fast enough to reach the nearest end of the Fitzgerald Fissure by mid-morning the following day. Once night fell, he could do nothing but build a snow cave and wait for dawn. At least he had a few more hours of daylight left, the sky was a dazzling blue and the mountain air still. As long as there was no wind – a rarity, he had to admit – he could follow the snowmobile tracks all the way to their camp. Following their exact path would also virtually eliminate the chance of falling into hidden crevasses.

The regularity of his breathing, the swish of his clothes and the crunch of his boots was all he could hear. He had always found solo treks exhilarating but now he craved company. He started talking to himself as he worked through a plan for Maddie's rescue. Could he capture the leader and threaten to kill him unless Maddie was released? Could he enter the camp unseen, find her and leave before the alarm was raised? The mountain peaks, which he had always regarded with joy, now seemed ominous and threatening. Would he even make it through the night?

Luke began to sing, the power of his voice sucked away by the vast emptiness. It was a French children's ditty, one his father had taught him, 'Frère Jacques'. It was simple and repetitive but gave him a good walking rhythm. Then he progressed to something less childish, 'Hymne à l'Amour', which his father used to sing amongst the clatter of pans and shouting in the kitchen.

Luke's voice trailed away as he thought of Jason. How would Jase remember him if he perished? Luke stumbled as his leg disappeared up to his knee in the loose ice. He yanked it free and continued. It was two days since he'd heard the news about Jessica's engagement, and he hadn't been able to speak with his son since. He imagined Jason, crestfallen at his daddy's silence. Would he always associate his father with disappointment and absence? Luke was determined to change that. He should never have left Melbourne, never allowed himself to be manipulated by Jessica. Maddie was right: there was still time to make amends.

Luke was determined to live. To make things right with Jason. To keep his promise to Maddie.

He took some comfort from the ice axe in his hand and the Lee-Enfield strapped to his pack. It wasn't much against modern weapons, but he'd have surprise on his side. Maddie had once called him a maverick. Being impetuous usually got him into hot water and this rescue mission would undoubtedly lead to trouble. He imagined Maddie tutting at him, and smiled.

He started to sing again, unwilling to think of the odds stacked against him.

★ ★ ★

Robert sat a safe distance from the test site, leaning back into his chair like a cricket enthusiast in a private box at the final day of The Ashes. His reluctant guest, Madeline Wildman, sat next to him. She was in fresh clothing, her wound seen to by his doctor. It was clean and would heal well. She had already tried to escape twice, leaving him no choice but to tie her arms behind the chair. She refused to look at him or speak, but this was better than the tirade of abuse she had hurled at him upon arriving at the camp – and the bite she had inflicted on one of his men.

He admired the contours of her profile, and Maddie held her head up disdainfully, aware that he was looking at her. The creamy pale skin of her throat, her bright round eyes and long golden hair reminded him of Botticelli's Venus. She was a rare, if only temporary trophy. A pity about the temper.

'Stop staring at me, you creep,' she said, her eyes fixed straight ahead.

Even when she was furious, the movement of her soft lips was an open invitation. How many women had floated in and out of Robert's life, all disappointing, all drawn to him by his power and wealth? All were insipid creatures with perfect proportions who only lasted a few weeks before he deleted their numbers from his smartphone. This woman, however, had guts as well as an unusual, earthy kind of beauty. What a shame she would have to freeze to death somewhere on the mountains, desperate to escape the murderous Luke Searle.

' "They look like rose-buds fill'd with snow",' quoted Robert, looking at her lips. She blinked several times in confusion. 'That beautiful line is from Thomas Campion's "Cherry Ripe". You see, we Chinese are not the uneducated peasants you think we are.'

'I don't think that,' she said, turning her head, her eyes scanning his face. 'I ask again: who are you, and what are you doing here?'

'You're a bright woman. I'm sure you'll work it out.'

'Are you General Zhao?'

Robert threw his head back in laughter, revealing two rows of pristine white teeth. He'd never before been mistaken for his father. 'Why do you think I am the General?' he asked, still chuckling.

'My mistake,' she mumbled. 'What did you mean when you said Luke can't hurt me anymore?'

'A private joke.' He sipped at his glass of champagne.

'So what do you want?'

'I want to save my people.'

Maddie raised an eyebrow and sneered. 'Sure you do. If this was a mercy mission you wouldn't be slaughtering people. And why the soldiers? Are you drilling for oil? Mining? Testing weapons? Dumping waste? What could possibly be worth all this bloodshed?'

Robert looked down as he experienced something akin to remorse. He had never intended to kill anyone. But he had to succeed, no matter the cost. He felt a sting of anger. 'How dare you judge me. What I am doing here is more important than you or your friends.'

'Then what do you want from me?' she asked.

'My men are idiots and lack refinement. I want to share my moment of glory with someone intelligent enough to appreciate its true significance. But don't flatter yourself. I had considered Searle for this role, but he's dead now. At least you, my dear, have a beauty he never possessed.'

Maddie tried to lunge at him. 'What did you do?'

'Don't shout at me,' he yelled back, standing and slapping her hard across the face. Despite her bindings, she managed to headbutt his stomach. He stumbled back, shocked and winded. 'Guards!' he croaked. Two men rushed over.

'You murdering bastard!' Maddie screamed. 'What have you done?'

As his men roped her chest to the back of the chair and bound her feet, Robert recovered his composure. 'I did nothing. He was dead when we found him. A leopard seal was enjoying his carcass.'

Robert delighted in the way Maddie's face crumpled, almost curling in on itself with despair. Then she looked at him, her eyes begging him to tell her it wasn't true – that Searle was still alive.

'I don't believe you. He knows the seals,' she said, but her words lacked conviction.

'Oh, dear. This man was more to you than just a member of your team, wasn't he? Yes, I've heard that happens at remote stations. Desperate sex with people you'd never normally find attractive. Lying to loved ones afterwards, claiming fidelity. But isolation and loneliness can do that to you. Tut, tut. Not the kind of behaviour I'd expect from a station leader.'

'Go to hell, you fucking nutcase!' She spat out the words through a tear-stained face.

Ignoring her insult, Robert reached for his champagne flute. 'To Antarctica's forgotten riches.'

Robert fully intended to enjoy this landmark moment. As he waited for the countdown, he surveyed the view. His camp was positioned perfectly: it had easy access to the glacier but was far enough back to avoid detection by any passing ships. It was reassuring to know that even though he was sitting on thick ice, somewhere beneath him lay solid bedrock. The Pine Island Glacier's ice tongue – the focus of his attention – sat on nothing more substantial than seawater. Further inland, he could make out the long gash of the Fitzgerald Fissure.

Tang, his explosives expert, was monitoring the countdown. Li sat next to him. Their equipment was spread out on a table outside Robert's tent. Maddie watched their every move.

Captain Wei marched over. 'Ready, sir. Lieutenant Tang will start the countdown.'

Robert nodded and Wei stood to attention to his right. Every now and again Wei glanced up the length of the glacier, inland, when he should have been looking seaward towards the point of detonation.

'What's so interesting out there?' Robert asked.

'Nothing, sir. Just low sun in my eyes.'

Tang began counting down from ten, and Robert's foot tapped out each second.

The explosion felt like an earthquake, except it wasn't earth shaking but ice. The boom was followed by a low rumble. Robert's director's chair shuddered and he had to lean forward to prevent it from tipping over. Maddie stared in horror at the spray of ice that shot skyward at the tip of the glacier's tongue.

Li and Tang huddled over their trembling monitors, which gradually stopped moving as the aftershock died away. An unnerving silence followed. Li shook his head, his eyes darting from the monitor to the mountains and back.

'Did everything function as it should?' asked Robert.

Tang saluted. 'Sir, the test is complete. The explosives worked well. The pentolite has not been impacted by the sub-zero temperatures or the wet, and the signal has gone the distance. We will be victorious.'

Robert stood and slapped Tang on the back. Wei again looked inland to where the glacier met the Hudson Mountains, and seemed to smile as he saw a cloud of snow in the air. Robert was too focused on the success of the test to notice. Li's lower lip was trapped between his teeth, and despite the cold, he was sweating. He remained glued to the monitors.

'Good work, men,' Robert said. 'I'll report our success to General Zhao and our backers. The tenth of March will be truly spectacular.'

Suddenly there was a crack so loud that Robert's hands shot to his ears. It was hard to tell where it came from. Li nervously started rocking back and forth. Another thunderous *crack*. It was behind them. Everyone except Maddie turned to face the Hudson Mountains. She struggled to peer around.

A gaping fissure was zigzagging across a section of deep snow covering the mountain, like a bolt of lightning. It continued for at least a kilometre. Li pointed, agog. Then the area of loose ice directly below the crack broke away and began to tumble down the lower slopes onto the glacier. Avalanche. Fortunately, the direction of descent was nowhere near their camp.

Robert was unaware he was holding his gloved hand over his heart until Maddie spoke.

'What have you done? Don't you know how unstable this glacier is?'

'I know that, Wildman, but my project won't harm your precious glacier.' She was beginning to annoy him. Perhaps he should dispose of her now?

Li was rocking more violently. 'No, no, no …' His seismometer was picking up another, more powerful tremor, this time in the direction of Cranton Bay.

'Stop that, will you?' Robert snapped.

'Sir, this is bad.' Li looked at Wei for guidance, his eyes fearful. Wei subtly shook his head and the glaciologist took the hint. 'Sir,' he said, 'I … I need time to work out what caused the avalanche.'

Tang spoke up. 'The aftershocks are a minor issue, sir.'

'No, they …' Li began. Wei glared at him to stop.

'Make sure this doesn't happen on the tenth,' Robert said. 'We could have been killed!'

Maddie leaned as far forward as her bindings would allow. 'Why are you blowing off bits of the glacier?'

'More than just bits, Madeline,' Robert replied. Why not tell her? She would be dead soon. 'We will blow away a perfect one hundred and twenty-five thousand cubic metre tabular iceberg and then another, and another.'

'But why?' she gasped. 'Why destroy the glacier?'

'Sir,' interrupted Wei. 'Permission to check the point of detonation before you report in?'

'Yes, go,' he said, flicking his wrist. 'And take Tang.'

The glaciologist would stay where Robert could keep an eye on him. Was he having some kind of breakdown? 'Li, I need you to model aftershock activity, based on the volume of explosives we're using on the tenth.'

The man stared at his screen like a rabbit transfixed by a car's headlights.

'Bring her inside,' Robert ordered another soldier. Maddie was released so she could walk but her hands were still tied. 'After you,' Robert said in mock gallantry. *A captive audience*, he thought smiling to himself.

The ice beneath Luke's feet shuddered. He looked up into the mountains and heard a roar that grew in volume. It sounded like thousands of wild horses galloping down the slope. Luke fell forwards as the ice beneath his feet shifted downhill. He scrambled to stand, whipping around on his unstable legs and trying to work out what was happening.

Then he heard a rolling, roiling, cracking sound, as higher up the mountain a deep gash tore across the ice. It seemed to resonate as the crack drove deeper and deeper towards the bedrock beneath. Snow was hurled into the air, forming a thick cloud. Simultaneously, the surface ice began to slide towards Luke – a tumbling, roaring mass, unified in one powerful motion. It gathered momentum and grew in height, like a tsunami.

Avalanche. Luke was going to be buried alive.

He desperately searched for somewhere to hide. To his right, a rocky outcrop poked its dark fingers through the thick ice. He ran towards it; it might protect him from the full force of the avalanche. He also had to create an airspace around his head. If he didn't, he would suffocate on his own exhaled carbon dioxide trapped beneath the snow.

The roar, now like a jet engine, was terrifying. The snow beneath his feet collapsed and began sliding downhill. Luke looked up as the wall of snow and ice raced towards him. He dropped his backpack – the weight would drag him down – and crouched low behind the rock, tucking his head in tightly and covering it with his arms, determined to keep an open airspace. His mind was screaming at him to prepare to swim: a flashback from avalanche survival training. If he wasn't crushed by the weight, he had to flail his arms and legs to try to reach the surface.

The force of the giant wave winded him. He could barely breathe as the roar was all around him. Luke was torn away from the rock, smashed by an icy wall. He tumbled, as if in a washing machine, with no idea which direction was up and which down.

Finally the movement stopped. Luke was buried, and he knew he had to get to the surface before the ice solidified. His arms still protected his face, and he created an airspace by pushing snow away. His mouth was dry with fear but he forced some saliva from it. It ran down his lower lip and onto his chin. As a result he knew his head was pointing towards the sky.

He crawled upwards but his limbs were so tired, and the weight of snow and ice so great, that he could hardly move. The longer he stayed there, the harder the snow would set. It already weighed like concrete. With sheer bloody-mindedness he punched his arms above him, then used his gloved hands as shovels to force a hole. His muscles screamed in agony. But there was nobody to rescue him. He refused to die like this – not now that he was going to turn his life around. He thrashed his legs and arms as best he could.

He caught a tiny glimpse of blue. Fresh air! The snow loosened and Luke managed to get his head and shoulders free. He gritted his teeth as he attempted to drag himself up and onto his stomach. The veins in his neck bulged with exertion.

The loose snow gave him no grip, and he could feel himself sliding backwards, sinking. It was like quicksand. No, not like this. He had to get his body free. He kicked his legs as if he were swimming, and first one and then the other came loose. All he had to do now was lie flat on the surface and crawl away to firmer ice. Loose snow continued to slide downhill, but no longer in a violent onslaught.

With each movement the snow beneath him sank a little, but he remained on top of it. How long he crawled for, he had no idea, but when he reached a boulder he used it to pull himself into a sitting position, with his back against the rock. Was it the same rock he'd hidden behind, or another? Luke was completely disoriented. He was nauseous and his head felt like it was being squeezed in a vice.

He passed out.

Robert had just finished relaying the good news to the select project team at Dragon Resources. His father had been unavoidably detained but the details would be passed on to him. Robert was on a high. Reluctant to let the buzz die away, he leaned over the bound and gagged Maddie. 'If I take your gag away, will you behave?'

She glared at him.

'Do you want to know what we're doing here or not?'

Either way he was going to brag, but he preferred an interactive audience rather than a silent one. Robert lived for moments like this. Whenever he outmanoeuvred a competitor, he took delight in seeing the mixture of hatred and bitter admiration written all over the faces of the defeated.

Maddie nodded, and Robert removed the cloth gag.

'My name is Robert Zhao Sheng,' he began. 'My father is General Zhao.'

'So what are you doing here, Robert?' she challenged.

He placed a chair in front of her and lit a cigarette. He inhaled deeply, making her wait, enjoying the forced intimacy.

'Water. The most precious resource in the world,' he said.

He waited for her response, but she waited for him to continue.

He inhaled again and then blew smoke up into the tent cavity.

'My people are dying, Madeline. The Party plays down the hardship, keeps the media coverage to a minimum, but our farmers can't produce crops, our industry is crippled, and our cities severely rationed. Our leaders have made terrible blunders, polluting rivers, building dams without thinking through the consequences. They have tried many ways to generate water but none as audacious as this. Our leaders worry too much about other countries' reactions. They forget those countries are our competitors – they are talking their own book, as we say in my business. Our government doesn't have the guts to do what is necessary. But I do.'

'So you're stealing Antarctic ice?' Her tone was scathing.

He wagged his finger at her. 'Theft? Pah. No one owns this wasteland.'

'Robert, I understand you need water. I really do. But China isn't the only one. Africa, the United States, the Middle East, Europe, my home – we're all suffering. But you can't just show up here, kill innocent people and start chipping away at a glacier. It's not yours to take.'

'That's where you're wrong, Madeline. The Madrid Protocol only prohibits activity relating to mineral resources. Not ice-harvesting. Anyway, Antarctica belongs to no one and to everyone.' He raised his arms and gestured all around him. 'This is my brainchild, and I, Robert Zhao Sheng, will be the first to successfully harvest Antarctic ice. Once other countries learn of my success, they will come clamouring to get their hands on all this frozen fresh water. You would be well aware that seventy per cent of the world's fresh water is right here in Antarctica? Seventy per cent! But …' he leaned back and placed his hands behind his head and gave her a glossy white smile, 'only I have the technology. Patented, of course. They'll have to come begging to me if they want to get in on the act. And for the right licence fee, I'm prepared to negotiate.'

'But how?' Her tone had changed, intrigued now. 'It can't be economically viable.'

'Madeline, Madeline. You obviously don't watch CNBC, do you? If you did, you see, you'd know water is now more valuable than oil. Have you been walking around with your eyes and ears closed? There are countries at war over access to rivers and aquifers. It is economically viable.'

Robert stubbed out his cigarette, collected his laptop and tapped a few keys. He returned to his chair and swivelled it to face Maddie. On the screen was a graphic of the Pine Island Glacier: two hundred and fifty kilometres long, forty kilometres wide and, at the very tip of the ice tongue, fifty metres deep.

'At the far left hand corner of the ice tongue. Here.' He pointed. 'We have calculated exactly how much explosive we need to blow off one hundred and twenty-five thousand cubic metres of iceberg.'

'But why use explosives? Why don't you simply chisel away at the glacier face?' She leaned closer. He had her hooked.

'Ah, there you betray your poor knowledge of glaciers. Your good friend Luke would have known this if he hadn't met with that tragic accident.' Robert couldn't resist reminding her. He just had to see the light in her eyes die, and it did. How easy it was to control people's emotions.

'It's suicidal for a ship to be under the front of a glacier and "chip away", as you put it. Glaciers calve all the time, and this one more than most. Too much risk, particularly considering my ninety-million-dollar purpose-built heavy-lift vessel. I certainly wouldn't want it damaged. And then there's the matter of refreezing, of course. We have to force a distance between the severed berg and the parent glacier, otherwise the two will simply freeze together again.'

Robert could see Maddie's mind ticking away. From the look on her face, she was buying into his ideas.

'That makes sense,' she said. 'And you'd need to control the shape of the berg. If it's tabular, it's less likely to flip ...'

'The vessel is equipped with lasers that can cut through ice with absolute precision. Every berg will be a perfect fit for our vessel.'

'Do you have a picture of her?' Maddie asked.

Robert was delighted. 'Of course. Here.' An image appeared on his screen. It resembled a supertanker but had a rectangular central section cut out so that the two ends of the ship were linked by a low-lying platform. Its ballast tanks could be flooded to lower the platform – the well deck – below the water's surface, allowing an iceberg or oil rig or even another vessel to float on board. Then the deck could be raised, lifting the cargo above the waterline. 'Four years in design and construction, two hundred and fifty metres long, eighty metres wide. There she is, the semi-submersible *Water Dragon.*'

Maddie stared at the image. Robert could see she was fascinated.

'She's designed to carry our icy cargo, but she can transport oil rigs. See, here,' he said, pointing to the well deck, positioned between a forward pilot house and an aft machinery space.

'Like the MV *Blue Marlin*,' said Maddie. 'Didn't that vessel carry the USS *Cole*, a destroyer, back to America after it was damaged by a suicide bomber?'

'Correct, Madeline, but ours is way bigger.' He threw his arms wide.

'A flo/flo,' Maddie whispered.

'Correct again. Float on, float off. And we'll be floating onto her deck a giant ice cube!'

'Amazing.' Maddie seemed impressed. 'But what are you going to do with the flo/flo for the seven months of the year when the continent's ice-locked?'

'Not seven. Four at most, and in those four months she'll be leased out. You see, one of my businesses is a shipbuilder, and it has built a new type of nuclear-powered, super-strong ice-breaker. It will work day and night to keep sea ice at bay so the tankers can come and go.'

'Tankers?'

'Yes. There's not much oil to transport these days, so they'll carry mulched ice instead. Soon the Amundsen Sea will be as busy as the Straits of Hormuz.'

Maddie nodded. 'So how are you mulching ice?'

'Great question,' he replied, carried away with excitement. 'You've heard of Whalers Island? The *Water Dragon* will carry the bergs into its calm harbour. There, we have an ice-pulping station. Once the ice is mulched – a bit like putting it through a wood-chipper – it will be pumped into the hold of the waiting supertankers. When it reaches China, any impurities will be removed.'

'Whalers Island?' Maddie shook her head, frowning, and Robert could see her putting two and two together. 'My God! You killed all those penguins. It wasn't bird flu at all.' She glared at him, and her sudden change of mood took Robert by surprise.

Despite the fact she was still tied to her chair, he took a step back. 'Madeline, stop being so emotional. We had to find a way to keep all those tourist ships away, and what better deterrent than bird flu? It worked a treat.'

'So you – what? Poisoned hundreds of thousands of penguins?' She screwed her face up in disgust.

'It had to be done.'

'They died in agony. How could you?' Her face hardened, which Robert didn't like. 'And our quarantine team? What happened to them?'

'Casualties of war,' he said, echoing his father.

'War?' she screamed. 'Are you out of your mind? There is no bloody war.'

'They were a small price to pay for the greater good.'

'The greater good!'

'Wise up, Madeline. The world is on the brink of a crisis. People are dying in wars over water: the Nile, the Jordan, the Congo. This is no different.'

'What a crock of shit! This isn't about saving China. This is about money. How rich will you be, Robert?' Her eyes were wet, and her voice hoarse. 'It's too high a price. Your thirst for wealth and power has blinded you to the real cost – human lives. Let alone the poor birds …'

He was about to dismiss her accusation but Maddie hung her head and her hair fell forward, hiding her face. He watched her for a while and then left the tent, feeling thoroughly deflated. How dare the bitch burst his bubble!

He needed someone to kick. Where was Li Guangjie? He must have snuck out during their argument. Robert was about to enter the techno tent when he overheard Captain Wei inside. Why wasn't he out inspecting the test site, as he should be?

'Keep your voice down!' Wei snapped to Li.

Robert stopped and listened.

'What does it matter?' Li was saying. 'This is madness! We only used a fraction of the explosives we'll use on the tenth of March, and already several new cracks have opened up either side of the initiation point. We caused that fracturing. Gao, I'm a glaciologist, so please listen. If we detonate one thousand two hundred tonnes of explosives, we could destroy the whole glacier.'

Robert's jaw dropped. What was Li talking about? They were only using a precisely calculated two hundred and forty kilograms, carefully positioned so the berg would break away in one piece. Why was Li twittering on about one thousand two hundred tonnes? That was the equivalent of sixteen truckloads! The man was losing his grip on reality.

'We proceed as planned,' said Wei.

'No, we can't! I always said this project was risky, but climate change has clearly had a much bigger impact on this glacier than we thought. It's fragile. I believe Project Eclipse will fracture the *whole* glacier.'

Robert burst into the tent. 'What the hell is Project Eclipse?'

Li made a whimpering sound but neither spoke.

'Answer me!'

Robert punched Li in the stomach and he dropped to the floor. The blow would have had little impact on Captain Wei, but Robert had deliberately picked the weaker of the two.

'Now, Li. What have you two been up to? Planning to sabotage the ice harvesting?'

'N … no, sir. Not at all. No, I w … want to make sure the water project is a success,' stammered the glaciologist.

Robert leaned closer to Li. 'So what the fuck is Project Eclipse, and why don't I know about it?' The man cowered and again glanced at Wei, as if seeking approval to speak.

'So, Captain Wei,' said Robert, shoving Li aside and pointing a pistol at Wei's stomach. 'Either you tell me what is going on or you die.'

Wei stared back defiantly. 'My instructions are to ensure the success of the primary mission – the detonation of explosives along the twenty kilometres of the Fitzgerald Fissure. The water project is secondary.'

Robert instantly noticed that he had dropped the 'sir' from his speech.

'Primary mission? What are you talking about? Water harvesting is the only mission.'

'Put down your weapon,' said Wei. 'I am not authorised to say any more. It's time to speak to the man in charge of Project Eclipse.'

Robert's face flushed pink with fury. 'And who the fuck is that?'

For the first time since Robert had known Wei, he saw the captain smile – and it was the smirk of the victorious. Wei jerked his chin forward and held his head high. 'General Zhao. Your father.'

Someone was shouting Luke's name from far, far away. He was so tired that he couldn't open his eyes. Better to sleep and dream. He was no longer cold or afraid and it felt good.

'Luke. Wake! You must wake now!'

That insistent, guttural voice. Where did he know it from? Luke became aware of hands gripping him, his warm snow blanket slipping away. He tried to look but his eyelashes were stuck together, each lash carrying a tiny ice particle.

'Wake up, you lazy son of a bitch.'

What? The accent was pronounced: it was Russian. Somebody was brushing snow from his face.

'He's hypothermic,' said a different voice. 'It's mild, but we have to get him warm, and he may have chest injuries.' Luke lost consciousness for a few seconds. 'Can you put up the tent? We need to get him into a sleeping bag fast. And make a hot drink.' The voice had an American twang, like his mate Bill at McMurdo Station. He must be dreaming again. He hadn't seen Bill for years.

'Luke,' said the American. 'Can you tell me if you're hurt?'

He heard the crackle of a two-way radio. 'We have found Luke

Searle. Repeat, we have found Luke Searle. He's alive but was caught in the avalanche, over.'

The voice sounded Scandinavian. His dream was turning into the United Nations. Was something or someone moving him? Yes, he was being lifted. He tore his eyelids apart, afraid. Perhaps the killers had found him? The leader of those bastards had had an American accent.

Luke wriggled his arms, trying to break free of their grip. But the face grinning at him was broad, the neck wide, and small blue eyes peered at him from behind puffy eyelids. He knew that ugly mug. Vitaly Yushkov.

'Hello, my friend,' said the Russian, his face cracking into a smile.

Luke tried to speak. He stuttered and realised he was shaking uncontrollably.

'You very cold. We must get you warm,' said Vitaly.

'Luke, where are the others?' It was that insistent Scandinavian voice again. 'Were they with you? Luke?'

'N … no,' Luke managed to say.

'Where are they?' the voice demanded. 'Come on, Luke, you remember Maddie Wildman, Craig Anderson, Pete MacNamara? Are they buried in the avalanche?'

'Dead,' he breathed. 'Maddie's gone.'

The voice was frantic. 'In the snow? Are they dead in the snow? Should we search for them?'

'I'm … alone.' Luke was pulled upwards, with a man on either side of him, and then dragged into a tent. 'Where did …' His freezer suit was being removed.

'Blood,' someone said. Was Luke bleeding, or did they mean the meat stains on the suit? He glimpsed another face: long, pale, baby-soft skin.

'My name is Rod,' the American said. 'I'm a doctor. You have mild hypothermia so we have to get you out of your damp clothes.'

Luke understood. They removed almost everything, checked over his body and placed him in a sleeping bag that felt so soft, so silky, that he fell back asleep immediately.

Some time later, Rod spoke again. 'Luke, we have some hot soup. We're going to sit you up.'

The doctor placed a spoon near his lips and Luke opened his mouth. The warm liquid slipped down his throat. He felt a chill in the pit of his stomach, but his skin was hot and tingly. When he finished the soup, he noticed the sides of the orange pyramid tent were buffeting slightly in the wind. A battery-powered torch hanging from the roof provided startlingly bright light.

Luke now recognised the bulbous eyes and agile movements of the super-fit expedition leader from the *Professor Basov*. Luke had met him only once, and he'd judged him as a man who was suspicious until you proved him wrong.

'Alrek Tangen,' the man said, by way of reintroduction. 'How are you feeling?'

'Better for the soup and sleep.' Luke croaked. 'Thank you … for finding me. But how—' Luke was suddenly feeling hot, his skin burning. He struggled to open the sleeping bag, and Alrek, who was kneeling, moved away as if from danger.

Luke felt a large hand on his shoulder. He moved his sore head around to catch a glimpse of Vitaly, who was sitting behind him.

'Stay still, my friend,' Vitaly said. His hand remained firmly on Luke's shoulder.

'We picked up your SOS,' said Alrek, still keeping a safe distance, his forehead creased in wariness.

Luke let his head fall back and laughed. He knew he sounded like a maniac but he didn't care. He couldn't believe the transmission had worked. His cry for help had been heard! Everything would be okay now.

'Vitaly. Good to see you.'

The Russian patted Luke's shoulder.

'How … how did you find me, here on the mountains?'

'In a moment,' replied Alrek. 'First, where are the others? At Hope Station?' Luke saw him glance a warning at Vitaly. But what could he be warning him about?

Luke sat bolt upright, taking even Vitaly by surprise. 'Maddie! They've got Maddie!'

'Don't move,' said Alrek, pointing a Makarov pistol at Luke.

Stunned, Luke froze. 'I don't understand. Who are you?'

'Exactly who I said I am. I need to know what you've done with the others. Tell me now,' said Alrek, his voice tense and shaky.

'Vitaly, what's going on?' Luke asked.

Vitaly was still behind Luke so he couldn't read his friend's expression. 'Your division,' he replied. 'They say bad things about you. They think you are a crazy man and you kill your friends. I say they are crazy people, but they will not listen to a sailor.'

'I didn't kill anyone. We were attacked. Chinese, I think. With rifles, like AK-47s. They burned down the station. Maddie and I are the only two left alive.' Luke shook his head. 'Why on earth would AARO think I killed them? That's absurd. I don't understand what's going on.'

'Alrek, this isn't necessary,' said Rod.

Alrek ignored both Rod's comment and Luke's question. 'Where is Maddie?'

'They have her. We were sheltering at Bettingtons and they hunted us down. Maddie was hurt. I hid her but they found her and took her. God, I left her defenceless.' Luke rubbed his hand over his face. Some of his fingers still felt numb.

'Where? Where is she?' Alrek demanded.

Luke looked up at him. 'Please, put the gun down. I'm not the enemy. They are. We have to find Maddie fast. They must have taken her to their camp. Help me find her. She's in terrible danger.'

Alrek lowered the pistol but kept his distance. 'Your SOS said one was wounded. That's Maddie?'

'Yes. Shrapnel in her calf from when the gas cylinders at Hope exploded. I removed it and sewed up the wound when we made it to Bettingtons.'

'Tell me about the operation,' Rod said. 'What did you do?'

'That's irrelevant,' snapped Alrek.

'No, it isn't. Luke, tell me how you sewed it up.'

Luke explained exactly what he had done. 'You did well,' said Rod, nodding. He looked at Alrek. 'I need to assess this man properly, but he doesn't sound crazy to me. He performed the operation well, given the circumstances. If he wanted to kill Maddie, why bother operating on her?'

Alrek nodded slowly. 'It could all be a lie.'

Luke's head throbbed. 'Think, man! Why would I leave the shelter of Bettingtons to tramp across a mountain in sub-zero temperatures to reach a camp that doesn't exist? Maddie is being held captive. God, she may already be dead. Look, I don't care if you believe me or not. Just let me go after her.'

Rod leaned over Luke. 'Hold it there, buddy. You're not going anywhere right now. You have frost-nip on some of your fingers, and on your nose and cheeks, and mild hypothermia. Night is closing in and we're staying put.'

'You'll come with us to the ship in the morning,' clarified Alrek.

'No,' said Luke. 'Maddie's in trouble. I won't just leave her. No way.' He was getting angry. What was wrong with these people?

Vitaly piped up. 'Luke not crazy. If he say there are killers and they take the woman, then this is the truth.'

'Vitaly, you watch him. He mustn't leave this tent, okay?'

Alrek was about to leave but there was something Luke had to know.

'How did you find me? On the mountain, I mean.'

'Well, it had something to do with the bloody big sign you left at Bettingtons,' Alrek said. 'We got there to find "Over Hudsons to Fitzy. Searle, 4 pm, 7 March". A novel use of zinc cream'. Luke had scrawled the words across the seaward side of the hut. Alrek paused. 'AARO helped us decipher the word "Fitzy". After that, it was a case of following your footsteps. Literally. Anyway, you were very lucky. Any further up the slope and the avalanche would've killed you.'

Alrek and Rod left. Luke could hear them in conversation but couldn't make out the words. Vitaly moved around to sit in front of Luke.

'Vitaly, what is going on?' Luke asked in a hushed tone.

'We hear your SOS. We reply, many times, but there is no response from you. We contact your AARO. They say that communication from Hope is broken, and families do not hear from their loved ones. They think something is wrong.'

Luke interrupted. 'But there's been *no* communication since the fifth. Two days ago! Why haven't they acted?'

Vitaly put out his hand to calm Luke. 'Not so, my friend. Someone from Hope is talking to your AARO people.'

Luke's bloodshot eyes widened. 'Not possible.'

'AARO, they ask us to sail to this Bettingtons and make a rescue if we can get through sea ice. And so, we cut through the ice and here we are.' The burly Russian gestured around him.

'But why would they think I'm capable of killing?'

Vitaly's blue eyes twinkled as he smiled sagely. 'My friend, everybody can kill. We defend the ones we love, and if we love life, we fight to live. But I do not know why they think you kill your friends.'

'Did they contact Rothera or McMurdo to see if they still have any planes? They could do a flyover and search for Maddie.' Luke was growing more agitated.

The British station Rothera was one thousand two hundred kilometres away from Hope, and McMurdo, the American station, was further still. Both had planes, but usually only until February when the aircraft left for the winter. *Perhaps McMurdo might still have a ski-equipped C-130*, Luke thought.

'I not know if they talk to these people. But nothing will happen until morning. It not possible for a plane to fly here at night. You know this.'

Luke leaned forward and grabbed the Russian's arms. 'At first light, I'm going after Maddie. Vitaly, will you help me get away?'

'Now you talk like a crazy man. You will die before you reach the camp.'

Luke stared at his friend, willing him to understand. 'You remember that night on the vodka when you told me the story of how you survived *dedovshchina*?' Luke had learned that *dedovshchina* was a brutal and sometimes lethal system of bullying of new recruits in the armed forces. Torture was the norm. It drove many to suicide.

218

Vitaly frowned, his eyes disappearing under his furrowed brow. 'Nyet. We will not speak of this.'

'You told me about your mate, Andrei. How you trained in bomb disposal together. He was like a brother to you. Then an IED killed him in Afghanistan. You deserted.'

Vitaly shoved his hand over Luke's mouth. 'Quiet! Nobody must know this.' Luke nodded and Vitaly released his grip. 'I had good reason,' the Russian added.

'I don't doubt it. You wouldn't choose the life of a fugitive, unless you had no choice. But my point is, you would have done anything to save Andrei and I'll do anything to save Maddie. She's like a sister to me.'

Vitaly nodded slowly and then grinned, his wide face flattening. 'I think maybe this woman is not like your sister!' His laugh sounded like the bark of a fur seal. In an instant, he was serious again. 'I understand. You cannot abandon a comrade. We will go to the ship in the morning. We get supplies and equipment. I will take the captain's pistol from Alrek. I will go with you, my friend, and we will find her, I think.'

As Robert stepped into his tent, he felt lightheaded. In his whole career, he had never been blindsided like this. Wei followed him. Furious that the soldier should assume he would be present when he spoke to his father, Robert rounded on him. 'Get out!'

Wei bowed slightly and withdrew.

Robert sat at his desk and stared at the Iridium satellite phone, trying to work out the best approach. A couple of seconds passed before Robert switched it on and entered his four-digit PIN. The bars on the display told him he had good coverage. He held the handset to his ear but didn't dial. Could it be true? Was his father running a secret operation? Would he really double-cross his own son?

Of course he would. What galled Robert was not that his father had betrayed him, but that he had, so far, outsmarted him. Robert should never have underestimated the General's ruthless ambition and cunning. Their thirst for power was matched, although Robert craved recognition more. He tried to calm himself and focused on dialling his father's scrambled line, which ensured their conversation would have no eavesdroppers.

'General Zhao,' his father said, the words snappy.

'This is Robert Zhao Sheng.'

'Wait. I must shut the door.' It was early morning in Beijing and the General was at work. 'The explosives test. I hear it was a success?'

'Which one, Father?'

A pause.

'Who betrayed me?' the General asked. No embarrassment. No apology.

'Nobody. I discovered your plan myself.' Robert kept his voice calm and measured. 'So, tell me about Project Eclipse.'

General Zhao grunted. 'You were to be told on the ninth anyway. No matter. Strategically, Project Eclipse is a thousand times more important than your water project and, therefore, need-to-know only.' He paused, clearly considering how much he should reveal. 'A scientist at Li Bai made a discovery that will give China unprecedented military power. I will be handing our leaders the chance to become the one true superpower. Greater than America. I'm talking about rare earth elements.'

Robert blinked. Rare earths were indeed extremely valuable, but he had not yet found a way to get into such a business. 'Go on, Father.'

'This scientist, Zhu Guoming, has spent the last two summers drilling samples along the length of the Hudson Mountains. I mean through the ice, down to the volcanic rock beneath. He discovered a precious mineral, bastnäsite, which contains …'

Robert heard rustling and realised his father had picked up some papers to read from. Soon he continued: 'Yttrium, neodymium, samarium, europium, terbium, dysprosium and praseodymium.' The rustling stopped.

In the late nineties, Deng Xiaoping had made a speech in which he said China would be to rare earth minerals what the Middle East was to oil. Robert knew that China already supplied ninety per cent of the world's rare earths, a fact that made several countries, especially the United States, very nervous.

The General went on. 'It's the single largest and most concentrated bastnäsite find in the world. You know what these minerals are used for?'

'Military technology.'

'Correct. China's military technology and everyone else's. Guided artillery projectiles, smart bombs, cruise missiles, stealth technologies, laser weapons, advanced armour and radar, night vision, jamming devices, unmanned aircraft. The list goes on. We will dominate the market. Can you imagine the United States begging for our bastnäsite? Without it, they can't equip their military machine!' The General sounded as though he were coughing, but he was in fact laughing. 'Think of the power this gives our great nation, Robert.'

'I believe South Africa and Australia have rare earth deposits.'

'Only in small quantities. The Hudson Mountains discovery is enormous, and it's only the beginning. Zhu reckons Antarctica is riddled with it, which means our leaders must be quick to follow through and claim as much Antarctic territory as possible. With me in command, naturally. Antarctica will soon become part of China. Mark my words.'

'Marie Byrd Land first, I assume?'

Antarctica's Marie Byrd Land was an enormous unclaimed wedge, which, from a point at the South Pole, expanded out to the Amundsen Sea. It was about the size of Pakistan. Robert glanced at the floor; he was sitting on Marie Byrd Land.

'Yes.'

'That could lead to war. You can persuade the Party to do this?'

'I can. Some members are already in the loop, but they are sworn to secrecy. The Party can claim complete ignorance and reap the benefits.'

I know which members you didn't tell, Robert thought. His father had many enemies.

'Why have you excluded me?' Robert spoke slowly but his fury was hard to control.

'I gave you the military support you needed for your water project. That should be enough.'

'So this is *your* project, is that it? You didn't want to share the glory?'

'How dare you speak to me like that!'

'So, when you and our advisers pushed me into harvesting ice from this glacier, it was all about efficiency: the two projects at the same glacier, same project team. Except I, as project leader and key investor, don't fucking know what's going on!'

'Go and cry on someone else's shoulder. I'll cut you in, but Wei will remain in charge of Project Eclipse.'

Robert clenched the fist on his good hand so tight that his knuckles turned white. 'You always thought me weak because I didn't go to military school. Doesn't it matter to you that I'm worth a fortune? I run one of the most successful private-equity firms in the world. I run deals worth billions, and yet you, Father, don't trust me!'

'I don't have time for this. Do you want to join me or not?'

Robert smacked his forehead as the realisation came to him. 'Ah, of course. This is really about you beating me. You can't be outdone by your weakling son, can you?'

The General gave a phlegmy sigh. 'You have always been a disappointment to me. Prove you have a backbone and work with me on Project Eclipse.'

The thick skin Robert had built up over many years peeled away and he felt as if his innards had been ripped from his body. He struggled to reply. 'I'll give you my answer when I've done my research. I choose my ventures carefully.' He was livid but he doubted that the General would notice his shaky voice. 'And the ice-harvesting? That must proceed as planned.'

'Naturally. But it is a secondary project – do you understand me? Nothing must get in the way of Project Eclipse.' The General's tone was threatening.

Robert swallowed. His father could still frighten him. 'What exactly is Wei in charge of?'

'Blasting a shipping lane. Our tankers have to reach the mining sites along the Hudson Mountains. He will open up a twenty-kilometre ice-free channel along the glacier's edge, so we can reach the Hudsons. Once the channel is open, our ice-breaker will keep it open.'

'I assume the detonations will be staggered, the iceberg first and then the shipping channel?'

'Correct. The berg will be blasted on the tenth of March, at ten hundred hours, your time. At twelve hundred hours, we will blast the shipping channel.'

'But that only gives the heavy-lifter two hours to secure the berg. That's too tight.'

'We cannot wait any longer. There is a risk that foreign military forces will try to stop us. By the end of the day more soldiers will arrive to secure the territory. They will parachute in and Wei will command them.'

The General ended the phone call and Robert stared at the handset for a long while. 'There's only room for one Zhao on Project Eclipse,' he hissed.

As he picked up his director's chair and flung it across the tent, he noticed Maddie for the first time. She was so still and so pale that, if her eyes hadn't been fixed on him, he might have thought her dead. Was it possible she had understood their conversation? It was time to get rid of her.

T MINUS 2 DAYS
8 March, 12:00 midday (UTC-07)

On board the *Professor Basov*, Captain Bolshakov and Alrek Tangen faced each other like gladiators in the ring. The beetroot-nosed, flabby-bellied Russian in his camel-coloured uniform glared at the stocky but athletic Norwegian expedition leader, who sported his tour company's branded fleece as if it were a royal insignia. If the matter hadn't been so serious, Luke would have laughed at the macho posturing. But Maddie's life depended on the outcome.

After the long morning trek down the mountain, and the boat trip to the ship, Luke had been allowed to shower and eat before he was locked in the surgery – one of the few cabins that actually had a key. Luke was amazed to learn that his house arrest was at the request of the Australian Antarctic Research Organisation's director, Andrew Winchester. Luke had demanded to speak to him, and a conference call was about to start. On the way to the communications room – escorted by Vitaly – they had passed the bridge and overheard the captain and Alrek arguing. Luke stepped onto the bridge, keen to dissipate the row. He could see the veins along Bolshakov's neck pulsating like tiny worms. Alrek's wide lips were clamped together and his muscular arms were folded tightly across his chest.

'*Kozel!*' shouted the captain.

Some spittle landed on Alrek's face and he wiped it away with his sleeve. 'How dare you insult me!' he seethed. Alrek had got to know some Russian swear words. 'I'm following protocols. We have to work with AARO. Wildman is their responsibility, and they must decide how to proceed. It's not up to us.'

Vitaly moved closer to his captain, ready to defend him if necessary.

'I captain this ship,' Bolshakov said. 'I decide where we go. I say we do rescue.'

'It's not that simple,' Alrek protested. 'Our guests are due in New Zealand at the end of the week. We are already two days behind schedule. And may I remind you that you are paid to get our guests back there – safely.'

'I don't give a shit about the tourists or AARO. It is the rule of the sea. We are the only ship near enough to find this woman. We will rescue her,' said Bolshakov, prodding Alrek in the chest.

'Stop this,' Luke said as he stepped between the two men, and, with firm pressure, pushed them apart. They stared stonily at him. 'Alrek, I don't care what you think I've done, but a woman's life rests in your hands. We have to sail to Pine Island Bay and send out a search party.'

Neither man moved.

Luke continued. 'Let's get this call over and done with, shall we? Precious time is wasting.'

Alrek shoved past him sourly and left the bridge.

'Captain, are you coming?' asked Luke.

'*Nyet*,' said Bolshakov, throwing his arms in the air. 'They think we Russians are stupid. AARO think Sergei does not know where your SOS come from. AARO say the SOS cannot come from Bettingtons. It must be from Hope Station. But they are wrong.' Sergei was the ship's radio operator. It was he who had been listening to the 500 kilohertz maritime distress frequency, out of idle curiosity. 'The AARO people insult Sergei. So I not waste my time speaking to them.'

With that, Bolshakov stomped away and relieved his second officer of control of the ship. He stood with his arms folded, staring out to sea. In front of him, the grey-painted radar tracked the ship's course.

'Captain,' Luke persevered, 'I need your help to persuade my boss that we should find Maddie.'

Bolshakov looked at him through bloodshot eyes. 'Vitaly tell me you are a brave man. He will go with you to search for this Maddie. If you wish, I will give you more men. But I will not speak to the Australian big boss.'

'Can you get us into Pine Island Bay?'

'I think, yes. Wind direction is good. It blows much ice out of the bay. This is very lucky.' The captain grinned and tapped the equipment in front of him. 'She is an old girl but bloody tough. She will break through the ice.'

'How long will it take to get there?'

The captain raised a pudgy finger and played with his handlebar moustache. 'That, my friend, I cannot say. You yakety yak with the big boss. I take us to Pine Island Bay.'

Luke knew that Bolshakov should not alter the ship's course without Alrek's agreement. After all, the tour company was paying the captain's wages. But he was grateful for the captain's rebelliousness and his old-fashioned heroic ideals. 'You are a man of honour,' Luke said.

As he and Vitaly continued on their way to the communications room, Luke stopped in the corridor. 'Whatever the outcome of this call, I'm going to search for Maddie,' Luke said. He kept his voice down. 'Can you get hold of Alrek's pistol? I lost my rifle in the avalanche.'

'*Da*. The pistol belongs to the captain. It is in the safe. I will take it.'

'Are there any other weapons?'

Vitaly's leathery face folded into a smile. 'I will get them,' he said knowingly.

'We'll need a tent, food, radios, head torches, ice axes. You know the sort of thing.'

'I will prepare,' said Vitaly, walking away.

In the ship's communications room, Luke sat down in front of a webcam mounted on a big screen. He exchanged an awkward greeting with the AARO head, Andrew Winchester, and the chief of station operations, Matt Lovedale, who were sitting at a long table in their Tasmanian headquarters.

Winchester, tall, lanky and white-haired, with a neat but nicotine-stained moustache, asked the first question. His voice had that gravelly tone that only a heavy smoker could muster. 'Luke, can you tell us what happened?'

Luke was desperate to understand why the director believed him a murderer, but he knew he had to demonstrate that he was calm and in control, and not the crazed killer they believed him to be. He spoke quietly, choosing his words with care.

'Some time after three am, my time, on the sixth of March, there was a fire at Hope Station. It was deliberately lit and they locked us in. Drilled the doors shut. Craig was on fire, screaming. We couldn't get out. The gas cylinders exploded, killing Blue. Sue was impaled on some debris. Maddie, Tubs and I escaped on snowmobiles, but they shot at us, hitting Tubs. Maddie had a piece of shrapnel in her leg …'

Luke cast his eyes down and squeezed them tight for a moment. He was back in the inferno again – he felt the heat, smelled the smoke, heard the screams. He broke out in a sweat. He forced his breathing to slow; he had to stay in control. Maddie's life depended on how he conducted himself in this debriefing. Now was not the time to crumble.

Matt Lovedale, whose head was disproportionately large for his body, seemingly reflecting his unusually long list of academic post-nominals, prompted Luke. 'Why do you think it was arson?'

'It *was* arson. The exits wouldn't open. We saw the intruders when we broke out. They had guns and they used them. I'm talking AK-47s.'

'Guns?' asked Lovedale. Luke saw incredulity on both men's faces.

'Who?' asked the director. 'Who wanted you dead?'

'You're not going to like this, given how important our relations are with them, but I believe they were from China. Maddie overheard them speaking Mandarin. She used to live in Hong Kong.'

'Pity Maddie isn't here to verify your story,' said Lovedale.

Winchester shook his head and clasped his stained fingers together on the desk. 'Luke, I'm sure you're aware by now that we have good reason to doubt your word.' Luke was about to interject when Winchester continued. 'The federal police have been contacted, but as there has never been a murder in the Antarctic before, they are trying to determine the best approach. Needless to say, the police and the Department of Defence want to speak to you, but I insisted that I speak to you first.'

'Thank you, Director, but I don't understand how you could possibly believe I would hurt my friends. I've been with AARO for seven years. You know me. I've saved lives. I wouldn't kill anyone.'

Winchester's blue eyes stared coldly at Luke. 'We know you've rescued colleagues before but you've also endangered them. We've put up with it because your research is outstanding.' He cleared his throat, like a rake over gravel.

'I have an email from Maddie to Matt,' he said, flicking a look at Lovedale, 'dated the fifth of March, expressing concern over your erratic, uncooperative and unbalanced behaviour. She thinks you are having a breakdown. This opinion is confirmed by Dr Frank Stone in a separate email. He describes your manner as "threatening" and "paranoid". On the seventh I received an anonymous call from someone claiming he was an old ham radio mate of yours. He said he was worried because you told him you were going to burn down the station because you couldn't stand the idea of spending the winter with "that bitch". I presume he meant Maddie, since it's clear from her reports that you two don't see eye to eye.'

'Who told you this lie?' challenged Luke.

'You tell me.'

Silence.

'How do you explain all this, Luke?'

If somebody had plunged their hand down his throat and yanked out his voicebox, Luke couldn't have been less able to speak. Everything that had happened over the last few days hit him all at once: the fire, the deaths, being hunted by killers, the dash across the mountains, his failure to protect Maddie and his burial in an avalanche. All his fight drained away.

He slumped forward and covered his pale face with his battered hands. How could Maddie have thought that about him? Had she been pretending to warm to him all this time because she feared he was a crazed murderer?

How could he explain her emails, indeed? Or the anonymous call? 'I can't,' he said.

Wendy Woo said goodbye to the last mourner. It was midday and already a humid twenty-six degrees Celsius. The air-conditioning didn't work and Jack's bungalow was an oven so her guests left early. Apart from Anthony Chan, only the caterers were still there, cleaning up after the wake.

Her father had been a popular and respected member of the community. More than sixty people – mainly immigrants like them – had attended the hurriedly organised funeral. Their tributes had been heartfelt. She had been surprised when a wreath arrived from Lenny Reid – the last client her dad had seen before he died. Of course, Reid's assistant would have ordered the flowers, but still, it was thoughtful.

Wendy shut the flyscreen door, leaned back against the sagging mesh and closed her eyes. Chan, his forehead beaded with sweat, hovered in the narrow hallway, his hands slightly raised, as if ready to catch her if she should fall.

'Do you want me to stay?' he asked.

'I feel so alone,' she mouthed, her words barely audible.

He took her in his arms and she wept.

The funeral had been a blur. It must have lasted an hour but it felt as if it had happened in five minutes. Wendy remembered everyone watching her as she spoke about her dad. They all knew they had fallen out. She had described their arrival in Australia as refugees, and how hard her dad had worked to build his business and to provide her with an education. She talked of his beloved friends, and she'd been careful to mention Anthony Chan, who'd sat in the front row, nodding his encouragement as she read the eulogy.

Her voice hadn't cracked, though, and she hadn't cried. She must have appeared pretty cold, but if she'd allowed her eyes to grow watery or her emotion to enter her voice, even for a second, she would have lost control and collapsed. So Wendy let them think she was an ungrateful bitch – as they probably already did. It was her way of getting through the funeral.

As her sobbing subsided, Chan handed her a handkerchief from his top pocket.

'I must look a mess,' she said, feeling awkward.

'You look lovely.'

Her short black Lisa Ho dress, with its beaded semi-circular neckline, was usually reserved for work functions. She remembered her dad asking her why she always wore black. Why not pinks, yellows and greens? At least it had been appropriate today. She squeezed Chan's hand.

'I'll be fine, Anthony. Really. You'd best get back to the office.'

He kissed her on the cheek and shuffled through the front yard to his car. She grabbed a half-full bottle of chilled sauvignon blanc and a glass, and walked into the backyard. It would be cooler under the liquidambar tree.

Settled into a plastic chair in the shade, Wendy could at last think about the post-mortem verdict. The pathologist had stuck to his original conclusion: Jack Woo had died of a heart attack. No poisons. Nothing unusual. No foul play.

One of the caterers popped his head out the door. 'We're off now,' he said. 'Everything's cleared.'

Wendy saw them out, leaving the front door open but the flyscreen door locked, and then returned to the garden. She scrolled though the stock market news bulletins on her iPhone. One headline immediately caught her attention: 'Dragon Resources on verge of big find'. It was all rumour, but the journalist had 'an insider' who claimed that Dragon Resources had discovered new oil deposits exceeding thirty billion barrels in an undisclosed location. If it were true, that would make the discovery one of the ten largest oil fields in the world, and new oil finds were unheard of these days.

It occured to Wendy that if she kept her mouth shut, and if Dragon Resources – legally or otherwise – found oil in Antarctica, then the shares currently in the name of Jack Woo Bespoke Tailoring would soon be worth a fortune. They now belonged to her. Far-fetched as it seemed, if she simply waited, she would be able to pay off the mortgage and have money left over. She gulped down the wine and poured another.

Would her conscience allow her to do something so very wrong? Dragon Resources was in breach of the Antarctic Treaty. Should she contact the authorities? Increasingly desperate oil companies had been lobbying for years to be allowed to drill there. They'd been like vultures, tearing at the flesh of their governments, threatening the collapse of the world economy if more oil couldn't be found. Oil was pushing two hundred US dollars a barrel now, which meant that the huge cost of drilling in such a remote place might become economically possible, especially given how difficult the commercial exploitation of oil sands was proving.

What was she thinking? She didn't need the money. Her dad had only invested in this venture because he wanted to free her mother from Heizuizi. Wendy stared up into the liquidambar's branches. She had climbed it often in her tomboy teens, entranced by its vibrant orange and red leaves. How many times had she sat in that tree and peered off into the distance, wondering where her mother was? Could she still be alive today?

Wendy licked away what remained of her Gypsy Rose lip gloss. She would do anything to free her mother, and if it meant raising two million dollars, then she would do it. The shares in Dragon Resources could be a way of generating at least some of that two million. She'd talk to Chan in the morning and see if he knew who her father was dealing with at Heizuizi.

She heard the familiar screech of the front door's flyscreen. She was sure she'd locked it. Wendy shuddered, despite the heat. Someone was in her dad's house. She grabbed her phone and, holding up the bottle as a weapon, walked towards the back window. Perhaps she was being paranoid? Perhaps the caterers had forgotten something and she hadn't actually locked the flyscreen at all?

Wendy saw something move in the sitting room and then it was gone. It looked like a man in black, wearing shades and a baseball cap. Had one of the mourners popped back? He had quickly disappeared from view.

Then Wendy heard a crash that sounded as if it were coming from her dad's bedroom. Terrified, she backed away and ran towards the neighbour's fence. Despite her dress, she easily clambered over it. Safe on the other side, she dialled triple-zero and requested the police.

Raising her head to look over the fence, Wendy saw a man calmly watching her through her bedroom window. He pointed his finger at her as if it were a gun barrel, then raised it a fraction as if he had fired at her. She ran.

***

Some hours later, after the police had come and gone, Wendy was back in the security of her hotel room nibbling on chocolate to calm her nerves.

Wendy was now more convinced than ever that her father had been murdered. The intruder's presence was a clear warning. She had been terrified at the time but now she was getting angry. 'Fuck you!' she said to the walls. 'I don't scare easily.'

Wendy pulled up the Australian Stock Exchange data to check out Dragon Resources' share price. Her almond-shaped eyes widened and she sat forward, peering at her smartphone. The company was up over forty per cent since the market had opened that morning. It had received a 'please explain' from the exchange, to which it had responded with a vague statement that left plenty of room for interpretation. They were milking the frenzy.

She couldn't help but smile. 'Well, I'll be!' she said aloud. 'You were right, Dad.'

If she was going to capitalise, Wendy had to act quickly. She hesitated for a fraction of a second and then rang Anthony Chan and asked him to find the paperwork that proved her ownership of the shares belonging to Jack Woo Bespoke Tailoring. She said she wanted it faxed immediately to her broker.

'What are you up to?' asked Chan.

'It's best you don't know.'

At a little after four in the afternoon, Wendy called her broker, who reminded her that the Hong Kong Stock Exchange was three hours behind Sydney, though he strongly advised her not to sell yet, believing the shares in Dragon Resources hadn't peaked.

'You can't be sure,' Wendy replied. 'This rumour could turn out to be hot air. No, I want you to sell every share immediately.'

Frustrated at having to wait, Wendy went to a café for a strong coffee. The market was in a frenzy of excitement about the company's mysterious new oil source, and every last one of her shares sold within an hour. She made a profit of almost four hundred thousand dollars. That, together with the money originally invested, gave her just over one point three million. It was bribery money, to free her mother. She didn't feel good about it.

As Wendy stared at the black stain in her empty coffee cup, she felt guilty. Logging in to her work server, she dug further into Dragon Resources. She found an announcement from a marine engineering company in Zhuhai. The company had been commissioned to build the world's largest semi-submersible heavy-lift vessel for Dragon Resources. Perhaps the oil was under the bay, rather than the glacier, and they needed to transport a rig?

There was a quote from the Hood Group's Chief Investment Officer, who had bragged about how he would turn around the company's fortunes and steer it to a new, highly profitable future. There was a photograph. She enlarged the image. Those eyes … She knew those eyes. Fear masked by arrogance.

A shriek escaped her mouth, her hand shot up and the coffee cup flew to the pavement and smashed. 'No, no,' Wendy cried.

'Please, God!'

She knew the eyes, but she didn't know the name Robert Zhao. Those eyes belonged to Zhao Sheng, General Zhao's only child. He must have changed his name.

The General had tortured and imprisoned her mother. Had the son, Robert, killed her father to protect his Antarctic venture? No, the boy she had met could not have done that. But what kind of man had he become?

'Are you all right?' asked the waitress, picking up the shattered cup.

'I'm sorry – can I have another?' Wendy stammered.

She googled Robert Zhao. Rich, respected and feared, he was a top dog in the world of private equity, a pillar of Hong Kong society and a supporter of worthy causes. But would he sanction murder? Would he come after her too?

Murder was more his father's style. Wendy struggled to control the hatred she harboured for General Zhao. Sweat dripped down her temples. Her father was dead but her mother might still be alive. She had to know.

Placing her life on the line, Wendy sent Robert an email at the Hood Group. She signed it 'Woo Huo'. He would recognise that name. They shared a terrible secret.

Robert brooded over his father's double-cross like a scab that had to be picked. He had discovered that Captain Wei and a much larger band of explosives experts had spent the ten weeks before his arrival at the camp laying explosives along the Fitzgerald Fissure. That team had left. After Robert's arrival onsite, Tang and Li kept a surreptitious eye out for any signs of malfunction.

Project Eclipse had a separate master controller and five signal relay boxes placed inside the fissure at four-kilometre intervals along the length of the crevasse. The electronic detonators were programmed to send a warning message if there were any problems. These Wei's team had secretly fixed while pretending to be working on the water project. Robert had been well and truly hoodwinked. Nobody at Dragon Resources had dared to warn him. They knew only too well how vengeful his father was. Robert would deal with those executives later. Most importantly of all, he would make his father pay.

But for now, he wanted to be satisfied that this new venture – mining bastnäsite – was as big as the General had boasted. He couldn't allow emotion to get in the way of business. His team at the Hood Group had sent him data on the rare earths industry, and he had received the investment proposal from his father – both as encrypted emails. After several phone calls, he made his decision.

'I'm in,' he emailed General Zhao. 'But dump your investors. You will do this with the Hood Group alone. My people will send the papers.'

He was distracted by an incoming email. The sender's name, Wendy Woo, was unknown to him but the subject caught his eye: Woo Ling. Oh yes, he remembered her.

Robert's right hand trembled as he opened the email and saw who it was from: Woo Huo, the daughter. Wendy must be her Western name. All his fury at his father faded. His brow uncreased and his face softened. He felt compassion, an emotion he hadn't allowed himself to experience for a long time. He remembered her terror and his powerlessness to protect her. He would never forget her screams. Why had she contacted him after all these years?

He breathed deeply and read through the email.

Robert

My mother, Woo Ling, was arrested twenty years ago for practising Falun Gong. You know the rest. I believe she may still be alive and imprisoned at Heizuizi Women's Forced Labour Camp in Jilin Province. You are now a man of considerable power and influence and I beg you to help me locate and free her. You owe me that much, Robert. I have never spoken to anyone of that terrible day.

Woo Huo

Her email address indicated she was probably living in Australia. He hoped she had made a good life for herself there. He lit a cigarette, but after one drag he left it in the ashtray.

Robert knew he should not reply. There must be nothing to link him to that family. It was exactly the kind of scandal he had engineered to destroy his own rivals. And he knew he could expect no better if the truth should come to light. But if there was one moment in his life that Robert allowed himself to regret – and regret was a luxury for losers, he knew – it was that terrible day when Huo's mother was arrested. None of it would have happened if his father hadn't hated Falun Gong so intensely.

From his clothes bag, Robert took a rolled-up velvet cloth the size of a placemat. He laid it out flat and touched a lock of perfectly straight black hair, tied in a white ribbon. He stroked its softness, careful not to pull any of the delicate strands from the ribbon. It was his mother's.

'Father blamed them,' he said aloud. 'But he drove you to it.'

She had lived in fear of her husband and sought solace from her miserable existence by secretly joining a small group of Falun Gong practitioners. But, ultimately, what drove her to suicide was the cruelty inflicted on Robert by his father. If she tried to stop Robert's beatings, she received them instead. She'd fallen into a deep depression and hanged herself in the kitchen.

Robert lifted his crippled left hand. 'He caught you teaching me the piano – do you remember, Mother? I was seven. You gave me lessons at school so he wouldn't know. My best times. I remember your smile. But someone betrayed you.'

He tried to straighten his damaged fingers, using his other hand. His own smile faded as he remembered the General's anger.

My son is going to military school. Music is for girls, not men! Never again!

'Remember, Mother? That's when he smashed his revolver down on my hand, just to be sure I never played again.'

Robert picked up a small hand mirror and stared at his face in the glass, then slung it across the tent. It bounced off the tent wall and shattered on the hard floor.

'You left me! Alone with *him*.'

He still had her suicide note. If his father had found her first, the note would have been destroyed. But Robert had discovered her when he came home from school. He'd instinctively known to take the letter, lying on the floor beneath her dangling feet.

Robert drew hard on his cigarette, then glanced back at the email illuminated on his laptop screen. Woo. Hadn't his father sent the assassin, King, to deal with an Australian tailor named Woo, who'd discovered their Antarctic project? It was a common name. Still, was it possible that their lives could be so intertwined that, yet again, the Zhaos had killed another Woo?

Woo Huo had kept their secret. He owed her the truth. He would choose his words carefully so as not to implicate himself. She would understand his meaning.

'It's too late,' he typed. 'So very sorry.'

T MINUS 1 DAY, 12 HOURS, 34 MINUTES
8 March, 11:26 pm (UTC-07)

Luke was woken by Alrek, who shook him brusquely, told him to dress and then escorted him to the comms room. On the screen, a dishevelled Lovedale was tapping his fingers as he waited for Winchester to join him. It was 5:26 pm of the following day in Tasmania.

'Matt, what's happening?'

'We must wait for Andrew,' Lovedale replied.

'What's the emergency response team doing?' Luke probed.

'The team's in place but we can't rush into this,' Lovedale said. 'We're talking to the Brits and the Yanks to see what they can do. You're on the only ice-breaker in the area. The director, the Department of Defence and the tour operator have to agree if the *Basov* should get involved.'

'Get involved? Christ!'

'Calm down, will you?'

Alrek stood, ready to escort him out.

'I'm okay, Alrek,' Luke said, then turned his attention back to Lovedale. 'Both Rothera and McMurdo have planes.'

'Gone for the winter. Anyway, you don't have a cleared runway.'

'Get the SAS, then. They can fly to McMurdo, refuel

and parachute in.' Luke was growing more agitated.

'Luke, you need to focus on clearing your name.'

'I don't give a shit about my name. We should be looking for Maddie. Right now!'

Lovedale folded his arms across his chest. 'Leave it to us, Luke.'

Luke sighed. If they didn't trust him, they wouldn't share their rescue strategy with him. He understood that. 'Those emails are fake,' he said as calmly as he could. 'That's just not how it was. Yes, I occasionally pissed Maddie off because I didn't follow protocols but I wasn't crazy, and Blue never said anything about my mental health.'

Matt shook his head. 'I'm sorry, but there's nobody to corroborate your story. All we know is this,' he said, holding an aerial image of the burned-out station close to the webcam so Luke could see it. 'Not much left, huh?' Matt said bitterly, as if it were all Luke's fault.

Luke checked the date and time at the bottom of the satellite image. 'This was taken yesterday afternoon,' he said. 'Surely you must have known something was wrong before then? Wasn't the complete communications blackout a big giveaway that we were in trouble?'

Matt leaned back, as if to distance himself from the big man glaring at him, even though Luke was almost six thousand kilometres away. 'None of the emergency systems were activated. Mac called in, on schedule, saying everything was A-OK. We only grew suspicious when family members told us they hadn't had any contact, that planned calls had been missed, birthdays forgotten and so on. And by the way, it's not easy to get the United States to move a surveillance satellite over Antarctica. We had to call in a big favour to get these images.'

Bloody red tape, Luke thought bitterly. Maddie might have been safely on board by now if AARO had asked for American assistance earlier. He was about to speak when Winchester entered the Tasmanian boardroom. He went straight to the phone on the sideboard and moved it to the table, then pressed the loudspeaker button.

Winchester addressed the person on the other end of the line. 'Miss, you're on loudspeaker.'

He then looked from Matt to Luke and Alrek. 'This caller wishes to remain anonymous, but she may have useful information.

Can you all please listen to what she has to say? Remember, our situation remains highly confidential.' He was telling them not to reveal anything that she didn't already know. 'Miss, can we give you a made-up name? To make things easier. How about Julie?'

'Fine,' the woman said. 'But I want to know who I'm talking to. Everyone listening. And no tracing this call. It's a pay-as-you-go mobile.' She had a strong Aussie twang.

Luke smiled despite the severity of the situation. Feisty. Reminded him of Maddie.

Winchester introduced everyone, then continued the discussion. 'Julie, can you tell them what you just told me?'

'I believe the Dragon Resources Corporation is drilling for oil in Antarctica, and they're doing it – or they're about to do it – right near your Hope Station.'

Winchester and Lovedale barely raised an eyebrow. They were hard men to convince. But Luke blanched. So that's what they were willing to kill for – oil! Was Dragon Resources a Chinese company?

Before he could speak, Winchester chipped in. 'The Antarctic Treaty forbids—'

Julie cut across his words. 'I know, I've done my research. But I'm telling you they are already there. Have you seen the market today? It's gone ballistic because of rumours they've found massive oil reserves in an "undisclosed location".'

'But that could be anywhere—'

She cut in again. 'I have the coordinates.'

'Go ahead,' Winchester said, and waited.

She was silent. Luke sensed that she was afraid to give them, despite her bravado. Luke alone appreciated that she might be putting her life in danger.

'Julie? Are you there?' Winchester prodded.

Luke stepped in. 'Julie, this is Luke Searle here. Please tell me the coordinates. Someone very dear to me is in danger, and your information could save her life.'

'Luke!' Winchester chastised.

'Seventy-four degrees and fifty-two minutes south, one hundred degrees and thirty minutes west.'

243

Luke gasped. He pulled a large map towards him and pointed. 'That's on the very edge of the Hudson Mountains, barely half a kilometre from the Fitzgerald Fissure.'

'That's the seaward end of the Hudsons, isn't it?' asked Lovedale.

'Yes,' Luke said. 'If this is correct, their camp is on the other side of the glacier from our station. Jesus, to think they were so near us and we never knew.'

Winchester cleared his throat loudly and frowned at Luke. Julie hadn't known that Luke was from Hope. He wanted her knowledge of the situation kept to a minimum.

Luke ran his hand over his unshaven chin. 'Julie, where is Dragon Resources' headquarters?'

'China. The head office is in Shanghai, but it's majority-owned by a private-equity firm in Hong Kong called the Hood Group.'

'Matt here. China has a station in the area. Perhaps you are mistaken and your data refers to activity at Li Bai Station,' he said, to test her conviction.

'Do you think I'm stupid?' Julie snapped. 'No, those are not the coordinates for Li bloody Bai.' With her voice ripe with sarcasm, she continued. 'Why don't you contact your station and ask them to take a look? They could walk on over and introduce themselves.'

If only they could, Luke thought.

Vast distances separated the woman they had named Julie from Luke and AARO's headquarters, but she sensed she had hit a raw nerve. 'Guys, are you still there?'

'We're here,' Winchester replied.

'Sorry I yelled, but I'm taking a big risk talking to you. I'm a little tense.'

'Let's move on, shall we?' Winchester suggested.

'Okay,' said Luke. 'Everything you've said makes perfect sense, but one thing worries me. Those coordinates are on the edge of one of the world's largest and most unstable glaciers. It wouldn't be possible to drill for oil through a moving ice sheet. The drill would snap, for a start. Why do you believe it's oil? Could it be something else?'

'Well, the news on the market is oil. And have you seen where WTI is trading nowadays? But yeah, it's possible the journos have it wrong. Dragon also mines coal, uranium, natural gas, iron ore …'

'What's WTI?' asked Lovedale.

'West Texas Intermediate,' Julie said. 'It's an oil price.'

Alrek spoke up. 'What about in the Hudson Mountains themselves? The mountains don't shift like the glacier does.'

Winchester tugged at the yellowing ends of his white moustache.

'If we assume that this Dragon Resources is in Antarctica, we have to ask, what would China risk war over? For what would they risk worldwide condemnation? Because if this is true and they've murdered our people to get at a resource, then it has to be something very valuable indeed.'

It dawned on Luke that Winchester, Lovedale and Tangen now seemed to believe in the possibility that a hostile group was on the Pine Island Glacier. He felt his energy returning, as if his batteries had recharged.

'Coal?' suggested Alrek.

'Not rare enough,' said Lovedale.

'Water?' Luke proposed.

Alrek snorted with derision.

Luke ignored him. 'Okay, it sounds crazy. But China's rivers are polluted and dying. The Yangtze supplies something like one hundred and eighty cities, and it's so dirty that it's known as the cancerous river. And their farmland is drying up.'

The woman agreed. 'Yeah, food security is a big deal when you've got over a billion people. And without water you can't grow crops.'

'I know China's spending billions on energy intensive desalination plants and their cloud seeding has never really got anywhere,' Luke said. 'They're running out of options.'

'Come off it,' Alrek said. 'Convert a glacier into water? And how do you transport it halfway around the world?'

'I have no idea,' said Luke, warming to the theory, 'but the tip of the Pine Island Glacier is perfect for harvesting because it's already floating on the sea.'

'But how do they get it back to China?' Alrek laughed. 'Tow it? Ridiculous!'

'Not as ridiculous as you think,' Luke replied seriously. 'Iceberg towing has been tried before, as far back as the seventies. I remember reading an article in 2006 about England's Thames Water considering towing Arctic bergs, and at least one Middle Eastern country was looking into the logistics of it.'

'That's true,' said Matt, whose engineering background was firing his enthusiasm for the idea. 'Oil companies have been towing bergs away from their rigs for years. But you wouldn't necessarily need to tow. If you found a way to crunch a berg into smaller pieces, you could do it piecemeal, carry it in one of those supertankers we found lying low inside Whalers Island.'

'Whalers?'

Matt nodded. 'The satellite images revealed two supertankers inside Whalers Island. The sulphurous mist cleared just enough for us to make them out.'

'It would cost a fortune,' Alrek protested.

'Cost is all relative,' Luke answered. 'Water is now traded on the stock exchange. If someone had enough money to invest in ice-harvesting, they could make a fortune. And given how desperate the Chinese are for water, they might just be crazy enough to try something like this.'

'I agree,' said Julie. 'I read a piece the other day that said the barrel price for water is over two hundred and fifty US dollars. That's more than the price of oil. You know, if that's what Dragon Resources is doing, they'd be creating a whole new industry: ice-harvesting. That's actually pretty clever.'

Winchester spoke. 'Luke, do you really think this could have legs?'

'I don't know. Maybe. Some things just don't make sense, though. It's hard to believe that the guys we know from Li Bai would do something bad for Antarctica. And I know their research is focused on the Hudsons, not the glacier. Zhu Guoming – one of their scientists – was drilling in the Hudsons to establish the age and volcanic history of the range. My point is – if they're after ice, why would they waste time in the mountains?'

'Perhaps Zhu's research isn't connected,' said Lovedale.

'I don't buy it,' Winchester said. 'There is no way this kind of activity would be sanctioned by the Chinese government.' Scepticism was setting in again.

'But what if it's not sanctioned?' Julie said. 'What if it's a venture the government knows nothing about?'

'Andrew here. Julie, do you have any actual evidence? Copies of documents from Dragon Resources, photographs of the site?'

'No,' she said.

Winchester continued, 'Where does your information come from?'

'Can't tell you,' Julie replied. 'Actually, there is one other thing. I don't know what it means or whether it's even connected. It could be a project name or a code word or something.'

'Go on,' Winchester said.

She paused, clearly feeling foolish. 'Does the word "shepherd" mean anything to any of you?'

Luke almost leaped out of his chair. 'Of course it does! It's Shepherd Dome – at the southern end of the Hudsons!'

Winchester cleared his throat. 'I think it's time to thank Julie and say goodbye. You've been enormously helpful. You may have saved a life.'

'Really? Okay, well, that's cool.'

'Wait,' Luke broke in. 'One more question. Does the name General Zhao mean anything to you?'

Silence.

'Julie? Who is he?' pressed Luke.

'Why? Why do you ask?'

Luke could hardly hear her, her bravado gone. 'I think he's here,' he said. 'Here in Antarctica.'

A gasp – more like sob. 'Then God help you all.'

'Julie, what do you mean?' Luke's voice betrayed his panic.

No response.

'Julie! Please.'

'Your friend is in terrible danger. He's very high up in the Chinese military. A brutal, cruel man.'

The line went dead. She'd ended the call. For a long moment nobody spoke, shocked by the revelations.

'Andrew, do you believe me now?' Luke said.

Winchester cleared his throat. 'Her story seems possible, but if this General Zhao is in Antarctica, this is much bigger than I can handle. We have to get Canberra involved.' He rubbed his forehead. 'In the meantime, Luke, you'll need to convince the police of your innocence.'

'I can prove I didn't start the fire. Let me go to Hope. I can show Alrek the bullets. The bolts drilled to the outside of the exits.

But for pity's sake, man, you have to get the SAS here. Maddie's in grave danger.'

A rough plan was forming in Luke's mind. Once at Hope Station, he and Vitaly could steal away. 'Do the satellite images show anything of the general's camp?' he asked.

'Nothing,' Lovedale replied. 'It must be well camouflaged.'

'Alrek,' said Winchester, 'ask the captain to take the ship into Pine Island Bay, as long as it isn't endangering the people on board. Then wait for further instructions. I need to talk to the Department of Defence and the PM. And Luke?' The director stared pointedly at his brilliant but rebellious glaciologist. 'Luke, you're already in more shit than you can imagine. Do not, repeat, do not attempt to find Maddie. Leave that to the professionals.'

★ ★ ★

It wasn't until she had ended her call to AARO that Wendy noticed a reply from Robert in her inbox. She felt sick opening his email, and even sicker once she had read it. She curled into a ball and cried.

The next morning, Luke stood near one of Hope Station's giant hydraulic legs, flanked by Vitaly, Alrek, Captain Bolshakov and Rod, the ship's doctor. Luke was glad he had managed to speak to Jason by phone last night. His son's joy in life and innocent chatter about a friend's birthday party had reminded him to stay positive. It gave him strength now, as he looked up at the blackened, gnarled devastation that used to be his home.

Vitaly whistled through his front teeth, shaking his head. Luke knew his friend had seen much destruction and death while in the army, but even he appeared taken aback. Bolshakov, the oldest and least fit of the party, was still puffing after the steep walk from where they had beached the Zodiac. His moustache carried ice crystals of frozen breath, and his head was covered by a fur-lined hat with earflaps. To the surprise of both Luke and Alrek, he had insisted on coming with them, leaving his first officer in charge of the ship.

Between gulps for breath, Bolshakov said something in Russian as he squinted at the collapsed roof. 'Holy Mother of God,' Vitaly translated.

Luke felt Alrek's eyes on him. 'I didn't do this. Look, man, for God's sake! Look. Why on earth would I do this?'

Alrek ignored his question. 'I'll check the exit doors for bolts. Luke, take Rod to the bodies. Captain Bolshakov and Vitaly, can you start to search for shell casings in the garage? Be careful, everyone. The structure looks close to collapse.'

The Norwegian had assumed the role of leader and Bolshakov hadn't challenged him; on land, he was out of his element. Luke was content to let Alrek think he was in charge. When the moment was right, he would put his plan into action.

'What if the soldiers are still here?' Rod asked, who had been brought up to speed on the situation.

They all looked around for signs of movement. Vitaly gripped the captain's Makarov pistol in his bare hand. He had removed his gloves so he could feel the trigger. Alrek, who was carrying an ice axe, had been furious that Bolshakov insisted that Vitaly have the Makarov. Luke was unarmed, at the Norwegian's insistence.

Bolshakov produced a flick knife. He released the blade, his eyes scanning the terrain. Rod carried nothing but his emergency medical pack. The wind was a low purr and Luke listened for any unusual sound. No gunfire. No unknown voices. No snowmobiles racing in their direction. They appeared to be alone.

Alrek was the first to climb the steps to the main entrance and the exterior walkway. Rod and Luke followed closely. Luke's heart was racing. He felt his stomach cramping, as if he were going to vomit. Luke stumbled on the top step. He recovered himself and pointed to the bolted exit door. 'Take a look. Bolts crudely drilled to the outside of the door. It's the same on the other exit. I was inside, trying to escape.'

'Show Rod where the bodies are,' Alrek said, unmoved.

Luke led them along the walkway and, dodging some rubble, stepped through the shattered window of Craig's room. Rod kneeled down and brushed the snow from Craig's skinned face, which was now glazed with an icy sheen. Luke turned away.

'Craig Anderson. Carpenter and fire chief,' Luke said, his mouth dry. He spoke quietly, with reverence.

Rod nodded, shaken, and staggered to stand. They moved on to what remained of the kitchen, passing the lift shaft.

'Sue Sadri, plumber, and over there is Dr Frank Stone, known as Blue.'

Luke looked away again. He heard the sound of retching and turned to find Rod being sick.

'I've never seen ...' the doctor began to say. He wiped his mouth with his sleeve, then looked up at Luke, his eyes wet. 'We must get them back to the ship.' But it was a while before he moved. 'Terrible,' he murmured.

Alrek had just joined them, and he reeled backwards when he saw the bodies. His gloved hand shot up to his mouth.

Rod pulled himself together. 'The others?'

'Pete MacNamara and Dave Cox were murdered before the fire,' Luke said. 'We thought it was a crevasse accident but it wasn't.' Luke shook his head at having been so easily duped. 'Their bodies are in the garage.'

Alrek frowned. 'Why?'

'That was the coldest place – except the food freezer, and we couldn't put our friends ...' Luke couldn't finish. He simply led Rod and Alrek out of the station and down the steps to the garage, where Vitaly and Bolshakov were searching for shell casings. The bodies of Dave and Mac were a macabre mix of scorched, blackened skin and melted white plastic.

'I see many bad things in my time,' Bolshakov said. 'Many deaths. But this,' he gestured around, 'this is act of cowardice. This is like the killing of sheep ... How you say?'

'Slaughter,' said Rod.

'That leaves one more person, excluding Madeline Wildman,' said Alrek. His practicality was jarring to Luke, but he knew the Norwegian was upset. He had turned very pale.

'Tubs, our chef. He's at a hut not far from here. Died of a bullet wound to the lung. There's proof for you. You'll find an AK-47 bullet in his chest,' Luke said bitterly. 'How the hell would I have an AK-47?'

Vitaly plodded over and held out his hand. In it was a shell casing, the size of an AA battery. '*Nyet*, not AK-47, my friend. People always think AK-47. Too many movies. This is from Chinese rifle, QBZ-97. Chinese army use QBZ-95 but it cannot take M-16 ammunition.

So they cannot sell this to other countries. They develop the 97 so it can take M-16 ammunition. This,' he held up the cartridge casing and swivelled it in his callused fingers, 'is a small casing. It come from Chinese QBZ-97.'

'How do you know that?' Alrek challenged.

The bull-necked Russian squared up to Alrek. 'In the Russian army we fight with AK-74s. Seventy-four, not forty-seven,' he emphasised. 'But I study the weapons of my enemy. I study American M-16 and Chinese QBZ-95 and 97.' He handed the casing to the Norwegian. 'Show your people. They will tell you Vitaly is correct.'

Alrek stared at the shell for a long moment and then looked up at Luke. 'I'm sorry I didn't believe you, Luke. It just seemed so ...'

'Unreal? Tell me about it,' said Luke.

Luke held out his hand. Alrek shook it, then spoke again. 'You've been through hell. I ... I'll report in to Winchester. The priority is to find Madeline.'

'Maddie.' Luke corrected him.

'Yes. I'll work on Winchester – we need the SAS here immediately.' Alrek left the garage, and soon they heard him talking into his satellite phone.

Vitaly turned his back to Alrek and checked Rod was out of earshot. He whispered, 'Snowmobile. It work?' He nodded at the last snowmobile parked at the end of the line. All the other vehicles looked too badly damaged to be useful. 'We take it?'

Rod joined Alrek outside and asked him to organise more men to help carry the bodies back to the Zodiac. They would also need the second boat for transportation.

Luke inspected the snowmobile. The compartment under the seat contained a complete recovery kit, including ropes, ice hammer and harness. He couldn't believe his luck. At last something was going right for a change. It needed fuel but the petrol storage tank had escaped the conflagration; it was situated some distance from the main building. Luke turned the ignition and it started perfectly. 'Let's fill her up and get out of here,' he said.

Bolshakov touched Vitaly's shoulder. He held up his flick knife, now closed. 'You take this,' he said. 'And give my Baikal-442 to Luke.'

Vitaly placed the second gun in Luke's hand.

'When were you going to tell me about this?' Luke asked, surprised to learn that the Russians had more weapons.

'There is a saying in Russia. "When two knows, then the pig knows." It means that once you tell your secret, everyone knows,' said Vitaly. 'I did not want Alrek to have this gun.'

Luke understood. He put the Baikal-442 in his inside pocket. 'Thank you, Captain.'

'You must go,' Bolshakov ordered. 'We will look after the dead. You have my word.'

The three men were huddled together in close conversation and hadn't noticed Alrek approaching. 'I'm coming with you,' the Norwegian said.

No one responded.

'Winchester is asking for immediate SAS deployment,' Alrek continued, 'but it will take them around nine hours to get here, weather permitting.' He looked up at the grey sky. 'Andrew says it's most likely they'll parachute in, but there's a blizzard warning for dusk. So,' Alrek clapped his gloved hands together, 'it could be up to us.'

'Are you sure?' Luke asked, stunned by his change of heart.

Alrek moved closer. 'I'm sure. After seeing this, I can't just wait here. Tomorrow could be too late.'

'They've killed six people already. If they catch us, they'll kill us.'

' "*For fred og frihet*." That's what my national service medal says. For peace and freedom. These people have threatened the peace of this place, and our peace too. I've made up my mind. I'm just sorry I didn't believe you earlier.'

Luke glanced at Vitaly, who shrugged his agreement to their third team member.

'Welcome aboard,' Luke said, slapping Alrek on the back.

'Captain,' said Alrek, 'will you liaise with AARO? Keep pushing for the SAS to come as soon as possible.'

Bolshakov nodded and took the satellite phone from Alrek.

'Okay, Luke,' Alrek said. 'What's next?'

'We have one working snowmobile. Two of us can ride it but not three. If we can find a trailer or sled, one of us can ride in that.

254

It'll be bumpy but it'll get us there. We'll have to cross the full width of the glacier tongue and then turn inland, following the line of the Hudson Mountains. We'll carry spare fuel.'

'Take this,' Bolshakov said, handing Luke his two-way radio. 'Good to have a spare radio.'

'Can we make it before nightfall?' asked Alrek.

'I hope so, but we've got a tent and sleeping bags. A stove. Enough food.'

'Only two sleeping bags,' said Vitaly.

'Well, we'll just have to huddle up,' Alrek said cheerfully.

Vitaly raised his eyes at the idea of huddling close to Alrek and Luke couldn't help but laugh.

It had taken all day to cross the width of the Pine Island Glacier and turn inland, following the lower slopes of the Hudson Mountains. Towing a trailer had slowed their pace, and Luke had begun to wonder if bringing Alrek was a good idea. They were only equipped for two.

As they'd got closer to the killers' camp, Luke had made the decision to leave the snowmobile behind, together with the spare radio for emergencies. He was afraid the engine noise might give them away. Now the three men were tied together in a line as they trudged the last one hundred metres. Daylight was fading fast and a storm was threatening. Luke was in front, taking the worst of the wind's pummelling, then Vitaly, and finally Alrek, who seemed to cope with the gusts and the snowdrifts as if he were strolling across a lawn on a summer's day.

Luke felt a tug on the rope behind him. Vitaly's foot had sunk knee deep into the soft surface ice and he'd fallen forward. Luke pulled him up.

'Do I need to carry you?' Luke grinned behind his balaclava. As he spoke, ice the size of sugar granules flew into his mouth and melted on his tongue. He clamped his jaw shut quickly.

Vitaly pushed down the scarf coiled round his mouth

and neck. 'You are very funny man. Ha!' He brushed the snow off his waterproof trousers. 'You want me to take the lead now?'

Luke imagined his friend parting the storm like the prow of a big ship, but he was best equipped to spot a crevasse hidden by snow so he declined the offer. He eyed with trepidation the looming clouds, which hung over the Hudsons like a filthy net curtain. He turned into the wind and began moving again.

A few minutes later, Luke held up his hand to signal a halt. According to Julie's coordinates, they should be almost at Dragon Resources' camp. The three men ducked behind an icy, dune-like sastruga and peered downhill. They could see nothing but a rolling expanse of ice below them.

Luke pulled out his binoculars. The snowy spindrift made visibility difficult. He scanned the area methodically, willing the camp to materialise. At last he saw something and pointed. 'There.'

The sun was low and light was poor, so the site would have been impossible to spot if a couple of tents hadn't glowed softly, like Chinese lanterns.

'Let's move closer,' Luke said. 'But keep your head down.'

They crept downhill and nearer the camp, then they hid behind a group of boulders, each one the size of a small car. By peering through a narrow gap, Luke could just make out some tiny triangular red flags on poles, which marked the camp's perimeter. But there was no national flag, which was unusual in Antarctica. The tents were a light colour – probably white – and white canopies covered what might be vehicles. No wonder the satellite image hadn't revealed their position. Even the generator had been painted white, as had a long line of shipping containers. Three Weatherhaven tents stood side by side, their entrances facing away from the wind. A snowmobile was parked outside one of them and its red paint drew Luke's attention like a beacon. Further along, there were six smaller pyramid tents.

'Why are there so many storage containers?' Alrek whispered.

'I guess they have a lot of equipment,' Luke replied.

'I hope they are not full of explosives,' said Vitaly, sucking on his teeth.

There must have been twenty containers, painted white, all of them the maximum size a tractor train could transport across the ice.

'Explosives?' Alrek frowned.

'*Da*,' said Vitaly, with no explanation. 'Why is there no guard?'

'The arrogant bastards assume no one's going to stop them,' Luke spat bitterly. Alrek looked toward the site warily. 'They can't hear us,' Luke continued, recovering his composure. 'The wind's too loud.'

'If they have a prisoner, then why no guard? I do not like this,' Vitaly warned.

'Too cold, perhaps,' said Luke.

'Now what?' asked Alrek.

Luke looked around. 'Can you two put up the tent? I'm going to watch for signs of Maddie. We need to know where they're keeping her. If we know, we might be able to sneak in under the cover of darkness.'

His companions nodded. 'The storm is settling in,' said Alrek, his voice raised above the gale. 'That means there will be no SAS. Nobody flies in a whiteout.'

'We're on our own, then,' said Luke, watching the camp through his binoculars.

A man, short but built like a bulldog, appeared from the first Weatherhaven, an assault rifle in his hand. He went into the second Weatherhaven. Another man appeared from that second tent and carried a tray of food into the first. He was unarmed. *So that's where the General is*, thought Luke. Only the leader would have his food brought to him on a tray.

Over the next hour, a lot of activity was focused on the second large tent, which Luke concluded must be the mess. Only one soldier exited the third Weatherhaven. His behaviour was odd. He paced outside the tent, then went inside, then paced outside again. Given the wind chill, it was madness for him to be outside. Eventually, the man battled through the winds to one of the canopies covering what appeared to be other snowmobiles and disappeared beneath it.

It was almost dark and all the men wore white parkas, so it was difficult to differentiate between them, but Luke thought he counted eight men. He was growing concerned that he had seen no sign of Maddie. Perhaps her leg was very bad and she couldn't walk? Or perhaps she wasn't there? Luke let the binoculars drop and he rubbed his tired eyes.

'Any sign of her?' asked Alrek, kneeling down next to Luke.

'No,' he replied, brushing snowflakes from his face. He filled Alrek in on what he had seen.

'Perhaps the tray of food was for Maddie, if she can't walk.'

'Possibly,' Luke said. 'I'm thinking that they'd hold a prisoner in one of those Weatherhavens. They could guard her better that way. If the middle one is the mess, it's either the first or the last one.'

'Seen General Zhao?'

'No, but I'm guessing he's in the first Weatherhaven.' Luke had seen photos of the General before he left the *Basov*.

With an exhaled 'Hmph', Vitaly sat on Luke's other side. 'I do not understand this "Weatherhaven".'

'The big, arched tents,' Luke replied.

Vitaly frowned. 'If she is just hostage, she will be with a soldier. If this general is a bad man, she will be with him. I am sorry, Luke.'

Luke knew what Vitaly was saying but it didn't bear thinking about. 'If we're going to get in and get out without alerting anyone, we have to know where she's being held,' Luke said.

'I'll keep watch,' said Alrek. 'You get inside and eat. There's nothing hot, though. We don't want them seeing a glow from our stove.'

'Call me if you see anything, won't you?'

'I will.'

Luke kept his head down as he made his way to their tent. His feet were numb; he hadn't realised how cold he had become. As he was about to enter, he noticed a solitary Emperor penguin a few metres away. It was standing upright, and at first Luke thought it was resting its beak on its chest. But on closer inspection, he saw that it was dead and its emaciated form had been freeze-dried. Luke felt a stab of sadness as he recognised the loneliness of its death. Emperor penguins survived the winter by huddling together. This one must have been left behind.

The sight of it dampened his mood further. What if Maddie was dead or had been left to die somewhere on the mountains?

'She is okay, my friend. Get inside and warm up,' said Vitaly, shoving Luke towards the tent entrance.

Once inside, they ate some protein bars in silence, then Vitaly pulled a small can of oil from his bag and used it to lubricate each pistol.

'If you have to use that gun,' Luke said, 'stay clear of the containers in case they're full of explosives and detonators.'

Two seasons previously, Luke had used seismic spectroscopy to build up an image of the seabed beneath the Pine Island Glacier's floating ice tongue. He'd set off a series of low-impact explosions and used a geophone to record the sound as it travelled up through the ice. He knew that high explosives – such as pentolite – and detonators had to be kept apart during transport and storage.

'Don't worry, my friend,' Vitaly replied. 'I am always careful with explosives.' He looked down at the pistol in his hand. 'We should not use guns, unless we must. Too much noise. I will use my knife and cut their throats.'

Luke swallowed. He had never killed anyone, or even imagined he might have to. Deep in thought, Luke pulled some chocolate bars from his pack and handed one to his friend.

'You speak to your boy?' Vitaly asked.

Luke's face lit up with a smile. 'I did, briefly, before I left the ship. It was so good to talk to him. He seems to be making friends easier these days. He was telling me about a party he went to and how much fun he had.' Then his smile faded. 'His mother was pretty pissed off that I hadn't called before. She wants to talk custody arrangements.'

Vitaly gave him a questioning frown. Luke clarified, 'She's getting married soon.'

The Russian ignored that piece of news. 'What did you say to your boy?'

Luke stared hard at his friend, surprised by the question. 'I told him about the station burning down and said that was why I hadn't called or emailed. I told him how much I loved him.'

'That is good. It is important you say this. Soon we may be dead, my friend.'

It was typical of Vitaly to get straight to the point.

'I also told Jase I was moving back to Melbourne so I could spend more time with him. I made a promise.'

'You said that? Then you must live and be a man of your word.'

'I'll try,' said Luke.

D-Day, and Robert was wide awake. He'd had an epiphany. His father hadn't tried to cut him out of the rare earths project because he thought him incapable. No.

While Robert slept, his ego had reasserted itself. He now saw that the General regarded him as a real threat. He feared that his high-profile, media-savvy son might steal his glory. That was it! And clearly, given that Robert was in Antarctica, the old man feared he might lay claim to Marie Byrd Land before he could win the Party's approval.

But just as Robert had underestimated his father's ruthless thirst for military power, the General had underestimated Robert's need to win. Particularly against his father.

'All my life you have belittled me,' he said aloud. 'No more.'

With his sleeping bag wrapped around him, Robert sat in his chair, crossed his arms and considered his strategy. There was no room for emotion in this equation. *What's my desired outcome?* he asked himself.

He lit a cigarette. For the next thirty-five minutes he remained still, except for the occasional head shake as he dismissed an idea, and the movement of his hand to and from his mouth.

Finally, he scrolled though a database on his laptop and found a phone number. He checked the time – it was 3:45 pm in Beijing – and used his satellite phone.

'General Guo Quiliang. This is Robert Zhao Sheng. Before you put down the phone, I have a business proposition for you.'

'I have nothing to say to you.' The voice was staccato.

'Wait! My father knows nothing of this call. I repeat, this is business. My proposal will not only make you an incredibly wealthy man but it will also ensure China's military supremacy for many years to come. Will you hear me out?'

A pause. He imagined the round face of his father's deadliest rival, his fat lip curled in distrust. Guo was second-in-line for the role of chief of the general staff of the People's Liberation Army, with only Robert's father standing in his way. Their hatred for each other was well known, if only ever spoken of in hushed tones.

'What is this? Has Zhao put you up to this?'

'No, sir. I understand your suspicion, but if you will just listen to me, I will explain how my father is the loser in this, and you the winner.'

'Go on.'

'As I'm sure you are aware, General, China leads the world in the mining of rare-earth minerals and the production of military technology. The two go hand in hand. But this can only continue if we find new sources of rare earths. What if I were to tell you that I have found a wealth of bastnäsite, a source so huge that China will become the world's undisputed dominant military power? The Americans and the Russians will quake in their boots.'

'Go on.'

'My investors and I are funding this top-secret project. I am onsite right now, and we are about to begin mining. My father is a backer and plans to take all the glory. His appointment as chief of the general staff is assured.'

'Does the Party know?'

'Only a select few.'

'Unsanctioned then.'

'The deposits are not on Chinese territory. There will be political ramifications, but the prize is worth it.'

'You must tell me where they are.' A slight lilt in Guo's voice revealed his excitement.

'Antarctica.'

Guo cleared his throat. 'Interesting. A continent that belongs to everybody and to nobody.'

'It's run by a useless bunch of do-gooder scientists and a worthless treaty. Perhaps it is time for China to claim new Antarctic territory?' Robert could imagine Guo's head spinning with the possibilities. 'Such glory! You would go down in history.'

'Where in Antarctica?'

Robert laughed. 'Come, come, General. You can easily track my location. I don't need to tell you. You will also be recording this phone call, just as I am.'

Guo chortled. 'Indeed. So, you would betray your father. Why?'

Robert hesitated. 'Why doesn't matter. What matters is that I run the project. The Party must guarantee my personal safety and enter into an exclusive partnership with the Hood Group for all mining and commercial activities in Antarctic territory controlled by our country. In return, I will cut you in. You will get the credit and be the next chief of the general staff. And, best of all, you will vanquish my father.'

'I cannot speak for the Party so cannot guarantee that.'

'Then we have nothing more to discuss.'

'Don't try to bully me,' Guo said sharply. 'I can stop this project.'

'It's too late. By twelve hundred hours today – that's in ten hours' time – the whole world will know about it and General Zhao will have claimed the glory. You must decide now if you are a partner in this or not. Why don't we say you'll get a two per cent carried interest in Dragon Resources? At present, it's a five-billion-dollar company but I have no doubt it will increase, let's just say … significantly after we announce our bastnäsite discovery.'

Robert gave the man some time to do the mental arithmetic.

'I will talk to the Party now,' he replied at last. 'As much as I can give you my word, you have it.'

'That promise is worthless. I need you to do something for me to prove your commitment—'

Guo interrupted. 'I will not—'

Robert cut in. 'I want my father to disappear. Tonight.'

He felt a tingle of fear at the back of his throat, but as soon as he said it, his heart sang like a bird in his chest.

The silence lasted for more than a minute. This time, Robert knew better than to interrupt. Killing General Zhao would give Guo huge satisfaction, but if the Party ever found out he would be tried for murder.

Eventually, Guo spoke. 'Consider him gone.'

T MINUS 4 HOURS, 30 MINUTES
10 March, 7:30 am (UTC-07)

It was almost dawn when the ferocious blizzard that had raged all night died away. Luke had barely slept. It had little to do with Vitaly's snoring, which was loud enough to register on the Richter scale, or the buffeting tent. It was because he had seen nothing to indicate that Maddie was alive, or even at the camp.

He pulled up his hood and crawled from the tent. Wispy clouds flecked the dark sky. The low sun was shining within a circular halo. Above the horizon, equidistant to the sun, two blindingly bright lights shone at the outer edges of the halo's arc. They were parhelia, caused by ice crystals in the high cold air, but it looked as if God's eye were peering at him through the last of the night sky. The sun looked like the pupil, and the cloud flecks like the iris, within a glowing outer rim.

Luke was not a religious man but he knelt for a moment. His body cast a long shadow behind him as he listened to the wind murmur. Then he crawled to the large boulders that hid them and peered through the binoculars at the camp below. No lights. No sign of movement yet. He unzipped his coat and pulled out a water bottle, then drank deeply.

Vitaly and Alrek joined him.

'Beautiful,' said Vitaly, nodding towards the spectacle.

'Any movement yet?' asked Alrek.

'I can't wait any longer,' Luke said. 'I'm going down there.'

'I have a bad feeling about this,' Alrek said. 'We don't know which tent she's in. We can't just open each one and hope we'll stumble on her. We'll be dead in seconds.'

'*Nyet*,' said Vitaly, 'but I can make a soldier tell me where is Maddie.'

'You speak Mandarin?' Alrek asked.

Vitaly pulled out the flick knife. 'I do not need to speak.'

'Let's think this through,' Alrek stammered. 'The storm's died away, so the SAS could get here by the early afternoon. I say we keep watch.'

'No way,' said Luke. 'We have surprise on our side. And if a plane flies over and drops troops, all hell will break loose. Maddie won't stand a chance.' Alrek looked unconvinced but Vitaly nodded. Luke continued. 'They won't be expecting me to steal into their camp. They think I'm dead, anyway. But I understand if you don't want to come with me.' He paused. 'Vitaly? Are you in?'

'Of course,' said the Russian.

'Alrek?'

He hesitated. 'No, I'm sorry. It's a death trap. I really think we should wait for the professionals.'

'Why have you come, then?' Vitaly asked in frustration.

'To help, of course. But we haven't seen any sign of Maddie. Why risk our lives when she could be dead? I don't think you should do it.'

Luke and Vitaly shook his hand and left. Luke carried the Baikal-442 and the ice axe. Vitaly had the Makarov and the flick knife. They stumbled a few times in the semi-darkness, but soon they were creeping around the back of the Weatherhavens, their two-way radios switched off to ensure absolute silence. The wind that whistled through the camp partially masked the creaking sound of their footsteps.

Two soldiers were coming their way, both carrying QBZ-97s, just as Vitaly had described. They were speaking in hushed tones. Luke and Vitaly hid in the gap between two tents. As soon as they saw the soldiers, Luke hurled himself at the wide-set man, and Vitaly at the slimmer one.

Luke clamped his gloved hand over his man's mouth and managed to knock away his rifle. Luke was a big man, fit and strong, but the stocky soldier was a bundle of muscle and reacted instantly. He bent down and threw Luke over and onto his back. Luke's axe flew across the ice.

The soldier reached for his rifle. Just as he grabbed it, Luke kicked it out of his hand and threw his full weight – ninety-five kilograms – on top of his adversary. He pushed his face into the snow and the man struggled. Luke knew that if he pushed hard for long enough, the soldier would suffocate. The man fought back, kicking and wriggling because his life depended on it. But could Luke kill?

Luke glanced up to see that Vitaly had his flick knife at the slimmer soldier's throat, his free hand over his mouth. 'The woman – where is she?' the Russian demanded, his voice low and threatening.

The soldier tried to shake his head.

'Where is the woman?' Vitaly whispered menacingly.

Luke watched in horror as the soldier pulled out a knife and was poised to plunge it into the side of Vitaly's stomach.

'Knife!' he shouted, forgetting their need to stay quiet.

The Russian caught the soldier's wrist and yanked the man's arm behind him, trying to force him to drop the knife. His frozen fingers lost their grip on the soldier's wrist and the man lurched toward his rifle on the ice. Vitaly threw himself on top of the soldier, whose eyes bulged wide in pain. He opened and closed his mouth like a fish out of water, and then ceased to move.

Vitaly struggled to stand. Luke then saw that the flick knife was buried deep in the soldier's chest, and his white parka was stained red around the blade. Vitaly had plunged it into the man's heart with military precision.

In shock, Luke almost released the soldier beneath him, who was growing weaker. Luke snatched the rifle from the ground and hit him on the back of the head with its butt then rolled him on his back. He was breathing but unconscious. Luke couldn't bring himself to kill in cold blood.

Suddenly, the whole camp was blindingly bright. It was as if someone had lit up a football field.

'Run!' said Luke. He didn't see where Vitaly went but he knew he had to kill those lights. People were shouting somewhere in the camp. Luke picked up his ice axe and ran as fast as his crampons would allow him towards the generator. He heard gunfire but didn't dare look around. More shouting, further away this time. Were they chasing Vitaly?

Luke reached the generator and ripped off the fuel cap. He gouged some ice from the ground and shoved it into the diesel tank, hoping to block its fuel line. Sweat glued his balaclava to his head. More ice. He swung his axe again then stuffed the shattered ice into the tank.

The generator spluttered.

'Come on,' he urged.

Luke kept shovelling ice until the generator shuddered to a stop. The camp was plunged into the dawn's muted light. Now he had a chance of escape, and so might Maddie and Vitaly.

He heard rapid gunfire and saw the sway of head torches moving in his direction. He dared not switch on his own, but there was enough daylight to see. He bolted up the mountain slope. It was hard work running on ice, but Luke was used to it. He guessed his pursuers weren't. His strong legs pumped like pistons and his crampons gripped the glassy slope well. He heard a snowmobile engine start up and disappear into the distance. Could that be Maddie or Vitaly escaping?

Despite his breathlessness, Luke shook his head. What a disaster! They'd achieved nothing except endangering themselves and Maddie. They should have listened to Alrek. Luke looked downhill and saw numerous head torches bobbing in the opposite direction. He was safe for now. When he finally got back to their tent, there was no Vitaly and no Alrek. And no sign of a struggle. Had Alrek gone to their rescue? He patted his chest, looking for his radio, but it was gone, lost in the fight. Without it, he couldn't contact them or call for help from the *Basov*.

He set off to find their abandoned snowmobile and the spare radio inside the seat compartment. He got a good pace going, almost jogging. The sun had brought with it a murky grey light, and from his high vantage point he could see Pine Island Bay and the *Professor Basov*, which was surrounded by a patchwork quilt of sea ice.

He reached the snowmobile and opened the seat. He turned on the radio and was about to switch to the marine voice distress frequency when he heard a voice he didn't recognise.

'Commander Scott to Luke Searle. Are you receiving? Respond immediately. Your friends' lives depend on it.'

Luke lifted the radio close to his mouth. 'Luke Searle receiving you loud and clear. Who the hell are you?'

'Make your way back to our camp where your friends are waiting. And do not, repeat, do not contact the *Professor Basov*. We are monitoring all VHF and HF frequencies. Do you understand? You have something of mine I want back. If you don't return it in the next fifteen minutes, Madeline will be executed.'

T MINUS 4 HOURS, 3 MINUTES
10 March, 7:57 am (UTC-07)

Breathless and alone, Luke peered down at his enemy. He had raced back to behind the boulders to get a view of the man calling himself Commander Scott. Looking through the binoculars, he saw Maddie, Alrek and Vitaly kneeling in a line, their hands tied. A soldier was standing behind each hostage with a rifle aimed at his captive.

The leader paced in front of them with an arrogant strut. Unlike the other soldiers, he had his hood down and wore sunglasses, rather than the soldiers' standard-issue snow-goggles. Even from where Luke hid, he could see a thick mass of black hair, perfectly neat. This man didn't resemble the photograph Luke had seen of General Zhao: late fifties, bushy grey eyebrows, shaved head, puffy face. This was not the General.

He checked his watch – it was eight minutes since he'd received the call. Seven minutes left. He looked at his radio. He needed help, but the man calling himself Commander Scott had anticipated his next move. Luke dared not risk contacting the *Basov*.

'Luke Searle calling Commander Scott.' The name stuck in his throat. What kind of prick would assume such a code name? 'What do you want from me?' Luke asked.

'You have the master controller,' the man replied. 'I want it back. You have six minutes and forty seconds before this beautiful woman's face is blown off.'

'Master controller of what? A detonation?'

'Don't treat me like a fool. Where is my laptop?'

'I don't have your laptop. I didn't even know you were using explosives.' He'd guessed a detonation had caused the avalanche, but a master controller suggested they were using a lot of explosives. 'We came for Maddie. That's all. Let her and the others go and we'll leave you in peace.'

Luke didn't need the radio to hear the leader's laughter echo up the mountain slope. 'Really, Luke, I expected better of you,' the man chided. 'Winner of the Seligman Crystal Award! Six minutes and counting before Madeline's blood decorates the ice.' The man waited for a response.

'I can't give you what I don't have,' said Luke. 'But I can give myself in place of Maddie. Let her go and I'll give myself up.'

'Go ahead.'

'I want to see her released first.'

Luke watched as Maddie's hands were untied and a soldier pulled her to her feet. She no longer wore the yellow freezer suit but was in their white uniform. She placed most of her weight on her strong leg but she didn't appear to be in great pain. Despite his terror, Luke felt a brief moment of joy. Maddie took a few steps away from the hostage line and then stopped.

'That's as far as she goes, Luke,' the voice continued. 'Your turn. Come down, and as you do, think very hard about my laptop. My patience is wearing thin.'

Luke shoved the Baikal-442 down the back of his boot and covered it with his leggings and waterproofs. He left the radio behind. He glanced at his ice axe, longing to take it with him. But there was no point; they would take it. He was terrifyingly vulnerable.

He stepped over the ridge with his arms raised above his head. Two soldiers jogged towards him and then frisked him. They found the pistol and removed it, bound his hands and escorted him to their camp.

As Luke drew close, Maddie mouthed, 'No,' but her eyes smiled in gratitude. Vitaly had a livid cut to a swollen lip. His eyes darted around as he looked for a means of escape. Alrek was crouched forward on his knees, trembling; he didn't look up.

Luke finally faced the man who had turned his world upside down. The man who had blackened his name, murdered his friends, and tried to kill him.

Smooth-skinned, slim, of Chinese origin, in his mid to late thirties, the man politely stretched out his right hand to shake Luke's. It was as if they were about to start a business meeting. Luke noticed a very expensive watch on his wrist, just visible between his glove and his cuff. He clearly wasn't from the military.

'May I introduce myself? I am Robert Zhao Sheng.'

'Son of General Zhao?' Luke guessed.

Robert raised a thin eyebrow. 'Indeed. What else do you know?'

Robert was dwarfed by Luke: the top of his perfectly parted hair only came up to Luke's chin. Luke took a step forward and blocked out the low morning sun, casting a long shadow over the man in front of him. To anyone less certain of himself, Luke would have been intimidating.

'Forget the games,' Luke said. 'Release Maddie now, as we agreed.'

'Answer my question first.'

With barely controlled fury, Luke replied. 'You are working with Dragon Resources and you have murdered six Australians. Whatever you are doing here is in breach of the Antarctic Treaty and your own country's laws. You must stop this. Now.'

Robert smiled. 'I knew you'd be a worthy opponent. I'm delighted to meet you at last. I must correct you, however. Firstly, I *own* Dragon Resources. Secondly, the Antarctic Treaty isn't worth the paper it's written on. Thirdly, I haven't broken any law. We are merely conducting scientific research here and had to defend ourselves from attack.'

Luke lost control. 'Liar!' He lowered his head and charged into Robert, who fell backwards, winded. Luke was struck by a rifle butt to his shoulder, the impact excruciating. A soldier gave a sharp kick to the back of his knees and Luke collapsed to the ground.

273

Robert brushed himself down and stood, apparently unfazed by the attack. 'Sadly, your interference is impacting my schedule. My explosives expert is dead, thanks to this brute.' He eyed Vitaly. 'My glaciologist has disappeared, and the master controller is missing. I am a patient man, but enough is enough.'

Explosives expert – so that was who Vitaly had killed. Their glaciologist must have left on the snowmobile Luke had heard earlier. But where would he go? Li Bai? He'd never make it.

'I have a deadline,' Robert continued. 'Tell me where my laptop is or she dies.'

The soldier next to Maddie forced her to kneel. She screamed as he yanked her head back by her hair. The stocky soldier Luke had fought with earlier glowered at him, as he drew a pistol from his holster and held the muzzle to Maddie's forehead.

'You've met Captain Wei, I think?' said Robert, tilting his head dismissively in the man's direction. 'He's very mad at you. It's humiliating for him to be overcome by a mere civilian.'

Wei kept his focus on his prisoner.

'You have ten seconds,' Robert said, pulling back his parka sleeve to better see his watch.

'I don't know – I've never seen it,' Luke shouted. He couldn't believe this was happening.

'We do not have this laptop,' growled Vitaly. 'You are a man of honour? Then free the woman. You made a promise.'

Maddie spoke, her voice high-pitched with fright. 'Luke, there are two detonations – one for ice, the other for rare earths.'

Wei smashed the side of his pistol into her left cheekbone, knocking her to the ice. Luke lunged forward in fury. He was kicked in the kidney and doubled over in pain.

Maddie cupped her bleeding cheek as she yelled, 'Today! At ten and midday. All along the Fitzy. They're blasting a twenty-kilometre shipping channel.'

'No, you mustn't!' spluttered Luke, struggling to sit up.

Robert began counting down to Maddie's execution. 'Four, three, two …'

'Someone tell him where the laptop is!' cried Luke.

'Stop!' Maddie shouted. Everyone looked at her. 'I have it.'

Luke was stunned; was this a bluff to buy time?

Robert approached and leaned over her. 'Where?'

'I hid it. When Li ran away, he untied me. I took it then.'

'Show me,' he ordered.

She was hauled to her feet. 'Now!' he shouted.

Wei and Robert escorted Maddie to the nearest in a long line of the camouflaged canopies, beneath which a metal walk-in storage container was hidden. She had tucked the laptop between the canopy and the outer wall of the container. She was marched back to her colleagues and made to kneel.

Luke watched as Robert took it and wiped some loose snow from the lid. 'You'd better hope it still works. You!' He beckoned a soldier. 'Change the battery. The cold will have drained it.'

The soldier disappeared into the third Weatherhaven.

Now that Robert had his laptop, Luke had no leverage. Perhaps he could reason with the man?

'Robert, please.' Luke cleared his throat. His mouth was dry, as if his saliva had retreated down his throat. 'Let the others go. You'll need someone who knows explosives. I know explosives.

'I'll help you, but the others must go free.' He was determined not to look at Vitaly, who was way more experienced than he was.

'Nice try, Luke. But I've read your file. You'll fight me all the way.'

'Hear me out.' He chose his words carefully. 'Harvesting water from ice. It's brilliant ...' Yes, he'd suck up to the little prick – whatever it took. 'But ...'

Robert folded his arms, suspicious at the compliment. 'I don't have time for a debate. You will—'

Luke cut in. 'No! Please listen, before you make a terrible mistake. I'm a glaciologist. I live and breathe ice. I know this glacier better than anyone. You remember when the Larsen B Ice Shelf disintegrated in 2002? The Pine Island Glacier is just like Larsen B, but three times its size and more important. It's on the brink. So is its sister glacier, the Thwaites. Together, they hold back the West Antarctic Ice Sheet.'

'Don't bore me with—'

'You don't understand!' Luke yelled. How could he get through to this man? 'Your explosives could destroy the grounding line. The PIG's bedrock is below sea level. So if the grounding line is damaged, there's nothing to stop the warmer seawater gushing in, lubricating the underside of the glacier. *All* of the glacier, not just your shipping lane! And if the West Antarctic Ice Sheet shifts and starts breaking up, the rising sea levels will flood Shanghai, Guangzhou, Tianjin, Shenzen – as well as all your low-lying coastal farmland. It will be a disaster for China, and irreversible. Millions will die and millions more will be made homeless.'

Luke saw Captain Wei stare at him and frown. *Wei understood English*, he thought.

Robert shook his head. 'Our scientists disagree.'

'Do they? Why did your glaciologist run away?'

Robert flicked his gloved hand in the air to dismiss the comment.

Luke had nothing to lose. 'A small explosion at the glacier tip – that probably wouldn't do much harm. But blasting twenty kilometres? That's madness. You'll unglue the glacier from the mountain walls. With the friction gone, it'll accelerate towards the sea and break up.' Luke tried to press his argument, but he was blocked by a soldier.

'Robert,' Luke persevered. 'If the PIG and the Thwaites collapse, we're talking a rise in sea levels of one and a half metres. That's enough to flood most of Bangladesh. Then there's India, Vietnam, the Netherlands, Florida, the Maldives. And the list goes on. But if the West Antarctic Ice Sheet melts, that's a rise of five metres. Five! Think about it. That's catastrophic.'

'This is scare-mongering, just like those climate change fanatics. Our modelling shows that the glacier will stay intact.'

Luke noticed Robert looked down the valley when he spoke, avoiding Luke's eye contact.

'It didn't, did it?' Luke pressed. 'What was the probability of collapse? Thirty, thirty-five per cent? More?'

Once again, Wei glanced at Robert.

'Less than twenty per cent,' Robert said. 'Barely material. And the rewards vastly outweigh the risk.'

Luke couldn't hide the contempt in his voice. 'Your money won't protect you, Robert. Food shortages. Rioting. Wars. Market chaos.'

'This is wrong, Robert,' said Maddie.

Robert flinched, stung by her words. Then he recovered. 'Wrong? You think what you in the West do is right?' He began to pace around. 'You pollute the planet and then you expect developing countries like mine to pay the price. You wail about Tiananmen Square and Tibet, yet you torture anyone you call a terrorist. What about Guantanamo? You invade and occupy, you meddle in the affairs of other countries and turn a blind eye to slaughter if it suits you. All the while, your thirst for oil funds the jihadi lunatics trying to kill you. What I am doing is no different from what you did in Iraq. But instead of oil, we need water. We took back Tibet to access their glaciers. And now we will take our share of Antarctica.'

'That's bullshit!' Luke shouted. 'Rare earths have nothing to do with that. They're used for military technology. For war. This is about your wealth and power. And everyone else be damned.'

'Enough. Now, I have one last thing you must do for me.'

Luke was about to tell him where to shove his request, then changed his mind. Perhaps it would give him some leverage. 'And what is that?'

'You'll call off the SAS. Tell Winchester you've found Maddie. Everyone is safe and our camp is deserted. The threat is over.'

'How you know the SAS, they come?' demanded Vitaly.

Alrek stared at Robert, open-mouthed, with despair in his eyes. He'd been relying on the SAS to save them.

'Webcam conversations are so easy to hack.'

Luke took a deep breath. 'I will not call off the SAS.'

'Then your friends will die, one by one.'

Luke looked into the eyes of each one. 'I can't let him do this. I can't … Once the glacier collapses, there's nothing we can do to stop catastrophe. Millions will lose their homes.'

'I understand,' said Maddie.

Vitaly bowed his head once.

'No, do what he says!' screamed Alrek. 'I don't want to die. Please!'

'I will not,' said Luke.

'I'll do it!' Alrek's voice was high-pitched and shaky. 'I'm the expedition leader. Andrew trusts me.'

'Alrek, it will collapse,' Luke said. 'Don't do this.'

'You don't know that!' he yelled.

In two angry steps, Robert was alongside Alrek. He drew a gun from his pocket and placed it in the middle of Alrek's forehead. He fired, and blood splattered over Maddie who was nearest. She screamed, her coat and face speckled crimson.

Robert stepped aside as Alrek fell forward, a gaping hole in the front and back of his skull. 'I hate cowards,' he said matter-of-factly.

'Oh my God! Oh my God!' Maddie rocked backwards and forwards.

'You!' growled Vitaly. 'You are a coward. You kill a man who cannot fight back.' Vitaly spat in Robert's direction.

'My first direct kill,' Robert said, as if to confirm he had actually done it.

'I will not make that call.'

Robert turned to him. 'I think your son may have something to say about that.'

Luke's eyes hardened to granite. His muscles contracted and he was ready to attack. 'Leave my son out of it,' he warned.

'I'm afraid it's too late for that.'

The prisoners kneeled on the floor of the Weatherhaven that housed Robert's IT and comms equipment. Luke and Maddie in front, Vitaly behind. Their hands were bound behind their backs. Facing them was a large monitor.

Robert sat behind his desk. 'Luke, I think you should watch this,' he said. 'A live feed.'

On the screen was a suburban street, in the middle of the night – or so Luke assumed. The sky was black and the streetlights illuminated pools of detail: cars and four-wheel drives, wooden fences, low-hanging branches of a gum tree, wheelie bins ready for collection. The camera bounced to a rhythm as the camera man walked.

'It's a head camera,' Robert said. 'You're seeing everything he does.'

The street looked terrifyingly familiar to Luke.

The cameraman stopped and glanced up and down. Not a single window was lit; all the inhabitants were asleep. The houses, although hard to make out, reminded Luke of the Federation cottages and brick terraces in many Melbourne streets. His body suddenly burned. 'No!'

Luke's heart almost stopped as the man stepped over a low picket fence and walked down the side path of a single-storey weatherboard cottage. It was Jessica's house.

'My son! Leave my son alone!' Luke tried to stand but Wei's strong grip on his shoulder pushed him down. 'Robert, what is he doing?'

'That's up to you.'

Luke watched as a hand gloved in black leather worked with a crowbar to force open the lower frame of an old sash window. Luke hoped the frame might squeak as it opened, possibly alerting Jessica, but no one else appeared. The man ducked low and stepped into the lounge.

'Stop him,' pleaded Luke.

The camera clearly carried its own dim spotlight. It was enough to see Jason's favourite robot toy on a low plastic table in one corner of the lounge room. Next to it was a child's palette and a painting, the paper warped under the volume of watercolours used. On the wall, his mother had displayed some of his work. This small room was the thoroughfare between the two bedrooms at the front of the house and the dining room, kitchen and bathroom at the back. The boy's bedroom was the first down the hallway.

'You kill the boy,' warned Vitaly, 'I kill *you*!'

'Robert, don't do this,' said Maddie. 'Not a child. Don't hurt a child.'

Underneath Luke's parka his muscles were as taut as a high-tension wire. He struggled to free his hands. His wrists bled but he didn't care. 'Tell him to stop,' he said through gritted teeth. 'I'll do what you want. I'll make the call.'

Robert nodded, his arms folded across his chest. 'Indeed you will. But just to make sure ...'

Outside Jason's room, Luke could see a soft glow under the door from a night light to keep the bogeyman away. Except this bogeyman was coming in.

Enraged, Luke charged at Robert. Vitaly roared like a bear set upon by dogs and hurled his mighty bulk into the soldier guarding him.

Wei smashed his rifle butt into Luke's back, over and over. Despite the onslaught, Luke managed to stand. He kicked high and hit Wei in the face. The captain staggered backwards, wailing, his nose broken, eyes screwed up in pain.

In the commotion, no one had noticed that Maddie was free of her bindings. She lunged for Robert's pistol on the table. She grabbed it with both hands and turned it on her captor, but her wounded leg made her stumble and a soldier knocked the gun away. She fell forward, clutching her fingers.

Automatic gunfire shredded a gash in the tent roof. They all ducked to the floor. Soldiers piled on top of Luke and Vitaly.

'Control them!' yelled Robert, who'd fired the rifle.

Luke struggled but was pinned down.

'I will kill your son!' shrieked Robert.

All three stopped thrashing, and Luke twisted his head so he could see the screen. The assassin was in Jason's room. On the polished floorboards in front of the bed was a circular rug, in the same pattern as the bedding: penguins on icebergs. The man walked quietly towards the bed and stood for a moment observing the sleeping boy: dark hair, pale skin, he made soft yappy noises in his sleep as if he were dreaming and trying to call out.

'You are disgusting!' Vitaly exclaimed.

The assassin leaned over Jason Searle and placed a large piece of gauze over the boy's mouth.

'God, no!' his father yelled.

Jason moved his head, and for an instant opened his eyes. Then he passed out.

'Chloroform,' Robert explained coldly.

The assassin shifted Jason's limp body so that he lay flat on his back and made himself comfortable on the boy's bed. He removed the pillow and placed it on his lap, ready to suffocate the boy when ordered.

'He's waiting for instructions,' Robert continued. 'He can wait there until sunrise, if need be. But I can't. You must convince Winchester to call off the SAS now. If you fail, or if you try to warn him, your son will die.'

Luke's choice was terrible: save his son or the lives of millions. But not both. He couldn't tear his eyes away from the pillow in the assassin's lap.

'Your director's line is ready,' Robert said. 'You'll be on loudspeaker.' He held the satellite phone close to Luke's mouth and ear. 'One word out of place, and King kills your boy.'

Luke registered the name but realised it was probably fake. Wei's head shot up in surprise, which worried him more. If a mercenary like Wei had heard of this assassin, then God help Jason.

Winchester answered after just one ring. He had been working through the night.

'Luke, where the hell are you? You're not on the *Basov* and Bolshakov won't tell me what's going on. Are you searching for Maddie?' His voice was hoarser that usual. Lack of sleep.

Luke's heart was racing. He had to get this right. 'I'm sorry, Andrew. I had to do it. But we've found her. She's alive and well.'

Winchester sighed with relief. 'Thank God for that. Does she need medical attention?'

Luke sensed danger. He couldn't allow anyone near the camp. 'No, she's fine. Her leg's healed well. I'm with Vitaly and

Alrek from the *Basov*. We'll help her back to the ship.' Alrek's name stuck in his throat. The poor man.

'That's a miracle.' Luke detected incredulity in the director's gravelly voice. 'Where did you find her?'

Luke looked up at Robert, who mouthed 'abandoned', and then signalled Luke to keep talking.

'She was at their abandoned camp, sheltering. That's how she survived. There's nobody else here. It looks like they're long gone.'

'Can you repeat that? Did you say the camp is abandoned?' asked Winchester, his astonishment obvious.

'Yes. It looks like some kind of research camp. Seems they were drilling for ice cores, not oil. There's nothing to indicate mining either.' The words tumbled out quickly but Luke hated the lies. 'From the chopper marks in the snow, it looks like they were airlifted out. Probably on their way home by now. So there's no need for the SAS.'

'That's not your decision, Luke.'

'Sorry, Andrew, I just know what a big deal it is to get the military here, and I don't want you embarrassed. Not to mention the cost.'

'Since when have you worried about embarrassing me?' Winchester paused. 'What's going on there, Luke? You're not telling me everything.'

Luke shot a look at Robert, who was pointing at the monitor. King sat on Jason's bed, the pillow poised. Luke swallowed a lump that felt the size of a country. 'Nothing,' he replied. 'I had to find Maddie to clear my name. If you don't believe me, ask her.'

Robert frowned and then nodded. He placed the phone next to Maddie's face.

'Hello, Director. It's Maddie Wildman here. I'm fine, and very thankful to Luke and the guys.'

'Maddie, it's so good to hear your voice. What happened?'

'Um, they took me from Bettingtons. On a sled. Their doctor checked me over. Then … they left. As Luke said, they were helicoptered out.'

'Were they the same people who attacked Hope?'

'I think so. But for some reason they didn't kill me.'

Maddie glanced at Luke. The story was lame.

'What did they want?'

'I have no idea.'

'They had guns?'

'Yes, automatic rifles. But they treated me well.'

'Where were they from?'

She glanced at Luke again, unaware of how much he had already told Winchester. 'I'm not sure – possibly China.'

'And you're okay with Luke and the others escorting you back to the *Basov*?'

'Of course. I'm fine. Seriously, Andrew. We don't need the SAS. Far better to manage this through diplomatic channels.'

A pause. 'Thank you, Maddie. I'd like to speak to Luke again.'

The phone was pressed against Luke's ear. 'Luke, you're a stubborn son of a bitch, but for once I'm glad you ignored me. It's good to have Maddie back.'

'Yeah, well, when I get back to Hobart we'll have a celebration, like we did for my last birthday. You drank me under the table, remember?' Despite the sub-zero temperatures, a trickle of sweat meandered down Luke's temple.

'Er … that's right, your last birthday.' Had Winchester noticed Luke's deliberate mistake? 'Truth be told, I've been up all night trying to get Defence to cooperate. They've been wanking on about international relations and how we can't go accusing Chinese citizens of murdering Australians without evidence. Bloody bureaucrats.'

'So the SAS isn't mobilised?'

'On stand-by. They haven't had the go-ahead yet. I'll update them on the situation. I suspect an international force is the likely answer. But now the culprits have left, I guess the pressure's off a bit. Just don't go moving any evidence, okay?'

Luke watched Robert's face. His captor nodded his approval.

'Okay, goodbye, Andrew. We'll talk again when we're back on board the *Basov*.'

The call ended and Luke looked from Maddie to Vitaly. He may have saved his son but he had condemned them all to death.

Nothing could stop the detonation now, and there was no longer any reason for Robert to keep them alive.

'Get their stench out of here,' Robert ordered in Mandarin. 'Get rid of them and make sure their bodies are never found.' The soldiers started to shove them towards the tent's exit.

'Wait,' called Luke, struggling hard. 'My boy – you'll keep your word?'

Robert glanced at the screen. He appeared to be making up his mind.

'He's a little boy. Let him be,' begged Maddie. No reaction. 'What would your mother think?'

The leader rounded on her in fury. 'You know *nothing* of my mother!' His face was screwed up in hatred.

'I heard you talking about her. Sound travels through tents,' Maddie explained. 'Robert, she loved you and protected you. She wouldn't want you hurting a little boy, would she?'

Robert's features softened, and he seemed unaware of the people watching him. He spoke into his headset and ordered the assassin to abort the mission.

Luke, Maddie and Vitaly tramped across the Pine Island Glacier, flanked closely by four guards. Their crampons – returned to them for the trek – crunched into the ice. They were walking to their deaths.

The wind blew a thick layer of white crystals across their path, which swirled around their legs like angry wraiths. On the featureless ice, there was nowhere to hide. With their hands bound and guns trained on them, escape was impossible. Two guards walked behind them, while the other two, including Captain Wei, were on a snowmobile. Wei had some surgical tape over his broken nose.

Vitaly broke their silence. 'Fuck! I not have a good day.'

Maddie and Luke couldn't help but smile at the understatement.

The soldiers were too far away to hear their captives' conversation, but still Luke kept his voice low. 'My hands are almost free.' He had removed his gloves. The colder his hands were, the more likely he could slip the bindings. He felt a click as his left thumb dislocated.

'I try. Mine are too fat,' said Vitaly.

'I'm going to reason with Wei,' Maddie said. 'See if I can get him to see sense. He looked shocked when you talked about the flooding.'

'Yeah, but he's a mercenary,' Luke replied.

'What have we got to lose?'

She pretended to stumble so that Wei caught up with her. She kept pace with his snowmobile's slow crawl.

'Where did you learn English?' shouted Maddie, so she could be heard above the rumble of the engine.

The Captain eyed her suspiciously. 'Quiet.'

Luke peeked around. He admired Maddie's resilience. Despite their plight, she was stubbornly determined to live.

'So where are you from?' she continued. 'Which province?' She repeated the question in her faltering Mandarin.

'It no matter. Keep walking,' he replied in English so Maddie did the same.

'I'm from Brisbane.' She had eye contact with Wei. She had to get a rapport going. 'My next-door neighbour's from Yunnan province. He introduced me to Yunnan tea. Delicious. Do you know it?'

Wei shook his head.

She tried a different approach. 'My uncle grows olives.' Wei looked blankly at her. 'He's a farmer.' She translated the words into Mandarin.

Wei nodded and said, 'Yes, my father farmer.'

'Where is his farm?'

Wei hesitated.

'We're going to be dead soon,' Maddie said, 'so it doesn't matter what you tell me.'

'Fujian province. He grow rice.'

Luke glanced around again. A glimmer of hope.

'Is that near the coast?' Maddie continued.

'I not understand.'

She screwed up her face. Luke knew that look. She was trying to remember something. 'Sea,' she said at last, in Mandarin. 'Is your village near the sea?'

'Yes. But it has wall to stop sea.'

Maddie moved fractionally closer to Wei. 'You understand that if the ice breaks up, the sea will rise and flood your village. Your crops will fail, your drinking water will be contaminated ... um ...' Maddie was searching for a simpler word. 'It will be full of salt. I

288

mean, you won't be able to drink it.'

Wei waved his gun, shooing her away. 'No, you lie.' A soldier shoved her back into line.

'I tried,' said Maddie, shrugging despondently. 'How are you going with the ropes?'

'Almost there. One more tug,' said Luke. With head jutted forward, his back and arm muscles strained as he gritted his teeth. For a fraction of a second his arms jerked up his back as he freed his hands. 'Done,' he panted. He pushed the rope up into the cuffs of his coat so his guards wouldn't notice.

'Look.' Vitaly raised his chin as he stared straight ahead.

In the distance, a line of poles ran parallel to the crevasse. The more distant flags were a hazy shadow of the nearer ones. All three prisoners squinted. The brightness hurt their unprotected eyes.

'Looks like they're taking us to the Fitzy,' Luke said.

'*Zhopa!*' Vitaly swore under his breath.

'Fantastic!' Maddie said sarcastically. 'So if the bullets don't kill us, the explosives will. Any ideas, anyone?'

Both Vitaly and Maddie were looking at Luke when his face broke into a huge smile.

'Why do you look like a man who just had the best sex?' Vitaly asked.

'Because we're not going to die,' Luke said. 'Before we get to the Fitzy, there's a slot, hidden beneath a weak snow bridge. I surveyed it back in October. That's how we get away.'

'I'm not understanding this,' said Vitaly.

'We can jump through the snow bridge into the crevasse, then escape by climbing out. It's shallow, maybe only two storeys deep.'

'This is a long way down. We could die. Ice is very sharp.'

'Yeah, maybe we will. But if we don't, we're gonna die for sure. This is a firing squad. I'd rather take my chances with ice than bullets.'

Maddie chewed her lower lip, unconvinced. 'Are you sure the slot hasn't changed since October?'

'No I am not,' Luke said. 'All I can tell you is that the bottom of this crevasse was like a bowl and should soften our fall. Regardless, this slot is our only chance of survival. You have to trust me.'

Her face muscles relaxed into a smile. She leaned into him and gave him a gentle nudge. 'This is totally insane. But, you know …' She paused. 'I will trust you.'

Luke was so taken aback that he almost forgot to pretend his hands were still tied. He wanted to put his arms around her and hug her. 'That means a lot to me, Mads.'

The ever-practical Vitaly chipped in. 'How do we climb out? No axe, no rope.' He eyed a soldier who carried a long loop of rope over his shoulder.

'Leave the rope and axe to me,' said Luke. 'The slot is up ahead. You can see it, where the snow sags. It's now or never.'

They followed his line of vision. A large area of ice, the length of a cricket pitch, appeared to have sunk a few centimetres. As a result, the snow looked slightly grey.

'Mads, when we get there, stumble. Tell them you can't walk any further. Beg them to get on with the execution. To do it then and there. Vitaly, you tell them you want to pray.'

'You want me to pray?' Vitaly looked astonished.

'Yes, you need your hands free in front of you. They cut your ropes, you hold Maddie and jump through the snow. Protect her injured leg. I'll follow.'

'Okay, Maddie?' asked Luke.

Her eyes sparkled. 'What the hell! Let's do it.'

'Vitaly?'

'*Da.*'

Within seconds, Maddie staggered, groaned and then fell. Her hand rested on the edge of the sunken surface ice.

'Get up!' Wei ordered, stopping his snowmobile.

Maddie clutched her wounded leg. 'I can't. My leg. Just get it over with, will you? For pity's sake? We're near enough to the crevasse.'

'If you're going to execute us, just do it,' pleaded Luke.

'I must pray. I pray before I die. You please free my hands. I will not go anywhere. You have guns.'

'You want to die now, you die now. But no pray,' said Wei.

'Captain, please,' pleaded Maddie. 'A man's last wish should be honoured.'

Wei thought for a moment, then ordered a soldier to free Vitaly's hands. It was the same soldier carrying the ice axe and the rope.

'Please? Me too?' said Maddie.

Wei again nodded.

Before the soldier realised what was happening, Luke had snatched the rope and ripped the axe from his hand. Vitaly grabbed Maddie's waist and fell backwards onto the weak snow bridge, which shattered. They disappeared.

Luke jumped through the gap and dropped into the darkness below.

Luke fell. He smashed into something hard and all the air was forced from his lungs. Distant shouting from above. Angry voices. Heavy clumps of snow hit his face and body like punches. Slowly, the cascade softened to a trickle of icy powder. Luke wiped it away and opened his eyes. He had to get his bearings.

He was on a narrow shelf. Instinctively, he flung his ice axe into the wall as an anchor. Directly above him, long icicles hung like a giant, glass pan pipe from the cathedral-like ceiling. The hole they had fallen through was almost circular and sunlight poured in, illuminating the otherwise dark cavern. He expected to see faces staring down or hear bullets pinging off the walls. But if their captors didn't have any way to secure themselves at the surface, they wouldn't want to crawl over what remained of a semi-collapsed snow bridge. Perhaps the soldiers assumed they were dead?

'Mads! Vitaly! Are you okay?' he called. It was unlikely their enemy could hear them in their semi-sealed icebox.

'Yes,' replied Maddie.

'I am very flat,' joked Vitaly.

'He's hurt his arm,' said Maddie.

Luke looked down. The wall supporting the ledge he lay on

sloped at a seventy-degree angle. The opposite wall was vertical. The floor of the slot was unusual: rather than the two walls narrowing to a point, the bottom curved like a bowl. It was covered in loose snow, which had softened their landing. Luke peered down into the depths: he spotted Vitaly's khaki green coat first. Maddie's white parka made her hard to see.

'I'm up here,' waved Luke. 'Don't move. The floor you're lying on may not be solid.' He knew it could be a false floor.

'What!' Maddie exclaimed.

'Keep still. You could crack it.' Luke saw her head of copper-coloured hair move as she tried to sit up. 'Maddie, you're the lightest. Can you brush the snow off the floor and check how solid it is? Be careful.'

Luke could just make out her silhouette as she gently swept the snow away.

'It looks rock-hard,' she called up.

'Good. Now, can you see any tunnels? Any daylight coming in through chinks in the ice? Any potential way out?' He waited.

'No, only the hole in the roof,' Maddie replied.

Luke scanned all that he could see of the chasm. Maddie was right. Their only way out was the way they arrived. 'Vitaly?' he called. 'How bad is your arm? Can you climb?'

'It is okay. It will not come out.'

Luke sighed with relief. With a dislocated shoulder, Vitaly would not have been able to climb.

Nearby, a piece of mottled ice protruded from the wall and pointed at the ceiling. It reminded him of a long, high termite mound. It was wider than Luke's shoulders but had a narrower section, much like a waist. He still had the coiled rope he had grabbed before he jumped. He guessed it was fifty metres – long enough. He tied a loop and tightened it around the giant stalagmite's waist, leaving both ends of the rope dangling. He tested that it could bear his weight, then coiled one loose end around his body as a make-do safety harness and pulled his axe out of the wall.

Above them, Luke heard a scream. Thick chunks of snow rained down. He looked up. One of the soldiers was dangling from a rope through a much wider hole in the ceiling. Clearly, he had tried to crawl across the overhanging roof to look for them and had fallen through. The beam from his head torch darted about like a fly trapped in a bottle.

Luke didn't move. The soldier was pulled back from the opening in rough jerks and disappeared. They waited in silence. Luke heard more angry words from the surface, then everything went quiet.

The minutes dragged by with no further sound from above.

'Have they gone?' Maddie's voice was tentative.

'I think so,' Luke called down.

Vitaly shouted, 'It is nearly nine. First detonation in one hour. I think soldiers are gone. Too busy to stay and wait for dead people.'

'I agree,' Luke called back. 'The first explosion shouldn't impact us. Maybe a little ground shake. But the one along the Fitzy … we're too near. It'll bury us.'

'I guess we're in what will become the shipping lane,' Maddie said.

'We need to hurry,' Luke called. 'We've only got three hours before they blow the Fitzy. I was hoping we'd see another way out, but I can't. We'll have to climb back the way we came.'

'But how?' asked Maddie. 'We haven't got any harnesses or pulleys.'

'We have a rope,' said Luke, 'and our crampons. Give me a moment to think this through.' He listened for any sound of human activity at the surface. Nothing. The sloping ice wall above him was covered with protrusions; these might give them something to grip. 'Mads, I can lower the rope and the axe and you can use them to climb up to this ledge. But how do you feel about free-climbing the last three metres to the surface?'

There was a moment's hesitation. 'I think I can do the rope climb. My leg should hold out. But the free-climb? That'll take the kind of strength I don't have.'

'Vitaly?'

'I am a sailor; I am good with rope. But my arm is not strong. I will try.'

Luke glanced at the icy stalagmite; perhaps it would not cope with Vitaly's tank-like weight. 'Okay, then,' he said. 'I'll climb to the surface and then you can use me as an anchor. If I can make it, you'll have a rope the whole way up.'

Suddenly, Luke heard an ear-splitting snap from down below. He leaned over the ledge, breathless with panic.

'The floor, it crack, I feel it,' said Vitaly, not daring to move a muscle.

'It's behind me,' shouted Maddie.

'Change of plan. Mads, don't move. I'm lowering one end of the rope and the axe. Use them to get yourself up to this ledge. I need to get one of you off that floor.'

Luke searched inside his cuffs for the bindings he had removed earlier, but they were lost. Damn! He removed his left crampon and pulled out the boot's shoelace. Using that shoelace, he tied a prusik loop to the long rope, the knot of which locked if you put weight on it but easily slid up or down the rope if you didn't. 'Use the prusik loop as an extra handhold,' he called down. 'As you walk up the wall, you can alternate using the axe and the loop. Okay?'

He tied the axe handle to the end of the rope and lowered it carefully.

A few seconds later it was dangling over Maddie's head. She reached up, untied the knot to take the axe and then used the rope to lift herself off the icy floor.

'Vitaly?' Luke called. 'Can you move away from the crack and find something solid to hold onto?'

As Maddie rose up the rope, Vitaly tentatively crawled back against the wall. Luke watched anxiously as Maddie got into an efficient climbing rhythm, digging the crampon spikes into the wall, pulling down on the prusik loop so that it took her weight, yanking the axe free of the ice and then slamming it into the wall higher up. Then she stepped up to repeat the same process. Within minutes, Luke was pulling her onto the shelf next to him.

'Thanks … Luke,' she panted, exhausted.

'Vitaly? Are you okay down there?' Luke called.

'*Da*, but I don't know how long it okay.'

'There's no room on this ledge for another person so I'm going to climb to the top and take the rope with me. When I'm set up as an anchor, I'll lower the rope for you.'

'Do not leave me here, Luke,' shouted Vitaly. His tone sounded a note of warning.

Luke knew that this was the closest Vitaly would ever come to expressing fear. 'Mate, I'll get you out. Count on it.'

Luke untied the loop and laced up his boot, then checked that his crampons were secured tightly. With the rope coiled over his shoulder, he said, 'Mads, I'm sorry, I need that axe.'

She reluctantly let go of the handle.

This was going to be the most difficult climb of his life: a free-climb in sub-zero conditions. With his right hand he smashed the axe's blade into the ice above him and clung to it. He then grasped a protruding piece of wall with his left hand. Digging his spikes into the ice, he stepped up. He found another wall cavity and used it as the next handhold. He made slow but steady progress up the wall. Gradually, the cold took away the feeling in his hands; he knew that was dangerous. He climbed further. Every muscle in his body shuddered with the strain.

He was an arm's length from the crevasse lip and could feel the sun on his face when suddenly he lost his grip.

Luke clung to the ice axe in his right hand, but his left swung away from the wall. His heart almost leaped through his chest. Thankfully, his spikes still held in the wall. He squeezed his eyes shut, sweat stinging them. He must not lose his nerve. Not now.

He opened his eyes and looked up, trying to work out what had happened. He hadn't lost his grip: the ice had broken away in his palm. He had to find a sturdier handhold. And fast.

He spied one that looked promising and stretched his arm up, hooking his fingers into it. It felt firm. He pulled the axe out and used it to test the edge he was about to climb over. It appeared that the soldier had demolished the weaker roof ice when he crawled over it.

Luke was nearly there. His ice axe crashed down on the top of the crevasse lip and wind-blown ice particles danced on his hand at the surface – a pleasant change from the tomb-like silence below. He moved his crampons up one at a time until he felt sure they were well embedded. He had to let go of his handhold and grab the axe with both hands. A blind leap of faith.

In one quick motion, Luke moved his second hand to the axe, praying it would stay wedged. The muscles in his neck bulged, his face crimson with the strain. He clenched his teeth and, with his last remaining energy, pulled his torso forward. His knees connected with the glacier's surface. Terrified that the lip might disintegrate, he crawled away quickly, hot sweat dripping from his brow onto the cold glacier. He had made it!

He struggled to a sitting position and looked around. He saw a stationary snowmobile in the distance, with a soldier on its seat. He was listening to the two-way radio. He hadn't yet noticed Luke; the moaning wind had masked the little noise Luke had made.

Without pausing to think, Luke yanked the axe free and moved on all fours towards the snowmobile. It was the one Robert had stolen from Hope. The soldier laughed, amused at something he had heard. Luke rose to a kneeling position. At last the man saw him. But before he could raise his rifle, Luke swung the axe into his arm.

The soldier cried out, dropped the radio and tried to raise his rifle with his remaining hand. Luke charged and crash-tackled him off the snowmobile. He tore the gun away and pointed it at the prostrate soldier, who clutched his bleeding arm.

Luke could barely stand. He kicked the radio away, gasping for air. 'Do … speak English?'

'Yes, little.'

'I don't want … to kill you. You understand?'

'Yes.' The man nodded as he held his limp arm. 'No kill me.'

'Lie on your stomach. I will bandage your arm, but if you move, I'll shoot.'

The soldier obeyed.

Luke opened the snowmobile seat and found the first aid kit, as well as a recovery kit and rope. The soldier stayed motionless but whimpered in pain as Luke tied him up. Luke hastily used the bandages on his captive and pocketed the radio.

Finding the snowmobile was a blessing. He switched it on and revved the engine. The rescue kit provided a pulley system but it would take too long to set up. Instead, he attached the harness from the rescue kit to one end of the rope he carried and tied the other to the snowmobile.

Luke quickly made his way to the crevasse's edge. 'Maddie!' he called.

'You made it!'

'Yup, your turn now. Get into the harness. When you're ready, I'll use the snowmobile to lift you. It could be jerky. Protect your face from sharp edges.'

'Did you say snowmobile?'

'Yes, they kindly left us one.' Luke used the kitbag as padding to stop the rope cutting into the crevasse lip, and lowered the harness.

'When you get near the lip, push yourself away from it so you don't get snagged.'

'Ready!' Maddie called out a few moments later.

Luke straddled the snowmobile and drove forward, watching for the rope to go taut. He needed enough power to lift her, but if he went too fast she might get bashed or sliced on the sharp ice.

In a few minutes Maddie lay on the ground near him. She was laughing with relief. 'Thank God! Thank God!' she repeated.

'I need your help with Vitaly, your weight on the snowmobile.'

'Of course.'

Luke threw the harness down to Vitaly. 'Mate, can you hear me?'

'About time!' Vitaly called.

'I'm using a snowmobile to pull you out. Try walking up the wall to avoid swinging. Do you understand?'

'*Da.*'

When Vitaly was ready, Luke revved the engine, with Maddie seated behind him. He inched the vehicle forward again and felt the rope go tight, but this time the snowmobile began to skid. Luke carefully accelerated some more. It crept onward, and then seemed to find some grip and jerked forward.

After a few seconds, Vitaly appeared over the crevasse lip and was dragged away from the edge. The Russian shook off a dusting of snow, like a bear coming out of hibernation. Luke braked and stopped the engine. All three were safe. For now.

Luke gave them a few moments to recover and then revealed his plan. 'We have two hours and ten minutes before the Fitzgerald Fissure blows,' he said. 'I have to try to stop it.

I don't expect you to join me.' He kneeled and patted the ice as if comforting a sick animal. 'If this glacier is destroyed, millions of human lives will be too. We're all linked. I don't understand why Robert can't see that.'

'My friend, two hours and ten is very little time,' Vitaly said.

Luke looked over at the soldier. 'Let's find out what this man knows.'

Vitaly took the rifle and pointed it at the wounded man.

'We're leaving you here,' Luke said. 'So, unless you help us, you'll be blown to smithereens. Do you understand?'

The soldier nodded.

'If you help us find the explosives, we can deactivate them. You'll live and I'll come back for you.'

The soldier glanced in the direction of the Fitzgerald Fissure, his eyes wide with fear, but he did not speak.

'Help me and you have a chance. The SAS are on their way,' Luke lied. 'I'll put in a good word for you. I'll tell them you helped us.'

Finally, the man spoke. 'Explosive on floor and in wall at eighteen metre depth. All the way.'

'The full length of the crevasse?'

'Yes.'

Luke moved closer. 'How can we find them?'

'Red flag. Many flag.'

'Where's the initiation point?' The man didn't understand. 'Where does it start?'

The soldier nodded inland.

'How does signal from laptop reach the detonator?' Vitaly asked, jabbing the man with his rifle.

'I not know how to say,' replied the soldier. 'Signal go from laptop to box and then to detonator.'

'You mean there are signal relay boxes at the surface?' Luke asked.

'Signal relay boxes, yes. But not at surface. They in the crevasse.'

'How many?' Luke demanded.

'Five.'

That meant they were every four kilometres. 'How do we find them?'

'Yellow flag.'

'How deep are the boxes?'

The soldier frowned, trying to remember the English word. 'Boxes at ten metre.'

Vitaly whistled through his teeth. 'I will go with you, but this is a big challenge, my friends. We must be clever with our time.'

Luke steered them away from their enemy's earshot.

'Is he telling us the truth?' Maddie asked.

'I think it is truth,' Vitaly said.

'I agree,' said Luke. 'Robert will transmit the countdown signal from his laptop. If we can't stop the signal transmission – and there's no chance of that – then we'll have to stop the detonators receiving that signal.' Luke glanced at Vitaly for confirmation.

'*Da*. We must find these signal relay boxes. Without them, the signal from the laptop will be too weak to reach the detonators. We must cut ... how you say, like insect?' Vitaly held both hands to his head and wiggled his two middle fingers.

'The antennae?'

'*Da*. We destroy the antennae,' Vitaly said, flexing his sore arm.

'What antennae?' asked Maddie.

Luke clarified. 'The explosive is probably pentolite – it can cope with the cold and wet. It'll be in holes in the crevasse walls, surrounded by compacted snow to keep it nice and snug. In each stick of pentolite will be an electronic detonator. There'll be an antenna protruding from each detonator that would normally pick up the signal from Robert's laptop. But because some detonators will be as much as twenty kilometres away, and eighteen metres deep inside the crevasse, the long antennae on the relay boxes will ensure the signal reaches the detonators.'

Vitaly whistled again, shaking his head. 'They must have new technology. I never heard of such a big detonation, ever.'

'So how do we destroy the antennae?' Maddie asked.

'We have two ice axes now, thanks to our friend over there,' Luke said, nodding in the direction of the bound soldier, who watched them nervously. 'We cut them.'

'Isn't there a danger you'll create a spark?' Maddie asked.

'*Nyet*,' said Vitaly. 'The detonator is very stable.'

'One of us can use the climbing harness in the recovery kit,' Luke said. 'The other can use the ropes. Only two of us can do this. Maddie ...' He paused, knowing she would resist the idea. 'Vitaly and I know explosives and you don't, so we'll go into the crevasse. You should save yourself and leave.'

'I'm not running away,' she replied.

They heard a low rumble, like a far-off road train on a bumpy desert road. The tip of the ice tongue was some kilometres away but the sound of the blast travelled up the length of the glacier like a shudder moving up a spine. It grew louder.

It was 10:00 am. Robert had blasted away his iceberg.

All three peered down the length of the enormous fissure, knowing it would be impossible to immobilise all the signal relay antennae in time. Some explosives, in fact most, would still detonate. The other thing they knew was that they would probably be too close to survive the blasts.

T MINUS 1 HOUR, 55 MINUTES
10 March, 10:05 am (UTC-07)

Luke had the recovery kit strapped to his back, the binoculars round his neck and an ice axe in his hand. Vitaly carried the fifty-metre rope, the second axe and the rifle.

'If we can disable two signal relay boxes, we'll stop an eight-kilometre section from detonating,' said Luke. 'We might even manage another, which means twelve kilometres won't blow.'

'It is enough?' asked Vitaly.

'It should be.'

Maddie was standing with her arms crossed as she stared off into the distance towards Robert's camp.

'Mads, can you radio for help?' Luke continued. 'Tell them about Alrek. And you have to get the police to Jessica's house. I don't trust that bastard. I need to know Jason is safe. Will you do this for me?'

'What's the address?'

Luke told her as he tuned the confiscated hand-held radio to 2182 kilohertz. 'I hope the *Basov* is still in range. I know they'll be listening.'

She took the radio. 'You know there's a danger Robert will be monitoring this frequency?' Maddie said. 'He could bring the countdown forward.'

Luke glanced at Vitaly. 'I have to know Jason is unharmed.'

'It is the right thing,' the Russian said. 'But we must hurry. There is little time.'

'With my gammy leg, I'm no help here,' Maddie said. 'So I'm going back to Robert's camp. I'm going to get my hands on that master controller. Second time lucky, I hope.'

'No!' Luke stepped forward and took her gloved hands in his bare ones. He was shocked by the urgency in his own voice. 'Mads, please! Get out of here. There's no point in all of us …' He looked down. He didn't want to say the word. 'Head for the Hudsons. There's a snowmobile not far from our tent. Here, take this. It's activated.' He handed her the snowmobile's locator beacon, which was the size of a car's keyless entry device.

'No way, Luke. I'm not running when you're risking your lives. I know where Robert keeps the laptop. The last thing he'd expect us to do is walk back into his camp.'

'But—'

'He's two men down. He'll be distracted.'

'No, they'll see you coming.'

'I'm taking a leaf out of your book, Luke. Breaking the rules.' Her fiery eyes challenged him. 'And nothing will change my mind.'

Luke took her in his arms. He leaned his cold cheek against the top of her head and felt its warmth. What he would give to be on the *Basov* with her now, secure and warm. 'Please, just go back to Bettingtons,' he whispered.

'No.' She kissed him.

Her warm mouth sent a charge through his cold lips. He wanted to say how much she meant to him, but he couldn't find the right words. 'Tell Jase how much I love him.'

Luke pulled Jason's crumpled photograph from his inside pocket. He looked at it for a moment and smiled, then held it out to Maddie. 'Take this,' he said. He had never parted from Jason's photo.

Maddie took a small step back, shaking her head. 'You always carry it,' she said. 'Keep it and give it to Jason yourself.' She refused to admit he wouldn't make it off the glacier.

Luke placed it back inside his coat. 'Be careful,' he said as she began to walk away. He and Vitaly jumped on the snowmobile and set off for the Fitzgerald Fissure.

* * *

Between the Walgreen and the Fitzgerald crevasses was a long, slim strip of solid glacier. The explosives and the signal relay boxes had been placed down the side of the Fitzgerald Fissure that was furthest away from Robert's camp, but closest to the Walgreen Crevasse. This meant that ten precious minutes were lost as Luke and Vitaly reached the other side. Robert's team had marked the location of the explosives with red flagpoles at the glacier surface. Through binoculars Luke spotted a yellow flag, marking the position of a signal relay box, and they headed over to it.

Once there, they began to set up and secure Vitaly's harness.

'I get it now,' said Luke. 'They're going to destroy the strip of ice *between* the two crevasses. That's why the explosives are all on one side of the Fitzy. The shattered ice has to fall somewhere. It'll collapse on either side, into the two crevasses. Clever. Like a river overflowing into parallel ditches.'

'I understand,' said Vitaly. 'The seawater, it flows in. It washes away the broken ice. Then Robert has the shipping channel.'

'Not if we stop him. If we separate, we'll get through them twice as quickly. I'll double back for you when I'm finished, and we'll move on to the third one – if we have time. You agree?'

'Agree.'

'When we've immobilised the antenna, we pull the yellow flag out as a sign.'

'*Da*. We must get away before detonation. Not leave too late.'

'Let's aim to be on the snowmobile and ready to leave at eleven-thirty.'

'Okay.' Vitaly's piercing blue eyes studied Luke's face.

'I won't forget, my friend,' Luke said. 'I will come back for you.'

Luke hammered some ice screws into the surface and set up the pulley system as Vitaly got into his harness. As Luke drove away to find the next yellow flag, he glanced back to see the burly Russian disappear into the crevasse.

By 10:38 am, Luke was also abseiling into the fissure. In his part of the crevasse the two walls were fairly close, so the deeper he went, the darker and narrower it became. Still, the signal relay box was easy to find because the two-metre long antenna stuck out and pointed to the sky. Luke raised his ice axe and hacked at the base of the antenna. If he could disable it, then none of the explosives in this four-kilometre section would blow. At the second attempt, he sliced it in two and it fell into the abyss.

Robert had been waiting for the right moment to play one of his favourite pieces. It was Prokofiev's 'Montagues and Capulets'. The Russians did occasionally get some things right. Music filled the tent as he tapped his boot to its emphatic and atmospheric beat. He took a deep drag on his cigarette, enjoying his success.

The iceberg had broken away exactly as planned, and was almost secured to the heavy-lift vessel. A cameraman on board was filming everything and feeding the live images to Robert, General Guo Quiliang and the project team at Dragon Resources. Nobody had dared question General Zhao's disappearance.

A second cameraman was positioned high up the Hudson Mountains to capture the moment of detonation along the Fitzgerald Fissure. Robert had also charged him with the important job of editing his personal video footage. He hoped the detonations would be visually stunning, like fireworks on New Year's Eve, as the chain of explosives went off, one after the other, down the length of the crevasse.

Robert checked the countdown clock on the laptop screen.

In one hour and twenty minutes he would make history.

In one hour and twenty minutes he would be relishing

the greatest victory of his career.

Suddenly Robert shot forward, staring at the warning on his screen. 'What the fuck is going on?' he shouted.

★ ★ ★

He raced from his tent and straddled his snowmobile. 'If you want something done right, do it yourself,' he muttered, furious.

After Tang's death and Li's desertion, only Captain Wei and Robert knew how to handle explosives. Robert had tried to get another explosives expert flown in. But it was too late. Too likely to draw attention. Because Searle had been blabbing to AARO, the Australians and the Americans were asking their Chinese counterparts awkward questions. It now looked as if all Robert's hours of training, as well as observing his men set up the explosives, were about to pay off. Out of curiosity, he had watched his men working on the ice tongue, and had handled the pentolite and detonators himself. Most importantly, Tang had explained to him how the signal relay system worked.

Two relay boxes had malfunctioned. One could be bad luck but two was surely sabotage. Clearly, one of the captives had survived the fall into the slot. Robert's gut told him it was Luke Searle. It had to be. Robert didn't believe in fate or destiny, only in his power to make his own fortune. But there was something peculiar about Searle's connection to Antarctica. It was almost as if this wretched heaving mass of ice was keeping its protector alive. Ridiculous, of course.

Wei, who carried enough rifles and ammunition to kill a platoon, revved his engine, eager to depart.

'Shit,' yelled Robert. 'I forgot my helmet. Go and get it, Wei. In my tent, by my bed.' Robert didn't give a damn about safety. He wanted the camera and head torch attached to the helmet. If he was going to save the day, he wanted every moment of it on film.

Wei glared at Robert but obeyed. When he came out he was holding more than the helmet. He had Maddie, her arm locked in his strong grip. She kicked and punched but Wei seemed impervious to her blows. 'Sir, she was trying to steal the master controller. Again.'

Robert rolled his eyes in frustration. 'Kill her,' he said, yanking his helmet from under Wei's free arm.

Wei drew his pistol and forced her to kneel. 'Your family, Wei,' she pleaded. 'Their farm will flood. Please don't ...' Maddie shook her head, her voice choked into a whisper. She looked into his eyes. They didn't show fear but sorrow. Sorrow at what he was party to.

It was as if Wei were moving in slow motion. His gun shifted from pointing at Maddie's head to Robert's chest. Straight-backed, his arm out at a right angle, he looked directly at his commander. He said something and a shot rang out, but it was not Robert who fell dead. It was Wei.

'Loser,' growled Robert.

He aimed at Maddie, fired and then sped off. He peered around briefly to see her motionless body lying on the ice.

T MINUS 59 MINUTES
10 March, 11:01 am (UTC-07)

Robert touched the yellow flag at the most seaward point of the Fitzgerald Fissure. This was the location of the first of two disabled signal relay boxes, or so his wrist-monitor advised him. He had three new boxes and spare antennae in his trailer. He stood over a length of rope that hung down into the dark chasm, his enemy dangling at its end. The Australian or the Russian?

'Goodbye, whoever you are,' he said, chopping his ice axe down on the rope.

His aim was slightly off and the sharp blade only cut through part of the rope. It gave slightly as it began to unravel. He raised the axe high above his head, and this time his strike was perfect. With a *zing* the rope whipped over the crevasse edge and disappeared.

But there was no scream. Robert listened for a few seconds. Then, to his relief, he heard a crash and guessed that the man, whoever he was, had gone quietly to an icy grave. Tentatively, he peered over the edge but couldn't see a body in the dimness.

Robert tested the ice screws left behind by his adversary. They were firm so he used them. He hurriedly set up his pulleys. His first attempt didn't work. Damn this freezing hellhole! He tried again and this time got it right. Once in the harness, he walked to the fissure's edge, a new relay box and tools inside his backpack. Two spare antennae were strapped to the outside of his pack.

He swallowed back the bile in his throat. It wasn't like him to feel nervous. He must stay calm and in control. He had a gun and an axe, and his enemy must surely be dead. All the greatest Antarctic heroes suffered for their cause. His bravery would ultimately add drama to his memoirs. None of his flabby-bellied, limp-dicked competitors in the finance world would have the guts to do what he was about to do. He switched on the camera, stepped over the lip and started to walk down the fissure wall.

Robert felt the temperature drop instantly. He lowered himself with care, avoiding sharp protrusions. The ice grew inky and slick. He was nearing the five-metre mark when he heard a crash – it sounded like rocks tumbling down a mountainside. He looked around, searching for the source of the sound. He reassured himself that ice calved away from crevasse walls constantly.

'Chicken,' he heard a voice call.

Where did the voice come from?

'Chicken,' the voice scoffed again. He wasn't imagining it. It was English but the voice had a strong accent.

Robert grabbed his rifle strapped across his chest and, using his harness, swivelled around and looked down. 'Show yourself!' he called out, squinting as he used his head torch to peer into nooks and crannies.

Silence, except for the creaking of his rope. His head shot from side to side, up and down, but there was no movement.

Robert began lowering himself again, his weapon pointed into the gloom. The silence was beginning to unnerve him. 'Show yourself, you Russian pig!' he called out. 'Your once great country has crumbled, your empire gone. Your people are desperate for water, like mine, but what do you do? Nothing! You are impotent!'

He flicked the gun from side to side but still there was not a sound. He dropped further. As the natural light faded, he was aware that his head torch made him a target.

Time to change tack. 'Luke, why are you doing this? Leave here, and see your family again. Your boy is safe.'

No response.

'Luke!' he yelled, angry that his goading had failed. 'Show yourself or Jason dies!'

Robert's feet were now dangling only a metre above the broken antenna. He heard panting. His head torch searched the shadows until he realised it was his own rapid breathing. He was being ridiculous; the man was dead. The video was recording everything and Robert was supposed to be in the starring role. Fortunately, the camera was facing away from him but it would pick up the fear in his voice. He straightened his back. He'd delete that bit later. Robert dropped down to the signal relay box.

He heard a roar and, looking down, saw a giant of a man, his teeth bared, about to grab Robert's legs. Instinctively, he fired and the Russian was jolted by a bullet graze. Vitaly had been clinging to a narrow ledge just below and to the left of Robert.

Vitaly attacked again. His toes still on the ledge, he stretched up to grab Robert's ankle with both hands. Robert felt the bulky man's weight and, in panic, aimed the rifle at his attacker. But Vitaly was now directly beneath him and he couldn't get a clear shot. The Russian's weight would break his ankle – or, worse, his harness.

Robert clawed at the man's hands but they clung to his ankle. He pulled out his ice axe and aimed the blunt end – designed as a hammer – at Vitaly's hands. He missed, whacking his ankle, which fortunately was protected by calf-high boots. Regardless, Robert gasped. Furious, he raised the hammer again, and this time he didn't miss.

Vitaly bellowed, and his damaged hands released their hold. The Russian slipped and fell back and off the ledge. Robert heard a loud crunch, and then another. Broken pieces of ice tumbled downwards, crashing deeper and deeper. Then quiet.

For a long moment he scanned the darkness. When Robert was finally convinced that Vitaly wouldn't return, he focused his attention on the severed antenna. He attached a new one and, to his relief, his wrist-monitor told him the controller's signal was now reaching this critically important detonator – the last in the sequence.

'Nice try,' he scoffed aloud.

He checked his watch: 11:21 am. There was not enough time to get to the second signal relay box, reactivate it and make it back to his camp safely. But given the glacier's fragility, he hoped the next section along would collapse at detonation, regardless. He heard a buzzing sound and, too late, recognised it as somebody descending. A boot kicked his face and the points of two crampon spikes sliced into his chin. Then a fist cracked his jaw with a snap, like the wishbone of a cooked bird.

Robert's head jolted sideways, and the force of the blow propelled him into the ice wall. How had Vitaly got up there? Completely mystified and crying out in agony, he blindly fired upwards.

T MINUS 38 MINUTES
10 March, 11:22 am (UTC-07)

Robert tugged at his harness, desperate to get away.

'No you don't, you murdering son of a bitch,' said Luke, his face an angry shadow.

Before Luke could force the rifle from his enemy's hand, a bullet nicked his shoulder, creating a fireball of pain. He flinched and almost lost his grip. Before Robert could fire again, Luke zipped down to the ledge below, but Robert dropped a fraction too, and kicked at him with all his might.

As if in slow motion, Luke registered the twelve claw-like points protruding from the underside of Robert's crampon – four at the heel, six on the sole and two at the toe. The front two were raised like the fangs of an attacking funnel-web spider. He wanted to lift his arms for protection but, having no harness, he had to cling on to the ropes.

Instinctively, Luke turned his head to one side and clenched his eyes shut. His mind told him that was dumb, as it exposed his vulnerable left temple, but in the millisecond he had to consider his options, his instinct to protect his eyes took over.

It felt like a surgeon was peeling away his face without anaesthetic. He groaned as the metal slashed three or four millimetres deep:

two parallel cuts just below his ear, and two into his cheekbone below his eye socket. The last two to connect slit his lip, the metal perforating through to his teeth. He tasted rust-like blood seeping into his mouth.

'Payback,' Robert managed to say through a broken jaw.

Luke swung out his axe and connected with one of the ropes supporting his enemy. Robert's harness jerked and he dropped his rifle. The other ropes held, but Robert was now unarmed.

Luke's face was on fire, his mouth full of blood, but he pulled himself level with his enemy. He lifted his axe again. 'Where's Vitaly? Where?'

'Stop! Don't!' Robert squeezed his eyes tight for a moment. Speaking was agony. 'Down there. He attacked me and fell.'

'Liar! You cut his rope!' With his axe still poised to strike, Luke called out to his friend. 'Vitaly! Vitaly!' There was a glimmer of hope he might be alive but Luke heard nothing but the snap of shifting ice.

'Spare me and I'll stop the countdown,' Robert pleaded.

'It's started?' Luke was stunned.

'Not yet, but it's programmed to begin at eleven fifty-seven.'

In fury, Luke swung his axe at the new antenna and it fell into the chasm.

'Disappointing,' Robert said. 'But the rest of the fissure will still blow. Can you risk the glacier's collapse, Searle? Huh? I can still stop it, if you let me go.'

Luke considered for a moment. 'Stop the detonation and I'll let you live.'

'This is the key,' said Robert, showing Luke something that resembled a USB memory stick. It was dangling from a chain around his neck. 'If I place it inside the master controller's port, the countdown will be terminated.'

'The laptop's at your camp?'

'It is.'

Luke thought of Maddie. Was she alive? He realised that if she had the laptop, Robert wouldn't be here.

He glanced at his watch. Twenty-six minutes and nine seconds to detonation. Only just enough time to get to Robert's camp. Luke was torn. With Robert at his mercy, he could stop the detonation. But first he had to find Vitaly.

'Give me the key.' Luke raised the axe higher, ready to strike.

Robert reluctantly handed it over and Luke placed the chain around his neck. From way below, he heard a moan. 'Quiet!' he hissed at Robert.

'Luke …'

It was hardly more than a whisper. Luke ripped Robert's head torch from his helmet, almost toppling the tiny video camera. 'Vitaly,' he called, as he shone the torch into the chasm.

Distracted, Luke didn't see Robert's hand slide into his coat pocket. In the split-second it took for Luke to raise his eyes, Robert had pulled out a pistol and was turning it in Luke's direction.

The ice axe was in Luke's hand, secured by a wrist loop. He swung it across his body and the pick struck the side of Robert's chest, sinking deep into flesh and gut and bone, like a butcher's knife slicing through a carcass. The killer dropped his gun, his face in a startled gasp. Luke retrieved the blade and Robert's head slumped forward like a baby unable to bear the weight of his skull.

'Luke,' called Vitaly, weakly.

'I'm coming,' Luke shouted back.

Blood dribbled from Robert's wound and his body twitched. His breathing was a wet gurgle. 'You lose.' He spat blood in Luke's face and collapsed.

Every muscle in Luke's body tensed, like a sprinter waiting for the starter gun to fire. He calculated time and distance. He could save his friend and stop the detonation, but only just. 'No, Robert,' he replied. 'I will win.'

Luke scanned the area around them and saw the ledge Vitaly had used to hide from Robert. He swung across to it, pushing Robert's limp and suspended body in front of him. With his crampons firmly set on the outcrop, he lowered Robert so he lay flat, then he unbuckled his harness and tore it away.

He began descending fast into the chasm, taking the extra harness with him. 'Keep talking to me, Vitaly. Where are you?'

'Lu … uke,' the Russian called.

It sounded as though Vitaly couldn't catch his breath. Luke remembered Mac's blue, parted lips, his chest wedged into a hole that crushed his ribs, suffocating him to death. Luke sped up, his neck craned downwards. It was very dark. In the torchlight he saw the khaki of Vitaly's parka. 'Mate, hold on! I'll get you out of there.'

He was now level with his friend, whose leg was trapped in a crack in the ice floor. He was lying on his stomach.

'You having a party up there … huh?' Vitaly's deep-set eyes almost disappeared behind his relieved smile.

'Robert's dead. Have to get you up fast. I've got a key that stops the countdown but have to reach his camp to use it.'

'*Blyad!* No time!'

'Fuck's about right, my friend. I'm going to have to be quick.' Part of Vitaly's right ear had been blown away and he had a deep gash above it in his scalp. 'How badly injured are you?'

'Broken leg. Bullet cut my ear. It is okay. Put me in the harness. Then you must go.'

'Can you make it up on your own?'

'*Da!*'

'Okay, this is going to hurt.' Luke got Vitaly under the arms; he must have weighed one hundred and twenty kilograms, and he was pure muscle. Luke was strong but he struggled. 'You need to go on a diet,' he joked, as he dragged the big man onto firmer ice.

With no time to worry about the pain, Luke roughly pushed his friend's legs into the harness and ignored the man's curses. 'Use Robert's snowmobile, okay?' Luke asked.

'No problem. You must go!' Vitaly demanded.

Luke hesitated. He checked his watch: eighteen minutes and twenty seconds left.

'Go!'

Luke ascended so fast that he barely noticed his muscles burning. As he crawled out of the fissure on his belly – his chest heaving, his whole body shuddering from the exertion – a snowmobile

317

skidded to a halt nearby, showering him in snow. Had he finally run out of luck?

'Luke! My God, your face!'

It was Maddie's husky voice. Was he imagining it? He lifted his head. She ran at him and held him tight. Just as quickly, she tore herself away and yanked the straps from a backpack off her shoulders. 'I've got the laptop – but how do we stop the countdown?'

She pulled the master controller from her bag and placed it on the snowmobile seat. Luke struggled to stand and had to lean on the vehicle for support. The laptop was switched on but in sleep mode. She opened the screen. Luke looked at the digital clock.

Ten minutes and two seconds to go.

Luke ripped the chain from his neck. His hand trembled so much that he struggled to insert the key into the port.

'It's in,' he said.

`Terminated at nine minutes and fifty-one seconds` appeared on the screen.

Both Maddie and Luke stared in disbelief.

'We did it,' said Luke, quietly at first. Then he yelled, 'We did it!' and he wrapped Maddie in his arms. 'How on earth did you get the laptop?' he asked, his chin resting on her warm head.

'Robert thought I was dead. He shot at me and missed, but I played dead.' Maddie pulled back and he released her. 'Wei tried to stop Robert … Robert killed him.' She frowned as she noticed Robert's snowmobile. 'Oh my God, he's here, Luke – that's his!'

'He's dead. He can't hurt us anymore. But Vitaly's still down there, injured.'

Luke handed her the laptop for safekeeping. He took one end of the rope he had used to climb out of the crevasse and tied it to the vehicle's handlebars. He threw the other end into the fissure. 'Can you call down to him? We're going to use the snowmobile to pull him out.'

She did so and then joined Luke on the snowmobile. He accelerated away from the fissure until Vitaly was safely on the surface. Maddie leaped off the vehicle and ran over to him. 'We stopped the countdown – it's over!' She danced around him in little circles, her arms held high, her long hair swinging in an arc behind her.

'I think I am dead and with an angel,' Vitaly said.

'Mate, that's the second time we've had to drag you out of a crevasse. You've gotta watch where you're going,' Luke joked.

Vitaly lay spreadeagled on the ice and laughed.

T MINUS 3 MINUTES
10 March, 11:57 am (UTC-07)

Robert is entering a tiny room, an airless cubicle with no windows. A soldier guards the door. A battered bedside lamp provides a pinkish glow of light. The walls are burgundy, like the red wine that makes his father loud and belligerent. Apart from the bed, there is a framed mirror on the wall and a small wooden chair, both amateurishly painted gold. Robert stands just inside the recently shut door and peers from behind his father's wide frame, like a shy toddler.

Robert is fifteen and the girl on the bed looks to be no more than twelve. She has no breasts and wears a simple smock dress, no ribbons in her hair. Her family is clearly poor, probably peasant stock. She sits on the edge of the bed, hunched over, her eyes darting from his father to him, one minute pleading, the other terrified.

'Mummy. Where's my mummy?' she says.

'Arrested this morning. You won't see her again,' replies his father, intending to be brutal. He swivels to face his son. He is not in his military garb but a civilian shirt and trousers, his expanding belly protruding over his belt. 'She's clean,' he says to Robert. 'A virgin. Happy birthday.'

Robert is appalled. He has always imagined he would meet a girl and fall in love. His beautiful mother had talked to him about the tenderness of making love, despite her husband's cruelty. But this? This is disgusting.

'Thank you, Father,' he replies politely, and waits for him to leave. Robert will simply talk to the girl and make her promise to pretend they had sex.

'Well, get on with it. Her name is Woo Huo.'

'I'm waiting for you to leave,' he replies, a tremor in his voice.

His father laughs, the same mocking laugh he's always used at Robert's expense, his mouth wide as if he were chewing up whole countries. 'Oh, no, I'm staying. I'm going to make sure my weedy son becomes a man. Now, get on with it. Show me you're worthy to be a Zhao.'

His father moves to stand in front of the door, folds his arms and waits. The girl cowers, shaking her head, her misery clear in her pleading eyes. Robert begins to unbutton his shirt. He feels sick. He doesn't want to do this but he is desperate to win his father's approval. But not like this; he can't rape a girl.

Robert stops unbuttoning his shirt and turns to face his father. 'I thank you for this gift, Father, but I want to make love to a girl who is special to me. I would like to leave now,' he says, and he steps closer to the door. But his exit is blocked.

His father's hand whips out and slaps him across the face. 'Show me you're a man,' he shouts. 'Take your clothes off now, and fuck her.'

Robert's eyes become watery and his father's narrow in scorn at his son's cowardice. Robert shakes from head to toe but he obeys and soon he stands naked, his small penis limp.

'Undress her,' his father orders.

Robert walks towards the girl, who scrambles onto the pillows, curled into a tight ball. 'Please, please don't,' she repeats, over and over.

'You fucking baby,' his father yells at him. He approaches and slaps the girl across the top of her bent head. She tries to curl into a tighter ball but he yanks her arms up and tears off her dress, then her panties, which are sodden with urine.

General Zhao glances at his son's flaccid penis. 'What's the matter with you? Doesn't this stir your blood?'

'No, Father,' Robert replies meekly, increasingly ashamed.

'Retard!' his father screams. 'Watch what a real man does,' he says, unbuckling his belt and dropping his trousers onto the stinking carpet.

★ ★ ★

Robert woke with a jolt. It wasn't a fantasy; he remembered every detail. Woo Huo – Wendy.

He was colder than he believed possible. Where was he? His vision was blurred; all he could see were patterns of greys and blues. He blinked and pain shot down the left side of his face, which seemed to hang oddly. He tried to move and coughed, almost choking on the blood from his lungs.

Breath. He had no breath. His lungs wouldn't expand. Then he remembered the excruciating pain of the axe slamming into his chest. He was in the Fitzgerald Fissure. But how could he still be alive? For a moment his heart beat a little faster with hope, but he couldn't catch his breath and he coughed up more blood. There was no hope.

Robert moved one hand, a few centimetres at a time, feeling his surrounds. He could see through only one eye. He was on his side, on some kind of ledge. He lifted his hand to his waist: he had no harness. The bastard had left him there to die.

He felt a momentary surge of anger but it didn't last long. His life-blood was seeping away and he was weakening fast. Anger would drain his energy. He couldn't waste it. He had a task to complete. His legacy must be a magnificent victory. His ego would allow nothing less. Above all, there was no way he would be beaten by that nobody, Luke Searle.

Did he still have his backpack? In flesh-tearing agony Robert raised his free hand higher up his chest and found a strap. Yes. And his wrist-monitor? It was attached to his left arm, which was numb, pinned beneath him. He tried to move onto his back but his parka was stuck to the ledge. His blood had glued his coat to the ice. Robert lay still, momentarily defeated.

'Call yourself a man?' he heard his father's voice shout.

'Yes,' croaked Robert. He remembered the video camera and hoped it was still recording. What had he been saying? His heroic battle with Vitaly would be on tape, and his attempt to shoot Searle. Now the camera would record his final act. He would be immortalised. The thought gave him a surge of strength.

Robert wrenched his left arm out from under his body. He undid the wrist-monitor's strap and raised it in front of his eyes. The movement felt like razor blades tearing at his guts. Did the screen say the time was 12:02 pm? No, it can't be! He blinked several times as he tried to focus on the message illuminated on the small screen.

Terminated at nine minutes and fifty-one seconds.

Luke Searle had stopped the countdown! Robert had to re-start it.

Resting the monitor on the ice, he undid the zip of his parka and began to wriggle free. He almost passed out from pain, and his lungs were on fire. First one arm and then the next, and he was free of both coat and backpack.

Robert peered down at the sodden red stain of his wound, then up at the signal relay box above him, its antenna gone. Did he have enough strength to fix it? He had to try. Gritting his teeth, he sat up. His scream was brief but intense, and he coughed blood, spraying it over himself. He could hardly catch a breath, barely enough to oxygenate his ever depleting blood supply.

In a dreamlike state, Robert took the second spare antenna from his bag. Now to stand. With his back to the ice wall, he used his legs to push himself up. The ledge, the wall, everything was moving, as if he were at sea. He was giddy with lack of oxygen.

Robert pulled himself level with the box. Reaching up, he unscrewed the remains of the destroyed antenna before doubling over and vomiting blood. The pain was unbearable but he just managed to screw the new antenna in position. He staggered, unable to tighten it fully, but it held in place.

Robert collapsed back on the ledge, which was to be his glassy

323

open coffin. He felt for a tiny rubber button on his wrist-monitor and pressed it. A cursor flashed on the small screen, asking him for his password. His hands were so cold that he couldn't feel the raised keys, but he knew their location. His vision was fading fast. He used the keyboard to tap in his password, changed only a few hours earlier.

W–E–N–D–Y.

Robert had never forgotten her. He had never forgiven himself for watching his father destroy her innocence, just as the bastard had destroyed his own sensitivity, his belief in human goodness.

Nine minutes and fifty seconds.

Nine minutes and forty-nine seconds.

Nine minutes and forty-eight seconds.

He had overridden the command to terminate. Not even the key Searle had taken could stop it.

'I win,' he wheezed, his last words recorded on a video camera that would never be found.

T PLUS 11 MINUTES
10 March, 12:11 pm (UTC-07)

Maddie, Luke and Vitaly were so filled with relief that a few minutes passed before Maddie noticed the countdown had restarted. 'No! It can't be,' she cried.

Luke was instantly at her side.

Vitaly stopped laughing and sat up.

`Six minutes and forty-six seconds.`

'How in God's name did that happen?'

Luke fiddled with the abort key. It hadn't come loose. It simply wasn't working.

'What?' demanded Vitaly.

'Countdown has started again and this section is going to blow too!' Maddie said. 'Look.' On the laptop screen each detonator was listed as working, except the one Luke had deactivated.

Luke shook his head in disbelief. 'Robert is still alive. It must be him.'

'Six minutes and forty-three seconds. What can we do?' Maddie shot an anguished look at Vitaly.

'Nothing,' Vitaly replied. 'We get the hell out of here.'

Maddie dropped the laptop as if she'd just been scalded. 'What if we smash it to pieces?'

'*Nyet*. Once the signal is sent, it cannot be stopped. We must leave very fast!'

Luke helped Vitaly to his feet. 'You come with me,' he said. 'Maddie, take the other snowmobile.'

Vitaly took his fractured leg in both hands and manoeuvred it over the seat, roaring in agony. He placed his bulky arms around Luke's waist. 'Go,' said the Russian.

Maddie was already on the move.

Luke pushed the vehicle to maximum speed and shot off towards the mountains. He guessed they had less than five minutes now – not enough time to escape.

All around him was the enormous expanse of gleaming white ice that he had fought so hard to protect. Even after thousands of years, the Pine Island Glacier felt solid, indestructible, eternal. It had stood strong while kings and queens and empires lived and died, most unaware of its existence. It had survived two world wars and nuclear bombs. Global warming was melting it, slowly, like a cancer devouring its host, day by day. Yet the glacier was still battling on. Luke knew it could be savage but its majesty was undeniable. Had Luke finally lost the battle to save it?

The first explosion reverberated through Luke's chest like the rumble from a distant cannon. He momentarily released the accelerator. The epicentre was behind him and to his right, much further inland.

The next boom was a fraction closer. Then another and another, like a series of blows from a heavyweight boxer, pounding on Luke's chest. His eardrums were pummelled and the ground shook.

Luke heard Maddie scream, and looked over to see her ducking low over the handlebars. It was an instinctive but futile reaction, since the threat was from below, not above. She looked up at him, her eyes wide with terror.

Luke released the accelerator and both snowmobiles slowed to a halt, Maddie following his lead.

'Why do you stop?' Vitaly hollered as Luke stepped off the vehicle. 'Drive!'

'What are you doing?' screamed Maddie.

'It's too late,' Luke replied. 'We're not going to make it off the glacier. And if I'm going to die, I'm not running. I'm sorry, Mads.' His words were drowned out by another explosion directly behind him.

Vitaly nodded. 'This is true.'

Yet another shattering detonation. They all ducked low and covered their ears.

Maddie dismounted and Luke placed his arm around her and drew her close. Vitaly stayed on the snowmobile. The ice beneath them shifted suddenly, like a violent earthquake. Maddie and Luke stumbled and fell onto all fours.

'But how?' she asked, trembling.

'Robert must have an override code. He start the countdown again,' Vitaly shouted.

'And he must have replaced the antenna,' Luke added.

Vitaly nodded. 'I am sorry. I should have known. That man is too rich and clever not to have backup plan.'

'There's no way you could have known,' Luke replied. 'I'm just sorry it had to end this way.' He felt the ice vibrating beneath his bare hands. He patted its surface. 'Not long now,' he said.

'I always say explosives will kill me one day,' said Vitaly. 'But, I die with brave friends.'

Luke gave him a wry smile, but an instant later it was gone. 'Jase,' he breathed. He wanted to say goodbye.

'He's safe,' Maddie said. 'I saw to that.'

The shockwave from the next detonation juddered through Luke's body and his hands and knees slipped. As the fissure wall shattered and collapsed, it creaked and groaned like metal in a car-crusher.

Maddie handed her two-way radio to Luke. 'Get a message to him,' she shouted.

The ground shook again. Luke managed to tune in to the right frequency.

Bolshakov's voice yelled, 'Where are you? We hear explosions.'

'There's no time,' Luke shouted above the noise. 'Tell my son I love him. You must tell him.'

There was a moment of stunned silence. 'I will.'

Luke offered the radio to Maddie. She shook her head and didn't take it. 'It's okay. I'll be with my baby girl.' She looked away, not wanting him to see her tears.

'Get out of there!' Bolshakov bellowed over the radio. 'The glacier – it collapse!'

'Vitaly?' Luke offered his friend a chance to say goodbye. He took the radio, said something in Russian and handed it back to Luke. Luke let it fall from his hand. 'What did you say?'

'I ask him to return my body home,' he replied. 'I have not set foot in Russia for thirteen years. At last I can go home.' He lifted his blue eyes to the pale sky and waited.

'Mads. I wish we'd had more time,' Luke said.

She hugged him. 'Why do I finally meet the right one when it's too late?'

Boom!

Boom!

Boom!

Explosions rolled onwards towards the bay, like a Mexican wave of thunder and destruction. Luke watched fragments of ice shoot into the air, like a fountain of snow. Then a vast, screeching, agonising, cracking sound as the stressed ice at the front of the glacier began to break up. The ice beneath their feet shifted with a neck-breaking jerk, and he felt the pull of gravity as the ground tilted a fraction.

'Vitaly, lie down!' he yelled. 'Use your axe!' Luke swung his own axe deep into the glacier's back. 'Maddie, hang on to me.'

The aftershocks pounded their bodies like a jackhammer. Luke felt the glacier's death throes, as if it were a desperate animal writhing in the jaws of a predator. Somewhere deep below them, the ice split.

Completely disoriented, Luke saw chunks of ice the size of ships hurled into the air. The white beast arched its back beneath him, lifting him up. Maddie clung to Luke in silent terror. The glacier shook, shuddering at its vulnerability. Luke's sense of balance was shot to pieces but he clung to the axe handle. He was determined to see it through to the end.

The glacier face was calving pieces of ice the size of office blocks into the sea. Massive waves crashed over what remained of the ice shelf, further weakening it. An immense rift worked its way inland from the ice tongue, splitting the glacier in half. A great mass of jade, blue and white ice shifted and pointed like an arrow towards the sky. It was breathtakingly, hideously beautiful.

Another crack opened up, and Luke watched, calmly fascinated, as it snaked towards them. The ice beneath him began to tip up at an alarming angle. He started to slide. Shards of crystal-like pieces flew at the sun, and through them he saw the colours of the rainbow, as if in final defiance of the inevitable.

T PLUS 2 YEARS
London

He had met his interviewer and they had shaken hands. The guy was a legend around the world, his talk show pulling millions of viewers each night. But Luke tried not to think about that as he stared around the brightly lit set, at the London skyline through the large windows, at the armchair where he'd be sitting in a few minutes, a microphone broadcasting his every word. This was his idea of hell, but if he could survive what he'd been through in Antarctica, then he'd get through this.

Over the last two years, Luke had been asked to speak at the United Nations, and to consult for his government and others. Tomorrow, he was leaving England to appear before the United States Senate Committee on Armed Services, where he was to present his views on climate change as a threat to global security.

He had also been offered an enormous sum of money to head up a new multinational, state-of-the-art Antarctic research station, to model and monitor the West Antarctic Ice Sheet's disintegration. But he couldn't go back. The men and women who had died there still haunted him. He had nightmares, their voices calling his name. Apart from that, he had made a good life with Maddie and Jason, and that was too precious to risk losing.

But just because he existed in a self-imposed exile from Antarctica, that didn't mean he cared any less about it.

A warm hand took his and he felt instantly better. 'You'll be fine,' Maddie said. 'You're an old hand now.' She gazed around the set, her eyes sparkling with excitement.

Their relationship had gone beyond the initial desperate clinging, beyond their guilt that they had lived and others had not, beyond their anger at the slowness of governments to react and at China's denial, blaming a renegade general and his son, beyond their disbelief as resource companies hovered like vultures, falling over themselves to cash in on the disaster. With the glacier gone, the continent was slowly losing its icy armour, and its riches were highly prized.

Antarctica was changing forever and, as a result, so was the rest of the world. Which was why Luke was hauling himself from country to country, spelling out very clearly that everybody's way of life was about to change, whether rich or poor, and that economies, defences, health, food and water – all the things he, like so many others, had taken for granted – were under threat.

'This is so awesome!' Jason said.

'Yeah, mate, it is.' Luke reached out and tousled his son's hair.

'Oh, Wendy called,' Maddie said. 'I've got to hand it to her, she's got the knack. Another donation. Five hundred thousand dollars. That'll keep the foundation going for a while.' The Searle Foundation provided much-needed aid and education in poor countries facing serious flooding.

'Let's use it for the refugee project in Vietnam,' Luke said.

Wendy had visited Luke upon his return to Australia. It was her money that had enabled him set up the foundation.

Luke heard his name being called. He turned towards the dimly lit auditorium, at the rows of empty seats that would shortly be filled. He searched the back rows and the man repeated Luke's name, his voice like sandpaper on rough wood.

'Hey! Mr Celebrity! You now too big to have a beer with me?' The man guffawed as he walked down the aisle, two steps at a time. Vitaly Yushkov first squeezed Luke, then Maddie and finally Jason, in a bear hug. He took a step back to gaze at Luke's neatly ironed shirt. 'You look very nice,' he teased.

Luke laughed. 'How's the Arctic touring business?' It was July; the *Professor Basov* was leaving for Spitsbergen the next day.

'Shithouse. No bloody ice!'

A production assistant beckoned for Luke to follow her to hair and make-up, but he politely declined. He wasn't going to hide the raised scars, six of them, that marked his left cheek and mouth, a reminder of Robert and his crampon spikes. She ran off to inform the producer, Larry, who shrugged and then called Luke backstage.

'The battered hero look – I like it,' Larry said.

Luke frowned. He had been asked to wear his Cross of Valour but had refused. He kept it locked away like the memory of his friends' deaths.

'It's all good,' said Larry. 'Let's rattle a few cages, shall we? Michael will start by asking you to tell your story and how you survived, then he'll move on to what you think can be done about the collapsing ice. Oh, and how we tackle all those displaced people. Okay?'

Every morning, when Luke first opened his eyes, he reminded himself how it was that he was still alive. How he had flung his ice axe into the tilting glacier, and hung on until its shifting mass had settled into its new position, upended at a twenty-degree angle. Vitaly had clung on too, the old sailor resolutely refusing to budge, the crampons of his good leg like claws in the ice.

Luke was eternally grateful to Winchester, who had realised something was wrong during their phone call, and had sped up the rescue mission. Luke's hint about their celebrating his last birthday together had raised the alarm. In fact, Luke had spent that birthday being reprimanded for delaying the departure of the *Aurora Australis*; he'd forgotten his camera.

Those days of irresponsibility were now long gone. The meltdown clock was ticking, and there was so much to do. Including these excruciating interviews.

'Sure,' Luke replied, but his voice lacked enthusiasm. He hoped Maddie would be in the front row, as she had promised.

'You don't like the attention much, do you?' Larry asked.

'Not much, but it's got to be done.'

Larry attached a microphone to Luke's shirt collar. 'Do you really think sea levels could rise by fifteen feet? Seriously?'

'Yeah, it's possible,' he replied. 'They're already up by just under a metre, or three feet. It'll be many years before it reaches five metres, though. We've got time to lessen the impact.'

The producer nodded, frowning. 'Really? I mean, that's London in trouble, Amsterdam, Manhattan …'

'Portsmouth, Hull, The Wash, parts of Belgium and Denmark. New Orleans could be wiped out. Florida's in danger. Most Pacific Islands, Egypt, Vietnam and Bangladesh are going to have serious trouble. Sydney and Brisbane airports look like they'll be underwater, and Port Phillip Bay – in my hometown of Melbourne – is under threat.'

Larry stared at him. The audience was arriving and the hum getting louder. He pulled himself together. 'Okay, we'll be going live soon. Are you ready?'

'Ready as I'll ever be.'

ACKNOWLEDGEMENTS

Writing this book has been an adventure in itself. I travelled to Antarctica on a former Russian oceanographic research vessel, the *Professor Multanovskiy*, to be awoken every morning by the Russian captain barking instructions to his crew through the PA system. It was like waking to find myself in a James Bond story: turbulent seas, glaciers the size of small countries, and abandoned stations eerily left as if the inhabitants would return at any moment. On board, I met two people whose advice has proved invaluable: Luke Saffigna who bears no resemblance to my hero, save for his initials and his passion for Antarctica, and Jeff Rubin – author of Lonely Planet's *Antarctica* guidebooks.

Thanks to the generosity of so many at the Australian Antarctic Division (AAD), I learned something of crevasse rescue techniques, avalanche survival, polar medicine and station life. Armed with this information I then took liberties and created my fictional world. I was lucky enough to interview one of the AAD's first female station leaders, Joan Russell, whose insights helped me create Maddie Wildman. The AAD's icebreaker, *Aurora Australis*, is like a small city and the ship's master,

Tim Sharpe, was kind enough to show me around. Thank you, also, to the crew of *L'Astrolabe* for having me on board.

I should state that there is no Hope Station or Bettingtons. The Australian Antarctic Research Organisation (AARO) does not exist and bears no resemblance to the Australian Antarctic Division, except for its location. However, numerous people at the AAD have generously contributed their time and knowledge. Thank you to Stuart Pengelly, Tom Maggs, Peter Yates, Dr Tony Worby, Patti Lucas, Peter Jansen and Dr Graham Denyer of the Polar Medicine Unit. At the British Antarctic Survey (BAS) in Cambridge, England, I spoke to some of the wonderful people doing research on and around the real Pine Island Glacier (PIG). A huge thank-you to Dr Julian Scott, Dr Andy Smith and Hugh Corr. Julian. I am grateful for your good humour when answering some of my more bizarre questions about my fictional plans. Athena Dinar and Heather Martin, you were amazing. Very few people have actually been to this incredibly remote and inhospitable part of the world. Yet the health of the Pine Island Glacier and its sister, the Thwaites, is believed to be critical. These two glaciers do, indeed, hold back the West Antarctic Ice Sheet, the melting of which could lead to catastrophic sea level rises.

A special thanks to Kate Perchina, Nathan Rosaguti, explosives expert Michael Fuller, as well as Tony Cooper, Jonathan Jutsen, Rob Thomson and Julia Davenport from climate change consultancy, Energetics.

Keir Vaughan-Taylor and Patrick W. Larkin – thank you for sharing your knowledge on climbing gear and abseiling. Thank you, Dom Bragge, for your help on radio communication. Once again, Fosm, I know I can rely on you for my imaginary hacking needs and Eon, you are a genius. Several people gave me valuable feedback on an early draft including: Jason Humphries, Louise Wildman, Lucie Stevens, Brian Bell, Harry Free, Patrick M. Larkin, Tim and Sarah Webster and Meg Wrixon.

I am very lucky to have such a supportive agent, Gaby Naher, whose advice on this manuscript was, once again, absolutely spot on. Thank you to my publisher, Melanie Ostell, for championing this book and for guiding me editorially, and to senior publicist, Ashlea Wallington, as well as the awesome design, sales and marketing teams at Pier 9. And thank you to all the bookshops and retailers who sell copies of *Thirst*, and all the people who buy them. Last, but by no means least, I cannot thank my husband, Michael, enough for coping with the endless brainstorming and for his unwavering support.

I love to hear from my readers, and can be contacted via my website at www.lalarkin.com.

Turn the page to read the first chapter of L. A. Larkin's *Devour*

1

Lake Ellsworth, Antarctica,
78°58′34″S, 90°31′04″W

On the flat, featureless ice sheet, katabatic winds swoop down the mountain slopes, whipping up ice particles and hurling them at a solitary British camp. The huddle of red tents, blue shipping containers, grey drilling rig, and yellow water tanks are so tiny on the vast expanse of white, they resemble pieces on a Monopoly board. Three kilometres beneath the camp, subglacial Lake Ellsworth, and whatever secret it may hold, is sealed inside a frozen tomb.

In the largest tent, used as the mess and briefing room, Kevin Knox stands before Professor Michael Heatherton, the director of Project Persephone.

'So how the hell did this happen?' says Heatherton, dragging his fingers through greying hair.

Knox brushes away a drip running down his cold cheek, as ice, frozen to his ginger beard and eyelashes, melts in the tent's comparative warmth. Outside it is minus twenty-six degrees Celsius but the wind chill makes it feel more like minus forty.

'Mike, we don't know exactly. The boiler circuit's broken. It'll need a new part.'

'Don't know?' Heatherton scoffs.

Knox clenches his pudgy fists. What a thankless little twat! For the last hour he and Vitaly Yushkov, the two hot water drillers, have been struggling to fix the damn thing.

A strong hand squeezes his right arm and Knox glances at

1

Yushkov standing beside him, whose penetrating blue eyes warn
him not to lose his temper. Knox gives the Russian an almost
imperceptible nod and Yushkov releases his grip.

Their leader gets out of his plastic chair and paces up and
down behind one of three white trestle tables. A marathon run-
ner of average height, he is lean, wiry and exceptionally fit for
his age. But, next to Knox and Yushkov, he appears fragile. Knox
isn't tall but he is chunky, and likes to describe his wide girth as
'love handles' even if the Rothera Station lads pinned a photo on
the noticeboard with his head photoshopped on to the body of
an elephant seal. Not that it bothers him.

Yushkov is six foot one. His neck, almost as wide as his head,
meets powerful shoulders, and his hands are so large they remind
Knox of a bunch of calloused Lady Finger bananas. Knox
knows little about Yushkov's past – conscription, ship's engineer, mechanical engineer – and the taciturn Russian doesn't
care to share. He is now a British citizen and the most talented
mechanical engineer Knox has ever worked with, and that's all
that matters.

'The eyes of the world are upon us,' Heatherton says, his
Yorkshire accent softened after years working with the British
Antarctic Survey in Cambridge. 'Everybody wants to know if
there's life down there.' He momentarily looks at the rubber
flooring beneath his boots. 'And we're only a kilometre away
from the answer. We have to get the drill working again before
the hole freezes over.' His voice is high-pitched with agitation.
'So what I need to know is, can you fix it?'

Yushkov speaks, his accent as strong as the day he last set foot
in Mother Russia, sixteen years ago.

'Boss, we built the hot water drill. We did not build the
boiler. So, we need time to understand the problem. We will
talk with manufacturer, get advice. We have spare parts at

Rothera. If we are lucky, we get new circuit in a day or two and all is hunky-dory.'

Yushkov grins, revealing surprisingly perfect white teeth given his heavy smoking. Heatherton opens his mouth but Knox jumps in.

'It's going to be okay, Mike. We'll get it running on a backup element and keep the tanks warm. Stop worrying.'

The taut skin around Heatherton's eyes is getting darker each day. He plonks down into a chair and rubs his hands up and down his face, as if trying to wake up. He looks exhausted.

'Look, Kev,' he says through his splayed fingers, then drops his hands to his sides. 'I'm a geoscientist, not an engineer. But to do my bit, I'm relying on you to do yours. I'm frustrated, that's all.'

That is as close as Knox has heard their leader get to an apology.

Heatherton cranes his neck towards them, frowning, and speaks quietly so nobody can hear through the canvas walls. Not that anyone could anyway, given the blustering winds.

'Could it be sabotage?'

Yushkov shifts from one battered boot to the other.

'Pardon?' Knox says. He can't have heard right.

'Has the boiler been sabotaged?'

'Jesus, Mike!' says Knox, flinging his hands in the air. 'What's got into you? We're in the middle of bloody nowhere trying to do something that's never been done before. Things go wrong. It's inevitable.'

'Yes, quite right.' He sighs. 'But a lot of things are going wrong. Too many. And we all know the Russians are trying to beat us.' Heatherton flicks a look at Yushkov. 'No offence.'

'None taken,' Yushkov replies, but the low rumble in his voice says he is not being entirely honest.

3

At that moment, BBC science correspondent, Charles Harvey, steps through the door, his black parka covered in snow, like dandruff. He's as blind as a bat without his glasses, which means he's constantly wiping ice off the lenses or cleaning them when they steam up.

'Hear you've had a spot of bother. Mind if I join you?'

Heatherton hesitates. Harvey continues.

'I see a great story here. Engineers struggle in howling storm to save project. That sort of thing.'

'An heroic angle?' Heatherton's hazel eyes light up. He runs his fingers over his smooth chin, the only team member who bothers to shave. Knox knows why: Heatherton wants to look dashing in Harvey's documentary. 'I see. Okay.' He looks at Knox. 'Well, let's get on with it.'

'Fine,' says Knox. 'But if that blizzard gets much worse we'll have to stop work and wait for it to pass.'

'Yes, yes, health and safety and all that,' Heatherton says, 'Quite right. But if you don't get the boiler working soon, this whole project is done for. Ten years down the toilet.'

Knox raises his eyes in exasperation. 'No pressure then.'

As he zips up his black parka sporting the Lake Ellsworth project logo, tugs inner and outer gloves on to his hands, pulls on his beanie and hood and places snow goggles over his eyes, he thinks for the thousandth time what a stupid colour black is for Antarctic clothing. Should have been red, yellow or orange so they can be spotted easier. Through the flimsy door he hears the wind has picked up speed. It will be near impossible to hear each other above the roar.

'Okay, mate,' Knox says to Yushkov. 'Let's get this done as quick as we can. Stay close. Use hand signals.'

Yushkov nods.

'Vitaly, a word,' says Heatherton, gesturing him to stay.

4

'Right. I'll get started then. But I can't do much without him, so make it quick, will you?'

Annoyed, Knox leaves, letting the fifty-mile-an-hour wind slam the door for him. The field site is a swirling mass of snow. He grips a thick rope, frozen so solid it feels like steel cable, secured at waist height between poles sticking out of the ice at regular intervals. Only thirty feet to the boiler. He carefully plants one boot after another. He staggers a few times. Head down, body bent, he throws his weight into the storm like a battering ram. Where the hell is Vitaly? That bloody Heatherton is probably wanking on about loyalty and reminding Yushkov, in his unsubtle way, that he now works for the Brits. The man is bloody paranoid.

Someone takes him in a bear hug from behind. He thinks Yushkov is mucking about, but when a cloth is held hard over his nose and mouth, he begins to panic. It has a chemical smell he can't place. Confused and disoriented, he tries to turn. He feels light-headed and his eyelids droop.

Knox wakes. He hears a high-pitched buzzing, then realises it's the retreating sound of a Bombardier Ski-Doo. Soon, all he can hear is the buffeting wind. He wants to sleep, but his violent shivering makes it impossible. He opens his heavy eyelids and sees nothing. Just white. Where is he? The hardness beneath his cheek tells him he's lying on one side. Knox tries to sit up, but his head pounds like the worst hangover, so he lies back down. He blinks eyelashes laden with ice crystals, trying to take it all in. Of course. The boiler. He must have fallen. Maybe knocked his head?

This time, Knox manages to sit up and waits for the dizziness to pass. He can't see the horizon or the surface he's sitting on, or even his legs. Like being buried in an avalanche; there is no up or down. He's in a white-out – the most dangerous blizzard. He sucks in the ice-laden air, fear gripping him. Ice particles get caught in his throat and he coughs. His heart speeds up and, instead of ener-gising him, it drains him. He racks his brain, trying to remember his emergency training. But his mind is as blank as the landscape.

Think, you fucking idiot. Think!

It's pointless shouting. He doesn't have a two-way radio. Nobody can see or hear him. Christ! What happened? His jaw is chattering, his body wobbling, and now he can't feel his hands or feet. He lifts his right arm so his hand is in front of his eyes, but it doesn't feel as if it belongs to him. His fingers won't flex and the skin is grey, the same colour as his dear mum when he found her dead in her flat. Frostbite and hypothermia have taken hold of him. What he can't understand is why he isn't wearing a glove. He checks the left hand. No glove and no watch, either. Nothing makes sense.

Knox attempts to bend his knees. His legs are stiff and move-ment is painful. He manages to bring them near enough to discover he wears socks, but no boots. The socks are caked in ice and look like snowballs. His shivering is so violent that when he tries to touch them, he topples over.

Stunned by his helplessness, Knox stays where he fell. He places a numb hand on his stomach but he can't tell if he's still wearing a coat. He can't feel anything. He blinks away the ice in his sore eyes and peers down the length of his body. He sees the navy blue of his fleece. No coat. The realisation that he will die if he doesn't find shelter very soon is like an electric shock and his whole body spasms. Terrified, he scrambles to a sitting position, battling the blizzard and his own weakness.

'Help!' he shouts, over and over, oblivious to the pointlessness of doing so.

For the first time since he was a boy, he cries. The tears are blasted by the gale and shoot across his skin and on to the woollen edges of his beanie, where they freeze, as hard and round as ball bearings.

Knox struggles on to his hands and knees like an arthritic dog, sobbing, a long string of snot hanging from his nose. Shelter. Must find shelter. Despite his numb extremities he crawls on all fours, around in a tight circle, hoping to see something, anything that will tell him where there's a tent or a shipping container. Any kind of shelter. But there are no shapes of any kind. Nothing but whiteness. The desperate man decides to go in one direction for ten steps, then turn to his right for ten, then again and again until he returns to his current position. The gusts are so powerful, it's pointless trying to stand. So he stays on all fours.

He tells himself that Robert Falcon Scott walked thousands of miles to the South Pole with frozen feet. Then he remembers Scott never made it back. Knox's head is tucked into his chest and the patches of hair sticking out of his beanie are stiff and white. He peers into the distance every now and again but the view doesn't change. Where is the rope, for Christ's sake? When Knox thinks he's done a full circuit, he stops, but there's no way of telling if he has returned to his starting point. He pants, exhausted. Perhaps he should build a snow cave, as all deep-fielders are trained to do, but he doesn't have a shovel or ice axe, and his hands are useless. Suddenly, he feels on fire all over and claws at his fleece, trying to remove it. But he can't even grip the hem.

Like a match, his strength flares ever so briefly and then vanishes.

He wakes with a start. How long has he been lying here? Minutes? Hours? The snow build-up is now a blanket over him. He pulls his knees to his chest, curling himself painfully into a foetal position.

He chuckles. What a tit! He's going to get such a ribbing when they find him, lost only a few feet from the camp. He'll never live it down. Oh well. Story of his life: always the butt of jokes. He isn't shivering any more and feels warm and cosy. Yushkov will know he's missing. They'll be looking for him. He's so tired. Tired and numb. He can't hear the wind any more.

When he closes his eyes, everything is peaceful. Knox hears his mother tell him it'll be all right. She's reported his bullying to the headmaster. His school blazer is ripped, but she's not cross. His head in her lap, she brushes his long fringe from his eyes. As long as she keeps holding him, he isn't afraid.